# ONCE a RAKE, ALWAYS a ROGUE

*Potions and Passions*
*Book 3*

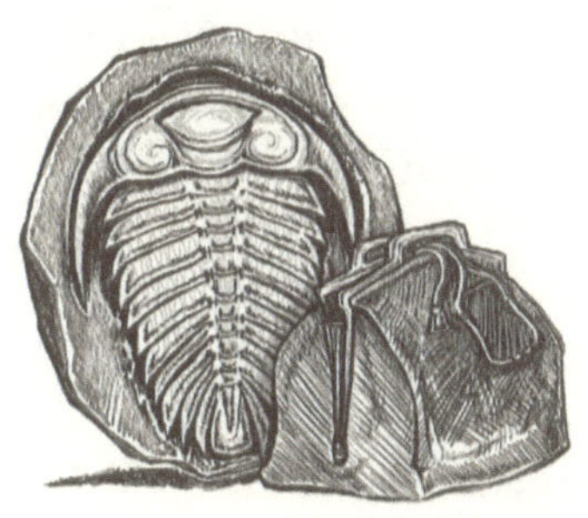

## CATHERINE STEIN

For everyone who has ever felt they didn't or don't fit in.
You are beautiful.

# PROLOGUE

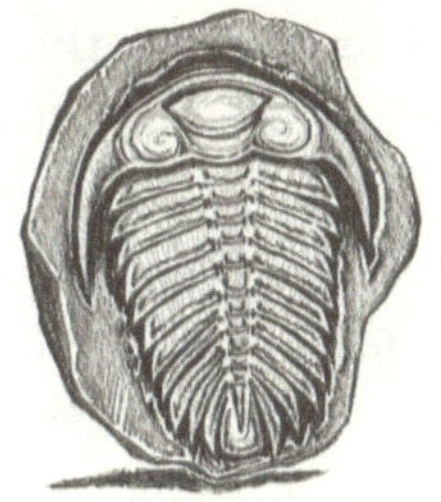

August 14, 1877

**A**STRID SKIPPED ALONG THE BEACH, turning her face up to catch the sun's warm rays. The ocean breeze tumbled her unbound hair and kissed the skin of her neck and arms.

*At last.*

Her entire body sang with relief to be here, at home, away from the madness of London and the strain of her first Season. If she had any say in the matter, it would be her only Season. She had no desire to ever repeat the last few months.

It wasn't that she hated parties. Astrid enjoyed dancing, and it was always interesting to visit new places and watch the array of ladies and gentlemen in their finery. But night after night of putting herself on display for people who saw her as nothing more than a large chunk of money had spoiled most of the fun.

Today, she was free. No maid had yanked her corset strings too tightly or pinned mounds of false hair to her head. Her clothes were simple, comfortable, easy to move about in. Her feet were bare to the tickle of the grass and the grit of the sand.

Tomorrow, she would return to her studies. She had three new books to read, and a dozen specimens lay in a box in her laboratory, awaiting cleaning and classification. The ancient creatures called to her, but they had been waiting millions of years. They could give her this one day to relax and recharge.

She paused to scoop up an interesting rock, gave it a cursory examination, and dropped it into her purse. The little bag thunked against her hip, loaded down with the day's collection. Today's findings were no more than ordinary rocks and fossils, but Astrid never came to the beach without taking something back for her studies. Sometimes a closer look in the lab revealed things she would otherwise never notice. Besides, "I need to return these rocks to the beach," made a convenient excuse for leaving the house.

As usual, she had promised to be back in time for tea, and it had been long enough since her lunch of fruit, cheese, and nuts for the first stirrings of hunger to set in. Astrid made her way to one of her favorite climbing spots and scrambled up the ten foot escarpment, foregoing the longer walk to the staircase her parents had installed years ago. When she reached the top, she turned, as was her habit, to survey the beach and the sparkling waters of the Channel. The sight never grew tiresome.

"Well, hello there!"

Astrid wheeled around to discover a handsome young man striding toward her. Dressed for sport, in buckskin breeches and riding boots, he looked as dashing as any man she had seen in town that summer. His clothes were perfection, hugging muscled thighs and a broad chest. He wore no hat, revealing hair the color of beach sand, attractively tousled by the gentle sea breeze. He took her breath away.

"Oh! Hello."

The stunning stranger could only be one of her brother's

friends from University. Cal had mentioned he might stop by with several "school chums" enroute to a hunting party. He hadn't mentioned those chums would wander down to the beach, startling her so badly her heart wouldn't stop thumping.

The man had drawn close enough that she could see the smoky gray color of his eyes, and his refined cheekbones. His smile was one of mischievous good cheer. Astrid tried to calm her silly enthrallment by dwelling on his hideous plaid necktie. It was rather sloppily knotted, in contrast to the rest of his ensemble.

His gaze traveled over her, from her unruly hair to her dirty, unshod feet. "And here I thought we had left all the beauties behind in London!"

A hot burst of humiliation flared in her cheeks. She'd heard so many similar, insincere flatteries during the Season. No one thought short, plump Astrid Wembley ethereal. She had heard the pitying whispers saying it was too bad she wasn't tall, lithe, and blond like her Swedish-born mother. If only the men would say what they really meant: *Your enormous dowry is so beautiful!* She would prefer an honest fortune hunter to any of the suitors she'd had thus far.

Astrid pulled herself up as tall as she could manage, prepared to tell him to save his breath for lying about all the things he wasn't going to shoot on his hunting trip, but he spoke again before she had the chance.

"You live in the area, I presume?"

She jumped, taken aback. Didn't he know who she was? "Y-yes," she stammered.

"Lovely place. I'm just passing through, sadly. I'm a friend of Lord Caladay, Whitehaven's heir. You must know of him, I imagine."

*He's my twin!*

So much for the hope that any of that Swedish beauty had passed on to her. Her brother's friend couldn't even tell they were related? Her heart began to race once more. If he didn't know who she was…

Those gray eyes were wandering again, over her breasts and hips, then rising to linger on her mouth. He closed the space between them. His voice dropped, low and seductive. "I would have asked to stay longer, had I known what a charming companion I would stumble upon here."

Astrid could hardly breathe. This gorgeous rogue of a man knew nothing of her title or her money, and yet, here he was, acting for all the world as if he wanted to kiss her. She'd been kissed a few times, by the flattering fortune hunters, and it had been nice enough, but to be kissed—desired!—for her own self? The mere thought was intoxicating. She swayed toward him.

"I'd love to steal a kiss," he murmured.

Astrid tilted her chin up. "Take it. It's yours."

His lips brushed over hers. She sighed and melted into him, her arms winding around his neck, returning the kiss with wanton abandon.

Glorious.

He was eager, but not demanding, welcoming her kisses as much as he offered his. The gentle press of his mouth grew firmer, hungrier, and he dragged her body tightly against his. Hot. Hard. Ravenous.

Astrid gasped in surprise when his tongue teased her lips apart. He plunged into her mouth, exploring and coaxing, urging her to follow.

Her head swam. She reveled in the taste of him.

*This.* This was how a kiss was meant to be. A wild, greedy, indulgence that made her forget the world and long for more— more of him, more of them—anything and everything he would give her.

A voice in the back of her mind told her she ought to protest when his fingers began to unlace her bodice. It grew louder when he tugged down the loose top she wore underneath, exposing her breasts. Something about impropriety and scandals. His hands felt so good on her, though. So right. She kept on kissing him, letting him touch her and tease her as he pleased.

When he bent his head to her bosom and laved one stiff nipple, she groaned in pleasure and threaded her fingers through his gold-brown locks. This was thoroughly wicked, and yet she couldn't stop.

And why should she? She refused to marry any of the awful men who had expressed interest. Another Season was out of the question, so she doubted she'd meet many eligible men in the future. Certainly, she didn't expect to meet any who would leave her to the life she desired. Giving up her studies was unfathomable. She'd rather be a spinster.

But spinsters missed out on kisses and bedroom intimacies. They didn't get frenzied, passionate embraces. This might be her only chance to…

"Gracious," she moaned. His hands had come up under her skirts, running over her bare thighs and squeezing her bottom through the thin fabric of her drawers.

"Indeed." He lifted his head to gaze into her eyes. His own had turned to the liquid silver of mercury. "You are delectable."

"You too," she breathed.

He pulled her hard against him, drugging her once more with kisses, grinding his hips into her. The sensation of his rock-hard arousal against her belly made her spring back with a yelp of surprise.

He meant to put *that* inside her? She knew something of anatomy and the mechanics of copulation from her readings, and she supposed it must fit, given that people did it all the time. Still, it gave her pause. Enough to regain some of her senses. Sexual pleasures came with consequences, risks beyond that of scandal, and she was unprepared to handle them.

"Too much? Too fast?" Disappointment shone in his eyes.

Astrid felt it too. That lack of fulfillment. The hunger to reach out and touch him once more. She forced a nod.

"My apologies. You drove most of what sense I possess out of my head." He smoothed out her skirts and pulled her top back up to cover her. "Perhaps another time?"

Her cheeks burned, and a grin spread over her face before she could stop it. The thought of a renewal of today's activities caused excitement to bubble up inside her. It would be thrilling. And dangerous. This time, her nod came eagerly.

For heaven's sake, she didn't even know his name! She didn't dare ask. That would only lead to him asking *her* name. Even if she lied, if she uttered more than a word or two, he would notice her upper-class accent and make the connection. Then he would tell Cal, who would tell her parents, and everything would turn into an awful mess. No. She would have to content herself with the memory of this one exquisite moment.

"I will look for you when I am next in the area," he promised. "May I walk you home now? Or wherever you are headed?"

Astrid shook her head. What could she do? Walk him back to Whitehaven Manor? Hardly. He would head there soon anyway, to continue on with the hunting party. She needed to go elsewhere until he departed. She would be late for tea. "No. Thank you."

His brows crinkled in an altogether too-attractive frown. "If you are certain."

"I am."

He sighed in resignation. Then he took up her hand and brought it to his lips. It was enough to send a tingle throughout her entire body. "Until we meet again, then."

"Until then."

Astrid hoped they would meet again, someday. She also hoped it would be far enough in the future that she could formulate a sound plan for what to do when they did.

She started off, in the opposite direction from home, trying not to glance back, certain he was doing the same.

After several agonizing seconds, she risked a look. Their eyes met. He, too, had failed in this. She lifted a hand in farewell, then continued on with a smile on her face.

I

# CRITICAL CORRESPONDENCE

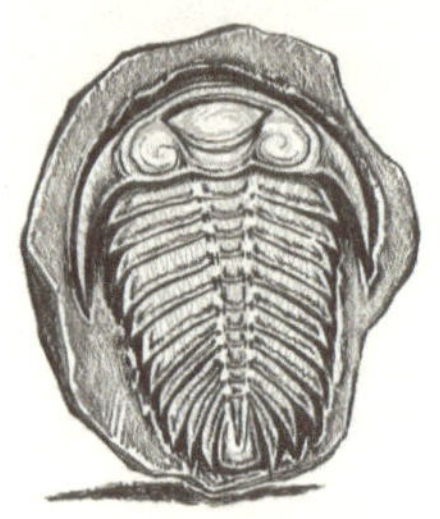

September, 1884

"GRACE! GRACE!"

Astrid flew into the laboratory, brandishing her letter like some plundering pirate waving a sword, proclaiming her victory to all and sundry.

"I have done it!"

She twirled in a circle, the fabric of the well-used carpet soft against her bare feet, the inviting yellow glow of the potion lamps like sunlight on her face, even in the cool basement room.

Her research partner looked up from the pile of fossils she was cataloging. Grace brushed back a strand of wavy, dark hair that had come loose from her ponytail. "Done what?"

"Lord Ayleston is *recommending* me for membership to the Institute!"

Grace sprang from her seat. The bangles around her slender wrist jingled. Her mother, a metalsmith, regularly sent newly crafted bracelets from India to match every outfit Grace owned. Today, their metallic clinks sounded like music to Astrid's delighted ears.

8

"That's wonderful!" Grace exclaimed.

"All those meetings and letters. Papers. Applications. Begging. It has all paid off! Finally! Oh, Grace, I'm so happy I could just burst!"

Astrid flung her arms around her friend and danced her around the room, dodging shelves and racks of specimens. They careened into a bookcase, which wobbled precariously, dumping a volume of *The Comprehensive Guide to Medicinal and Potional Uses of the Flowers of the British Isles* on her head.

"Ow! Damned silly, out-of-date book!"

She scooped it up and shoved it back into place, dissolving into giggles. All this excitement made her giddy. Ridiculous, she supposed, for a grown woman of twenty-six, but Astrid never managed to behave as she ought.

"May I read the letter?" Grace inquired.

"Of course!" Astrid handed it over. "It has a rather somber tone, I'm afraid. One of Lord Ayleston's colleagues died unexpectedly, which is why there is an opening for a new member."

Grace nodded, reading. "He does sound delighted to recommend you for the position, however."

"Yes. I feel a twinge of guilt for profiting from a man's death, but not enough for it to dampen my spirits, as I hadn't met him but in passing."

"You should feel no guilt at all. They ought to have voted you in years ago. It's hardly your fault the current membership is set against increasing its numbers."

"I think they are set against letting a woman in. But Lord Ayleston doesn't give a fig about a person's sex, only about their work. And now he has given me the director's recommendation. Voting against that is simply not done."

Grace's brow furrowed. "Some of those men will do it, regardless."

Astrid drew herself up as tall as her five-foot-one-inch frame could manage. "Not enough of them," she declared with supreme confidence. "Too many of them know me and know my work. They will accept me, though perhaps grudgingly."

Grace grinned. "And I will help make your official application sparkle with such brilliance that anyone who does choose to reject it will feel an acute embarrassment."

"Thank you. We will make it not only professional, but pioneering. We will use true-color photographs." Never mind that the last batch developed had a decidedly sickly look to them. Between herself, Grace, and Cal, they would soon perfect the apparatus.

"I made the necessary adjustments to the developing potion," Grace said. "Has your brother tweaked the machine like he promised?"

"No, but he will. I'll go pester him now, and give him the good news."

"And I will get back to work sorting." Grace gestured at the collection scattered on the desk. "Thus far I've only found two specimens worth keeping from this week's excursions."

A touch of pink colored Astrid's cheeks. "I may have been daydreaming on a few of my walks."

And how could she not? They'd had a spate of unseasonably warm weather, and she'd spent much of it roaming the beaches with her feet bare and her hair flying loose, imagining far-away lands, great adventures, and—she had to admit—mysterious encounters with a handsome stranger. These moments of escape and fantasy were vital to her well-being.

It had been just over a year now since her father had died and her whole world had ground to a sudden halt. Cal had become Whitehaven. Astrid had become the lady of the house when her mother's nerves had failed to recover from the blow. It had been—was still—hard, but they were coping, and life was improving. The letter from Ayleston was her new beginning. She would travel again, put more effort than ever into her research, and drag her brother into the sunshine with her.

She had just reached the top of the stairs when she spied

him rushing down the hall toward her, all but running.

"Astrid! Thank God. I was just coming to find you."

Cal's light blue eyes blazed with an all-too-common expression of panic. His fair skin was paler than usual, combining with his white-blond hair to give him a ghostly mien. Once, he had spent hours of every day outside. His struggle to take up the Whitehaven name had left him too often indoors, fading his once-bronzed complexion and leaving crinkles of stress around his eyes.

"I was on my way to find you as well," Astrid replied, feigning good cheer. Her brother's distress had quashed her enthusiasm. Sharing her news became an afterthought. Right now she only wanted to hug him.

She couldn't recall the last time she had hugged him. Ages ago. Months, perhaps. They'd been so close, once. How had it come to this?

Cal's gaze fell to the paper in her hand. "You received a letter as well?"

"Yes, from Lord Ayleston."

He blinked in confusion. "Ayleston?"

"Yes. He is recommending me for membership in the Institute."

"Oh!" A flash of happiness passed over his face before the despair took hold once more. "Oh, Asti, I'm so sorry. Someone is trying to destroy everything you've worked so hard for."

"What?"

"Come into my study. I think we'd best be sitting down."

Astrid's heart thudded in her chest. Good heavens, what dire news had he received? Had one of the Institute's less agreeable members written a nasty letter? She'd been sneered at before. She could take it.

She took a seat in her favorite chair in the study, perching on the edge rather than sprawling as was her habit. Cal took his place behind their father's big desk, shifting uncomfortably. Somehow all six-foot-two of him still looked like the little boy who used to clamber up into the chair and pretended to run the estate.

"I've had a letter."

Astrid nodded, folding her hands in her lap and waiting for him to continue.

"It comes from Mr. Fawdry at the Cliffsdale Ladies' Convalescent Asylum."

"The lunatic asylum? Whyever would he write you?"

"It seems there have been… complaints."

A heavy dread settled in Astrid's stomach. "About me?"

"Yes."

"Bugger."

Cal's eyes narrowed. "Don't let anyone hear you talk like that, Astrid. It won't help your case."

Their matching eyes locked. She didn't need to remind him that he was the one who had taught her most of the naughty words she knew. For a silent moment they shared the bittersweet memory of those mischievous childhood days.

He pushed the letter across the desk. "Here. Read it for yourself. There's no sense in me reciting it for you."

Astrid retrieved the paper and gave it a quick perusal. Anonymous complaints, naturally. No one would dare criticize her to her face or confess to their shameful backstabbing. Mr. Fawdry insisted upon an immediate evaluation and threatened legal action. He believed she should be committed at once, "for the safety of her own person as well as that of the public."

"I didn't realize I was so dangerous to the local populace," she scoffed. "One would think I was a well-armed brigand from this report. Little do they know I wield only a pocketful of rocks and fossils."

"I wish I could laugh it off as you do."

"I had rather laugh than cry."

Cal reached out and covered her hand with his own. "I won't let them take you, Asti, I swear it. They can file all the complaints they want. They can start legal proceedings, charge us with crimes. I don't care. I'll find some way to get past it."

"I could always leave the country." The thought caused a stab of pain. Leave Cal and Grace. Leave her mother who needed her. Leave her laboratory, her work, her beloved home. As much as she craved adventure, Whitehaven was her refuge, always waiting to embrace her upon her return. She would fight for it. "No, that won't do except as a temporary measure."

"We will think of something. As a peer of the realm, I have some influence, but given my age and our family eccentricities… Goddammit!" He shoved his chair backward, raking his hands through his hair. "Who would do this to you? I'd like to pound him to a bloody pulp!"

"I honestly couldn't say. Everyone thinks I'm strange. I have dozens of disappointed suitors."

"Bleeding fortune hunters."

"Exactly. Any of them could hold a grudge. Or it could be someone in town who is having the vapors because I don't have a constant chaperone."

She flipped over the paper to examine the list of complaints against her. It was lengthy and spanned the full range of her supposed sins.

"Heavens. I *am* a menace to society, it seems. Just listen to this: 'Reads novels in public. Wears clothing unbefitting her station. Shows a disinclination for marriage. Uses technical and/or scientific language. Runs about unshod, like a wild hellion.' I suspect I'm not supposed to feel proud of that, am I?"

"There is a certain wildness in our blood. We're not meant for confined spaces and strict rules. I hadn't thought it so bad a thing until now."

"Well." She sat back in her chair, her mind abuzz. "We both know I'm quite sane, despite all this so-called proof. We simply must prove it to everyone else."

"Easier said than done."

Astrid winced. "I'll have to go out in public and follow all the rules, the way I attempted to do when Mother and Father insisted that I at least *try* to have a Season."

"I would say you should marry, but I refuse to see you shackled to any of those wastrels who see only your handsome dowry."

"I appreciate that."

"Very well, then." He scooted his chair back into the desk and took up a sheet of paper and a pen. His anxiety had dissolved into determination. "You do everything you can to discover who might be behind this. We will all endeavor to act as normal as possible. In the meantime, I will summon help."

"Help from whom?"

"Monte. Dr. Montford, that is."

"Ooh, isn't he the friend who's a complete rakehell? The one you said once convinced half-a-dozen young ladies to join him for a naked sporting competition in the style of the ancient Greeks?"

"We have long since grown up, Astrid. He's a respectable physician now."

"Oh. That's too bad. He sounded interesting."

"Well, now he is proper and boring. But knowledgeable. Go work on a plan. Tell Miss Fairfax about this mess. Her head is filled with ideas. I must write this letter."

"Tell your doctor friend I don't do any sporting activities in the nude. There's too much possibility for chafing."

"Astrid! For God's sake. Normal. Act normal."

"Is there an instruction manual for that?"

Cal let out a choking sort of laugh. "I wish!" He sobered quickly, walking around the desk to help her to her feet. "Better to laugh than cry, eh?"

"Yes."

He wrapped his lanky arms around her, and for a few moments they held one another, needing no words, easing their worries in their togetherness. Nothing and no one would separate the Wembley twins.

## II

# (NO) INTRODUCTION NEEDED

To: *The Honourable Ernest Montford*
From: *Frederick Wembley, Marquess of Whitehaven,*
*Viscount Caladay*

MONTE,

It has been too long, my friend, since we have corresponded, and I wish I could say that I write you merely to remedy such failure on my part. Alas, I am not so earnest a friend. I must beg your immediate assistance with a problem of grave importance.

You may recall my twin sister Astrid. Or, rather, you may recall my tales of her, as I do not believe the two of you have met. I do remember there was a time I threatened you to keep away from her under pain of death. Regardless, you have heard me speak of her and joke of her eccentricities. It pains me to say that I no longer consider them a laughing matter.

We have received a letter (A letter! How can I term it such? It is all but blackmail.) from a nearby asylum, asserting that numerous complaints have been made *regarding her unusual habits and bluestocking tendencies. I love my sister and would not change her for the world, but her lack of interest in settling down with a husband and her constant drive to join a scientific society mark her as peculiar, and many, I am unhappy to report, take this as a sign of madness. The letter states that for the good of the local population and Astrid's own safety she must be evaluated and likely incarcerated for an "indefinite duration."*

*I am at my wit's end. I fear I have not given her as much attention as I ought to have done in this year since our father's untimely passing. She has always tended to wildness, and she has been free and often on her own these past months. I cannot even say what she has been up to much of the time. I also cannot deny that I, too, am worried for her mental state, given my own difficulties and the hysteria and instability to which our mother has succumbed of late.*

*My own word as regards her sanity may not suffice to keep her here at Whitehaven where she belongs. You, my dearest friend, with your piles of books and dedication to research, may be her only hope. If you could observe her and offer a learned, professional opinion on the soundness of her mind and decency of her habits, it could free us from this sudden and terrible burden. I promise a handsome payment and all conveniences at my disposal.*

*If you are able, please accept the invitation to my home at once, that we may benefit from your professional advice.*

*I hope to see you soon, and wish it were under happier circumstances.*

*Sincerely,*
*Cal*

Whitehaven Manor had changed little in the years since Monte had last seen it. The gardens were a bit different, but the house was as colossal as he remembered. The towering foyer contained the same furnishings, including a peculiar aquarium that had captivated him on his previous visits. Raised on a pedestal in the center of the hall, the open-topped octagonal tank teemed with water-loving plants and brightly colored fish. Monte trailed a finger through the water as he stared down at the circling goldfish, watching them dart in and out of the greenery. Wild creatures, slipping from sight. In the confined space, they would soon appear again. The girl would not. Each time he'd passed through, he'd looked in the village, wandered the farms. She was but a brief interlude, burned in his memory, once flesh and blood, but now insubstantial as a phantom.

*"Ah-hem."*

Monte whirled at the sound. Crippens, the butler, stood scowling, an expression Monte remembered from long ago visits.

"If you would follow me, sir. His lordship will see you in the study."

Monte nodded, chiding himself for letting his mind wander. He wasn't here to toy with the household pets, nor to reminisce about lost women. He'd left that sort of deplorable behavior behind him. Besides, he expected she was long since married to some unappreciative bastard.

He followed Crippens deeper into the mansion than he'd ever been, admiring the craftsmanship and tastefulness of the decor. The walls and tabletops sported a cheerful clutter of photographs, art, and bric-a-brac. Old candle holders had been replaced by modern lamps that glowed steadily with high-quality illumination potions, brightening the corridors and rooms. Such a massive house could have been ostentatious, but the family had made it warm and inviting. It was a home, and he could see why Cal was so fond of it.

It would be good to see his friend, even under unusual circumstances. They hadn't spent nearly enough time together in the past year. Only a few, brief visits in London. Cal—

Whitehaven, he was now—had new responsibilities as marquess and head of the family. Monte had patients to attend and his research. He'd shoved those to the side. Cal needed him, and Monte had sworn to always be there for him.

The first order of business was to meet the 'crazy' sister. Monte had dug through some of his old correspondence to refresh his memory of her. Cal referred to her often, in that loving, teasing way that made Monte envious. His own brother was nine years older and had always watched him with a wary frown, as if he were a bandit, hiding in the shadows, waiting to do him in and inherit in his stead. The good-for-nothing spare. Now that Osmund had two sons of his own, he'd deemed Monte irrelevant.

*Lady Astrid Wembley,* Monte mused. *Free spirited. Obsessed with science. Spends inordinate amounts of time outdoors. Collects and studies rocks.*

She sounded like any other Wembley. Eccentric. Descended from madmen, people said. Both parents had been amateur botanists and had written a textbook together. They had educated their children at home, rather than sending Cal to Eton and Astrid to a ladies' boarding school. Cal had made himself into a champion cricketer at Cambridge by studying the game from a scientific perspective and thought swimming in the ocean in November was perfectly reasonable.

No wonder Lady Astrid had been declared insane.

"Dr. Ernest Montford here to see you, your lordship," the butler intoned, waving Monte through the study door.

Cal looked up from a pile of correspondence. His blond hair needed trimming, and his complexion was uncharacteristically pale. His eyes, however, flashed with pleasure, and he sprang from his seat.

"Monte! It's been an age." He raced around the desk and Monte found himself subjected to an enthusiastic bear-hug. "I can't thank you enough for coming."

A moment later, Cal stepped back and coughed awkwardly,

straightening his shoulders in the guise of a stoic British marquess. "Right. Good to see you."

There was no hiding his roiling emotions behind those pale blue eyes, but Monte had years of practice feigning ignorance of that hot Swedish blood. No need to add to the embarrassment by acknowledging the sentimentality.

"Indeed. Let's to business. Where is this sister of yours, Whitehaven?"

Cal winced. "Please don't call me that. Yes, I'm Marquess of Whitehaven, but I'm also still Viscount Caladay. I can't abide giving up the name I've used my entire life, and I haven't a son to use the title for me." A mischievous gleam sparkled in his eyes. "And if you insist upon using my proper title, I will retaliate by calling you Ernest."

"Not even my mother calls me Ernest, as you well know. Now, your sister. Where is she?"

"Late. She was supposed to be here to meet you, but punctuality is not her strongest point. She gets caught up in things."

"Her studies?"

"Anything. Work, the book she's reading, her pets, an unusual pebble in the garden. Whatever sparks her interest."

"I see."

"It's not that she's incapable of paying attention, it's just that she doesn't bother. What much of the rest of the world considers important she considers tedious."

Monte nodded. "I can see how that would cause trouble. Lithe, blond beauty ignoring one's advances in favor of a stone on the ground? Bound to infuriate a man."

Cal laughed. "You really haven't ever met her, have you?"

"No. Why do you say that?"

"Turn around."

Monte swiveled just in time to see a woman step through the doorway—a dark-haired, curvaceous, and far-too-familiar woman.

"Oh, fuck," he blurted.

By some miracle, his profanity was lost beneath Cal's introductions.

"Astrid, please allow me to present my dear friend, Dr. Ernest Montford. Monte, this is my sister, Lady Astrid Wembley."

Monte was dead. Deceased. Bereft of life. Cal was going to drag him into the well-trimmed gardens and beat him senseless with the rocks Lady Astrid was so fond of. He would be left for the ravens to pick at. Then the young lady would be sent to the asylum and Cal would return to kill him once again for his failure to help. Maybe he was dead already. This certainly felt like hell.

Why now, of all times, must he reap the reward of his misspent youth? It put not only his friendship at risk, but her future as well. He had envisioned finding her in a hundred different ways, but never had he even considered something like this. This was the price, it seemed, for attempting to seduce an innocent young lady.

*It's been seven years,* he told himself. *Perhaps she doesn't remember you.*

"I'm pleased to make your acquaintance at last, Dr. Montford," Lady Astrid greeted him, eyes sparkling. Her plump, pink lips grinned up at him. "It feels as though we ought to have met years ago."

So much for that hope. She not only remembered, but she was taunting him. Her piercing gaze caressed him head to toe, just as it had that day on the beach, sending a rush of arousal straight to his cock. Damn. Thank God long coats were in fashion.

"Yes," he replied idiotically.

His memory was faulty, it seemed, because she was vastly more beautiful than he recalled. Or perhaps she had simply fully grown into her womanhood. Her face transfixed him, so round and cheery, with clear, wide eyes. Her shapely little nose sported a small silver ring in the left nostril that he found curiously appealing.

And those lips. Lush, kissable lips. Monte remembered the taste of those lips. Crisp, tart, with a deep, subtle sweetness. As perfect as a fruit plucked at the peak of ripeness.

He had to wrench his gaze from her mouth, but only made the situation worse by allowing himself to examine the rest of her body. Someone had forced her sumptuous figure into a rigid, conservative day dress of the type worn by any number of respectable ladies. It did nothing to flatter her, though it couldn't disguise her generous bosom. Monte would much rather have seen her in peasant dress.

"I understood you to be a dissolute rake," she said, "but Cal tells me you have become quite respectable and boring."

Lord, but she was impertinent. Her sass made words like "delightful" and "refreshing" spring to mind. Why did he like that about her? He oughtn't like that. He glanced over at Cal, because looking anywhere in the vicinity of Lady Astrid caused nothing but rakish thoughts.

Monte steadied himself with a deep breath and addressed the lady, determined to proceed in a calm and civilized fashion. "Er, yes. I admit to a certain foolishness in my youth, but I believe any man can reform himself should he make the effort. I do my best to live by moderate and healthful habits."

"How interesting." Her flat tone implied he was the dullest man she'd ever met, but her eyes had lost none of their sparkle. Tantalizing, teasing woman.

He wanted to push her up against the wall and smother her taunts with kisses. His disobedient body took a step toward her. Hell. He needed to escape before the situation got any more out of hand. Before he did something unforgivable. Before Cal began to suspect he already had done.

"You must excuse me, but I need to check that my trunks have been delivered and get settled in. We needn't conduct any interviews or the like until tomorrow."

"Interviews?"

He gazed into her eyes, narrowed in puzzlement but deep with curiosity. Sharp, intelligent eyes. Studying him like a specimen in her collection.

"I must conduct and record proper medical examinations if we are to prove you to be of sound mind and body."

"Ah. So that is how you are to 'help.'"

"You disapprove?"

"I'd hoped for something more like advice. Ideally better advice than, 'act normal.'" She cast an irritable look at her brother.

"I will do my best to offer what professional wisdom I possess. Please excuse me. I will see you at tea."

Assuming he could get himself under control by tea time.

*Act normal.*

Would that he were able.

# III

# TROUBLES UPON TROUBLES

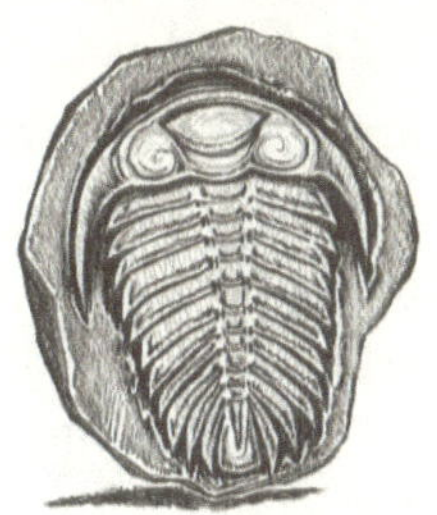

Tʜᴇ ɴᴏᴛᴏʀɪᴏᴜs Mᴏɴᴛᴇ was her erstwhile mystery suitor.

Astrid wanted to laugh. And not in a good way. In an anxious, maniacal way that would be taken as further proof of her insanity.

She ought never to have teased him. She'd taken one look at those misty, gray eyes and that fine figure, and her brain had turned to mush. Flirtatious words had spewed from her mouth.

She'd horrified him. He'd gaped at her as if she were a fiend sprung from the depths of hell. Perhaps there was some truth to his claim of respectability.

Not only would she have to see him again at tea, but they would be in the same house for an indefinite period of time. He would ask her questions and study her habits. That would be awkward under any circumstances, but how much worse would it be because it was *him*?

This wasn't at all how she'd envisioned their reunion. It had been years since she'd actively planned their next meeting, but he did cross her mind from time to time. She'd always imagined he would sweep her into his arms and kiss her until her toes tingled and her skin burned. He would say, "God, I've missed you," and she would drag him to her favorite secluded cove where they would make passionate love. Because she would be sophisticated and prepared. But she was neither.

"Astrid? Is something wrong with the apparatus?"

Astrid blinked and turned toward Grace. "Oh. No. Sorry. Cal did make the adjustments I asked for, and the new plates are of much higher quality."

She pushed her mind back to the camera, turning knobs to adjust the angles for the best lighting. Their design had been tweaked to perfection, if only they could get the potion right. Magic was so… finicky. She could mix ordinary chemicals with exacting results, but add serum and everything went awry. It seemed potions were more art than science. Beyond the realm of Astrid's understanding, certainly.

She shifted the fossil. No sense in taking a crooked photograph. This particular trilobite wasn't the best for showing off colors. It was only a dark brown fossil in a bed of lighter brown rock. It was one of her best-preserved examples, however. If this latest test was successful, she would move on to photographing more colorful pieces. She had several beautiful rock samples and hundreds of fossils. The trilobites, though, were her specialty and first priority.

"I'm one hundred percent certain the developing potion is correct," Grace informed her. "It handles our traditional photographs beautifully. I have hopes the new batch of color fixative will be clearer than the last."

"You would know better than I. I'm no potions talent. They simply never come out quite how I plan. When I was sixteen, I tried to make a potion to cure my cold. My nose stopped running, but my eyes itched for a week. I've only used real medicines since then."

Grace chuckled. "When I was a girl in India I used to mix up 'potions' with muddy water and things I found on the ground. Then I would ask my parents to drink them. One day I grew angry that they only pretended and drank my concoction myself. That was the end of that."

"Ugh! How revolting," Astrid laughed. "How have I never heard that story before?"

"Because we don't do potions often. And you know I rarely talk about myself. I prefer to hear the stories of you and Lord Caladay as naughty children."

Astrid grinned. Grace was the only other person who continued to call her brother Caladay instead of Whitehaven. It was a peculiar little intimacy that made her feel like family. Astrid loved her like a sister. They had long been friends, but were growing ever closer.

Astrid returned to her work, adjusting the position of the trilobite once again, and rechecking the angles. The longer she fiddled, the more the lighting changed.

"Do you want to tell me what's bothering you?"

"Nothing's bothering me," Astrid lied. She turned the knob one final click and declared it good enough.

"Is it the trouble with that man from the asylum? Your brother assured me his physician friend is well-regarded in medical circles and people will respect his opinion."

Astrid tried to hide a wince. "I'll have to sit for interviews and probably a medical exam. It will be embarrassing."

*It will be worse. He knows I'm abnormal. He must think me loose also. I must have been one of dozens of girls to fall for that smile and that voice. Maybe hundreds. But now he's reformed while I am as wild as ever.*

"I didn't think you so easily embarrassed."

"Grace, he will have to lie. I can't be normal. It isn't in me. I rejected eight proposals in the first half of my one Season. Do you know why they stopped coming? Because by then everyone had figured out I was strange. And that was when I was trying my best!"

To be honest, she *had* called a number of those men fortune hunters to their face. And rather strongly hinted that many of them were less than intelligent. Her best was, at best, problematic.

"Then we shall have to address the problem in a different way," Grace declared. "Who would do this to you?"

"I have no idea. I have no enemies."

"You have at least one. Think of it like a mystery in a sensation novel. What is his or her motive? Who stands to gain if you're locked away?"

"Someone who wants my place in the Institute." It seemed so obvious now she had said it. She had achieved something others envied. "I have Lord Ayleston's recommendation. Even with a few rabid anti-feminists in the group, I will have the votes. I can't be supplanted unless I am gone entirely."

"Good. Bring an extra notebook when we go to the lecture series this weekend. We can record names of attendees and discover who might be coveting that position."

"Cal doesn't want me to go. He's afraid I'll be kidnapped or some such nonsense. And he won't come along. You know how he's gotten, with all those worries about 'duty' and the like."

Grace grimaced. "Yes. The poor man. The stress is…" She turned away. "It's not good for him. I wish there were more I could do."

Astrid put a hand on her friend's shoulder. "It's not your burden. You have been a true friend to us and done more than anyone would expect of you. Why, you are standing here helping me with yet another trouble!"

Grace whirled about. "And I think I have an answer. At least for this weekend."

"What? Ignore my brother and hop on a train by myself? That was my plan."

"No. We ask Dr. Montford to join us."

"Oh." The urge to laugh nervously took hold once again. "That makes sense." It did. Cal would think it reasonable. They could utilize the time aboard the train to get through some of the ridiculous interviews. It was an excellent idea.

It was also, perhaps, the worst idea ever.

# IV
# BILLIARDS AND BRAN CAKES

Tea was awkward. Dinner was worse. Monte contemplated drinking himself into a stupor. It wouldn't take much these days. He rarely indulged in more than a single glass of wine or a snifter of brandy. It came as a relief to disappear into the billiard room with his friend, well out of sight of the ladies.

Thus far, he couldn't stop himself staring at Lady Astrid, as if somehow he could turn her from a marquess's daughter into a lowly farm girl through sheer force of will. He would meet her on the beach, they would have a romp, and be done with it. Not that he ought to be indulging in sexual dalliances with farm girls, either. Even if they had eyes like the sky and hips just begging to have a man's hands on them.

His cue ball caromed off in entirely the wrong direction. All these lustful thoughts were not good for a man's brain.

"You're out of practice, old chap," Cal chuckled, taking up his own cue and quickly sinking the red ball. "Whatever are you doing with yourself these days?"

"Treating rich patients with dubious problems."

"Sounds like a delightful hobby."

"It pays the bills. The remainder of my time is spent on potions work."

Cal potted the red ball for the third time in a row. Thank God they had only made a token gentleman's wager.

"Potions, is it? What are you trying to make?"

"A cure for hysteria."

Cal's cue slipped, and he missed completely. "I thought that was a joke."

"Not at all. I am determined. You know how I felt about that asylum."

A shudder ran down Monte's spine. He could never forget those horrible months he'd spent working with the institutionalized women. Deplorable, unsanitary conditions. Isolation. Straitjacketing. So-called treatment with electric shock inducers and electropotion ingestion. All the methods meant to confine or subdue patients revolted him. What the women needed were therapies or medications to ease their symptoms. He'd helped a few, but failed so many.

Cal's hand clenched around his billiard cue. "Those things you wrote about: that's what they want to do to Astrid."

Monte squeezed his friend's shoulder. "I won't let anyone commit her. I swear it."

"She's not insane. She's unusual, but not insane."

"I agree. Even on so brief an acquaintance."

Cal gave him a quizzical frown. "Is that so? It seems to me you don't like her very much. You look pained whenever you are forced to converse with her."

*You have no idea.*

"On the contrary. I find her fascinating."

*Much too fascinating.*

"You and she exchanged barbed words over a roast chicken."

"I merely noted that cream sauces ought not be slathered over one's meat, as the aggregation of too much rich or heavy food can lead to indigestion, which in turn upsets the temper. She then proceeded to eat far too much of the sauce, which no doubt precipitated her insolent remarks."

"She wasn't wrong calling you pompous."

"A moderate diet is essential to good health and mental stability. I see no reason why I shouldn't encourage others in good nutritional habits."

"Monte." Cal's voice held a warning.

"What?"

"You're an ass. Also, it's your turn."

Monte took up his cue and returned to the game. Cal's mistake had left him a good shot, and he potted both the red ball and his own. He retrieved the balls and lined up his next shot.

Just as he was poised to strike, Cal said, "You will be escorting my sister to London for the weekend."

Monte jerked, sending the cue ball sailing across the room.

"Dashed bad luck, that," Cal remarked. "Two points more to me."

"That wasn't very sporting of you, Whitehaven," Monte shot back, emphasizing Cal's title.

"I was merely making conversation."

"You can't send me off all alone with your sister! Are you mad?"

"Miss Fairfax will be with you. There ought to be no trouble." The laughter faded from his eyes. "I'm counting on you to ensure there is no trouble."

"Of course."

*You are setting me up for trouble. Lady Astrid is nothing but trouble.*

And Monte had left trouble far behind him. He was respectable now, dammit.

"Let's play," Cal offered a conciliatory hand. "Fairly, from now on. Would you like a drink? It might improve your game."

"Yes." *To hell with moderation.* "Make it a double."

Monte's foolish overindulgence left him waking with a throbbing headache and a short temper. He stumbled down to breakfast and requested a pot of tea brewed extra strong, resisting the temptation to dull his pain with more of Cal's brandy.

Cal and Lady Astrid were already seated at the table, along with a woman Monte had yet to meet. Tall and dark-haired, with a bronze complexion, she had a confident, no-nonsense air about her. She wore a flattering, but modest green dress, accessorized only by a pair of matching bracelets around her left wrist. Her posture was perfect and she sliced her food into precise bites. Everything about her proclaimed her to be smart and sensible. A good companion for Lady Astrid.

"Monte, do join us," Cal called, waving him to the table. "And permit me to introduce you to my sister's research partner, Miss Fairfax."

"Dr. Montford," she greeted him, not waiting for further introductions. "It's a pleasure to meet you. Thank you for agreeing to accompany us to town this weekend. It will set Lord Caladay's mind at ease. You must excuse him, but he is under the mistaken impression we ladies are incapable of taking care of ourselves."

Definitely smart. But bold. Monte revised his opinion. Miss Fairfax might not be a moderating influence on Lady Astrid.

Cal's features were twisted in pain. Monte suspected his head was pounding as well. "I do not think you incapable of anything, Miss Fairfax."

"Oh, excellent!" Astrid exclaimed. "Then we shall go on our own." She stabbed a large bite of boiled egg and popped it into her mouth.

"That's not what I meant."

Astrid stared him down until she finished chewing. "You were lying, then?"

"I was not."

"Then why don't you trust us?"

"See here, I'm only trying to..." Cal put a hand to his head. "No. I'm not going to argue. You must excuse me. I have business awaiting me." He abandoned the remainder of his breakfast and fled the room.

A short time later, Miss Fairfax excused herself as well, leaving Monte alone with Lady Astrid. He eyed her across her questionable breakfast of eggs, greasy meats, and cheese. She wore another drab, constricting gown this morning, and her soft, brown curls had been yanked into a tight knot. The lack of any stray wisps suggested her hair had been fixed in place with a bandoline solution. Monte couldn't fathom why ladies insisted on mistreating their tresses with gummy concoctions. Perhaps she simply didn't know better. He would advise her of the potential ill-effects.

And perhaps offer to help her wash it from her hair. It would necessitate she strip down to her underthings. He would bury his fingers in locks damp with rose-scented water, while he molded his body to hers...

"Aren't you eating?" she inquired. "I believe there is leftover chicken with cream sauce, if the current selection is unpalatable."

The edge beneath her conversational tone sent another stab of pain through his head. He was in no mood for an argument. He wanted to be back in bed, preferably with a warm woman snuggled up beside him.

He cursed silently. This favor he was doing his friend was detrimental to his moral fiber. If Cal weren't his best friend in the world, he would have left for home by now.

"I believe your kitchen maid is bringing my breakfast just now," he answered, straining for civility.

The young woman placed a plate and a steaming pot of tea

before him. He smiled up at her and thanked her. She bobbed a little curtsy, her cheeks flushing a lovely pink.

"You're very welcome, sir." She fluttered her eyelashes at him and scampered away.

"Women really do fling themselves at you." Lady Astrid sounded not quite annoyed, but certainly grim. "I suppose I oughtn't be surprised about that."

"I don't encourage it."

She raised her dark eyebrows. "Oh, is that so?"

He winced. "I apologize for my behavior toward you in the past. It was deplorable and I am heartily ashamed of it."

She stabbed another bite of egg. "Of course you are."

She didn't sound mollified, so he pressed on, determined to convince her of his sincerity. "I should never have taken advantage of you. It doesn't matter that I didn't know you to be a well-bred lady. Touching you was wrong. All I can say is I was a stupid, randy boy. I assure you, it won't happen again."

Astrid continued to maul her egg, her lips pinched into a tight line. Monte's gut tightened. She wouldn't forgive him.

"I would like to begin again," he offered. "I genuinely wish to provide assistance with your current predicament. I wouldn't presume to claim your friendship, but can't we be civil acquaintances?"

A long silence passed between them before Lady Astrid sighed.

"Very well. I shall practice my social niceties. Lovely to see you, Dr. Montford. How are you this morning?"

*Hungover and lustful.*

"Very well, thank you."

"What are those peculiar little cakes on your plate?"

Monte glanced down at the small round cakes. The cook had done a masterful job, making them perfect circles of a lovely dark-brown color. "Bran loaves. I eat them every morning. Your cook was kind enough to make a batch for me."

"How curious. May I try one?"

"Certainly." He sliced off a small bite and transferred it to her plate. "You would do well to eat them, yourself. They are most healthful."

She chewed her bite slowly, and her nose wrinkled in distaste. "Ugh. It's like eating paper."

"The rich foods you've eaten of late have no doubt overstimulated your palate. I assure you, if you were to eat them every morning as I do, you would find them appetizing."

"I doubt that."

Monte sipped his tea. It was as strong as he'd hoped. "The bran loaves stimulate healthful digestion and do not overset the stomach. This allows both the body and mind to begin the day in a restive state. Unlike your cheese, which may well cause dyspepsia when ingested so early in the morning."

Astrid's brow furrowed, but her tone remained even, "I'm very fond of cheese."

"I never eat cheese," Monte explained. "Nor do I adulterate my tea with milk. It adds an unnecessary richness and dilutes the beneficial properties of the beverage."

"How unpatriotic of you."

Was she mocking him again?

"What *do* you eat, Dr. Montford? Other than your revolting little cakes, I mean."

"Vegetables."

She gave him a skeptical arch of her brow once more. "Vegetables."

"Yes."

There was a distinct lack of vegetables at the breakfast table this morning. Dinner had provided only a few withered specimens with most of the nutrition boiled out of them.

"Nothing else? You did eat some of the chicken last night, though you avoided the sauce."

"Moderate portions of meat. Nuts and beans. But primarily vegetables."

"No fruits?"

"Rarely."

"That's a pity. I love fruit. There's nothing quite like biting into a perfectly ripe apple, don't you think? It floods one's mouth with that crisp, juicy taste. So sweet, with just the right tart bite."

Monte swallowed a groan. Now he was fixated on her mouth again. He gulped his tea to prevent himself saying anything he would later regret.

Astrid hopped from her seat, forcing him to set down the cup and rise.

"It was interesting chatting with you in a civil manner, Dr. Montford," she said. "I must go and prepare for our journey. Enjoy your tasteless breakfast."

He nodded and watched her leave before resuming his seat and pouring himself another cup of tea. He wished it were a good, strong whisky.

"Cal, you bastard," he muttered. "You haven't just asked for a favor. You've asked me to do the impossible."

# V

# ENEMIES AND ENIGMAS

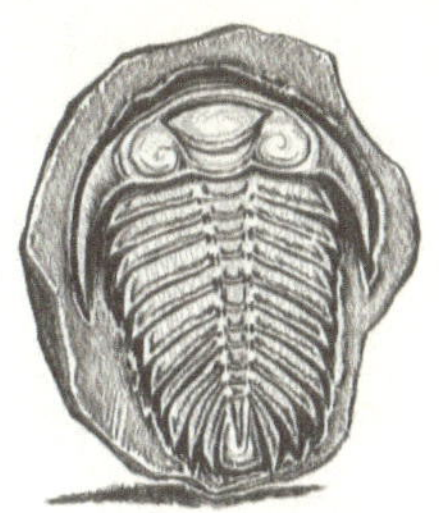

"ERNEST MONTFORD IS AN insufferable know-it-all." Astrid shifted in her seat and tried not to stare at him across the crowded lecture hall.

"Hmm?" Grace looked up from her book.

"Don't you agree?"

"Pardon? I'm afraid I was caught up in a particularly fascinating anecdote. Did you know Iceland is covered in volcanoes?"

Astrid was almost certain she'd read that exact same book. "In fact—"

"It has been devastated multiple times in its history due to eruptions that send clouds of ash and smoke into the air. It has peculiar hot springs and places called geysers where steaming water sprays from the ground. I should very much like to visit, though it's a cold, strange place."

"I'm not especially bothered by cold, as you well know."

"Yes, well, I wouldn't travel there except in summer. On the short winter days, the sun is up for no more than five hours. Though that isn't so bad as places even further to the north,

"

where it's said they have no sun at all." Grace snapped out of her reverie. "I'm sorry, what were you saying?"

Astrid laughed. "Something about insufferable know-it-alls."

Grace's cheeks reddened. "I didn't mean to be."

"No. You were simply excited. I didn't mean you in any event. I meant Dr. Montford."

"Oh. He seemed nice enough to me. Was your interview on the train ride so terrible, then? I admit I was lost in my book, and I thought it best not to interrupt while he made flirty-eyes at you."

Astrid sighed. He had *not* made flirty-eyes. He made you-are-the-most-abnormal-person- I've-ever-met eyes. She had spent two and a half hours answering absurd questions about her health while he frowned suspiciously and criticized her habits.

"All I wanted was to read my novel. He wanted to lecture me about nutrition and the ill-effects of, oh, everything I like to eat."

"But you finished the interview?"

"Oh, yes. We covered diet, exercise, sleep, diet, exposure to chemicals during my research, clothing choices for outdoor activities, potion ingestion, oh, and diet. The man hates cheese. I don't know what's wrong with him.

"Then he asked about today's lecture and when I told him it was concerning germ theory, he launched into a half-hour diatribe about micro-organisms and hygiene, as if I were the stupidest, most slovenly person on earth. Did you know the whole of my life I have been bathing at the wrong time of day?"

Grace's dark eyes widened. "There's a wrong time of day for bathing?"

"Indeed. And a wrong temperature. The bathing chamber must be heated just so, and one mustn't bathe too soon after eating, as it can upset the tempers. Well, I can tell you my temper is rather upset just now."

She glared across the room at Montford, who was engaged in an animated conversation with Lord Ayleston. She was certain Ayleston had been on the way to speak with her when Monte had intercepted him. He'd probably done it deliberately. Pompous arse. She'd liked him much better as a rake.

Today's speaker took the podium, and Astrid turned her attention to the stage. For the next hour, at least, she could relax. As much as it was possible to relax in an ugly, too-tight dress and a corset that jabbed her painfully if she didn't sit rigidly upright. She already regretted the part of the plan that had her dressing as respectably as possible. Worse, it was her own idea. People were so easily swayed by the looks of things. They forgot that sometimes exquisite cheekbones and a perfect chin hid an insufferable know-it-all.

The lecture was brilliant. The speaker was engaging and the topic fascinating. As was typical for an event at the Scientific Institute for the Progression of Rational Thought, the audience asked insightful questions that further enhanced the experience. Astrid did her best not to be annoyed that Dr. Montford asked two excellent questions while she had none of her own.

Tomorrow, though, the talk would cover the exposure of stratigraphic layers through erosion and upheaval. That, she could discuss for hours. Anyone who didn't know her would understand Ayleston's recommendation after tomorrow.

"How did you enjoy the talk, Lady Astrid?" Lord Ayleston inquired when enough of the crowd had wandered away to finally give them the freedom to converse. "I found it most interesting. Today's microscopes can show us so much."

"I loved the talk, Lord Ayleston, thank you for asking. I use my own microscope often to examine the details in small fossils."

"Have you ever examined bits of foodstuff with a microscope?" Dr. Montford cut in. "I should like to give a greater study to yogurt, in particular. It appears to be full of healthful sorts of microbes. I recommend it as a substitute for cheese in a moderate diet."

Astrid glared at him. Grace looked to be trying not to laugh.

"I have also done studies on putrefaction and the growth of molds and bacteria on foods exposed to air," Monte continued, a gleeful gleam in his eyes. "Without proper storage, the little beasts multiply rather vigorously. However, if one follows Dr. Harvey's recommended preservation techniques, their growth is drastically reduced."

"Well, I assure you no unpleasant creatures are growing on the food we provide here," Ayleston chuckled.

"Actually—" Montford began.

It would have ruined Astrid's attempt to be normal to tell him to shut up, but he was standing near enough that she just so happened to turn in a way that caused her elbow to jab him in the ribs. He made a rather delightful grunt of pain.

"Might I persuade the three of you to join me for tea?" Ayleston offered.

They readily agreed, and soon were settled comfortably in the director's personal office, munching on goodies and sipping a full-bodied Assam. Monte ate nothing but cucumber sandwiches, leaving Astrid free to swipe an extra scone. She gave him a defiant look as she took her first bite.

Lord Ayleston stirred his tea in a distracted manner, frowning and staring somewhere past Astrid's head. She had noted this sort of behavior from him in the past, where he appeared to be pondering heavy questions.

"I'm sorry to disrupt your happy afternoon, Lady Astrid, but I think the possibility exists that we have an enemy in common," he said at last, still gazing into the distance.

Her scone froze halfway to her mouth. "An enemy?"

"Just so. Dr. Montford was telling me earlier about your current troubles."

Astrid rounded on Monte. "You did *what*? That's private!

How could you? Why not just wave a sign around? 'Here is Lady Astrid Wembley, lunatic.'"

"It only made sense to bring the issue to Lord Ayleston's attention after your brother told me you suspected the complaints may have originated with someone who wants your place at the Institute."

"That scoundrel! I told him that in confidence!"

Grace laid a hand on Astrid's arm. "Cal is doing what he can to help."

"As am I," Montford insisted.

Lord Ayleston cleared his throat, and they turned back to face him. "Rest assured, Lady Astrid, no information regarding you will leave this room. In fact, nothing we discuss here will leave this room, is that understood?"

"Perfectly." She would hear him out and rail at Montford later.

"As I was saying, I have been apprised of your unusual problem and the suspicion it may be connected with our organization. That supposition, I believe, is a good one, given what else I believe regarding recent events."

"Something bad has happened to you as well," Astrid guessed.

"More than 'bad.' Tragic. Heartbreaking. But, of course, you will have heard. I mentioned it in my letter." His chest rose and fell in a sorrowful sigh. "My longtime friend and colleague, Dr. Stephens, passed from this world recently. His heart gave out suddenly."

"I'm most sorry for your loss," Astrid replied. She knew well the weight of grief. The pangs of the loss of her father came less frequently these days, but she never knew when one might sneak up on her.

"Thank you, dear girl. You should know he greatly admired your work and would be proud to have you as his successor."

"Thank you. That does make me feel less awkward. But there is more to his death? Some connection to me?"

"I believe him to have been murdered."

No one in the room gasped, or even flinched. It was, after all, the logical reason for Ayleston's grim assertion they had an enemy.

"Was a post-mortem examination conducted?" Dr. Montford inquired.

"It was. According to the report, there were no signs of poison."

"A potion-based poison can leave no obvious signs if properly concocted," Monte asserted.

"You are certain of that?"

A flicker of anger darkened Monte's eyes. "I am."

Ayleston nodded. "I appreciate the confirmation of my suspicions."

"You have given thought to motive, I assume?" Grace asked. She had her notebook in hand.

"As I am certain you realize, there are factions within the Institute with differing visions for its future. Stephens was my greatest supporter. Anyone wishing to undermine my position as director would benefit from his absence."

"And it is much less suspicious to kill him than to kill you," Astrid observed.

"Suggesting to me the murderer is no fool. Not that anyone associated with the Institute could be termed a fool. It's difficult to imagine any of our membership would do such a terrible thing, but the minds of men are still very much a mystery to us."

Astrid tapped a finger on the table. "We had considered my antagonizer might want my place in the Institute. Could he have killed to create an opening and then contrived to keep me away?"

"No one outside the Institute knows of my recommendation besides your family and friends," Ayleston said.

"And anyone a member may have told," Astrid pointed out.

"That is suggestive of a conspiracy. A member colluding with an outsider."

"Someone who is eager to join and willing to support one of those factions you spoke of. Are there faction leaders? They would be the most obvious suspects."

"Yes, and I will keep a close eye on them. I can't rule anyone out, however. This is a group of intellectuals. The scheme could have more layers than we can think of now. I caution you to take the utmost care with your safety and to keep me informed of any discoveries you may make. If I learn anything that might help you, I will let you know. If there is anything I can do, please let me know."

"If anyone mentions me, it might help to give the impression I am entirely normal."

Lord Ayleston laughed. "Lady Astrid, you wouldn't be the wonderful woman you are were you 'normal.'"

Happiness burbled through her. She had little recollection of her grandparents, but Ayleston had come to fill that void for her. He had watched her grow, encouraged her passions, and had pride in her as a person and a scientist. Anyone wishing to thwart him would be wise to get rid of her.

The group finished the last of their meal in pensive silence. Grace jotted in her notebook, and Montford fidgeted. He might strive for restrained and sober behavior, but there was a great deal of restless energy in him.

He gripped Astrid's arm as they descended the steps of the Institute headquarters. A prickly sensation spread across her skin. She remembered those hands on other parts of her body.

"We must return to Whitehaven at once," he insisted. "It's not safe for you here."

Astrid jerked from his grasp. "I will not! The lecture I came here for is tomorrow, and I won't skip it because you think I'm a helpless girl."

"That isn't what I think," he argued. "I think we are too close to a number of people who might wish you harm. At home you can keep strangers away. In the city, they are everywhere. I swore to your brother I would see to your safety."

Astrid stared up into those striking gray eyes. "I won't go home."

Shadows of emotion flickered across his face, but she couldn't interpret them. He may have been angry or worried. Possibly he was simply hungry because he ate nothing but vegetables. Whatever he felt, it ran deep.

His head jerked in a gruff nod. "I will accept that so long as you don't leave my sight. When at the hotel, you and Miss Fairfax will remain together in your room and keep both the door and window locked."

Astrid bit her lip, considering defiance.

"It's a sensible plan, Astrid," Grace said. "Until we know more, we must assume the killer might attack more than your reputation."

"Very well. Let's return to the hotel. I feel the need for a hot bath." She shot Monte a look. "Even though I have just eaten."

# VI

# OF SOUND MIND AND BODY

**N**O ONE WITH A LICK OF SENSE could doubt that Lady Astrid was of sound mind. In fact, she was indisputably brilliant. Had Monte believed in astrology, he would have said the Wembley twins had been born under a genius star. Instead, he suspected intelligent parents had conceived them under optimal conditions and their mother had lived a healthy and abstemious lifestyle throughout her pregnancy.

Monte had long admired Cal's sharp wit and creative mind. Astrid, he had discovered, was every bit as intelligent as her brother, and more focused. Whereas Cal dabbled in everything and seldom bothered to master anything, Astrid showed herself to be a dedicated researcher and true expert.

Monte lounged in his seat, his legs crossed at the ankles, admiring the straightforward way she demolished the man on stage with her. One insightful comment had sparked an hour-long debate that now culminated with her taking the stage and proving her point, complete with photographic evidence. She had come prepared.

The lecturer, one Lord Smyth, appeared mortified to be outsmarted by a woman, a fact which entertained Monte to no end. As a long-time worshiper of the fairer sex, he knew from experience women spanned the same range as men—from dim as a rock to so brainy he resembled a rock by comparison. And yet man after man fell victim to the fallacy that a woman's smaller brain was a mark of inferior intelligence. A man of science ought to know better. Dr. Harvey's latest paper theorized that the female brain was denser than the male brain, thus making up for the size difference.

"I concede the issue, Lady Astrid," Smyth said. He sounded magnanimous and gave her a bow of respect, but his cheeks were hot. "Your study into these phenomena is much more comprehensive than I had realized."

"I think what you meant to say is, 'Lady Astrid, you ought to have been the one giving this lecture,'" Monte commented.

From his seat in the back, Smyth couldn't hear him, but several people nearby snickered.

"I think now you understand why she insisted on being here today," Miss Fairfax whispered.

"Indeed. She was spectacular. Ayleston is right to think she belongs."

Miss Fairfax smiled at him fondly. She was pretty. Tall, slender, elegant. Not his preferred type, fortunately. If she meant anything beyond friendship with that smile, he wouldn't struggle to resist it.

"I trust this has given you ideas for your report? You can attest she is articulate, rational, and entirely capable of engaging in civilized public discourse."

If only those were the qualities her detractors had a care for. They would call her unfeminine. They would attack her unusual habits. Monte knew of only a few of those, but he expected to uncover many more. He had a list of reasons patients might be committed to an asylum, and already he'd checked off half-a-dozen that applied to Lady Astrid.

She wouldn't win any points for style, either. To be perfectly blunt, she had the fashion sense of an inebriated gnat.

Today's dress was a putrid color between orange and pink that left her with a sallow complexion. It looked to be strangling her. The waist was cinched so tight he didn't see how she could breathe, let alone talk. She resembled a poorly-whipped meringue, when he knew she was anything but.

What Lady Astrid needed was a rational corset and a gown that flattered her figure. A trim, little hat perched atop her curls would help, along with real gems to indicate her noble station. He hadn't seen a single bit of jewelry on her except for the ring in her nostril. She ought to do away with that, also, but Monte rather liked the way it drew attention to her finely-formed nose. He would be unable to put up a convincing argument against it.

"I have revised our plan," he informed Miss Fairfax. "We will take the later train this evening."

She quirked an eyebrow. "Oh, we will, will we? How interesting."

"You have a very cultured impertinence, Miss Fairfax. Less frank than Lady Astrid, but just as biting."

"And which style do you prefer, Dr. Montford? Though I think I can guess."

"I prefer none at all."

"If that were true, you wouldn't be the dearest friend of Lord Caladay."

Astrid raced across the auditorium toward them. "That was exhilarating," she said in a breathy voice that made Monte want to tear the unhealthful corset from her body. He didn't permit himself to reflect on possible ulterior motives for this corset-ripping desire.

"Just now I had three people tell me how wonderful my explanations were!" she continued. "I'm going to add topics I should like to speak upon to my application to the Institute. Then Lord Ayleston can schedule me for a lecture the moment I am voted in. Shall we head for home? I have some notes I'm eager to look over, and this lecture ran so long we might have to hurry to make our train."

"I have decided to remain in town until this evening," Monte informed her.

"What?" She snatched hold of his coat sleeve and dragged him away from the crowd. "You made me remain locked in my room because of so-called danger here and now you tell me you want to stay longer? Have you lost your mind?"

"I've determined what we must do to convince the world of your rationality, and the first step is to look the part. We must go shopping."

"Look the part? What do you think I've been doing? Why do you think I squeezed myself into this awful dress, if not to look normal?"

"That dress is three years out of style and it doesn't fit."

Her blue eyes turned to ice. "None of my fashionable gowns fit. Stylish ladies aren't supposed to be fat."

Monte winced at the pain in her voice. "Please don't describe yourself with a word you find hurtful. There is absolutely nothing wrong with the shape of your body. You are merely inappropriately attired."

"That's not what everyone else says. 'Fat' is one of the nicer descriptions they use. And don't think I didn't see you look daggers at me when I ate an extra scone."

"Scones are unhealthful, particularly when slathered with jam. If you eat fruit, it should be fresh, not mashed and boiled with sugar."

Astrid crossed her arms beneath her sadly-restricted breasts. "Not everyone is so fortunate as to be able to afford fresh fruit in any season."

"One needn't import one's fruits," he explained. "Seasonal eating is sufficient. Many fruits, such as apples, can be stored for some time after harvest or dried for further preservation. More importantly, a root cellar will do for keeping an ample stock of vegetables during the winter months. I recommend beets, in particular, as they are an excellent source of nutrition and can be enjoyed year-round."

She rolled her eyes. "I think I will give up vegetables entirely. It's clear they make a person annoying."

"But what is to blame for your own disagreeableness?" he shot back. "Excessive consumption of cheeses, I should imagine. Or do you simply suffer from irascibility of the feminine variety?"

Monte caught a glimpse of a dainty, ungloved hand before it made contact with his cheek in a reverberating smack.

He staggered under the force of the blow. Her strength surprised him, though it shouldn't have, given her inclination for outdoor recreation. He watched Lady Astrid stomp from the room, then lifted a hand and gingerly touched his face.

"Ow."

"You deserved that." Miss Fairfax smiled at him in the same affectionate manner as before. He wondered if she was taunting him.

"Yes. That was intolerably rude. Lady Astrid has a knack for making me forget myself. I will find her and apologize."

"I suggest you hurry. I imagine she's headed directly for the train home."

Monte forgot himself again and swore.

# VII
# BUST OF THE BALL

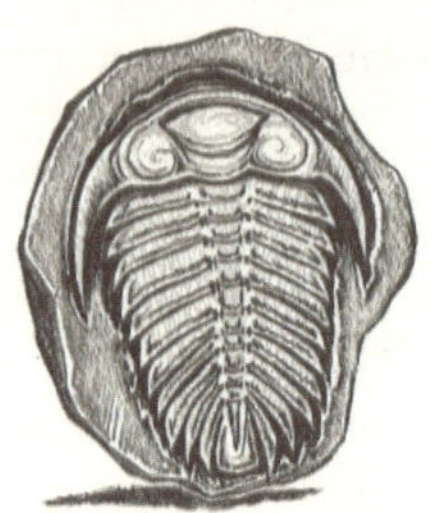

Astrid's fork dropped back down onto her plate. Most days she loved their garden luncheons, but she was certain her brother had just ruined this one.

"A ball? Tomorrow?"

Cal let out an exasperated sigh. "That's what I said, wasn't it?"

"I arrived home yesterday. You couldn't have given me more time?"

"We received an invitation, Asti. I can't ask our neighbors to change their plans to suit you. We're out of mourning now. We must go out. It's vital we be seen as social and courteous."

"Ugh."

"I know, I know. You hate going out in Society. But a few events to show you aren't so different than anyone else will go a long way toward chasing off that horrid Mr. Fawdry."

"I can't help but be different from everyone else. Also, I have nothing to wear."

He looked her up and down. "What's wrong with the dresses you have?"

"They're all three years out of style and they don't fit."

"Why didn't you mention that before?"

"I was only recently informed of this problem by your learned doctor friend."

"Ah." Cal chuckled. "Well, if anyone would know, it would be Monte."

"Is that so?"

"Oh, yes. Sometimes all he needed do was bat his eyelashes and ladies would come running. But other times he would dazzle them by knowing intricate details regarding their clothing, accessories, hairstyles, and so on. Allow me to demonstrate." He turned and shouted across the terrace in a manner unbefitting a marquess, "Monte! What did Lady Cassandra Peabody wear to that party at your father's house in '79?"

Monte looked up from his plate of vegetables. "The orange brocade? A House of Worth creation, I believe. The height of fall fashion. It had a button-front bodice and short, gauzy sleeves. She had matching silk slippers and her jewelry was amber. Orange from head to toe, and all the way down."

Astrid leaned toward the other table. "All the way down to what?"

He stared at his plate and speared a chunk of salad. "I misspoke."

"No, you didn't. You meant her underthings were orange, too. You remember her dress because you stripped it off of her."

Her brother jabbed her in the ribs, though she hardly felt it through her rigid corset. "Astrid, a lady doesn't speculate on such things, and no gentleman would ever discuss such matters with her."

"I wager he discussed it with Lady Cassandra."

"Stop antagonizing Monte, Astrid. He's going to be selecting what you wear to the ball tomorrow."

"Oh, no. Absolutely not. Just look at that abomination of a waistcoat. Green and red plaid? It's painfully loud. I don't trust his taste."

Despite her protestations, Astrid found herself in the ballroom an hour later, with all of her "ladylike" dresses spread across the floor. Grace and Cal watched from the comfort of a sofa while Dr. Montford wandered about, rejecting things. Servants flitted in and out, grins on their faces. The entire household thought this a jolly good time.

"Did you really choose these?" Montford wondered.

"They were chosen and purchased for me. I don't like shopping because I don't like these sorts of gowns."

"What do you prefer to wear?"

"Nothing appropriate."

Their eyes met and heat flared between them, that same wild desire that had overcome her upon their very first meeting. She took an instinctive step toward him.

He flinched and turned away. One hand gestured at another dress. "No good. Not your color." He turned toward Cal. "She needs to go shopping. At a proper dressmaker who will see her properly fitted. Do it soon so she can have multiple dresses before the house party."

Astrid rounded on her brother. "What house party?"

"I want to hold an event here. Only a few days. It's our duty to extend invitations to those who have invited us."

Astrid threw up her hands. "I have work to do," she lied. She was going for a walk on the beach. This house was stifling.

As she strode from the room she heard Monte's voice sighing. "The dark blue will have to do. But swap out the underskirt for the gold."

· · ·  · · ·

Astrid couldn't breathe. She could barely walk. She certainly couldn't eat any of the delicious pastries spread across the refreshment table. She gazed down at them, her lashes fluttering, willing herself not to cry.

*Astrid Wembley does not cry. Astrid Wembley is strong. She climbs cliffs and does scientific research. She knows how to throw a punch. She will not be laid low by a pinchy corset and snobbish guests.*

The words were becoming her mantra. If only she could take deep breaths to accompany them.

"Potion, miss?" asked a rangy man behind the table. The faded Marvale livery hung askew on his bony frame. The new earl appeared as stingy as his predecessor. Nothing in the house had been updated since Astrid had last seen it five years prior.

She frowned at the small cup the servant had indicated. "What does it do?"

"Why, it increases your allure, naturally. You will seem nobler, taller, thinner."

Astrid glared at him and grabbed a pastry. She wandered away, keeping to the edges of the room, nibbling tiny bites she hoped wouldn't upset her squashed innards. She didn't want to be taller and thinner. She wanted to be herself, dammit.

This party had her feeling nineteen all over again. Marvale's estate bordered Whitehaven, and only ten miles separated the two houses. Astrid had expected a smallish, local affair. What she'd found was a massive crush. Dozens had come from London just for one evening's entertainment. Others had come further. She'd heard one man boast of driving six hours and hitting speeds of thirty miles per hour in his steam car. People she hadn't seen in years had gaped at her and whispered, just as they had done during that one miserable Season.

Tonight, she suspected they were adding, "I heard she's crazy," to their catalogue of insults.

Another servant wandered by with a tray of drinks. "Potion, miss? If you're feeling shy, I have one to give you courage. Or there's allure to catch the eye of the gentlemen."

Astrid gave him a false smile that might have been nearer a grimace. "No, thank you."

All she needed to do to attract the men was to shout, "I have fifty thousand pounds to my name!" She wasn't such a spinster yet that the fortune hunters would ignore her, though some might balk at courting a lunatic.

She had no inclination to draw attention to herself anyhow. Better to be a wallflower and loiter along the edges of the room in peace. She would have loved to dance, but she was loathe to put herself on further display this evening. Showing up at all had caused enough rumors to fly. Also, her shoes pinched something fierce.

She took another step backwards, forgetting the enormity of her bustle, and crashed into the wall. The unexpected collision caused her to stumble, arms flailing in an ungainly attempt to keep her balance. Stupid dress. She was never awkward in her ordinary clothing, but truss her up in a ballgown and she became a bumbling fool. She may have been a lady by birth, but not by nature.

"Lady Astrid, how lovely to see you."

The familiar voice startled her, and she whirled toward it. "Lord Smyth! Hello." He was grinning. He was a handsome fellow, much more so now than when he'd been scowling after the lecture. His dark hair was tidy, his sideburns short, and he sported a curling moustache. Fashionable. The sort of man who could find any number of young ladies to dance with.

So why was he here, smiling at *her*? Had he noticed her near fall? Her embarrassment might make a nice revenge after she'd proven him wrong in front of so many others two days ago.

"I hadn't expected to find you here," he continued, the smile not wavering. "I suppose I didn't think to find you anywhere except the halls of the Institute. Which is nonsense, of course. You have a life beyond science, just as I do. And tonight those lives happen to intersect. How delightful!"

"Yes, it is," she replied, a slight hesitation to her voice. She'd thought him furious at her. Why was he now chatting as if they were old friends?

"You trounced me rather thoroughly the other day, did you

not?" he laughed. "I was stunned, I must say. Lord Ayleston's recommendation seemed peculiar until that moment. I suppose I shall have to cede my expertise in the field of geology to you when you join our ranks. How are you in chemistry?"

"I follow the latest developments in the scientific journals, but I don't study it myself."

"Excellent. I shall devote myself to that, and let you be our rock lady."

Astrid didn't find the term "rock lady" to be particularly flattering. In fact, she rather thought it belittled her work with trilobites and their importance to the understanding of stratigraphy and the theory of evolution.

On the other hand, Lord Smyth wasn't snarling at her and had accepted she was more expert than he. That was enough to please her tonight. With each small victory, she made strides toward equality.

He took a step back and cocked his head to one side, looking her up and down. "I say, you are looking very fine tonight, indeed. At the Institute your mode of dress is so ordinary, but this is quite lovely, and that color flatters you."

Her cheeks flamed. It had been ages since anyone had complimented her in such a fashion. Years, perhaps. Smyth had done a better job of it than the fortune hunters, too. They tended to compare her eyes to oceans and her lips to roses, usually while gazing at her bosom.

"Might I have the next dance?" he asked.

"That would be lovely, thank you."

She allowed him to take her hand and lead her to the dance floor. Forget the pinchy shoes. Here was a man who knew about her bluestocking ways and still wanted to dance. It was possible he was a fortune hunter, but she didn't care. All that mattered was that she could be herself.

What could be better? A pleasant, handsome partner, who wore a suit well and had the sense to avoid plaid waistcoats.

"Do you like cheese, Lord Smyth?"

He blinked at the non sequitur. "Er… Yes, I suppose. One cannot go wrong with a good Cheddar."

"I met a man once who despised cheese. I couldn't fathom it. Do you think it peculiar?"

His eyebrows had lifted in a way that made his eyes appear round and frozen, like a startled deer. Astrid was certain he found *her* peculiar, but they were already dancing, and he couldn't escape.

"I suppose we all have our little quirks," he replied diplomatically.

"Some of us more than others."

Her thoughts were still on Montford. Why? Why think of cheese and plaid and smoky gray eyes when she had a perfectly agreeable gentleman in her grasp? A gentleman who probably hadn't seduced Lady Cassandra Peabody.

Astrid made up her mind to focus on her companion and how he had complimented her, even though she was crammed into a dress much too small and with a bustle that made her wobble. He had a nice, firm body, and was an excellent dancer. He had lips that could possibly be pleasant to kiss. A bit thin, perhaps, but that could be an illusion caused by the bushiness of his moustache. She preferred a shorter, trimmer style.

Like Cal's. Definitely like Cal's, and not at all like Monte's. Her eyes sought her brother in the crowd. Was he dancing? He'd made some despondent remarks about needing to marry. Astrid hoped he found all the ladies here as unpleasant as she did. She couldn't stand the thought of him taking a wife out of a sense of duty and against his own desires. She also didn't like the idea of relinquishing control of Whitehaven Manor. She'd come to enjoy working with the staff and the household accounts her mother could no longer handle.

Lord Smyth stopped abruptly, and she realized the dance had ended. Astrid thanked him and looked around for the nearest sofa. Exerting herself in her too-tight corset had left her breathless, and her feet ached. He followed her and offered to fetch refreshments.

She almost asked for cheese, but it was no fun to spite Monte when he wasn't around to see it. Instead she declined everything and pleaded a headache. Smyth hurried off and returned a few minutes later, potion in hand.

Astrid stared at the concoction. To not drink it would be rude, and probably make her lie apparent. It felt wrong, however, to ingest a magic brew from a man who was all but a stranger. She knew his work from the Institute. She had argued with him at one lecture and shared a dance with him. For all she knew, he could be Dr. Stephens' murderer.

To kill her here, in public, would be idiotic. The killer wasn't so stupid. She ought to be perfectly safe, but the logical reasoning didn't diminish her unease.

She took a small sip. The potion tasted vile, in the way of tea that had been over-brewed and left out to go cold. She chanced a few more swallows and then handed the cup back.

"That will do, thank you."

"The whole dose ought to clear your head entirely."

"I prefer not to overindulge in medication, nor in fact in anything. For instance, I have had only one tiny pastry tonight and taken only one turn about the dance floor. My personal physician encourages moderation in all things save for vegetables."

Smyth's eyes went deer-wide again. "I see."

"It is most healthful."

"Of course. Excuse me, I will go dispose of the remainder of this potion. How is your head?"

*Unchanged, though my stomach is now protesting.*

"Better, thank you."

He bowed and departed. Astrid hopped up from her seat and went in search of her brother. Moderation might not be good enough where balls were concerned. She would advocate for total abstinence.

## VIII

# INDELIBLE INK

"THAT IS NONE of your business!"

Monte reined in his temper. Hadn't he begun this conversation by saying he needed to ask her a number of private health questions? He called on his best professional manners. "It is a standard question for all female patients, and I am required to make note of it if I am to fill out a proper evaluation."

Lady Astrid brandished a bite of sausage. "My menstrual cycle is of no concern to you and that is final."

As a physician, it was, in fact, of concern to him. If she were suffering from any complaints of that nature, he knew how to make a potion to alleviate her symptoms. The potion also doubled as a contraceptive, but that was neither here nor there.

"It *will* be asked of you. If I don't note it, someone will ask why. It's always taken into consideration where a woman's mental health is concerned."

"Because you idiot men think our wombs make us feeble and insane."

"We do not," he snapped. He paused and took a sip of tea

to calm himself. It was difficult to be clinical Dr. Montford around her. "Or, at least, I don't. There is a great deal we don't understand yet about women and the preponderance of hysteria. We're always learning. That is the way of science, as you know. It's proven, however, that unhealthy habits and troubles of the body are directly linked to diseases of the mind, regardless of sex."

"Proven by whom?"

"I couldn't say. If I were to look through all my books, I'm certain I could find you many references to those who have researched the subject. The mind-body connection is a well-known fact."

"I've found that many 'well-known facts' are the result of someone stating a thing at random and then later referring back to his own comments on the subject."

Monte shook his head. "You have led us off topic. If my report is to convince Mr. Fawdry of the soundness of your mind, we must cover all aspects of your health, unpleasant or not."

"I called nothing unpleasant. I merely said it was none of your business. What comes after that? Warts? Unsightly birthmarks? Frequency of water closet usage?"

"Any urinary or bowel troubles would need to be noted, naturally. And eventually we must cover sexual habits and troubles."

He feared for a moment she might fling a glob of greasy meat in his direction. Why did he continue to hold these discussions at the breakfast table? Cal was too early a riser, and Miss Fairfax dined with the family only sporadically. Monte needed to stop seizing this time alone with Lady Astrid for work purposes. It was killing his appetite. Perhaps tomorrow they might discuss the weather instead.

"Isn't it obvious, Dr. Montford?" She smirked at him. "I'm a world-famous courtesan with dozens of lovers. The only trouble I have is tripping over all the men who fall at my feet in unending devotion."

"I can understand how that might happen." He would love to fall at her feet, tug her stockings down, slide his hands up underneath her skirts. Damn. Every day the same problem. He'd been far too long without a woman. Perhaps if he hadn't been such a bounder in his youth, his current abstemious habits would feel less like torture.

"You needn't mock me," she retorted. She tugged at her dressing gown as if it weren't already covering her neck to toe.

"No mockery was intended."

Astrid threw him angry looks over her last bites of sausage, then hopped up in her usual abrupt manner.

"I'm going to go take a bath—right after eating, and in an unwarmed room. Then I have work to do. You may as well make up lies for all your inappropriate questions. You will need the practice for when we get to my dissolute novel reading and rock climbing."

Monte finished his meal in contemplative solitude. Why must she question everything he said? It wasn't as if he hadn't studied. He had a degree from Cambridge and was now a Fellow of the Royal College of Physicians. He'd treated hundreds of patients, most of whom were well-pleased with his treatments and advice.

Needing to clear his head, he abandoned the house for the half-mile walk down to the beach. He slowed when he reached the modest escarpment, wandering along the edge until he reached the very spot where he had met Astrid. Minutes ticked by while he gazed out at the ocean, watching, listening. The contours of the beach had transformed over the years, but it was unchanged in essentials. Green grasses gave way to white rock. Beyond, the sea water lapped at smooth sand and scattered pebbles Astrid would no doubt find fascinating.

It was little wonder he hadn't realized who she was when they had met here. High society wasn't her natural habitat.

This was. He could feel her in the whip of the wind through his hair and hear her in the crash of waves upon the shore. Free. Untamed. A force of nature. He could as soon tell her what to do as he could command the ocean to lie still.

Monte turned back to the house, determined to start anew. He would show her he meant to work with her, not against her. A full evaluation required that he observe her, learn her habits, come to know her. It would be a step, he hoped, toward earning her trust.

He found Lady Astrid busy in her laboratory, a basement room that had once been part of the working rooms of the house (in the days when the house was simply grand and not yet colossal). A wooden floor had been laid atop the stone, and it was warmed by a sturdy, though well-used carpet. The walls were papered in a soft blue, and the room amply lit by potion-fueled sconces. Additional lamps sat on tables and counters.

The back wall was lined floor-to-ceiling with bookcases, all of which were full, and a closet to the left of the entrance looked to hold racks of specimens. Additional racks had been wheeled into the center of the room. Above her desk hung an annotated drawing of a layered rock formation.

Monte turned to examine the wall to his right and nearly jumped out of his skin. A monstrous bug jutted out at him, easily twenty inches long, with a segmented body and ghastly spiked protrusions.

"Christ!" he swore, staggering backward. "What the fu… deuce is that?"

He recovered himself enough to take a second look at the thing. A plaster casting, it appeared. A reproduction of an enormous fossilized creature.

His obvious horror had Astrid grinning. *"Terataspis grandis,"* she replied, rising from her seat. "The largest species of trilobite known to man. That model has been reconstructed from the fragments we have found."

"You found that appalling thing?"

"Oh, no. It was found in America. Most of the specimens I have found myself have come from my excavations in Wales and West Midlands. Many wonderful fossil beds have been found near the Welsh-English border."

"You make excursions across Britain to dig up giant fossil insects?"

"They aren't insects. They are arthropods, but distinct from any modern creatures we know of. You can't tell from that model, but they would have had legs. Many legs, I believe, like a centipede."

Monte shuddered.

"In fact, one of my biggest projects in recent years has been to corroborate Mr. Walcott's findings about trilobite legs. I have personally found evidence of legs in half-a-dozen species thus far. The legs are seldom preserved, and the soft under-portions of the body are even more rare. Another of my current studies is an examination of preserved trilobite tracks. We uncover more examples of these with every new excavation, and they are giving us a deeper understanding of trilobite underbellies. This is why one must take great care with fossil specimens and examine them thoroughly. Even the smallest trace of an appendage or other feature can advance our knowledge of these creatures."

"Indeed."

Monte stepped away from the terrifying giant trilobite and took a moment to study the rare and elusive Astrid Wembley in her burrow. This was the girl he remembered, grown lovelier and more womanly. She wore a loose, cream-colored top with short sleeves and a low, scooped neckline. A simple blue skirt fell to mid-calf, revealing a bit of white stocking above her sensible walking boots. She didn't look constricted or uncomfortable. Without the multitude of layers, he could fully admire the curve of her hips and the thrust of her bosom. She must have had a corset, because her breasts didn't jiggle when she moved, but it seemed to be a sensible, supportive one, and not the body-malforming torture device she had worn under her other dresses.

Her blue eyes gleamed in the warm, yellow light, and a soft flush had stolen over her cheek. What a remarkable woman. Who else would be so enthused about trilobite underbellies and hang stratigraphic diagrams on her walls?

"Won't you show me around your laboratory, Lady Astrid?" he asked. "It seems a very pleasant and organized place. Conducive to productive study, I imagine."

"Oh, yes. Quite. Grace is to thank for keeping it so very neat, however. I have a tendency to pile things on and around my desk. In case I need to call upon them at a moment's notice, you understand. I dislike having to disrupt my thoughts by walking clear across the room."

"You prefer to disrupt them by digging through piles?"

She laughed. "Not at all. It always makes me wonder what I was possibly thinking by not organizing things. Which is why I compromise with small piles and file most things away using the shelves and the rolling cabinets. That was Grace's true genius idea: specimen cabinets we can roll in and out of the closet. It has helped me to no end."

"How long has Miss Fairfax been living here with you?"

"Almost four years. Cal and I traveled to India on a combination sightseeing and charity mission in autumn of 1880. We met Grace there and I knew immediately she was just what I needed in an assistant. Since then she's become more of a partner. She's an organizational mastermind. Let me show you around the lab. This is my working area, obviously."

Astrid waved a hand at her desk and Monte caught a glimpse of some sort of marking on the underside of her right forearm. Before he could take a good look, she turned away.

"I was writing up ideas for a lecture on the geology of this region, so this cabinet, here, is full of local rocks and fossils." She pulled open several drawers to show him. "I also have photographs, most of which are my own, and maps, which are not. I'm not a skilled hand at drawing, so I photograph specimens rather than attempting to render them with pen and paper."

Monte thumbed through a number of images. "You *are* a skilled photographer, it appears."

"Thank you. I enjoy photography, and the need for proper lighting provides yet another excuse to go outside. I like working here, where there is nothing to disturb me, but I need my time in open spaces. Follow me, and I'll show you what's in the closet."

She waved her hand again, giving Monte another peek at her arm. Whatever was there was neither natural nor accidental. He tried to maneuver around to her opposite side for a better look.

"These are my trilobite cabinets," she announced, proudly. "All carefully classified and labeled. Please don't touch, as some of the pieces are quite fragile."

Monte took a look out of politeness, but he had lost interest in her work. The tattoo on her arm—if that's what it was— had become an obsession. He needed to know what it was, where she had gotten it, and why. Staring was rude. Asking about it was rude. Casting surreptitious glances was beneath his dignity, yet he found himself doing it anyway. She refused to stand in a position that afforded him a good look.

"This is my very own fossilized trilobite track." Her voice held a deep reverence for the foot-long section of rock in front of her. "Look how you can see the markings from the little legs."

She pointed at a particular location, and Monte could no longer contain his curiosity.

"Lady Astrid, I hope you don't find me as rude as you clearly found me at breakfast, but I can't help but wonder about the ink on your forearm."

"Oh!" She flipped her arm over and held it out to him, a touch of color rising in her cheeks. "It's a trilobite, of course.

*Olenus micrurus.* A Welsh specimen. Isn't it a beauty? Most people don't see it, because either my sleeves are long or my gloves cover it."

"The artist did a masterful job." Monte focused on examining the tattoo from an artistic perspective, trying to ignore the bug-like, segmented form. "Where did you have it done?"

"London."

He laughed. "There are a great many tattoo parlors in London."

"I suppose there are, but I admit that I'm not certain what street this particular shop was on."

"Oh?"

"This was about five years back, shortly after our twenty-first birthday. The whole family was in town, and Cal and I were supposed to stick together. I slipped away without him."

"This doesn't surprise me."

"I took a cab until I came to an area that looked interesting, upon which I hopped out and began to explore. I imagine it wasn't a part of town young ladies are supposed to visit, but I was dressed similar to this and wasn't a target for pickpockets."

*But perhaps a target for men with certain ideas*, Monte refrained from pointing out.

"When I stumbled upon a tattoo shop, I knew just what I wished to do with my afternoon. I had a photograph of this specimen in my purse, because it was the finest fossil I had discovered and cleaned, and I wished to present it to the scientists at the Institute. They declined to look, by the way, which was quite a disappointment."

Monte grinned at her. Astrid was exactly his kind of woman—brave and smart, with a rebellious streak.

*No*, he corrected. *Not my kind of woman.*

She was Monte-the-rake's sort of woman. The sort of woman he would've had a fling with, once. Not the sort of calm, sensible sort a respectable physician would spend time with. Perhaps he needed a wife. A quiet, demure woman who sat at home with her sewing and would make a good mother for his proper, respectable children. The very thought made him shudder. A holdover from his wild bachelor tendencies, no doubt.

"You aren't the sort of woman to let a little disappointment discourage you," he observed. "I assume they eventually allowed you to show the fossil?"

"No, not that one. But I have brought in other photos and even some of my more robust specimens since then. I started sending them every paper I wrote, and eventually Ayleston, at least, began to read them. But I've never shown anyone at the Institute my tattoo, because I need to look a respectable scientist."

Monte shrugged out of his coat and draped it over the top of one of the cabinets. Astrid's eyes widened in surprise.

"Scientists are an unusual and varied group," he said, unbuttoning his cuff and beginning to roll up his sleeve. "I expect there are many of us who have gotten some ink over the years."

He held out his bared arm to display a tattoo of his own. "The Rod of Asclepius."

She leaned toward him, resting her fingers on his wrist. Her touch burned through him, sending a raging desire pounding through his veins.

"The physician's mark. I like it."

"Thank you." His voice came out thick and low. Her head snapped up, those clear, blue eyes finding his, rooting him to the spot. His heart was racing, his breathing ragged. Her fingers hadn't moved from his arm. His skin was afire.

"Astrid," he gasped. His fingers flexed, longing to grab her, haul her against him. Her full, pink lips invited him to plunder her mouth, to taste the sweet tang of her. Her tongue darted across her lower lip and he groaned.

"Montford!" The offended masculine voice shook Monte

from his trance, and he whirled about to find Cal standing just outside the closet door. "Just what do you think you're about, alone with my sister and half undressed?"

"We're comparing tattoos," Astrid explained. Her cheeks were flushed, her voice a touch breathless. She lay her arm alongside Monte's. The snake winding along his skin looked to stare at her trilobite. His wrist still tingled where she'd touched him.

Cal fixed him with a furious glare. "That's not going to help anything."

Monte yanked his sleeve back down and buttoned it closed. "It's helping me get to know your sister." He grabbed his coat and stepped back into the laboratory. "Thank you for the tour and the conversation, Lady Astrid. I will leave you to your work."

"Thank you, Dr. Montford." She nodded politely, but he could still see the blush on her skin.

"If you mean anything unseemly by 'getting to know' her—" Cal began, the moment the men were out of earshot.

"I meant what I said," Monte snapped. "I'm not a rake anymore, Caladay."

"I know, I know. I'm sorry. I'm just so bloody worried about… well, everything. You should get to know her. It might make the two of you less contentious."

"That's my hope."

Monte didn't want to argue with her. He damn well wanted to kiss her. And the more he learned of her, the fewer reasons he could think of not to do just that.

## IX

# AT THE ASYLUM

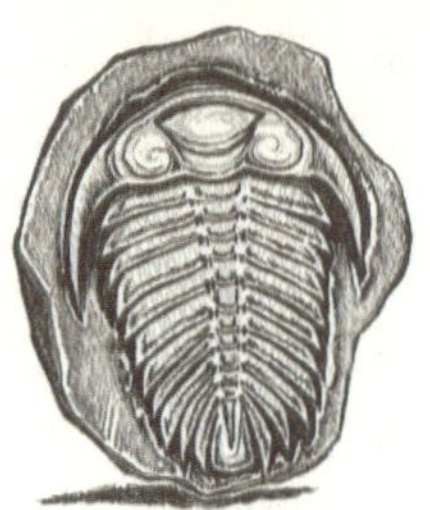

Astrid stashed the bicycle in some shrubbery that hadn't been trimmed in her lifetime, if ever. Cliffsdale Ladies' Convalescent Asylum was noted for its commitment to privacy. This included letting the hedges surrounding the property grow to ludicrous proportions, so that no one might see through or over them and disturb the patients at rest.

The rich patients, that is. The asylum was well known for its lavish care of "temporary patients." Wealthy women who wanted a week or a month to hide away from the stresses of their daily lives paid great sums of money to visit. Astrid, who counted among her faults a tendency to eavesdrop, had heard a group of ladies speak of it during some dull party years ago. An "ailing" lady could spend all day in bed if she wished, or simply sit in the garden sipping lemonade. Restful activities such as reading and painting were available—though no novels were to be found—and the treatments included warm baths, sleeping potions, and as much soup as one wished to eat.

Astrid crawled beneath the bush to get a look for herself. In her sensibly-fitted corset and an altered pair of Cal's trousers, she had enough freedom of movement to slide between the branches. The shrubbery was so dense it caught on her hair and clothing, but with a bit of effort, she burrowed deep enough to peek out the other side.

The main wing of the asylum was comprised of an old country home that had once belonged to some member of the gentry. The portion of the building Astrid could see was in good repair. It backed up to a small garden, bordered on two sides by the concealing hedgerow, and on the third by smaller, neater bushes.

Half-a-dozen ladies lounged in the sun, some beneath parasols or blankets. A few sipped at tea or soup, while the others simply rested, eyes closed. Astrid suppressed a giggle at the sight of the very rigid and particular Countess of Reybourg flat on her back in the grass, asleep. A bored servant—who was supposed to be holding a parasol to shade Lady Reybourg's face—sat cross-legged beside her, plucking blades of grass.

It seemed ridiculous that these women needed to pay exorbitant prices to do things anyone could do at home. It was all the result of this absurd sense of decorum the world had cultivated. Lady Reybourg couldn't lie in the grass on her estate, because "such things were not done." The young woman swinging on a hanging bench, dressed in her nightgown and kicking her bare legs up in the air, likewise couldn't repeat her behavior outside the asylum.

These women pleaded temporary insanity, relaxed themselves in ways Astrid considered perfectly ordinary, and then returned home to act as if it had never happened.

*I am not entirely peculiar,* she thought with a little laugh.

What made her peculiar was only that she saw no reason to follow ridiculous rules. These ladies would all return home and go back to being whatever society said they ought to be. Astrid couldn't help but be herself. Her own tendencies and opinions couldn't be suppressed, even when she was on her best manners. Inevitably, she would say something scientific, or sneak outside without a chaperone. Her brain simply couldn't handle irrational social constraints for any length of time.

"As you can see, Dr. Montford," the voice of Mr. Fawdry drifted across the lawn, "our patients are able to recuperate under the safest and most restful conditions."

Astrid shrank back further into the bush. She couldn't let Monte discover she had followed him here.

"Some of these ladies need be here but a few days more," Fawdry continued. "Others have only just arrived."

The girl on the swing giggled in a crazed sort of way Astrid was certain was false. Her slim legs were visible almost up to her knees. She cocked her head in a flirtatious manner. Looking at Monte, no doubt.

"Do not stay outside too long, young lady, or you shall catch a chill," Monte said in his pompous doctor voice.

She giggled again and flopped on the bench, causing it to sway precariously. She began to sing.

"Doctor Foster went to Gloucester in a shower of rain."

Perhaps she actually *was* crazy.

"What of the more difficult patients?" Monte inquired. "I understand you have a wing devoted to the care of those who need more specialized treatment or who may never recover."

"Indeed. We do not often invite outside physicians into those areas. As I am certain you know, a strict routine is essential to keep patients sedate. I shall make an exception, however, seeing as you are on the Psychical Health Board."

He was? He had neglected to mention that fact to Astrid during any of their so-called interviews.

"Thank you," Montford replied. "If it's anything like the rest of your facility, I shall be pleased to take a positive report back to London."

"I'm certain you will find everything meets your approval. Won't you follow me?"

Astrid risked peeking further into the garden, and watched them disappear into the house. Monte looked perfectly calm and continued to converse with Fawdry in an amiable manner.

She felt a pang of betrayal. Fawdry wanted her committed for life, and Monte was smiling at him and praising his horrid asylum. How could he?

That morning in the laboratory, she'd thought she sensed a flicker of the desire he'd once shown for her. He'd seen her as more than a difficult patient, or Cal's sister. They'd bonded over tattoos. Or, they would have, if Cal hadn't stomped in and ruined everything.

Men.

If Montford returned to Whitehaven proclaiming the asylum a fine, healthful place Astrid would do well to visit for a time, she was going to punch him in his lovely mouth. Perhaps she might punch him anyway, and Cal, too, for not telling her about this visit. She'd only known about it by eavesdropping outside Cal's study.

She slipped out of the hedge and circled around the back of the asylum toward the wing for long-term patients. It was a dreadful addition, done up in a late-Georgian style that tried to crunch an overabundance of classical features and a great many large windows into a space much too small to do them justice. She wondered if the bricks felt the same way she did when squeezed into a fashionable ball gown.

Another crawl into the bushes showed her a grassy lawn similar to that used by the temporary patients, but entirely empty. The difficult patients didn't go outdoors, it seemed. This didn't surprise her.

Rumors about this place had flown through Whitehaven her entire life. Children whispered that if you were bad you'd be shipped off to Cliffsdale, never to be heard from again. They scared one another with tales of gruesome scientific experiments, potions that sucked your life away, and dank dungeons. The way adults had shuddered at the name had made a young Astrid believe all the stories were true.

Now, she suspected the children's tales were nothing more than fanciful imaginings. It was the underlying reality—

the original impetus for the stories—that worried her. The exterior of the building was tidy and cheerful. Carriages of the wealthy came and went, taking satisfied ladies to and from their appointments. On the surface, it was just what it claimed. Somewhere beneath lurked a rotten core.

Astrid pushed her way clear through the hedge and stepped out into the unoccupied garden. The grass here wasn't as neatly trimmed. Flowerbeds were dotted with weeds. A glance out the window wouldn't show the neglect, but up close, Astrid could see this area was tended merely to keep up appearances.

She crossed the lawn to peer into a window, but thick curtains blocked any glimpse of the interior. She slid along the wall, trying one window after another, hoping for a place where the curtains were pulled back. She found one at the far end of the wing, up against the six-foot divider hedge that blocked her from the view of the recuperating ladies. On the other side of the bush, the swing creaked.

"Mary, Mary, quite contrary," the voice of the girl sounded through the hedge.

Astrid shielded her eyes to look through the window. The room inside was no more than an office. She could see a bit of a shelf, and part of a desk.

"What do we see?"

Astrid spun around. The girl—actually a woman not much younger than herself, now that she saw her up close—must have stood up on her swinging bench, because she now leaned precariously over the hedge, looking straight at Astrid.

"Does the boy look a girl or the girl play a boy?"

Astrid put a finger to her lips to shush the other woman.

"Nothing is there, nothing at all," sang the woman. "Float away, up, up, up."

"Come down, Lady Ophelia," a soothing voice coaxed. "We wouldn't want you to fall."

"Up, up, up," Ophelia continued. "Nothing down, boy-girl. All up!"

Astrid's gaze traveled up the side of the building to the floors above.

"Yes, yes," Ophelia sang.

Astrid jolted. Ophelia was speaking in riddles, but her words were neither random nor meaningless. She was acting. For what purpose, Astrid didn't know, but she'd been most helpful.

"Down, dear," the nurse said. "Give me your hand. That's right."

Lady Ophelia disappeared behind the hedge. Astrid eyed the first floor above her, and the second floor beyond. It only made sense to keep the things they wanted to conceal above the ground floor, where accidental curtain openings wouldn't reveal secrets.

"I know a hawk from a handsaw." Lady Ophelia's sing-song voice faded into the distance.

Astrid took several steps backward and surveyed the building, looking for places where one might be able to see through an upper window. She settled on a few choice locations and began to climb. The overdone architecture made her ascent simple. She could stand upon the massive stone lintels jutting out above each window or the hefty sills below. The slats dividing the window panes and the shutters surrounding them provided hand and footholds aplenty.

The first room she investigated was tidy, and empty, save for a few simple cots. A dormitory room. Innocuous enough. She clambered over to the next window.

This room was quite dark, the curtains only the smallest bit ajar. Astrid adjusted her position, pressing her face against the glass. What she could see made her shiver. An unfamiliar machine stood in the center of the room, with several chairs nearby. Chairs augmented with straps and chains. She couldn't make out anything else beyond the chairs, and wasn't certain she even wanted to.

Regardless, her determination to understand this place

and the man who wanted to trap her here propelled her on. She continued climbing up to the second floor, edging closer to an open window. If the room was empty, perhaps she could slip inside for a look.

She stretched past the shutters for a glimpse, only to pull back with a start. Not only was that room not empty, it was cramped with women in tattered clothes with wild hair. One foot slipped from her precarious perch, and she clung to the woodwork, her breath coming in rapid pants as she steadied herself.

Astrid braced herself and leaned over for a second glimpse. She risked a longer look this time, before pulling away once more, her heart pounding.

Those women were drugged. Every one of them had a strange, glassy-eyed expression. Staring, unseeing. Or perhaps seeing things that weren't there. A deep pain spiked in Astrid's chest. She knew that look. Her mother wore it most of the time, trapped in the thrall of the laudanum.

"Well, what have we here?"

At the voice from below, Astrid's fingers clenched tighter on the shutters. She glanced up. Could she scramble up to the roof and make an escape down the opposite side of the building?

"You may as well come down, little monkey. Are you an intruder or an escapee?"

Astrid glanced down at the man and was a bit surprised to see a face she recognized. "Lord Marvale?"

She wasn't entirely certain. The man had been her neighbor—if ten miles between them could be considered neighborly—only six months, and their introduction at the ball the other night had been brief. This man had the same gray-black hair, a sober, but elegant manner of dress, and an aristocratic attitude that would do a duke proud.

"Lady Astrid," he chuckled. "What an interesting surprise."

He didn't sound surprised in the least. No doubt he knew

of her reputation. She'd been spotted and recognized. There was nothing to be done about it. She made her way back to the ground.

"I almost didn't recognize you in your... intriguing costume," Marvale said. The tone of his voice was pleasant, but the gleam in his eye suggested contempt.

"Yes, well, I cannot cycle in my skirts. What brings you here, Lord Marvale? Are you donating to the asylum? Or visiting a patient? Any ladies of your acquaintance would be on the opposite side of the hedge, I imagine."

His eyes narrowed, mouth twisting into a calculating frown. "You are of my acquaintance, Lady Astrid."

"Barely." After the word escaped her mouth, she realized it must have sounded rude.

Marvale's expression didn't change. "On the contrary, Lady Astrid. I have known you for years."

"What? I'm certain, sir, I had never seen you until our visit the other day."

He bared his teeth in a predatory smile. "There may have been no formal introduction, but I know you from your regular attendance at lectures given by the Scientific Institute for the Progression of Rational Thought."

"Oh!" It was true she'd never been shy about asking a question or making a comment on a topic that was of interest to her. It was a peculiar notion, however, that she might be as well known as all that. In many of the lectures she was no more than an attentive observer.

"Are you a frequent attendee, yourself, Lord Marvale?"

"I am a member."

Astrid blinked. She was certain she had never seen the name Marvale among the membership.

He chuckled. "I admit a tendency toward lurking. I am a researcher, not a lecturer. You might know me by my family name, Pierce. I have kept it as my professional name since inheriting the earldom."

"Dr. Pierce. Yes, I have heard of you. You specialize in psychological studies, is that correct?"

"I do. I am on the Royal Psychical Health Board."

*With Montford.*

"You are here in a professional capacity, then?" He had yet to answer her original question.

"I am. I pay weekly visits whenever I have a patient here for treatment. I am also occasionally called in for a consultation with difficult inmates."

Astrid bit her lower lip. Pierce wasn't easing her concern that the women here were more prisoners than patients. The fact that he was a regular part of the operations meant she didn't trust him in the slightest.

"Now, Lady Astrid, might I inquire as to *your* reasons for being here? Certainly you are no physician, and your method of entry is unsavory at best."

"I was here to visit a friend, and I had no intention of entering in such a fashion. I was only taking a peek to see where they might be keeping her."

He sniffed in disbelief. "What is the name of this friend of yours?"

"Lady Ophelia," Astrid replied, with a smile.

It was time to get out of here. She didn't trust Marvale, and she couldn't risk waiting and letting anyone else learn what she was about. She darted past him, making for the place where she had entered through the hedge. By the time he realized what had happened and ran after her, she was deep into the greenery. Marvale would have a difficult time following, if he could get through at all.

She popped out the other side and ran all the way to Cal's bicycle. Moments later, she was pedaling furiously down the road, leaving Cliffsdale Asylum and her frightening findings far behind.

# X

# CONFESSIONS OF A REFORMED RAKE

"**W**HERE IN GOD'S NAME have you been?"

Monte hung back from the confrontation, watching Astrid storm up to her brother, her face like a thundercloud. Such emotional people, these Wembleys. Sometimes he wondered if they had any British blood in them at all.

"Out for a ride," she snapped. "And what of it? What gives you the right to think you can say what I do and do not do?"

"I am the head of this family, and it is my responsibility to see to your well-being. Given your current situation, I would have thought you would have better sense than to go gallivanting about—"

"Oh, shut up. I'm so tired of duty this and responsibility that. It's all you care about anymore. It's ruined you, Cal."

"You have no idea, Astrid. You have no idea how hard I have worked and how difficult this is."

"And what do you have to show for it? Nothing. Just a stuffy personality and constant misery. Well, I won't let you go dragging me down with you. I might be 'just a girl,' but I know how to take care of myself, thank you very much." She turned and stomped away, her eyes swinging to meet Monte's as she walked past. "As for you, Dr. Montford, I don't care how many degrees you have or how many boards and committees you are on. You don't get to tell me what to do, either. Good day, gentlemen."

Monte watched her depart, her rounded bottom swaying as she walked, displayed to fine advantage by her trousers. He shifted uncomfortably, trying to ease the sudden tightness in his own apparel.

Cal flung himself on the sofa. "I try, Monte. I swear, I do. Why can't she see that I'm trying my best?"

"Perhaps what Lady Astrid means is that you're trying too hard," Monte offered. "Your heated relationship makes it hard for her to put it in words or for you to interpret the words she says. You both focus on the shouting, not the intent."

"You're making my head hurt."

"Another sign you're working too hard. Perhaps a bit of time away from it all. You will accomplish more if you approach your work with a sufficiently rested mind and body."

Cal rubbed a hand across his face. "I can't go away with Astrid in jeopardy of being taken from our home."

"Astrid will be fine. She is strong and smart. I'm here to lend my professional assistance."

It occurred to Monte that no one had told Cal about the suspected murder of Dr. Stephens. He would counsel Astrid and Miss Fairfax not to mention it. The last thing Cal needed was another reason to panic.

"I can't imagine what I would do if you weren't here," Cal said. "What of your visit to the asylum? Did you learn anything of use to us?"

"Let's go to your study and I'll tell you the whole tale. I'll have some tea brought 'round. It will ease your nerves."

Cal heaved himself off the sofa with a sigh. "Ask for some biscuits, also."

"You oughtn't eat sweets in the middle of the day. It's not good for the digestion and might aggravate your headache."

"Oh, stuff it. I swear, Monte, you are the dullest man I've ever met. Eat a biscuit. It might do you some good."

Monte relented on the biscuit issue, though he had no intention of indulging in such foul refreshments himself. He'd begun to think it was Cal who truly needed his help. The man was stressed near to the breaking point.

At Monte's insistence, they settled into armchairs facing the hearth, rather than sitting at Cal's desk. Outside, a cold, gray drizzle had begun, an early-autumn harbinger of the long, chilly winter to come. Monte scooted his chair closer to the fire, basking in the warmth. Cal edged his further away. He had the enviable trait of rarely being cold. Monte could get cold in July while wearing a full suit and standing in the center of an inferno.

"Tell me about the asylum," Cal insisted. "What did you learn?"

"Very polished on the surface. The wing for recuperating ladies of means has earned its reputation. The patients are treated in grand style and left to do as they please. I imagine it's most restful, and of great benefit to those of them that do suffer from true nervous complaints."

"But that's not where Fawdry wishes to send Astrid."

"No. The accusations against her state she is a danger to herself and others. She would be confined to what they refer to as the 'hospital wing.' Again, on the surface it looks a legitimate facility. I observed many methods that I don't personally agree with, such as the use of straitjackets and small chambers for confinement, but these are widely-accepted practices, and were said to be used only for patients in the throes of a fit or presenting a danger to persons around them."

Cal snagged another biscuit. "What of the patients themselves?"

"Of those I saw, some appeared to have genuine mental distress, whether grief, paranoia, or unspecified hysterical complaints. Others, I suspect, were poor and without a place to go. They or their families chose the asylum over the workhouse. They appeared in good physical health, all things considered."

"What, then, is beneath the surface?"

"I don't know, but there must be something. I saw no more than a quarter of the rooms in the hospital wing. Most doors were closed, and locked, I suspect. It was a calculated tour. Intended to show me just enough to allow me to make the report that was my stated purpose. The only unusual thing I saw was the potions laboratory. Fawdry takes pride in mixing up many of the medicinal potions himself. He was well-stocked with ingredients and praised his own experiments."

Cal leaned forward in his seat. "Experiments in what?"

"That is the question, and I don't like any of the answers I have thought up."

Cal's voice dropped to a fierce whisper. "No one will experiment on my sister."

"I suspect she will have similar feelings on the matter," Monte replied quietly.

Silence fell over the room. The two men sat sipping their tea, the fire dancing before their eyes.

"Tell me something happy," Monte suggested. "Something we would have talked of in the past. You haven't traveled recently. What of your projects? Have you built anything interesting?"

Cal shrugged. "I haven't had much time for working. I've repaired a few things around the house, worked on Astrid's camera. Nothing worth chatting about."

"I can't imagine you've gotten up to much carousing of late. Ill-advised bets? Tattoos like your sister?"

"No," he chuckled. "Astrid is much bolder than I in that respect. What of you? When did you have your arm inked?"

"Three years ago. Haven't I shown you?"

"You haven't. And I never have the opportunity to see you unclothed anymore, since you've given up taking stupid dares and fooling with lusty women in semi-public spaces. Or have you? I suppose I'm never in town these days."

"I strive for moderation in all my habits, and have done these past several years. As you know."

The firelight glinted in Cal's eyes. "No visits with Lady Cassandra?" he teased.

"She's a duchess now. And happily rusticating in the country. Which was the entire purpose of our affair in the first place."

"There must have been someone interesting."

"Not especially." *Not as interesting as your sister.* "What about you? Your habits haven't changed at all, if that empty plate of biscuits is anything to go by. And yet I can't even recall the last time you told tales of your conquests. You can't have been celibate for an entire year."

A rosy tinge shaded Cal's pale cheeks. "No, I certainly haven't."

"Tell me, then. What sort of women? How many? What public spaces have you defiled with your wicked ways? Confess to everything and I will determine exactly what sort of harm you have done yourself with your overindulgences."

Cal smiled a smile unlike any Monte had seen on his face, joyful, but tempered by a touch of sadness.

"One woman. Quick-witted, spirited, beautiful, and tall enough not to break my neck when I lean down to kiss her. Sadly, the only public spaces we have defiled are my own gardens."

Monte studied his friend's face, unravelling the peculiar expression. "You're in love!"

"Dreadfully."

"For how long?"

"It feels like forever. We've been lovers for nearly three years."

Monte's jaw dropped. "Three years?"

"Anything I've told you about in the last three years, it was her. It's been no one but her. I can't even imagine anything else anymore."

"Bloody hell, Caladay. How could you not tell me?"

"I haven't told anyone. Not you, not Astrid. No one."

"Miss Fairfax?"

Cal's clear blue eyes confessed everything, even before he nodded. "You always were sharp."

"She's the logical choice, and she fits your description. You have my word I won't tell anyone. I won't put her reputation at risk."

"Thank you."

Monte shook his head, then laughed. "Three years, Cal. Damn. I suppose I always expected it of you. You have that certain loyalty that makes a man suitable for one woman alone. You've made an excellent choice. Smart woman. I like her."

"It wasn't a choice. It simply happened. I had no control over it."

"Terribly fatalistic of you, old man."

"I'm not jesting, Monte. It hit me like nothing I've ever known. Even now sometimes I look at her and my heart aches with the force of it. No matter what happens, she will never leave my heart. I will never be the same man I once was."

Monte opened his mouth to speak, then snapped it closed again. He couldn't find the words. For years he had teased Cal about the women that captured his attention. But what did one say to a man who had just laid his heart bare? Monte did the gentlemanly thing and sipped his tea and said nothing.

Cal stared into the fire, pain furrowing his brow. "I don't know what I'm going to do, Monte. I must marry and marry well. How can I choose a wife when I love another? How can

I bear to leave Grace? I can't ask her to share me. That would be an insult to all we have had. I must let her be free to make a life of her own. God. I can't stand it."

Monte couldn't understand this titled obsession with marrying other titles. It was so off-puttingly elitist. In fact, as a second son with shamefully little inheritance due him, he found the entire concept of inherited nobility a trifle distasteful. Not that he would admit to such a sentiment. He wasn't an American, after all.

"I'm sorry." Cal sat back, shaking his head. "Hell, Monte, listen to me. Such a maudlin wreck. We were supposed to be discussing happier things. Tell me about your women. You won't go to pieces over them."

"I haven't any."

"Nonsense."

"I swear it. Not a one in the past six months or thereabout. I told you. Moderate habits."

"That's not moderate. That's insane."

"I'm trying to put my energy into my work and my research, not waste it in sexual excesses."

"You're cracked." Cal set his tea aside and rose. "Get up. We're walking down to the tavern."

"Why?"

"Because you need a girl, and I need a drink."

Monte finished his tea, considering the idea.

Cal tapped his foot impatiently. "Come on, then. I'm not going to wait all day. Wasn't there a woman you fancied hereabouts years back?"

"Yes."

"Maybe we'll find her at the tavern and you can have another go."

"Never 'had a go' in the first place. Only enough time for a few kisses."

"Ah. That explains the infatuation. You never did like

missing out. Now get your arse out of that chair and let's see if we can find her."

"Unlikely."

If he found Lady Astrid at the tavern, he was hopping the next train back to London.

"There are other nice girls. What are you in the mood for? Tall? Short? Thin? Plump? Pale? Dark? Old? Young?"

*Dark brown hair with a gentle curl. Sun-tanned skin. Eyes like the sky. Curves that would shame Aphrodite.*

Cal was right. He needed to get out of this house. Perhaps a pretty girl would do him good.

Which was how he found himself some half-hour later at the farthest end of the village of Whitehaven in a tavern of questionable repute with an amorous woman in his lap. She was friendly, cheerful, and full-figured, with bouncing curls and smiling eyes. Cal had picked her out and brought her to the table. He knew Monte's tastes.

Her hands had long since burrowed beneath his waistcoat, and she had taken to wriggling her generous bottom against his groin. He was plenty aroused, but couldn't work up the enthusiasm to carry her off upstairs. His brain wouldn't stop picturing Astrid in her trousers. What in hell was wrong with him?

"You want to go someplace private, love?" his companion cooed in his ear.

"Not particularly."

"Well, I ain't the sort of girl to do things in public."

"Certainly not. You're a lovely woman."

"Then what's the trouble, dearie?"

Monte gave an awkward cough. "I have a terrible hereditary condition that could cause my heart to give out should it be overstimulated by amorous congress. My father succumbed to it, and his father before him. It grows worse with each passing generation. I'm afraid I may not even live long enough to father a child of my own."

She wrapped her arms around his neck and planted a kiss on his brow. "Oh, you poor dear. You've never known the pleasure of bedding a woman?"

"No, never."

Across the table, Cal sat with his face buried in his hands, shaking with suppressed laughter.

"And such a handsome thing you are, too." The woman climbed from Monte's lap. "Let me fetch you another mug of ale, dearie."

"That won't be necessary."

"It's the least I can do. It'll help you take your mind off your troubles, and we serve the best ale in the county, we do."

"Thank you. You are very kind."

She bobbed a curtsy. "You're welcome, love. You let me know if you'd like me to sit with you longer, or if you prefer time to yourself."

"I will not impose on you further, but thank you. It's rare for me to have the company of a beautiful woman, given my condition."

Cal's head didn't lift until she had walked away. He had turned an embarrassing shade of scarlet. "Oh, God, Monte. You've told some wild lies before, but that might just be the funniest thing to ever come out of your mouth." He wiped a tear from his eye. "I'm dying. And I still think you've lost your mind."

"That's entirely plausible."

"What was wrong with her?"

"Nothing was wrong with her. She's delightful. Clearly something is wrong with me. Perhaps I've been working too hard, myself. I may need to take my own advice and rest."

Cal's brow furrowed. "Sometimes I can't tell if you're serious or sarcastic."

"I'm not altogether certain."

"Quit having me on. What's troubling you?"

*Your sister.*

"Nothing," Monte replied. "You are simply unaccustomed to my respectable and healthful lifestyle."

"Very well. I will pretend to believe you reformed and we will drink in companionable silence."

Silence was an unfamiliar concept to the patrons of this establishment. A glance around the room told Monte he and Cal were the only people not talking. Shouts between tables punctuated the general clamor. He nursed his beer and listened in on what bits of conversation he could make out.

"…Lady Astrid?"

Monte's head swiveled at the sound of her name.

"What's she done this time?" someone asked.

"Rumor is she was caught trespassing and indecently dressed."

"Never took her for a criminal."

"Madness runs in the family, they say."

A hand clamped down on Monte's arm. "We're leaving," Cal hissed.

"Good idea. The ladies will be wondering where we've gotten to."

"I meant we're leaving Whitehaven. First thing in the morning. We'll stay in London until this is resolved. I can't take it anymore."

"That may not be the best of ideas."

"Why not?"

Monte cleared his throat. "Uh, because we think there's a murderer in town, and he may be a danger to her."

Cold fury swirled in Cal's eyes. "Why am I just now learning this?"

"We didn't wish to alarm you further."

Monte held his ground and took the punch like a man.

# A CHAT OVER BREAKFAST

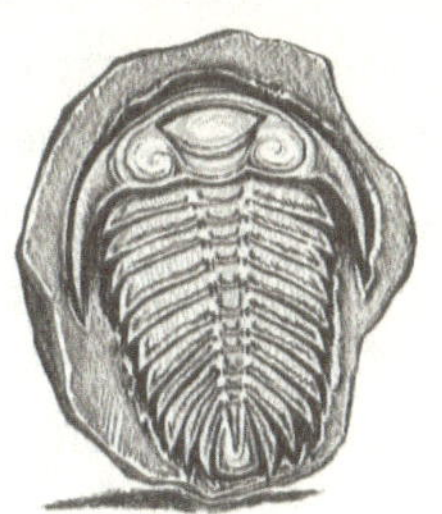

ANOTHER DAY, ANOTHER BREAKFAST alone with Dr. Montford. Astrid had passed Grace and her brother in the hall, both of whom had finished with their own meal before she'd even reached the breakfast room. Their shared habit of retiring and rising early mystified Astrid. Morning was a time of sleepiness and irritability. She wanted it to be as short as possible.

She took a seat directly across from Monte, running through witty retorts she might use when he inevitably began to lecture about nutrition. Yesterday had been a pleasantly rant-free day. He'd gone off somewhere with Cal in the afternoon, and then the two men had disappeared into their rooms upon their return, not even coming down to dinner. She suspected they had gotten into a terrible row. They were both obstinate sorts, and Cal's university stories had taught her that shouting matches and even fistfights were not uncommon among his circle of friends.

Monte was eating his revolting bran things and staring down into a book. Whatever it was had him riveted, as it took several seconds before he realized he was no longer alone.

When he finally did look up, it knocked the breath from her lungs. Hot desire flared in his silvery eyes, and his kissable lips twitched in a wicked smile. He was fully Monte the rogue this morning. His sandy hair was mussed, his necktie sloppy, and a ghastly blue-purple bruise ringed his right eye. What a peculiar sort of man, to engage in fisticuffs one moment, and then sit himself down at the table to read as if nothing untoward had happened. Why did that make her heart race and her stomach do queer little flip-flops?

He quickly schooled his features into an impassive expression, but Astrid had caught him in an unguarded moment, and she couldn't unsee that instant of longing. He did want her. Even if he thought her crazy. Even if he were truly reformed. He still wanted her.

She tempered her excitement with a reminder of all the farm girls and Lady Cassandras he'd seduced over the years. He probably wanted her because he wanted everyone.

The decision came to her, all of a sudden. If she had to put up with interviews and medical advice, she was going to get some flirting and kissing out of it. She would begin by being cheerful, and not asking the burning question of why her brother had hit him.

"Good morning, Monte."

His brow furrowed at her informal address. "Good morning, Lady Astrid."

"I see you had some sort of mishap yesterday. I do hope it doesn't pain you overmuch."

"I will recover."

"I'm glad to hear it." She scooped up a forkful of eggs. They had been scrambled up with cheese and onions, her favorite way to eat them. "You will be pleased to learn my eggs have onions mixed into them this morning. I am eating a vegetable with breakfast."

"I'm afraid I don't wish to discuss your dietary habits this morning. You have made it clear you have no intention of heeding my advice, and I have no desire to begin yet another day with an argument."

Astrid bit back one of her rehearsed retorts. Flirtation wasn't as easy as others made it appear. Should she tease him or flatter him? When should she bat her eyelashes? Or would it be better to play with a loose tendril of hair? She strove to continue her overture of affability.

"Very well, then. What would you like to talk about?"

"Nothing. I should like to read my book."

"Ah. That's not especially sociable of you."

"No. Which is why I am conversing with you, regardless of my feelings on the matter."

"You are a terrible grump this morning."

And now she had further upset her plan by insulting him. Those who said honesty is a virtue must not have the forthright manners she did.

"I didn't sleep well last night," he sighed. "What is your excuse?"

"I'm always irritable in the morning, but I was doing my best to be friendly. I shall try again. What are you reading, Dr. Montford? There. If you can't read your book without being rude, you can at least talk to me about it." She shoveled eggs into her mouth, forcing him to take over the conversation.

He turned the book so she could read the title. "It's Dr. Harvey's text on the benefits of an abstemious lifestyle, the dangers of unnatural and immoderate behaviors, and advice for adopting and maintaining healthful habits."

"That sounds dreadfully boring."

"Not at all."

"Does he advise eating bran cakes?'

"He invented them."

Astrid caught a peculiar gleam in Monte's eye.

He continued on in an eager voice, "Dr. Harvey is working to open a bakery that will produce bran loaves on a large scale and market them for sale across London, and from there spread the product to other portions of the country. The ultimate goal is for people the world over to benefit from wholesome foods."

"This Dr. Harvey is your idol," Astrid said, identifying his boyish enthusiasm.

"I wouldn't term it as such, but I do greatly admire him. He has studied a long time and is a very learned man who has committed himself to improving the health of the general populace."

He could term it however he wished. She recognized the signs of hero-worship. She had a few heroes herself and wouldn't deny it.

"Dr. Harvey cooks large bran loaves and has them sliced like bread or cut into smaller squares, but I must admit that I'm rather fond of the way your cook makes them in little tart cups. I might write to the good doctor myself and recommend it."

Color rose in his cheeks at this suggestion of correspondence with the man. Astrid dared not laugh at him.

"Why not simply distribute the recipe?" she inquired.

"Oh, it's written out in his book, but too many people do not read widely."

"You could hand out pamphlets. I can picture you standing on a street corner, waving them about and shouting at the passersby all the healthful advice you have learned from the great Dr. Harvey."

Monte's jaw tightened, but he didn't reply.

"I'm sorry. I only meant to tease, but that came out very sarcastic. It's a bad habit of mine. 'Uses sarcasm.' Is it on your list?"

"What list?"

"The list of reasons to send me to the asylum. I know you have one, because I've seen you shaking your head and making little checkmarks."

"I won't commit you to that horrid place."

"Oh, good, then you don't approve of it? I was concerned when you were so friendly with the proprietor *and* on the same

Psychical Health Board as that Dr. Pierce."

"You followed me? That explains the trespassing rumors."

"You wouldn't have allowed me to accompany you."

Monte glanced at the ceiling, as if begging for divine intervention. "It would have blown my cover. I had one chance to investigate while it's yet unknown that I am here at your behest."

"Did you learn anything useful?"

"Not especially, no."

Astrid struggled to keep her smile from becoming too smug. "I learned the women are drugged."

"Drugged?" His posture stiffened. "Are you certain? How did you discover that?"

"Well, I climbed, to be frank. After I went through the hedge—"

A knock at the door caused Astrid to pause and turn. Elsie, her lady's maid, stood in the doorway, a bundle of flowers clutched in one hand.

"Beg your pardon, my lady, but a gentleman stopped by to leave his card for you." Her cheeks pinkened. "And he left these for you, also." She thrust the flowers in Astrid's direction.

Astrid blinked at her. "You must be joking."

"Highly irregular," Monte growled.

Elsie skipped across the room and presented the flowers to Astrid with a wide smile. "Crippens was most disgruntled by it all and couldn't determine whether to bring you the card and the flowers or not. So I took the task upon myself. What young lady doesn't like a gift from an admirer?"

Astrid suspected something was wrong with her eyes, because they had grown very round and she couldn't seem to stop blinking. "I have an admirer?"

Monte used her distraction to take the calling card and read it himself. "One who, it seems, has the nerve to call upon an unmarried lady with not the slightest attempt to address himself to her relations. I don't approve of this Lord Smith or Smythe or however he pronounces it."

Astrid yanked the card from his hand. "You know it's pronounced 'Smith' like a blacksmith. You were in attendance at the lecture."

"Oh, that fellow! The one whose reputation you left in tatters. You must have terrified him, if he's making peace offerings."

"Actually, I think he likes me. He danced with me at Lord Marvale's ball and was kind and complimented me even though I was scientific and unfashionable. Elsie, could you find a vase for the flowers, please?"

"Certainly, my lady." She scampered off toward the kitchens.

"Smyth is staying at the inn in Whitehaven, it seems," Monte commented, his voice still reproachful.

"Why do you say that?"

He pointed at a handwritten number on the back of the card. "That will be his room number. He must think you fast. Don't go there, or he will be expecting certain things of you."

"And what if I *am* fast and I want to go?" She tried to inflect her voice with the confidence she suspected a brazen woman would have.

"Then I shall have to put a checkmark beside that item on my list."

He said this without even a hint of humor or irony. Rogue Monte would have made it a joke. Rogue Monte might even have given her that smoldering look and suggested his own room was much closer than the inn. But he was Doctor Monte now, and so frustratingly proper. The estimable Dr. Montford did not make bawdy jokes or kiss young ladies on the beach.

Another knock drew her attention back to the door. Crippens held a tray with a letter on it.

"Additional correspondence for you, Lady Astrid." His face scrunched up in a frown even grimmer than his usual mien. "I trust Elsie informed you of the visit of that presumptuous young man."

"She did, thank you. And thank you for bringing the letter."

Astrid accepted the missive and he bowed and returned to his duties. She tore open the paper and began to read.

"Oh, bugger."

Monte leaned across the table, concern creasing his brow. "What trouble now?"

She flattened the letter on the tabletop to allow him to see it. "I am accused of criminal insanity and summoned to appear before a judge to determine my fate."

"Bugger, indeed."

"I suppose I shall have to comply and endeavor to act the sanest, most normal woman in the country."

Monte bent over the letter. "We have two days. We finish the interviews. Then you and I will sit down together and write the report. I will put in as much truth as I am able, but there will be places where we need to invent plausible lies. We must also explain your unusual habits in as innocuous a manner as possible. We will choose the most well-known of your eccentricities and present them as harmless and rational. Your beach-going, for example, can be associated with your work. Come up with a reason you must do it barefoot, if you please."

"Because I like to feel the grass and the sand beneath my feet. Also, shoes full of sand are dreadfully uncomfortable."

"I can work with that." He rose from his seat, his bran cakes only half-eaten. "Please excuse me. I must retrieve my notes. Then we must find a quiet location where we can talk undisturbed. Keep in mind that it could take hours."

"People will think we are having an affair."

His mouth twisted in a frown that looked almost painful. "Better me than Lord Girls-Can't-Understand-Geology Smith-Smythe."

Astrid had to agree.

## XII

# FLINGS AND FLOWERS

"THIS NEXT BIT WILL BE the worst yet," Monte warned. He shifted his position on the elegant settee in the cheerful, sunny room they called the "large parlor." Sadly, this conversation was nowhere near as pleasant as his surroundings.

Astrid raised a single, dark eyebrow. She had neat, pretty eyebrows. And just when the devil had he begun thinking of eyebrows as pretty? Cal was right. He was cracked.

"Worse than the menstruation questions?"

"Invasive questions on sexual habits. Questions about things you oughtn't even know about, to be honest."

"Oh, yes. Don't you remember? I told you I was a courtesan."

She plucked one of her flowers from its vase and twirled it around in her fingers before lifting it to her nose and inhaling deeply. Another irrational surge of hatred for Lord Smyth-with-a-y burned through him.

"I have known courtesans, and you, my dear, are clearly not one of their ilk."

"We are different now. You wouldn't know, being so entirely reformed."

How was it that she could make him feel a fool for adopting

a lifestyle the rest of the world considered morally and socially admirable?

"I can tell you aren't a courtesan, Lady Astrid, because you are enthralled with your new bouquet. A courtesan would be indifferent to such gifts, having received hundreds from her many admirers."

Astrid stroked the petals of her flower. "This is my very first."

Monte dropped his pen and nearly his notebook, and spent several very ungenteel seconds attempting to keep everything from clattering to the floor.

"You can't be serious."

"I'm sorry to startle you, but it's the truth."

He continued to gape at her. "No gentleman has ever given you flowers until this moment? You? Impossible. Your brother told me you've rejected a dozen marriage proposals."

"I have. They only wanted my money. Fortune hunters would meet me at an event and propose that very night, whereupon I would reject them. None ever sent flowers. And the flood of proposals fell to a trickle as it became known how peculiar—and plainspoken—I was."

"But surely there have been some who like a woman who speaks her mind?"

She shook her head.

"And what of those who take one look at you and are entranced? Do you scare them off so quickly with your eccentricities?"

"Dr. Montford, you appear to be under some delusion that I am pretty. Most people don't find me so."

He plucked the flower from her fingers, and when she reached for it, he let it fall, catching her hand instead. He pressed her fingertips to his lips and held them there until her eyes locked with his.

"You are gorgeous. These paltry blooms cannot begin

to convey a proper appreciation for your beauty. You shame diamonds. You could send Venus into a jealous rage."

"You're crazy." Her words were a breathless whisper.

"I am not." He kissed her fingers again, lingering a moment in the taste of her. Her skin was warm and soft, smelling of berries and a whiff of serum. She must have used a moisturizing potion to protect her delicate hands while digging and studying her rocks. "Smyth isn't writing room numbers on calling cards because he admires your brain. In fact, I'm certain he's terribly jealous of your brain. He probably wishes to reassert his masculinity by conquering you in a different way."

She jerked her hand away. "Well, that's obnoxious. You love to make everything unpleasant, don't you?"

He retrieved her flower and held it out as an offering of peace. "He struck me as an obnoxious fellow. But, I admit I did only observe him the once. He may simply be wild for you. As I said, you are gorgeous."

Astrid shoved the flower back into the bouquet and folded her arms across her chest. "Let's move on, shall we?"

"Yes. Let's." He stared down at his notes, willing his brain to make sense of them. At the moment, it was screaming, *Lady Astrid smells like berries and tastes like an ocean breeze*, which was certainly not what he had written. "Um…"

"Embarrassing sexual questions?" she prompted. "Ask me about the things I'm not supposed to know of, and I will tell you whether Cal told me all about them—probably wrongly— when he first went to University."

*Bloody hell.* This was the last thing he wanted to discuss with Astrid. He suffered enough fantasies under ordinary circumstances. He didn't need the reminder of the feel of her body against his, and her enthusiastic response to his touch. He absolutely did not want to know what other men had fallen prey to her amorous charms.

"I shall move through the list as quickly and tactfully as

possible." His voice came out choked, though with anger or desire, he couldn't say. "Do you currently have any lovers?"

"I do not."

"I'm glad to hear it. Have you any past indiscretions, and if so, how many? It is important we note all occurrences of this kind, as there is the possibility of the other parties involved being used as witnesses against you."

She sniffed. "I assume I needn't worry that *you* might speak out against me?"

"Certainly not! I have already apologized for that incident, and I shall do so again and again, with the hope that someday you might forgive me."

"Oh, enough, already," she sighed.

"Pardon?"

"Stop apologizing."

Monte's brow furrowed. "For anything?"

"For that day on the beach. You're acting as though we did something horrible, and that isn't how I remember it."

He grimaced. "My behavior was unpardonable. It was terrible of me to take advantage of your innocence in such a fashion."

"You were nineteen. You were hardly some aged lecher preying on young girls. We were excitable youngsters. That's all."

"I was enormously more experienced than you, and I fully intended to have my way with you right there at the top of the cliff."

"And yet you stopped the moment I wished you to stop." She lay back in her chair, a smile of triumph on her face. "You accepted my decision without hesitation and then left it to me whether we might ever renew our activities. That is not the behavior of a deplorable villain. That is the behavior of a man who respects a woman and her body and her choices."

Monte opened his mouth and shut it again, swallowing

words of protest. "Very well," he said at last. "I rescind my previous apologies."

"Thank you. I have rather fond memories of that day, and I would prefer you not ruin them just because you are on some peculiar crusade of moral purity. I don't think it's having the desired effect, to be honest. You seem irritable much of the time. Perhaps that is nothing unusual, but it seems to me that in the moments you forget yourself you are much happier."

"Which one of us is conducting this interview?"

"Ah, yes. My 'indiscretions.' I met a handsome man on the beach years ago, and thankfully he is no longer apologizing for the kissing and fondling, because it was most pleasant. Since then, I have kissed a handful of men, but none of them were especially good at it. I shall try to endeavor to remember their names for your notes. They were all very dull fortune hunters. I smacked one of them who tried to grope me."

He frowned at her. "That's all?" In seven years she had done nothing but kiss a few men? A woman of her passions? It was the most appalling thing he'd ever heard.

*No. It's not appalling. It is perfectly sensible and respectable, and I ought to be applauding her for her character.*

"Yes. Did you prefer the courtesan story?"

"I prefer the truth."

She was lying. That had to be it. He couldn't imagine her alone all these years. He clenched his teeth. Imagining her with other men wasn't an improvement. Either way, he hated it.

Astrid shrugged. Such a casual, unladylike gesture, and so much herself. "Well, there it is, in all its sordidness. I have kissed you and half-a-dozen boring men who couldn't even be bothered to gift me flowers. Perhaps I should try kissing Lord Smyth. He might be better at it, since he appears more romantically inclined."

"No." The word came out unintentionally, and with a vehemence that surprised even himself.

Astrid arched an eyebrow. "Would it cause a problem for

the report and the inquest? Because if not, I don't see how it's any business of yours."

"Yes, the report." A convenient excuse. "Don't even mention that you have an admirer. I should like to be able to say that you are a perfectly innocent young lady with no knowledge of or interest in any carnal behaviors."

"That's silly."

"Maybe so, but it's what they will wish to hear."

"I find I don't like this lying business at all. I would prefer if I could just say the truth. You will write it down in your notes, won't you? The real Astrid Wembley is a somewhat innocent, not-terribly-young lady with quite a lot of interest in carnal behaviors, but not as much knowledge of the subject as she would like. Though, I wager you could teach me, Monte. You probably know the answers to all my questions."

Good God, was she flirting with him? He was dying to respond with a salacious remark. To hear her questions. Offer to show her the answers. She was slowly driving him mad. He was going to end up the one in the asylum.

Desperate to change the subject, he said, "I think that's good enough for the interview. I'll report all your habits as moderate and respectable. We shall make the case that all your so-called abnormalities are the result of your being a bluestocking. You are devoted to your research above all and haven't time for frivolous things such as parties and fashion. Time spent digging for rocks and unusual clothing choices are a necessary part of your work. You have no romantic entanglements because you have little interest in marriage. You have long since embraced the truth that your intellectual tendencies make you best suited for studious spinsterhood."

Astrid's gaze dropped into her lap. "When you say it like that, I sound the most tedious person alive."

"I'd rather they believe you tedious than insane."

Her hand reached for her flowers, stroking the petals once more. "I'd rather people like me as I am, but that, it seems, is too much to ask." She stood up and picked up the vase. "We're done, then?"

Monte rose to see her to the door. "Yes. I'll write up a draft report. Tomorrow we will review it together and make any changes. Do you mind if I get the input of your brother and Miss Fairfax, as well?"

"Not at all. Thank you for your help. At least with a deadline it will all be over soon, one way or another. Good afternoon to you, Dr. Montford."

"Astrid," he called after her retreating figure.

She glanced back over her shoulder.

"I don't think you tedious. Not in the slightest."

"Thank you."

He watched her leave, then shut the door and paced the room, too anxious to sit and write. Where was the relief he ought to have felt upon her departure?

He didn't doubt his report would work. Just a spinster. She sews—did she sew?—and she reads. A woman of science. Unusual, but sane. Harmless. Of little interest to anyone.

Astrid had the right of it. Lying left a bitter taste in his mouth. But it was necessary. Two days and it would all be over with.

Monte wasn't certain he wanted it to end.

Astrid moped away the remainder of her day. The insanity charge was giving her a good hard look at the way people saw her, and it only reinforced all the unhappy things she had thought before. She tried her best to shake the sullen mood. She drank her favorite tea and ate scones flavored with cinnamon. A reread of her letter from Lord Ayleston gave her a moment's pleasure. She kept her flowers with her all day, to brighten the room and remind her that someone thought her worthy of a gift. Mostly, though, she thought of Monte's eyes, and how deadly serious they had looked when he told her she was beautiful.

And yet, he reacted with horror to all her attempts at flirtation. He wanted her against his will. Because he knew the truth. She was crazy. Not needing-an-asylum crazy, but too-strange-to-be-seen-in-public-with crazy. Besides, he hated all the food she ate, her bathing habits, her clothes, her tendency to go outside without a hat or parasol or in cold weather, and he was disgusted by her trilobites. He might think her beautiful, but he didn't like her at all.

She turned in early, took up her favorite novel, and read until all was forgotten and the only world that existed for her was that of Victor and the monster. When she awakened late the next morning, the sun was bright and high in the sky.

"Oh, blast." She snapped the watch shut. "I shall miss breakfast entirely."

She tumbled from the bed, pulled on a simple, black dress with a bodice laced over the top, and tied her hair back into a tail. Good enough.

She froze when she opened her door. Scattered on the floor in front of her room were half-a-dozen tiny bouquets.

Astrid scooped up the scraggly little bundles. More grass than wildflowers, slightly wilted, but pretty, and tied neatly with bits of twine. Curious, and cautiously pleased, she carried them down to breakfast.

Six more bundles sat by her seat at the deserted table, along with some toast and boiled eggs. She wolfed down the breakfast, gathered up all the flowers, and hurried down to the laboratory to consult with Grace on the matter.

Astrid raced through the door and froze. All around the room were more tiny bouquets. They sat on bookshelves and atop cabinets. Her desk was strewn with them. One even lay across the top of the *Terataspis grandis*.

"What is all this?" she blurted.

Grace grinned at her. "I can't say for absolute certain, but I would guess you have an admirer."

"I… But…" She stared down at the bundles clutched in her hands. Little autumn blooms of purple, white, and yellow. Not grand or fancy, but wild and sweet. Tiny bursts of beauty and joy. She loved to look at them on her walks. As a child she had gathered enormous bunches of them to decorate the house. Sad, wilted blooms she had adored nonetheless.

"I believe there is a note for you on the desk. I promise I didn't read it."

Astrid walked to her desk and unfolded the paper. The note was short and candid.

*Now you have received dozens. As you have long deserved.*
*–Monte*

She retrieved the biggest, heaviest book she could find and pressed the note and the prettiest flower from each bouquet between the pages, then stuffed it back on the shelf. The rest, she gathered up and carried out to the gardens, scattering them along the paths to share her bounty with the world.

As she walked, her mantra echoed in her head.
*Astrid Wembley does not cry.*

# XIII
# INQUISITION

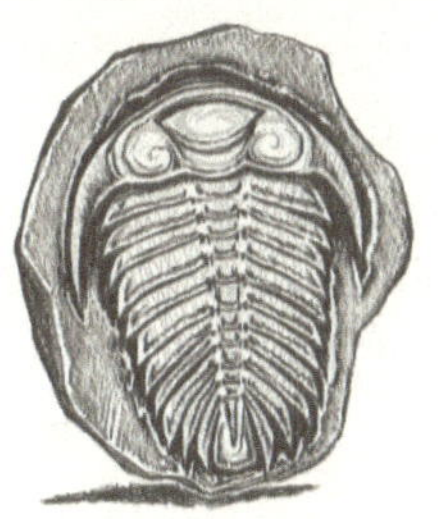

Cᴀʟ ꜱᴀᴛ ᴘʟᴀꜱᴛᴇʀᴇᴅ ᴛᴏ ʜᴇʀ ꜱɪᴅᴇ. Astrid nudged him again, but he refused to give her more space, and even lanky as he was he was too big for her to move.

All day it had been like this. He walked with her, sat with her, clutched her arm or her hand. She didn't think he'd been this clingy since they were in the womb.

He was also every bit a marquess. He boasted a flawless appearance—severe, with costly accessories and an expression of fierce superiority as he looked down on mere mortals from his stately height of more than six feet. Cal was prepared to use his rank to protect her. Or his fists, she suspected.

"Freddie, dear," she murmured, using his little boy nickname, "I appreciate your desire to keep me safe from asylum owners and murderers, but I'm bloody sick of being squashed!"

"Hush! Don't let anyone hear you talking like that."

"No one can hear me but you, because you're all but on top of me. Stop it."

"We're nearly done. A few minutes more and the judge

will set you free and we can all return home and forget this ever happened."

"And if he doesn't?"

"I shall commence a public tirade the likes of which you have never seen."

Astrid couldn't suppress a smile. "I do love you, Cal."

"I love you, too." He slid over to give her a bit more room, taking hold of her hand instead.

Astrid's gaze drifted back to Monte, who sat apart from their group in his role as expert witness. He'd worn a plaid waistcoat again, but in a more subdued style than his usual choices, dark blue with subtle yellow and red striping. His suit was tidy and well-fitted, and every hair was in place. His necktie, though, was a mess. The man couldn't fashion a tidy knot to save his life. Astrid thought it gave him the look of a man who couldn't quite grasp fashion because his mind was so preoccupied with important doctoring things. She hoped that was the impression it gave to everyone else.

The bruise around his eye, fortunately, had faded enough not to be obvious unless you were standing near to him. It was now a disgusting greenish-yellow color Astrid found fascinating. Many disgusting things fascinated her, to be honest: insects, worms, fungi, rotting logs, even dead animals. She found detailed medical descriptions of diseases and surgeries interesting rather than off-putting. It was a very good thing no one had asked her about any of this as part of her sanity evaluation.

"Dr. Montford," the judge boomed. His low, echoing voice gave Astrid chills. It was just the sort of voice perfect for making such pronouncements as, "To the gallows!"

Monte rose to address the question. "Yes?"

"The one omission I have noted in this report is the lack of a direct response to the charge of indecent dressing."

"You refer to the reports of Lady Astrid attiring herself in men's trousers?"

"I do."

"That would be the costume she adopts in order to ride a bicycle. The vehicle allows her to cover more ground than she would be able to on foot, which can be necessary when she must study or photograph large areas of the countryside. With no bicycles yet in stores that make allowances for skirts or riding clothes designed for a lady, she must make do.

"But, as I understand it, she intends to do away with the contraption altogether by learning to drive a steam car. Isn't that correct, Lady Astrid?"

"It is indeed," Astrid replied, though she had no intention whatsoever of ceasing to ride. She sprinkled in some truth, because she was a horrid liar. "It's a new trend among ladies of quality to learn to drive, and I believe this will provide a far more genteel mode of transport."

This was the longest statement she'd made on behalf of herself the entire day. Monte had done most of the talking, and even Cal had been asked more questions than she had. The judge, her accusers, and most everyone else seemed to think her incapable of all but the simplest tasks. Sometimes she hated being a woman.

"Thank you." The judge gave her a nod. "That is all."

Monte slid back into his seat and picked up his pen. His habit of touching the end of it to his mouth was the only sign of his restlessness. Astrid's resultant contemplation of the fullness of his lips had provided a much-needed distraction from her fears.

She reminisced about the tender press of those lips against her fingers while Fawdry turned a simple question into a final plea regarding her danger to herself. His monotonous, long-winded explanation amounted to nothing more than, "bicycles are precarious and unchaperoned ladies are in constant peril of eternal damnation."

Even the judge looked bored. Astrid amused herself by

imagining him shouting, "eternal damnation," in his rumbling voice.

"Thank you, gentlemen," he said instead. "I have no more questions." He sat back, tapping his fingers against his chin as he pondered Astrid's fate.

Cal squeezed her hand. On her opposite side, Grace patted her arm.

"From all I have read here, and the questions I have posed, the evidence points in favor of Lady Astrid's sanity. I have some misgivings, however, about the fact that she has been evaluated by only one physician. Your credentials do you credit, Dr. Montford, particularly your membership on the Psychical Health Board, but your youth and lack of experience make me feel another opinion is warranted."

Monte bit the end of his pen, his expression hard as rock. Astrid's heart threatened to pound straight out of her chest. Cal's fingers clenched on hers.

"I should like to reconvene three weeks from today for a final review of this case. I am appointing Dr. Pierce, Lord Marvale, to conduct an independent evaluation during that time."

"No," Astrid gasped.

Thankfully, the judge continued on, not appearing to have heard her.

"He is a peer of the realm and member of the Scientific Institute for the Progression of Rational Thought as well as the Psychical Health Board. If he can corroborate Dr. Montford's report, I shall consider the matter closed."

The small assemblage began to rise and move toward the exit. Astrid remained frozen in place, trapped beneath a flood of horror. Three weeks. Three weeks of freedom, and then her life would be over.

"No," she whispered. "No, no, no."

"Asti." Cal patted her hand and helped her to her feet.

"Everything will be fine. Marvale is a man of science. He has seen you at lectures. He knows you are sane."

She shook her head, not daring to air her concerns in so public a space. She allowed Cal and Grace to lead her out to the steam car, her body moving of its own accord while her mind spun off in all directions.

*Outmaneuver Marvale. Discredit the asylum. Flee the country. Find the murderer. Find my attacker.*

Hows and what-ifs bounced around her head. So many questions. Her eyes darted back and forth in confusion.

"Where's Monte?" She needed him. He had some of her answers, though they might only lead to more questions.

"He hired a cab. He's not part of our party today, remember?" Cal frowned at her, his hand still on the car door. "Asti, are you certain you're well?"

No, she wasn't. Her mind was racing, her thoughts clouded by fear. Her ghastly spinster/bluestocking dress was crushing her body, and probably her soul as well. It was past time for lunch, and she was starving. She wasn't well at all.

"Take me home. Please, Cal, take me home. I can't talk about it here."

By the end of the drive home, she had settled somewhat. Food and a change of clothes revived her, and determination supplanted her anxiety.

Hands clasped behind her back, she walked the border of the dining room carpet, plotting her next move. Cal and Grace remained at the table, patiently waiting for her to gather her thoughts. Monte, late to lunch because his cab had lagged well behind the steam car, attacked his salad with a vehemence that made her wonder what the poor lettuce had ever done to him.

"Perhaps the reason you're always so irritable is that you're in a constant state of hunger from eating nothing but vegetables," she speculated aloud. She meant it as a scientific hypothesis, but as usual where he was concerned, it sounded more like criticism.

He glared up at her. "I am not always irritable, nor am I hungry, except near mealtime. In fact, I find my wholesome diet prevents me from the sorts of dyspeptic attacks that can only be alleviated by indecorous pacing."

She gave him a nasty smile and continued to walk. "You have misdiagnosed my complaint, Dr. Montford. The only pain I am suffering at the moment is the headache brought on by your self-righteous proclamations."

He skewered a radish. "You must suffer frequent headaches, Lady Astrid, if they are brought on by so slight a thing as someone daring to disagree with you."

"Actually…" She drew the word out. "They are most infrequent. What surprises me is that you do not suffer from them, being so entirely disagreeable yourself."

"Have you considered, Lady Astrid, that your compulsive need to lash out at me might, in fact, be a defensive reaction caused by an aversion to the introspective contemplation of your own flaws?"

"My flaws are a point of constant public scrutiny, Dr. Montford, or hadn't you noticed? Perhaps if you spent less time lecturing me on the evils of my ordinary habits you might have been able to put together a better defense of my character than 'she's a boring, old spinster' and I wouldn't find myself in a worse mess than ever."

"Better?" he sputtered. "A *better* defense? I could, without thinking upon it, list a dozen reasons you might be committed to an asylum. I made your wholly abnormal lifestyle appear both innocuous and rational. The only possible way I might have done better would have been to replace you with someone entirely unlike yourself."

Astrid stopped pacing and stared him down, filled with equal parts fury and dismay. "Thank you for clarifying. I had very nearly made the mistake of liking you. Please excuse me. I need to go and completely rework my plans. I wouldn't wish to inconvenience you any further."

She spun on her heel and stormed out. She'd had enough of men. Starting right now, she was handling things her own way.

· · · ༼༽ · · ·

Monte muttered a string of invectives under his breath, making another violent jab at his food. The poor radish had been mauled beyond recognition.

"Goddammit, Monte." Cal clearly felt no need to control his language. "Why is it so difficult for the two of you to converse like civilized people?"

"Because your sister isn't civilized?"

"Neither are you, whatever you pretend."

"Are the two of you going to fight as well?" Miss Fairfax asked. "Had I known there would be such drama at lunch, I would have sold tickets."

"No, we are not," Cal insisted. "We're all going to calm down, and then we're going to determine why Astrid is in such a state. I'd thought the hearing went well."

"Marvale is the problem," Monte explained.

"Why? We didn't stay for the entirety of his ball, but Astrid handled herself respectably and even danced, so he can't fault her for her social behavior. He also will know her from her connections to the Institute. I see no reason to think he won't support your statements that she is a devoted scientist and mentally sound."

"I don't like him."

"How is that relevant?"

"I know him somewhat from the Psychical Health Board, where he goes by his professional name of Pierce. He's a potions regulation advocate."

"What's wrong with that? After that rash of potion-related deaths in London this summer, I can understand why anyone might feel we should give some consideration to what goes into our potions and who is making and selling them."

"The regulation faction isn't concerned with safety. They're concerned with control. The techniques to identify small sources and extract serum from soil have resulted in a potions revolution in just two years. Potion use is spreading to working class families and rural communities who couldn't afford such things in the past. Health potion prices have plummeted, and many new medicines have been developed. I've heard tell of a potion that can heal ordinarily fatal wounds if ingested in time. I know for a fact that a potional vaccine for tetanus is now available, and there is a rumor one has been made against bubonic plague."

"Monte, you are ranting. What is the trouble with Marvale?"

"He and the other regulation advocates wish to do away with small sources and independent harvesting—the very thing that has brought about these important advancements. They will put individual entrepreneurs, experimenters, and small, local potion shops out of business, claiming safety. Their goal is a regulatory committee with the power to approve who can harvest and from where, who can sell, and what they can make. A new monopoly to undo all the good that has come from the demise of the Imperial Potions Company."

"That does sound self-serving, but how does any of this affect Astrid?"

"I'm not certain. All I know is Marvale is not to be trusted. I also trust no one from the Institute, including that Lord Smyth who is acting so taken with her."

"Is it really so shocking that any man might admire my sister?"

"I hadn't thought so until she informed me his was the first bouquet of flowers she had ever received. I hadn't realized how many men would be intimidated by her brilliant mind and her unrestrained honesty."

"Ah. That explains the wildflowers." Miss Fairfax gave him that friendly smile. It no longer looked at all flirtatious, now he knew she and Cal were together, but he still couldn't determine whether it was sincere or ironic.

"What wildflowers?" Cal asked.

"Dr. Montford used wildflowers to make a point regarding the inferiority of all of Astrid's previous suitors."

Cal's face scrunched in confusion. "Pardon?"

"It's not relevant to the current situation," Monte replied. "I know you had intended for me to return home following this hearing, but I must beg you to allow me to stay. There is more to this than a disgruntled man wishing to rid himself of an inconvenient female. Something untoward is happening at Cliffsdale. Astrid told me she thinks the women are being drugged."

"Why does she think that?"

"I don't know. We were interrupted during the conversation, and then I forgot to ask her during our subsequent interview."

*Because I can't spend any amount of time with her without my mind becoming clogged with impure thoughts.*

"We shall get to the bottom of it. I can't help but think the asylum and the Institute are connected in some nefarious fashion, and whether through bad luck or some rival's jealousy, Astrid has landed in the middle of it."

Cal put a hand to his head and winced. "You needn't beg, Monte. I'll do that for you. Please stay. Your expertise is invaluable, but even without that, having you here means so much. I don't know what I would do without so great a friend to rely on."

Monte placed a hand on his friend's shoulder. "I will always have your back, Caladay. Always. Because I know you would do the same for me."

# XIV

# INTO THE MADHOUSE

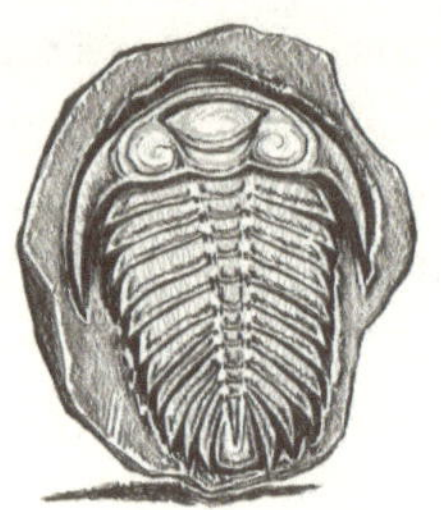

"I MUST SAY, YOU ARE LOOKING lovelier than ever I have seen! That dress is most flattering."

Astrid gave Lord Smyth her best fake smile and thrust his new offering of flowers at Crippens. The butler took them with a look of disgust that mirrored her own feelings. Of all the inconvenient times to gain an admirer. Not only had Smyth barged in at a most inopportune moment, but she found his aggressive friendliness a trifle off-putting. Particularly when he complimented her on a costume meant to make her look as little like herself as possible. Her nose twitched. It felt naked without the ring in it.

"Thank you, Lord Smyth, for your gifts and the honor of your visit, but I'm afraid I was just going out. I can't stay to chat. My brother is home, if you should like to call upon him."

A moment's displeasure flashed in his eyes, but he maintained his affable smile. "You are going out? I would be happy to escort you."

"No." A long, awkward moment passed before she added, "Thank you."

"It wouldn't be a bother." The insipid smile remained plastered on his face.

"I'm leaving to visit a friend. You may not accompany me. You have my apologies."

*You do not have my apologies. I told you no. Now, go away.*

"Please allow me to show you out, Lord Smyth," Crippens murmured, his tone deferential. His customary scowl twitched slightly, as close to a smile as he ever managed.

"Yes, of course. I shall call another time. Enjoy your outing, Lady Astrid."

By the time the door closed behind him, Astrid's face hurt from the forced smile.

"What shall I do with *these*, Lady Astrid?" Crippens dangled the flowers from his fingertips.

"Put them in the dining room. No sense in wasting something beautiful." She snagged her cloak from its hook rather than waiting for him to fetch it for her. "If anyone asks, I have gone to visit a friend, and I will be back in time for dinner."

"Of course, my lady."

She ignored the reproachful tone and slipped out of the house. Crippens hated her unladylike behavior, but his loyalty to the family was absolute. He would scowl and grumble, but leave her to do as she pleased.

The autumn air was crisp this morning, with a brisk wind and gray skies that presaged rain. Astrid tugged her cloak tight around her shoulders and started down the lane toward her first visit of the day.

The potions shop run by Miss Mary James was a repurposed shed at the edge of the James' family farm. Astrid stepped into the warmly lit room, smiling at the new racks and the hundreds of little bottles on display. Miss James's business was thriving.

"Lady Astrid!" the proprietress greeted her, rising from her seat in the corner to grasp Astrid's hand. "I'm pleased to see you. How are you today?"

"Uncomfortable."

"I'm sorry to hear that. I have an array of medicinal potions. What is your particular complaint?"

Astrid chuckled. "No, I'm not sick. I'm in disguise."

She flipped her cloak back to reveal the most slimming dress she owned, a black mourning costume from her uncle's funeral, back during her sixteenth year. It hadn't fit her then, and it certainly didn't fit now. It had been restyled after her father died, but she'd never worn it until now. She could feel the seams straining with every movement. The large bustle wobbled precariously behind her. She put the odds of making it home without any tears at ten to one.

"Those sleeves do look somewhat tight."

"Everything is tight. If I sound breathless, it's because my corset is cinched as tight as it has ever been. It's horrid, but I wish to look as different from myself as I can manage. That's where I need your help."

"Aha." Miss James turned to her merchandise, one end of her mouth twisting up as she thought. "I think I have a potion or two that will be just the thing."

Twenty minutes later, Astrid bade goodbye to her friend and continued on her way, now a ginger-haired, green-eyed, freckled beauty. Or some approximation thereof. Her face itched a bit from the potion-laced face cream that had created the freckles, and she knew if she touched her hair it would feel oily from the potion she'd combed through it. But Mary knew her craft, and the magic in the cosmetics meant everyone would assume what they saw was real. Astrid pulled up her hood to protect her red tresses and put her feet to walking the miles to Cliffsdale Asylum.

A gray-haired woman waved Astrid through the entrance and took her cloak, welcoming her to the asylum with a well-rehearsed speech. Astrid took a moment to look around the foyer. It reminded her of an opera house, all marble and gilding. A glittering chandelier cast pools of potion-fueled light across the floor. Vases of flowers added cheery spots of color to the opulent space.

"A lovely place you have here," she said, meaning it. The main entrance was welcoming, for all its lavish decor. Astrid would have been happy to attend a ball or a dinner in such a house.

"Thank you, Miss…?"

"Ada Anning," Astrid introduced herself. "I have come to visit my cousin, Lady Ophelia."

"Welcome, Miss Anning. If you would step into the parlor, one of the nurses will be with you shortly. Shall I ring for tea?"

"No, thank you."

Astrid perched on the edge of a chair, afraid to sit back lest she stretch too far and bust out of her dress. She did want the tea. Breakfast had been small, and she'd had nothing to eat or drink since. With her stomach squeezed beneath the corset, she feared even a small drink might make her ill.

She examined herself in a nearby mirror. From this distance she looked like another person altogether. The red hair didn't suit her, she decided, and her poor, crushed breasts looked so small. She did look fashionable, though. All in all, she preferred to be herself in her ordinary clothing, even if no one else liked it.

"Miss Anning?" a nurse inquired.

Astrid stood. "Yes."

"You are here to see Lady Ophelia?"

"I am. Is she available? How is she? I do hope her time here is doing her good, the poor dear."

Astrid detected a bit of pity in the nurse's smile. "I assure you she is comfortable and in the best of hands."

"Thank you."

"Follow me, please."

Astrid followed her guide deeper into the house, through halls and rooms every bit as beautiful as the entrance. The furnishings were costly and comfortable, with many of the nicest spaces occupied by patients at rest.

"Lady Ophelia spends most of her time here in the music room," the nurse told Astrid, leading her into the wide, high-ceilinged space.

All over the room, patients relaxed in much the same way they had in the garden, lounging on chairs and sofas. A few had books, and one was painting, but most sat resting, or even dozing. The beautiful pianoforte sat in the corner, untouched and silent.

In the dead center of the room lay Lady Ophelia, clad again in only a nightgown. She sprawled on her back, staring up at the painted ceiling, jabbering to herself.

"So many clouds. Such a sunny-dark day, and I cannot see but for the clouds. Do you think it shall rain? No, certainly it shall not, for look how very many clouds there are today."

Astrid's eyes drifted to the ceiling. It had been painted up with a garish Baroque-style fresco, teeming with clouds and angels, and looking not at all as if the space opened to the heavens.

Lady Ophelia flapped her arms. "I should like to fly like the rain. How wet I would be. And falling, always falling."

"Lady Ophelia." The nurse bent over her, speaking in soothing tones. "You have a visitor."

"Oh, but I cannot. For I am a cloud and much too high to be seen."

The nurse held out a hand. "Come, dear, and see."

Lady Ophelia allowed the nurse to help her to her feet.

"There you are, dear. Do you see? Here is Miss Anning, come to visit."

"Hello, Cousin," Astrid greeted her. "How are you?"

"Cousin?" Lady Ophelia studied her with a penetrating gaze. Recognition flashed in her eyes. "Oh, but I know you. Changing, always changing. Boy, girl, brown, red. Is this the real you?"

"Yes, it is I, Ada."

"Hello, Ada. I am Lady Ophelia, and most awful melancholy."

Astrid offered her hand, and Ophelia took it, giving her a squeeze.

"Would you like to sit and talk, Cousin?"

"Oh, but I cannot, because there is so much noise I cannot hear. Do you hear it? All around and in my head."

"Yes. Perhaps if we were to sit alone?" She glanced out the window at the empty garden. The cool, gray day had kept everyone indoors.

"Oh!" Ophelia pressed her face to the glass. "You wish to travel. I long to travel. But it is so far to Africa, and so very hot there."

"Yes, dear. You would need your boots and stockings. And a cloak or jacket to protect from the sun." Astrid glanced at the nurse, then back at Ophelia. "If you will wear those things, I will take you on a journey. There is a lovely boat waiting for us."

"Oh, yes! I have been on it. It sways in the waves and I can feel the breeze in my hair."

Astrid turned to the nurse once more. "Is it possible to fetch her things so I might take her outside?"

"Yes, of course. I shall return shortly."

Ophelia rambled on about the heat and the sun of Africa during the minutes that they waited for their things. Sprinkled into her nonsense were real facts about the climate and geography of Egypt. Lady Ophelia had a quality education.

The nurse helped Ophelia into her boots and cloak, then gave Astrid permission to walk her out to the garden.

"Thank you. I don't think we will be long. I don't wish my cousin to take a chill, but she does love the fresh air."

"That she does. The swing is a great favorite of hers. Only take care that she does not stand upon it."

The two young women hooked arms and stepped out into the garden.

"Yes, do take care, Miss Anning," Ophelia muttered once the doors had closed behind them. "They should hate for me to fall and mar their pristine reputation."

"If I didn't fear to blow our cover, I would go and stand with you on the swing, one of us on each side, and we would soar like the wind."

Ophelia's genuine laugh was a glorious, joyful noise. "Wouldn't that be fun? I know that is why many of the ladies come here—to have a chance to do things ladies oughtn't do."

"But that isn't why you are here."

"Nor you. Let us sit, and talk."

The two women sat side-by-side on the swinging bench, rocking slowly.

"Let me introduce myself," Astrid began. "I am Lady Astrid Wembley, daughter of the late Marquess of Whitehaven and twin sister to the present marquess. I'm widely reputed to be peculiar, if not insane. I'm convinced the glittering surface of this institution conceals a terrible enterprise where poor and ill women are imprisoned and maltreated. I wish to discover what they are doing and why, and put an end to it. And what of you? I know you are putting on an act."

"My name is Lady Ophelia Barnard. A dear friend of mine was sent to this facility at the behest of her wretch of a husband. He squandered her money and now seeks to marry another."

"And what better way to rid oneself of an inconvenient woman than to send her to an asylum," Astrid seethed.

"Precisely. He had her declared insane and the marriage dissolved on the grounds that she was not sensible enough to enter into a union. She is free of him, now, if only I can get her out."

Astrid nodded. "So you have pretended to be insane in order to get close to her."

"Yes. It is my hope that if I can act unusual enough for long enough they will transfer me to the hospital wing, even though I am a paid client."

Astrid gripped Ophelia's arm. "No. You don't want to go there."

Her eyes rounded in alarm. "Why? What have you seen?"

"When I was here the other day, sneaking around, I saw a group of patients in an upstairs room. I believe they had been drugged. I know that glassy-eyed look. Have you noticed that there are no bars on the windows? That is peculiar for an insane asylum. They employ a different technique to keep the patients from attempting escape. You can't let yourself go to that wing, or you, too, will be drugged, and then you will both be trapped."

Lady Ophelia dragged her feet on the ground, pulling the swing to a halt. "We must do something. I didn't come here to fail."

"Nor did I. I would like to propose a partnership, if I may. You remain here, learning all you can. It will be a delicate balance, being odd enough that you must stay, but not so much that they take you away and drug you."

"I can do it. I've learned much already. I recognize all of the doctors, because they come and go through the main entrance. I know many of their names as well. People talk when I'm around because they don't think I will even hear what they are saying."

"You were most helpful the other day, suggesting I look at the higher floors."

"The second floor is often mentioned. Nothing specific, only vague references, such as, 'Miss Jones was promoted to second floor,' or 'have the tea sent up for second floor dinner.' It's the only part of the asylum mentioned in such a fashion. Something is special about it."

"Something is terrible about it. That's where I saw the drugged women."

Lady Ophelia hugged her arms to her chest. "I will learn all I can, and I will find a way to write it down so I might pass you notes when you next come by."

"Excellent. I will investigate from the outside and learn about the men who run this place. If I must, I will come sneaking again, but perhaps at night when I won't be so obvious. And I will visit as often as I am able. My story will be that I'm staying at the inn in Whitehaven."

A fat drop of rain splashed in Astrid's lap, and she looked up to the sky.

"I should be going soon. Dressed as I am it will take me a good two hours to walk home, and this rain will only be growing worse as the afternoon wears on."

"Yes. And your freckles are beginning to fade."

Astrid's hand went to her cheek. "Oh, dear. I hadn't thought to ask how long the potions would last. I shall take that into account next time. I must also practice with the steam car. Driving would make visits far more convenient."

"I should love to learn to drive. When we free Beth from the hospital wing, you must teach us both, and then we can drive away to our freedom."

"I would love to do that. I promise to practice for both of our sakes and that of your friend."

Ophelia squeezed her hand. "Thank you. I knew when I first saw you you were someone special, and I'm more grateful than you know to have an ally in this."

"I do know," Astrid replied. "Because I feel the same."

The two women—friends now with a common goal—walked hand-in-hand back into the building, where the nurse waited to take Ophelia's cloak, and the boots she kicked off immediately.

"I shall take you to the Whitehaven beach someday," Astrid whispered, "and we shall run about on the sand in our bare feet."

"Yes, Cousin Ada, we shall travel," Ophelia pronounced, slipping easily back into her persona. "We are home from Africa, but we shall go to the Caribbean and to China and

Canada. Canada is so sunny-dark, did you know? So many clouds and no rain at all." Her gaze drifted up to the ceiling.

"No rain in here," Astrid promised. "Goodbye, dear. I shall visit again when I can."

"Goodbye, Cousin. Fly back soon. I shall be here. Or there. But I do not know." She flung herself in a chair and waved until Astrid disappeared out the door.

A steady drizzle had begun, and Astrid had gone no more than half a mile before it grew to a downpour. She held her cloak closed against the wind, keeping her head down and the hood low over her eyes.

She tried to pick up her pace, but the constriction of her corset allowed her only shallow breaths, and she grew winded quickly. Her stomach ached, and her legs wobbled. She had gone too long without food or water. She *would* learn to drive that car for her next visit.

The minutes slogged into hours as the mud made her footing treacherous and slowed her progress. The closer to home she came, the harder she pushed herself, eager to reach the warmth of a fire and dry, comfortable clothing. By the time she ascended the front steps, her head was spinning.

Crippens opened the door for her and took her arm to help her into the house. She was soaked through and dripping on the floor. Cold, stiff fingers tugged at the clasp of her cloak. She couldn't seem to catch her breath.

Monte came rushing toward her. "Lady Astrid, there you are. Your brother has been beside himself with worry."

His words sounded oddly distant to her ears, and her vision blurred at the edges. She took one step, then pitched forward into his arms.

# XV
# THE EYE OF THE BEHOLDER

"**A**STRID!"

Monte yanked the wet cloak off her and flung it aside. Little good it did. She was soaked through to the bones. What in hell was she doing, out in the pouring rain dressed like this?

"S-sorry," she stammered, trying to right herself. Her words were raspy, her breath coming in small, quick pants. "A little dizzy."

He grasped her with both hands and studied her face. Her skin was pale and her eyes dull. Her wet hair was streaked orange-red. She swayed on her feet and tried to speak again, but all that came out was a gasp.

Monte grabbed for the buttons along the back of her dress. He didn't know what she had done or why, but he needed to get her out of that corset and breathing normally. The slick buttons slipped under his fingers while Astrid sagged against him.

He cursed and clenched the delicate fabric in both hands. With a ferocious jerk, he tore the bodice open, sending buttons flying across the foyer. Through some miracle of fate—or, more likely, the fact she couldn't fit another layer—Astrid hadn't

120

bothered with a corset cover, and Monte found the laces of her stays exposed to his fingers. Thanking God for his unsavory past, he made short work of the knot, tugging the strings loose until he felt her suck in a full, deep breath.

He held her in his arms, keeping her upright, listening to her breathing slow and regulate itself, feeling his own heart rate doing the same.

"Thank you," she said, sounding more her usual self. "I shouldn't have run, I think, in this corset."

"You shouldn't have worn it at all. "

He released her, but she wobbled without his support. He grabbed her arm to steady her.

"Would you walk me to the kitchen? I feel weak from hunger."

"I will not." He scooped her up in his arms, and she let out a squeal of surprise.

"Mr. Crippens, Lady Astrid is unwell. Please have tea and food sent up to her room at once, and send her maid to help her into clean, dry clothes."

"Yes, sir. Shall I send for a doctor?"

"I *am* a doctor. I shall attend to her myself. Thank you."

Astrid squirmed in his arms. "Monte, what are you doing? You can't carry me all the way upstairs."

"I most certainly can." He strode off down the hall to prove his point. "Though the task would be easier if you wouldn't wiggle so much."

"But you're not a terribly muscular man. I'd hate for you—"

"I'm fine."

He did his best not to grunt going up the stairs. When he had estimated his ability to carry her, he hadn't considered that her sodden clothing must weigh at least two stone all on its own. By the time he set her down outside her door, he was breathing hard.

Astrid gave him a smug smile. "Thank you, Dr. Montford. I hope you didn't overexert yourself."

"I am perfectly well. You, on the other hand…"

He lost his train of thought as he stared at her. Her torn dress had slipped down, exposing the top of her corset and the swell of her now-unconstricted breasts. A few quick flicks to unlatch the corset busks, and he could have those luscious globes in his hands.

"Yes? What about me?"

*You are delectable.* "You're shivering. You need to get out of those wet clothes." *Please don't ask me to help you out of those clothes.* "Your maid will be along any moment. I will give you some time to rest and eat, but I will return later to check that you have suffered no lingering ill-effects."

"I feel better already. Only hungry."

"Good. Have something to eat, and I will see you again shortly."

He turned away from her indecent state and hurried down the hall to his own room to splash himself with cold water. After half an hour of reassuring Cal that his sister hadn't irreparably harmed herself, Monte returned to her room, medical kit in hand.

The door stood ajar, and when he knocked, Astrid called to him to enter. Attired now in a dressing gown of burgundy velvet, she sat cross-legged on her bed, sipping tea and reading a novel. Her hair had been brushed out and braided, and she had restored the silver ring to its customary place in her cute, little nose. Her delicate teacup touched her lips, the warm liquid leaving them moist and red.

His eyes darted around the room. Anywhere but her face. She had eaten, he noted with pleasure. A few crumbs on the tray beside her were all that remained of her food.

A bit of movement at the edge of his vision caught his attention, and he turned toward the window. Atop a low shelf sat a terrarium that contained a fern, a few chunks of log, and a giant, hairy, multi-legged *thing* crawling up the glass.

Monte sprang back with a cry of alarm. "Christ!"

"Monte, really. There's no need to be blasphemous."

His eyes were locked on the terrarium, wide with horror. "What in God's name is that hellish beast?"

Astrid set down her book and came to stand beside him. She popped open the top of the cage and picked up the hideous arthropod.

"This is Bristles. She's a spider." She ran a finger affectionately across the monster's furry back.

Monte retreated, gaping at Astrid's pet. "A spider? It's the spawn of Satan. It's as big as a house."

"They call them bird-spiders. Supposedly some species can eat small birds and grow to be as big as a dinner plate. Bristles is no bigger than my hand, though."

"Yet."

Astrid laughed. She petted the spider once more, then returned her to her enclosure. "I've had her for six years and I am convinced this is her full adult size."

"Six years? Lord. How long do they live?"

"No idea. I suppose I will find out."

Monte's shock had begun to subside, and his breathing slowed to normal. "Where the devil did you get it from?"

"A scientist at the Institute brought a pair back from South America. A mating pair, it happened. The female laid eggs on the voyage and he decided to raise the baby spiders and distribute them to anyone who wanted one to study. Most were mounted for display. I had similar plans at first, but I came to like her."

Monte wanted to laugh. Never had he ever met any woman so delightfully unconventional. "So you keep her in a wardian case in your bedchamber. As one does."

She grinned at him. "Monte, was that a joke? How shocking."

"It is either make a jest or run away in terror, and that is unbefitting a gentleman."

"Another joke! Oh, dear. Are you certain you are well?"

"Perfectly well." Reminded of his purpose here, he opened his medical bag, withdrawing his stethoscope. He slung it around his neck and set the bag on the shelf beside the hell-spider. "But what of you? Have you fully recovered?"

"I believe so. The food made a significant difference. Along with being able to breathe."

"Pardon my language, Lady Astrid, but what the bloody hell were you thinking? I can accept that you aren't afraid to be out in the rain, but to be wandering about all day exerting yourself in such a costume? Running in it? For that matter, why would you wear that dress at all? Why do such a thing to yourself?"

She sighed, her expression contrite. "I was in disguise."

Monte stepped closer, reaching out to touch a lock of her hair that still held a reddish tint. "Disguise."

"Yes. I visited a friend at the asylum, and I needed to change my looks. I used potions to color my hair and eyes and I chose a dress that gave me something like a fashionable shape."

"You chose a dress that cut off your air supply!"

"It worked. No one even cast me a suspicious glance. When I looked in the mirror, I could hardly recognize myself. Miss Ada Anning had nothing in common with Astrid Wembley. She was slim and redheaded, with an adorable sprinkling of freckles, whereas I am—"

"If you call yourself 'fat' again," he threatened.

"What? You'll lecture me? Tear all my best gowns?"

"I will kiss you until you believe me when I tell you how beautiful you are."

Astrid froze, her perfect mouth agape.

Monte took a step backward, prepared to apologize for his impulsive words. He didn't want her ever to think he might kiss her without her permission. Before he could speak, her hand shot out and clenched on his waistcoat. She hauled him against her, sending his stethoscope tumbling to the floor and pressing her soft bosom into his chest. Blue eyes riveted him to the floor. Glistening, pink lips tilted up at him, begging him to bend for a taste. His breath caught.

"I think you should know, Dr. Montford," she murmured, "I am the fattest fatty who ever fatted."

The man was neither a doctor nor a rake. He was a magician. It was the only explanation for how he could turn the entire world upside down with a press of his lips.

Astrid clung to his shirt, his solid form her only anchor in the raging sea of pleasure and desire. How could she have forgotten this? She had always remembered his kiss as an all-encompassing thrill, yet somehow the true magnitude of the sensation had become hazy with the passing of the years.

She groaned against his mouth, inviting him in with parted lips, reeling beneath the onslaught of his expert tongue. Hot. Wet. Spicy. His taste was smooth as the finest brandy and rich as the darkest chocolate. His arms enveloped her, sheltering her from anything that might dare try to drag her from him.

He needn't have bothered. She wasn't going anywhere. Not until she had fully explored the curves of his lips, the depths of his mouth, and the taste of his skin.

She kissed him with a reckless hunger born of years waiting to reacquaint herself with his electrifying touch. This wild, so wrong and so right sensation had eluded her since that crazy day on the cliffs. Now it had come raging back, urging her to throw caution to the wind and surrender to physical passion.

Her hands roamed the contours of his chest. Her kisses nipped the corner of his mouth, then down his chin to the thrumming pulse of his throat.

"Astrid," he moaned, his fingertips skimming down her back. "Astrid, you make me so damn hard." He cupped her buttocks and pulled her tight against his heavy erection.

Desire slid over her skin, sunk into her body, and penetrated down to her bones. It vibrated through her, from the tips of her fingers where they brushed his chest, to the wet, aching core of her sex. Never had she felt so beautiful.

He drew back just far enough to look at her, his gray eyes gleaming with undisguised lust.

Her mind reeled, drunk on the possibilities. She was ready to give herself up to him, fully and completely. If only she were more sophisticated, more knowledgeable. Should she unbutton her dressing gown? Her nightdress was plain and modest. Should she stop everything now and ask him about the best way to prevent conception? Was it a sign of her craziness that she wanted to fling herself at him?

He released her and staggered backwards, running a hand through his hair. It only served to make him more attractive.

"Hell," he gasped. "I am out of control."

"That's how I feel as well," she admitted.

"I didn't come here to seduce you."

"No, but you offered to kiss me and I…" Her cheeks burned, thinking of how eagerly she had snatched at the opportunity, how hungrily her mouth had claimed his. "I thought I would like that."

His smoldering gaze caressed her, head to toe. "And did you like it?"

"Very much."

"I'm glad." He took another step backward, shaking his head. "I need to leave, Astrid, before this goes any further."

*But why?*

The words hung there, unspoken. She took in the open door and the empty tray waiting to be taken away. Her brother's room was only two doors down. Perhaps now was not the time.

Monte scooped up his stethoscope and dropped it into his medical bag. "I think we can forgo the examination. From what I felt, your heart and lungs are in perfect working order."

For some reason, those words only made her blush harder.

"Monte?" she called as he stepped through the door.

"Yes?"

"I don't believe you yet. About being beautiful. You're going to have to try again."

*And again and again.*

# XVI
# PLANS OF ACTION

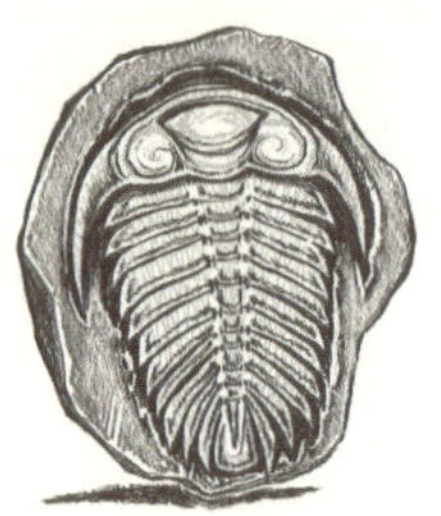

Astrid held the straining carpet bag closed with one hand as she fumbled to fasten the buckle. The satchel wasn't large enough to hold everything a lady needed for three days—even a lady of as little style as Astrid considered herself—but it would have to do. She couldn't pack anything she couldn't carry on her own.

She took a final look around the room to check that she hadn't forgotten anything. Bristles was happily stalking a cricket and wouldn't need another before Astrid returned. Her notes, photographs, and specimens were tucked into her shoulder bag, along with a novel and a few snacks in case of emergency. Nothing obvious was lying out.

Satisfied that all was in order, she slipped from the room, made her way through the silent house, and stepped out into the still early morning air. The soft glow of the first light of dawn drew her eyes to the horizon. A momentary pang tugged at her heart. A few minutes walk and she could be sitting in her special cove on the beach, watching the sunrise.

She turned toward the carriage house. Cal would be rising

soon, and most of the servants. She needed to be on her way before anyone could interfere.

The steam car rested in its customary location, beside the beautiful mid-century horse-drawn carriage the Whitehaven family still used for local jaunts or when the car was otherwise in use. Astrid lifted the hatch covering the engine and tried to remember her brother's usual routine. She could tell the potion tank was full. Peters, their driver and maintenance man, kept the vehicle at the ready.

Astrid pulled a lever to ignite the fuel and started up the engine. A shiver of nervousness ran down her spine. Starting from cold, it would be some minutes while the water heated and the steam compressed. She tried to pass the time by sitting in the driver's seat and familiarizing herself with the steering wheel, the throttle and the brakes. Only twice had she ever tried driving, and both times Cal had been sitting at her side and directing her. Making the three or four hour drive to London on her own was terrifying. And thrilling. By the time she arrived, she would be an expert, and assured of proper transport for future visits to Ophelia at the asylum.

When at last the gauges read the proper temperature and pressure, Astrid eased the car out of the carriage house, then hopped out and closed the door behind her. Whitehaven Manor was quiet and dark, no one the wiser. It was time to be off.

Four hours later, Astrid stopped the steam carriage in front of her hotel and stepped down, legs a touch stiff and shaky, but wearing a grin of triumph ear-to-ear.

"Good morning, my lady," a porter greeted her. "Would you like me to park your vehicle for you?"

"Yes, please. I won't need the car again until I return home. Please see that it is cleaned and refueled."

"My pleasure, my lady."

She had done it. She was a lady driver. The first half-hour had been a whirlwind of experimentation, and once in the middle of the journey she had needed to hop out and push the car to get it going again, but she'd succeeded in getting herself into town on time and unharmed. She had her bag sent up to her room and started off on the short walk to the Institute. It felt good to stretch her legs.

Determined not to make the mistake of skipping meals ever again, she bought an eel pie on her way, and sat eating it on the steps outside the Institute entrance in a very unladylike fashion. She wondered what Monte thought of eel pies. He probably wouldn't touch them. Too much eel and not enough vegetables. Stomach pleasantly full, she checked her pocket watch and made her way inside, satisfied she had enough time for a quick chat before the day's lecture.

The door to Ayleston's office stood open when Astrid arrived. She could see him inside at his desk, talking to a woman with more style in her little, modern hat than Astrid had in her entire wardrobe. In fact, Astrid was unpleasantly reminded she had completely forgotten to bring a hat, a parasol, or any other means of keeping the sun off her face. She hoped her mistake might at least remind her to pick up a new bottle of the skin-protection potion that kept her from burning during long hours at the beach. She'd used up most of her store during the summer months.

Astrid knocked on the office door, hoping she wasn't committing a terrible error in protocol. For all her independence at home, she was entirely unused to time on her own in the city. On most visits she came with Cal or Grace or the both of them. Her parents had accompanied her often when her father was still alive. The last time she'd spent a day alone in the city, she'd ended up with a trilobite tattoo.

She tugged up the end of her sleeve just enough to see a bit of ink, smiling at the memory. It had hurt, but she'd braved it out and now had beautiful body art to show for it. Her nose ring had come about in much the same way, when she slipped away from her brother for an afternoon during their travels in

India. She pondered what she might do this weekend, with no one nearby to temper her eccentricity.

"Lady Astrid?" Lord Ayleston sounded surprised to see her, but it took him only an instant to regain his customary sober temperament. "Please, come in. Allow me to introduce my niece, Lady Vayne. Patricia, this is Lady Astrid Wembley, whom, as I have told you, I am recommending for membership to our esteemed club."

The finely dressed woman held out her hand. "A pleasure to meet you, Lady Astrid."

As they shook hands, Astrid tried to remember what she might have heard of Lady Vayne. There had been an Earl of Vayne who had died some years back. Perhaps she was his widow? She looked to be in her early thirties and the ideal picture of poise and elegance. She gave Astrid a friendly smile.

"My uncle tells me you are brilliant."

Astrid blushed. She worked hard and had accomplished much, yet she still felt a fraud when people praised her. "Thank you. That is very kind."

"What brings you to town, Lady Astrid?" Ayleston asked. "It had been my understanding you meant to remain in the country for a time."

"I wished to consult with you on my findings and inquire as to what your own have been." She hoped the words sounded enough like a work matter that Lady Vayne wouldn't suspect anything of the truth.

"Ah. Of course. Patricia, could you shut the door, please? Thank you, dear." He turned to Astrid. "You needn't fear to speak openly in front of Lady Vayne. She is assisting me in my investigations, and may even have insight into your questions that I do not."

"You're wondering about the murder?" Lady Vayne inquired. "We have found two possible poisons that could have been used. They both produce the symptoms and manner of death observed, and neither would leave clear signs during a post-mortem examination. Both are potion-based. The ingredients necessary to produce the potions are common enough that it would be senseless to pursue that angle. Anyone with the recipe and a moderate amount of potions knowledge could make such a poison."

"Which narrows down our list of suspects not at all," Astrid sighed.

"Sadly, such is often the case with criminal investigations. Many leads result only in dead ends."

"What of the factions within the Institute and possible motives for the murder?"

"The obvious motive is to supplant me," Ayleston replied. "Nothing thus far has suggested otherwise. Voting me out is within the realm of possibility for either of my two greatest rivals, though each would need to steal a number of votes from the other. Neither man, though, has behaved suspiciously that I have been able to detect."

"Is either Lord Smyth or Lord Marvale a faction leader?"
"No. Why?"

"I have encountered both men of late. Marvale is my neighbor, of course, but he makes me suspicious because he tends patients at Cliffsdale Ladies' Convalescent Asylum. Smyth has begun courting me for some unfathomable reason."

Lady Vayne laughed. "You are an eligible young lady. I think that is reason enough."

"I am rather older than desirable and not at all a refined lady."
"You underestimate yourself."

Astrid shrugged, a good indicator of her unmarriagability.

Ayleston stroked his short beard. "Have you anything else of note to report, Lady Astrid? I understand there was a hearing the other day."

How had he known that? "Yes. The judge's impression of me was favorable, but he won't make a final decision without a second medical opinion. Unfortunately, he has appointed Lord Marvale to do the examination. I'm concerned by his connection to Fawdry and I know he dislikes me."

"I will investigate Marvale, and Smyth as well."

"Thank you. And anything you know of Fawdry and the asylum would be helpful as well. There is underhanded business at that institution, and I mean to bring it into the open."

"If anyone can do that, Lady Astrid, I'm certain it is you. Your determined spirit is what first caught my attention, and it has never waned in all the years I have known you."

"Thank you. I will try my best."

"I know you will. I believe it's time we were getting to the lecture. Shall we all go together?"

"That would be nice, thank you." No sense in striking out on her own in a location that still held the possibility of housing an enemy.

The small group made their way to the auditorium, which had filled mostly to capacity for today's talk on astronomy. Astrid scanned the room for open seats. Ayleston had a seat reserved near the front, but she doubted an extra place could be made for her.

"Lady Astrid."

The enticing, baritone voice sent a rush of pleasure straight through her chest, until the reality of his presence sank in and hot anger blazed through her. She rounded on him, fists clenching in fury.

"I saved you a seat," Monte said, mouth curving in a dazzling smile.

"What are you doing here?" she hissed. Only their public location prevented her from shouting.

"I caught the 7:10 train. It's faster than driving."

It wasn't the answer she wanted, and he knew it. She glared at him, but he continued to smile.

Her companions had turned toward the conversation.

"Monte!" Lady Vayne exclaimed. "How are you? It's been an age."

He gave her a slight nod. "Lady Vayne."

"No kiss for an old friend?" Her mouth twitched in amusement. "I recall a time when I was Tricia to you, but these things never last. Ah, well."

Ugh. Had he bedded every woman in London?

"It's good to see you," he said. "You are looking lovely, as always."

That was certainly true. Her expensive, fashionable gown highlighted full breasts and an elegant figure. She had naturally rosy cheeks and a pleasing expression. She was friendly and intelligent. Astrid couldn't very well fault Monte for liking her.

"I hadn't realized you had an interest in the sciences," he continued.

"I don't, particularly. I'm here to visit with my uncle." She gestured at Ayleston.

"Ah." Monte's gaze turned to Ayleston, who stared him down with a menacing frown befitting a man who had just caught a young rake behaving inappropriately with his niece.

Monte had probably received many such looks, as it didn't appear to faze him. "Good to see you again, sir."

"The lecture is about to begin. I suggest you escort Lady Astrid to her seat. Come, Patricia, I have a place for you."

Astrid took the seat beside Monte, mostly because she couldn't see anywhere else to put herself.

"I'm relieved to find you all in one piece," he whispered.

"What, did you think I had been kidnapped and murdered?" she scoffed.

"No, but I feared you may have had an accident along the way. It was badly done, sneaking out in the dead of night and stealing the steam car."

Astrid kept her eyes fixed on the stage and her hands clasped in her lap. It wouldn't do to jab him with her elbow during a public lecture. "I stole nothing. It belongs to my family."

"It belongs to your brother, and as I recall you hadn't learned how to drive it."

"I have remedied that situation."

"Apparently."

"As you can see, you have needlessly followed me. You may leave at any time."

"I think not."

"You have come, then, to lecture me on my wild behavior and drag me home?"

"No."

That surprised her. "Then why are you here?"

"Because there is the potential for danger and I promised your brother I would keep you safe."

"You always keep your promises, I suppose?"

"I do my very best to. Some present more difficulty than others."

"Are you saying I'm difficult?"

He huffed a short, mirthless laugh. "You have no idea."

Astrid straightened her shoulders and determined not to speak to him for the remainder of the lecture, and perhaps the remainder of the day if she could manage it. His presence distracted her from the talk. In the warm, crowded room he felt perilously close. Each time she moved, her skirts flounced against his leg. Twice, when she tried to adjust her clothing, her fingers brushed his thigh. The second time it may not have been entirely accidental. What made this one man so enticing and simultaneously so infuriating?

Despite Monte's annoying presence, Astrid found the visiting scholar a delightful speaker, and the subject matter engaging. It had been too long since she'd taken her telescope out to the beach at night and sat gazing at the stars, but today she felt a renewed enthusiasm and determination to do so again soon.

When Monte offered his arm to escort her to the nearby ballroom for refreshments and the opportunity to mingle with the guest of honor, she could think of no logical reason to refuse him. Her fingers, still twitching from their brief skim across his trousers, settled on his arm with a minimum of hesitation. She did her best impression of Lady Vayne's regal carriage and tried not to fondle his muscles. It was time to focus on her true reason for being here.

She spied her quarry shortly after entering the room, engaged in conversation with two other members of the Institute. She watched him for a time, noting who he was with and how friendly they appeared to be. When he turned in her direction, she shook Monte off.

"Excuse me, Dr. Montford. I have work to attend to."

"Work? What sort of work?"

She ignored him. She had caught Lord Smyth's attention, and they strode toward one another.

"Lady Astrid, I'm so pleased to see you again," he gushed. "I had high hopes you would come to town for today's talk."

"How fortuitous. I had much the same hopes regarding you. I'm sorry to have thrown you out so abruptly the other day, but it really was a case of terrible timing."

He placed a hand over his heart. The man was needlessly theatrical. "The fault is entirely mine, my lady. I ought to be more formal in my addresses to you, but I find myself acting on impulse, a weakness for which I grievously apologize."

"No need to come over all mawkish, Smyth," Monte interrupted. "Lady Astrid has a fondness for indulging her own whims and won't hold it against you."

Astrid glowered at him. Smyth gaped in offended shock.

"I'm sorry, do I know you?"

"Dr. Ernest Montford."

Smyth looked down his nose at the boorish commoner with the ill-knotted tie and unsightly waistcoat. Orange and blue today. It was the worst Astrid had seen, yet he still managed to come off as devilishly handsome. How annoying.

"Dr. Montford lives in town and had intended to show me the sights tomorrow," Astrid informed both gentlemen, flinging her plan into action. "Unfortunately, he was unable to make time during his day, due to the demands of his patients. I understand that, among very many others, he tends an afflicted woman who needs vigilant care."

Monte's mouth pinched into a tight line. Eyes hard as steel bore into her own. "Some say she ought to be institutionalized."

"How tragic."

"Indeed. Most especially since it might be prevented would she only heed my professional advice."

Astrid gifted him with a saccharine smile and an icy stare. "I can't imagine what might make a woman disinclined to listen to you, Dr. Montford."

Smyth's eyebrows had crinkled until they were almost touching. He glanced back and forth between Astrid and Monte. "Do you two need a moment in private?"

"No," they snapped in unison.

"Right, then."

"Dr. Montford was just leaving," Astrid declared.

"Yes," Monte replied. "Back to my daily exertions with troubled ladies."

"Do try not to exhaust yourself." Astrid gave an exaggerated sigh. "It's most unhealthful."

"I shall do my best, Lady Astrid, but when it comes to my patients I am ethically and morally obligated to see to their well-being, no matter how difficult that may prove. Good day to you."

She watched him wander off and casually insinuate himself into a conversation with several Institute members.

"Terribly unpleasant fellow," Lord Smyth remarked.

"Yes, well…" Astrid stopped herself, because her first instinct was to jump to Monte's defense, and that would not help the plan.

"Most ungentlemanly of him to leave you in the lurch like that."

"Quite."

"I don't suppose you might allow me to escort you about town in his stead?"

"That would be wonderful!" She fluttered her eyelashes, though she feared she looked silly doing it. "How very obliging of you, Lord Smyth."

"Think nothing of it. And please, call me Gideon."

"Of course." Astrid had no intention whatsoever of doing anything so intimate. She would have to ponder ways to avoid addressing him by name.

"Tomorrow morning, then. Shall I meet you—"

"Here at the Institute," Astrid jumped in. "I have proposals I wish to present to Lord Ayleston and the lecture committee in the morning."

"Ah. Excellent. I'm certain you have many clever things to say. Let us convene by the front entrance at, say, ten o'clock?"

"That would be perfect, thank you. Now, I'm afraid you must excuse me. I must find Lady Vayne, as our earlier conversation was interrupted by the lecture and we cannot part without proper closure."

Did that sound genteel? Or simply peculiar? It had been much too long since she had engaged in any regular socializing. Not that she had been any good at it to begin with.

Lord Smyth seemed to think it a sufficient excuse, as he bowed graciously and kissed her—thankfully gloved—hand.

"Until tomorrow, then."

"Until then. Good day."

Astrid hurried off, looking for Lady Vayne and pondering topics of conversation that were neither, "Which of these men looks like a murderer to you?" or, "What does Monte look like with his clothes off?" It took several minutes, but by the time the two women met in the throng, she had thought up an idea.

"My brother insists upon throwing a house party, including a fancy dress ball, and I have nothing to wear. Do you know a good dressmaker?"

Lady Vayne took her arm, smiling. "You've come to the right woman."

# XVII

# THE FIELD OF HONOR

AFTER THREE HOURS of trailing Astrid and Lord Smyth as they walked the entirety of London, Monte had run out of creative curses and had stooped to muttering, "Cal, you fucking wanker," every few minutes. Giving up, however, wasn't an option.

It wasn't merely a matter of a promise made. It was an unbreakable vow of honor and loyalty. It was a dozen sworn oaths, several made while drunk, and one made in blood. It was fistfights over stupid things, followed by laughter and tending one another's injuries. It was standing guard outside a bedroom in a house of ill repute, because it was Cal's first time and he was terrified he might panic.

It was kissing his best friend—and not chastely—in front of fifteen other men so Cal wouldn't lose fifty pounds to a drunken wager. Then wasting those same fifty pounds, plus the winnings, on more drink and frivolous clothing that did nothing to impress the ladies.

It was long hours talking about life and death, worries and fears, anything and everything. Late night outpourings of emotion that were forgotten by morning because gentlemen did not discuss such things.

It was loving someone so much he would take a bullet for him, even if he'd never say so to his face. Monte didn't need to. Cal knew. And Monte knew Cal felt the same.

Monte had reached the point where a bullet sounded less painful than following Lady Astrid.

After a stroll that seemed destined to cover every square inch of Hyde Park, Lord Smyth took her out in a boat for an interminable row along the Serpentine. Monte prowled the bank like an amateur cutpurse, creeping along from tree to tree, prepared to throw himself into the water and swim to her rescue, should Smyth attempt to drown her.

And she would drown, should she go overboard in her voluminous dress. An utterly astounding dress he had gotten no chance to see up close. He had no idea where it had come from, but it was entirely unlike anything she'd had in her closets at home. Striped red fabric with a solid silk underskirt, all gathered in a tidy bustle at her rump. A bodice that flattered rather than constricted. A daring little riding hat to match. Sometime between yesterday afternoon and this morning Astrid Wembley had become fashionable, and he was missing out on it.

Smyth turned the boat toward shore at last, and Monte found himself a good vantage point behind two ladies with abundant headgear. Astrid and her admirer chatted as they disembarked, and she looked to be smiling. The pair of them had been conversing all day, and Monte couldn't fathom what all they might be talking about. He hadn't seen the slightest hint of an argument. How was it possible a lady of such strong opinions could spend an entire day with a man without even the smallest squabble? When Monte was with her, they could hardly manage breakfast.

Astrid made several animated gestures, which Monte took to be an indication of where she wished to go next. Smyth made a gesture in the opposite direction, but was summarily rebuffed. He tipped his hat and allowed her to lead the way.

Perhaps that was the secret to their harmonious discourse. Smyth couldn't match her for either wit or tenacity, and therefore went along with whatever she wanted. It might even be what drew him to her. Some men did best when they had a more forceful personality to tell them what to do. Or else he was a villain trying to lull her into complacency with his agreeableness, that he might have a better opportunity to murder her.

The longer the day wore on, the less likely Monte found that theory to be. If Smyth had meant her harm, he would have had plenty of opportunities.

They were headed in his direction, so Monte ducked behind a nearby tree to keep out of sight. As he had done before, he would give them a moment to pass by and pull ahead before he stepped out into the clear.

He never had the chance.

A heavy weight slammed into him from behind, flattening him against the solid mass of the trunk. Pain blossomed across the left side of his head, and his ears rang. He had just enough sense to twist away from a second attack. The thick wooden club caught him with a glancing blow across the shoulder.

"You're meddling where you don't belong," his assailant snarled, swinging the baton again.

Monte ducked out of harm's way, staggering slightly. His head spun and blood ran down the side of his face. He needed to put his opponent at a similar disadvantage. He feinted with his left arm, and when the attacker dodged, Monte landed a powerful punch with his right. The man swayed, and Monte kicked at his weapon, sending it skittering across the grass. Much better.

The footpad lunged at him. Monte swiveled, planted his feet, and threw up his elbow, catching the man under the chin. The brute stumbled back but didn't fall. Tough son of a bitch.

"They said you was a prissy doctor," he mumbled, shaking off the hit.

"I am."

A prissy doctor with friends. Cal was no longer a wanker. He was now a bloody angel. Monte had taught Cal about women and sex; athletic, outdoorsy Cal had taught Monte how to fight. Fists, knives, swords, pistols, he knew them all. He could size up an opponent with a glance, and fight dirty if needed.

This footpad, or whoever he was, was strong and fast, but none too bright. They traded a few more jabs, neither landing a decisive blow.

"Didn't want to have to do this," the man mumbled, a hand delving into his pocket.

Monte sprang at him, grabbing his arm and wrestling the pistol from his grip before he could even lift it to aim. The thug drove Monte into the tree once again. He saw stars, but maintained his grip on the weapon. His assailant snatched up the fallen club, simultaneously drawing a second pistol from his other pocket.

Monte's head throbbed. Blood and sweat obscured his vision. A wave of nausea turned his stomach, and the world spun around him. Disoriented and fading rapidly, he could see only one option. He pulled the trigger.

# XVIII
# RECUPERATION

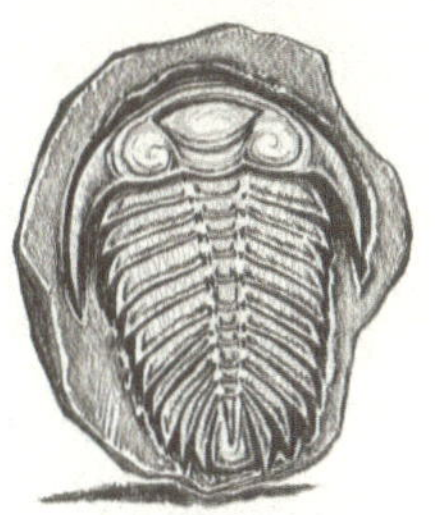

"How the hell did I get here?" Monte rubbed his eyes, his mouth turned down in a confused frown.

Astrid set down Dr. Harvey's unintentionally hilarious textbook and moved to sit at his side.

"Oh, good, you're awake. I was worried I might have to send for a real doctor."

"I *am* a real doctor."

"Yes, but at the moment you are the patient, while I am doctoring by making things up and reading your medical texts. I'm beginning to see where you get all your peculiar notions."

He looked all about him. "We're at my flat."

"I'm happy to see you talking sense. That's a good sign, according to the books."

"How did we get here?"

"You gave the cab driver your address, at my prompting."

"I don't recall that."

"You were having a rather difficult time keeping your feet. I had to make Lord Smyth help me with you, and he was none too pleased. He didn't want to ruin his suit with blood, and he thinks you're a cad."

"He's a buffoon. I do remember that."

"What else do you remember?"

Monte winced, whether out of pain or displeasure, she couldn't tell. "Nothing good." His eyes drifted toward the window, where the light was beginning to fade. "I've been out all afternoon?"

"Yes. Since I gave you the healing potion."

"What healing potion?"

"The one I had in my purse, naturally, in case it turned out Lord Smyth was our villain and he tried to do me harm. I told you I didn't need you to protect me."

Monte groaned. "When did I die and go to hell?"

A knock sounded at the door, and Astrid sprang to her feet. "Excuse me one moment. I must go and chase away another admirer. Or perhaps the police."

Astrid hurried to the front door, where she was relieved to find not another admirer, but a boy with a reply to her note to Ayleston. She thanked him and gave him a coin. She was down to only a few shillings after the rash of unexpected expenses. Tomorrow would require a stop at the bank if she wished to eat anything.

She read through the note as she walked back to Monte's sparsely furnished living quarters. The little waiting room and the office at the front of the apartment were tasteful and exactly what one would expect of a physician. The back room was one large, almost entirely empty space. The bed was quality, and seemed comfortable from the few times she had sat on it. There were few other furnishings to speak of. Only a bookshelf, a simple washstand, and a table with a pair of unpadded wooden chairs.

"Lord Ayleston says to remain here until morning, and he will come by and speak with us then."

She left out the part of the message where he said he would send Lady Vayne along to act as a chaperone during the night.

Astrid had locked the door and had no intention of opening it again for anyone.

"A sound notion," Monte agreed. "What were you saying about admirers?"

"Three ladies have come by this afternoon to wish you a speedy recovery, and half-a-dozen others have sent calling cards."

He frowned at her. "You're not joking."

"No, I'm not. Before you were the Notorious Ernest Montford, seducer of women. Now you are the Infamous Ernest Montford who fought a duel in Hyde Park."

He sat up, causing the blanket to fall away. He looked dangerously rakish, all scarred and bruised, attired only in his shirtsleeves.

"I did not fight a duel. I was attacked by a bandit."

"So you said. And so I told the police. But the rumor is you fought a duel. And you can't deny you shot the man and you both had pistols."

"What sort of lunatic fights a duel at no more than three paces, in a well-traveled area, at two o'clock in the afternoon?"

"It only makes the story more exciting. Broad daylight. Genteel ladies all about. You may not remember it, but there was a remarkable clamor after the gunshot. Ladies screaming and swooning and weeping. I had to pry one over-enthusiastic girl off your prone body and promise her she could lead the mourners at your funeral. She called you 'the most dashing scoundrel to grace our fair city.'"

"You're having me on."

"Well, perhaps that last bit wasn't strictly true, but you did inspire much weeping and excitement."

"And who am I to deny the good ladies of London such fine entertainment?"

"You're joking again. That's a wonderful sign."

Astrid did her best to ignore the little shiver that raced through her. The last time he had made jokes in her presence they had ended up kissing in a most sensational manner. That couldn't happen tonight. He had suffered a head injury, and various other ailments, and he needed to rest overnight for the healing potion to achieve full effect.

Or so she thought. She hadn't read the directions before feeding him the potion. Mrs. Ainsworth, a highly respected potion maker here in town, had assured Astrid the health potion was top-quality, so she expected a full and rapid recovery.

"I'm famished," Monte said, pushing the blanket off and swinging his legs over the side of the bed. "I don't imagine you might have any dinner prepared?"

"No, don't get up," she urged. "Though it's a very good sign that you're feeling hungry. The chapter on head trauma said—"

"I know what it says, and I should like to get something to eat."

"I have something. It's staying warm by the fire. Let me fetch it." Astrid hurried over to the hearth and dumped the tepid pie onto the pre-prepared plate. "I don't know how to cook, but I did go out and purchase some food. I don't know if you will like it, but it was what I could find on short notice."

"What is it?"

She passed him the dish. "Eel pie. And a cucumber."

He looked down at the food and chuckled. "A whole cucumber."

"It was the only plain vegetable I could find, except squash, which isn't especially practical."

"Squash is a fruit."

Astrid crossed her arms and frowned down at him. "So is a cucumber, biologically speaking."

He saluted her with the fruit in question. "Touché."

Monte bit off a chunk of the cucumber and chewed slowly. Astrid watched him eat in silence, reviewing the day's peculiar events in her mind.

"I don't think this was an accident," he said.

"The cucumber? I admit I didn't go far in search of food, but it did happen to be the only vegetable within a reasonable distance."

"Now you are the one joking. You know that isn't what I meant."

"You think the attack wasn't random. Not a botched robbery."

"The details are coming back to me now. He said something about meddling. He meant to beat me senseless to scare me off. Or perhaps kill me, if necessary."

"Thank God he didn't."

"Thank your brother. He taught me how to fight."

Astrid smiled at that. "Cal has always been very athletic. He teaches riding and cricket to all the local children and organizes competitions for them. Or, at least, he did before…"

She let the grief of her father's absence wash over her and then settle, taking a steadying breath.

"I know." His voice was soft. The sympathy and understanding in his gray eyes hit her like another wave.

Astrid pushed the feeling aside and steered the conversation back to the attack. "I think you're right about the attack. It explains the distraction."

"What distraction?"

"A lady collapsed in some hysterical fit not far down the lane from where you were. She made quite a bit of noise, and everyone around had rushed to help her. In the midst of the chaos we heard the gunshot. Only then did anyone notice your situation. I think I scared poor Lord Smyth half to death when I saw you. I screamed your name in a rather appalling high wail and ran to see if you'd been killed."

"He is 'poor Lord Smyth' now, is he?"

Astrid grinned. "Yes, actually. He is 'hard up for money and trying to hide it Lord Smyth,' as a matter of fact."

"You found that out on your tryst today?"

"It wasn't a tryst, it was an investigation. And I found out more than I ever wanted to know. The man talks about himself to no end. He is painfully dull, Monte. I thought the boat ride would last forever."

"So did I."

Her eyes narrowed. "You didn't need to follow me. All of this might have been avoided."

He squeezed his eyes shut. "Please. I have a headache. Let's not argue."

"I'm sorry. Is it very painful? I can get you a cold compress. Or should it be warm? I don't remember what the book recommended."

"I don't need either. The food will suffice. No loud noises or bright lights and no arguing and I shall be fine."

"Good."

Monte poked at the eel pie with his fork but didn't take a bite. "What else did you learn about Smyth?"

"He didn't mention the money straight out, but he was stingy with his coins. When we discussed travel, he made complaints that suggested to me he had ridden second class on the train. He mentioned 'current investments' in a vague way that sounded like get-rich-quickly schemes."

"He may be after your fortune, then."

"Yes, he may be. I have met many fortune hunters, however, and he has behaved somewhat differently. I'm not certain, but he may truly be growing fond of me. Whatever the case, he's not so terrible a man in my opinion. Certainly he isn't a murderer. He nearly fainted at the sight of all the blood after your duel."

"It was not a goddamned duel!"

"Don't shout, Monte. It's not good for your head, and what will your neighbors think?"

"I don't give a damn what they think." He sighed and scooped up a bite of his pie. "Please pardon my language, Lady Astrid. I am out of sorts."

"Think nothing of it."

Monte ate a few bits of pie, then asked, "What of the man I shot? Did he confess anything? Did I kill him?"

"I don't know. He looked to be in a bad way, and the police took him away. Will it bother you if it turns out he has died?"

"Honestly? No. He would have killed me. I don't feel sorry for it."

"Good. I would hate for you to suffer any more than you have done. How is your pie?"

He shrugged. "Edible. It will likely give me a stomach ache, but at the moment I don't care."

"I ate one yesterday and another this evening, and I haven't suffered in the least. Is your stomach so terribly sensitive as all that?"

"It's fine so long as I eat moderately and sensibly and avoid rich and fatty foods. The pie is good enough for tonight."

Astrid nodded, keeping to herself the opinion that Dr. Harvey's book and its extensive nutritional advice were quite silly.

"To change to a less controversial topic," he wisely suggested, "that is an astounding dress you are wearing. Tell me about it while I finish this dinner."

Astrid blushed. "Lady Vayne gave it to me. She insisted I have something, since my new gowns from the dressmaker won't be ready for weeks yet. She gave me this dress and had two more sent off to Whitehaven. I was rather surprised how little alteration it needed."

"Why? She's taller than you, I suppose, but beyond that you look to me a similar size."

"But she's so fashionable, and elegant, and..." Astrid let the sentence trail off. Lady Vayne wasn't slim and wasp-waisted like the women in the fashion plates. She never seemed uncomfortable in her clothes. Yet she radiated beauty and poise. How?

Monte studied Astrid for a moment, then shook his head and climbed out of bed. He walked over to her, pulled her up out of the chair and looked her up and down, mimicking her curves with his hands.

"Yes. Proportionally, you two are much alike. Any dress that looks good on her will look good on you. As this current outfit proves." He grasped her waist and drew her close. "Remember, Astrid, you are beautiful."

The kiss was soft and short, a sweet tease that left her body humming with desire.

"I should love to spend more time convincing you," he said, "but my head continues to ache, and I'm feeling sleepy again."

"Yes, get back in bed at once. I haven't tended you all day just to have you go and ruin all my hard work."

He transferred his mostly-eaten dinner to the table and slipped beneath the blankets. Astrid watched him until he was breathing the slow, even breaths of deep slumber, then picked up Dr. Harvey's book once more. She had yet to find the section on the unhealthfulness of cheese.

A knock came at the door only a few pages in. She set the book down with a sigh and went to greet her visitor.

"Good evening, Lady Vayne. I was told to expect you."

Astrid showed the other woman into the small parlor, where they perched on the single sofa.

"Good evening to you, Lady Astrid. How is Monte?"

"Fully clothed, I'm sad to say."

Lady Vayne's lovely, deep laugh echoed through the chamber. "Oh, dear. He must be in a bad way."

Astrid sighed. "It's worse than you know. He is reformed. He has adopted a lifestyle of abstemious and wholesome habits."

Lady Vayne's neatly manicured eyebrows twitched. "That *is* tragic. Is there no hope of recovery?"

"Well, he has kissed me twice in the last few days."

"I'm only surprised he hasn't done so every day, given the way he looks at you. I imagine you will un-reform him soon enough, if that is your desire."

"It is. I'm tired of waiting, and I want him to teach me all the wicked things I wish to know." It was refreshing to say the words aloud. What a strange and wonderful thing, to have a female companion willing to cheerfully discuss such topics. Perhaps they could become real friends.

Lady Vayne laughed again. "In that case, I will leave you be, as you clearly have no desire or need for a chaperone."

"Thank you. I trust you will tell your uncle nothing of this conversation? I believe he is terribly concerned for my virginity."

"Virginity is a state of mind, Lady Astrid, and it's obvious you've done away with yours."

"No, not I. Monte stole it years ago, at the top of a cliff beneath a beautiful summer sun. But if he doesn't hurry up and do something with it, I'm going to demand it back."

"Might I suggest you tell him so? I don't think he likes the idea you might consider another man."

Astrid didn't particularly want another man. She wanted Monte, and chatting with his former lover only made the longing worse. How dreadfully unfair that Lady Vayne had known him intimately and Astrid hadn't.

"You can conclude such things based upon seeing us together for so brief a time yesterday?" Astrid asked.

"Subtlety is not Monte's forte."

Astrid's thoughts drifted to the overabundance of bouquets. "No, I suppose it's not."

"Before I go, do you need helping out of that dress?"

"Please. I don't wish to sleep like this. Why don't you come into the bedroom?"

Lady Vayne glanced around as they entered the austere living area. "This is the emptiest house I've ever seen."

Astrid presented her back to allow Lady Vayne to work the buttons. "I told you, abstemious and wholesome. It apparently translates to 'boring.'"

"Does he still eat those awful bran loaves for breakfast?"

Astrid swallowed a giggle. When had she begun to find

Monte's rigid dietary habits oddly charming? "Every day. I don't know what I will do to feed him in the morning."

"I will ask my cook to make up a batch and have them sent over."

"Thank you. That's very kind."

"I'm happy to help. I'm very fond of Monte, and not merely because he made a good bedfellow. I also hope you and I will be friends."

"I hope so too. Oddly, I'm making many friends as a result of being called insane." Astrid slipped out of her bodice and draped it over the single chair. "And I must thank you for the dress."

"You're most welcome. It wasn't quite right for me, but it's perfect for you."

Astrid ran a finger over the smooth silk fabric. "Monte liked it. Perhaps I might learn to be fashionable after all."

Lady Vayne's smile was warm. She leaned toward Astrid, like a true friend and confidant would do, and whispered, "Would you like to hear my secret to fashion?"

"Please."

"Be yourself and wear what makes *you* feel beautiful. Comfort and confidence make all the difference."

Astrid considered those words as she showed Lady Vayne out and finished preparing for bed. She felt perfectly comfortable in her chemise and drawers. Comfortable was easy when she chose clothes entirely for herself. Confidence was another matter.

Worn down from a long and stressful day, she doused the lights and turned in earlier than was her habit. She slipped under the blankets, intending to keep to her own side of the bed and leave Monte undisturbed. Mere minutes later, she found herself snuggled up against his body, his arm around her waist.

"Love this dream," he murmured.

"So do I," she replied. She squeezed her eyes closed and let herself drift off to sleep in his embrace.

# XIX
# INTERVIEW, AGAIN

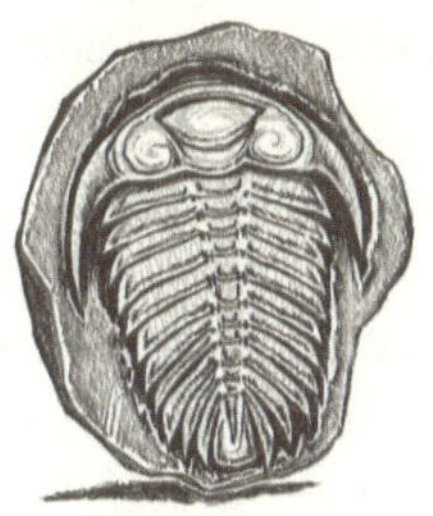

"How do *you* feel about being alone with him?" Grace asked. "That's the most important consideration."

Not pleased, if Astrid had to be honest. Nothing she had seen at the Institute had marked Marvale as an enemy. He had been unobtrusive, cordial with everyone, and not attached to either faction leader. Still, she couldn't shake her unease at his association with Cliffsdale.

She had persevered with Smyth, however, and conducted a successful investigation. She could do the same with Marvale.

"I shall be fine. He is more apt to accept my answers as true if I'm alone, and I feel I will be better able to question him."

Cal paced the parlor, hands clasped behind his back. "It won't do, Astrid. You can't be shutting yourself up all alone with a man. You're an unmarried young woman."

*Don't look at Monte. Don't look at Monte.*

Her eyes flicked toward him for only a second. He stood by the window, staring out, his back turned to her.

Yesterday morning he'd woken by her side and smothered her with kisses, only to break it off with a curse after a few lovely minutes. Since then he'd been distant, quiet. Even while

153

sitting beside her for the four hour drive home he'd given the impression of avoiding her.

"Monte, you agree with me, don't you?" Cal pleaded. "She cannot sit for this interview alone."

Monte didn't turn from the window. "Lady Astrid is fully capable of taking care of herself. Particularly in her own home."

"How can you say that so casually, after what happened to you?"

He turned, finally. The healing potion had done a fine job, leaving no indication any harm had befallen him. His face was unscarred, all bruises vanished. Yesterday his lower lip had still been slightly swollen. She had run her fingers over the sensitive spot and soothed it with her kisses.

"If anyone had wanted to harm Lady Astrid, he would have done so by now. Our criminal wishes her removed by other means."

"Might I propose a compromise?" Grace, ever sensible, waited for the men to pause and look her way. "Astrid will take the interview here, in this parlor. We can arrange the furniture in such a way that she won't sit uncomfortably close to Lord Marvale. The door will remain open, naturally. One or all of us can wait and listen in the next room. If she is distressed for any reason, she need only call to us."

Astrid beamed at her friend. "Thank you, Grace. I would be happy to have any of you near, so long as you're not interfering with my investigation."

"You're not a detective, Asti," Cal groaned. "We're trying to keep you out of an asylum. That is the priority."

"It's all connected, Cal. The more we can learn, the better we can defend me."

"Fine, fine. I accept Miss Fairfax's plan. But I can't be the one to listen or I might go bursting in. I'll be in my study." He spun and walked out. Astrid heard him mumble, "None of this would've ever happened if Father were still alive."

Less than an hour later, Astrid sat straight upright on a

high-backed chair, attired in one of her new dresses from Lady Vayne. Lord Marvale surveyed her from his armchair, pen and notebook in hand.

"You aren't often in Society, Lady Astrid, is that correct?"

"Yes."

"And what are your reasons for this unsociable behavior? You have professed excellent health and no melancholia. What is it, then, that is keeping you at home?"

"Isn't it obvious, Lord Marvale? I have very little in common with most others of my social class, particularly when it comes to those things we value."

He touched pen to paper. "Do go on."

Fine, then. If he meant to hear her out, she would give him what he asked for.

"To be blunt, I am different, and Society is unforgiving to those who are different."

He nodded, scribbling. "Could you give an example of what you mean?"

"Have you copious amounts of ink? My list could become quite lengthy."

He scowled at her irreverence. That would be another checkmark on his list.

"Example one: Miss Fairfax is one of the finest people I know, yet Society shuns her because she is half Indian. Two: Society sneers at Mr. Furbush because he is in trade."

"Who is this Mr. Furbush?"

"The bookseller. He is actually Lord something, but he rarely gives his title because he has been treated so ill. His predecessors squandered the family fortune, until he was left with nothing but his library. So he opened a bookshop. He is actually quite wealthy now and owns shops all over the country, including in London, but he personally runs the shop in Whitehaven because it is quiet and he likes the company here in the country. Society will have nothing more to do with him, even though he has money, is respectable, and is a very nice man."

"I see." Marvale scrawled more notes.

Astrid had considered marriage to Furbush, were he ever to ask, since he was a Very Nice Man and they got on well. Those thoughts had always come with a dose of uncertainty, because she couldn't imagine kissing him the way she kissed one Dr. Ernest Montford. Furbush would never spark those raw, carnal feelings in her. Feelings that Society told her ladies weren't supposed to have.

"I've met people that were looked down on for being American, or French, or Italian," she continued. "Some snub families that have had their titles for only a few generations. Women who don't marry are called 'crazy.' People cut off their own family members for marrying the wrong sort of person. My brother is driving himself mad trying to behave according to Society's rigid standards. It will destroy him. He's too indulgent, too liberal, too all-embracing. He loves the people Society hates."

Marvale's pen stopped moving. "Are you quite done now?"

"Hardly. I haven't even touched on my own treatment by so-called respectable people."

His jaw tightened. "Might you summarize in ten words or less?"

"I am mocked, sometimes openly, because I'm scholarly, and I am called dull and fat." She stared down her interrogator. "And insane."

"That was more than ten words, Lady Astrid." His voice remained calm, but his dark eyes and tight expression left no mistaking what he thought of her.

"I believe I did rather well keeping it under twenty, given the circumstances."

He flipped back in his notebook and made another mark. *Sarcasm, check. Impertinence, check. Defiance, check.*

"I can't profess to know you well, Lady Astrid, but it is clear even from our short acquaintance that you conduct yourself in an entirely unladylike manner. The questions remaining are, 'Why?' and, 'What can be done about it?'"

*'Because that's who I am,' and, 'Nothing.'*

"It's apparent I cannot make a proper evaluation through conversations such as this," he continued, "though I do have other questions that must be covered. I will need to observe and record your daily habits here at home as well as your behavior in public spaces and at social events."

Astrid didn't intend for her horror to show on her face. By the time she realized she was gaping, Marvale had begun to smirk.

"I'm sorry, Lord Marvale, but I am not at all comfortable with that plan. You are all but a stranger to me, and I cannot condone the idea of a man trailing a young lady about wherever she goes. Perhaps were I better acquainted with you we could make some sort of allowance, but I am not even familiar with your professional credentials. I cannot agree to being observed at all hours of the day, and I am certain my family will not agree either."

"You don't have a choice, my dear. Unless, of course, you feel that a stay at the asylum would do you good? Many ladies find great relief from their afflictions there."

Astrid's gaze was stony. "I have no afflictions."

"That remains to be seen. There is some reason for your strange behavior, and I mean to uncover it. We can't treat the problem until we have identified it."

She hopped up from her seat. For a moment she thought he would remain as he was, staring rudely up at her, but soon enough he hauled himself from his chair.

"I believe our time is up," Astrid said, though no duration had been agreed upon for the meeting. "Please permit me to walk you to the door."

*Walk to the door or I shall have you thrown out.*

"It would be my pleasure, Lady Astrid. This has been an illuminating conversation. I look forward to the next. I shall send you a note when my plans for observation are finalized. Remember, a woman with nothing to hide has nothing to fear from my examination."

She put on her fake sweet smile. "Of course not, my lord. You must consider, however, that a lady doesn't put herself on display for every Tom, Dick, and Harry. And I'm certain you wish to encourage me in all ladylike habits."

Astrid strode out into the hall, not bothering to look whether he was following. The door to the next room over opened, and Monte walked out, medical kit in hand. He gave her a nod, but his eyes were locked on Marvale behind her.

"Montford," the earl sneered.

"Pierce," Monte replied, interposing himself between Astrid and Marvale.

"I'm surprised to find you here. I would have thought you would be in London. I hate to think you might be neglecting your patients."

"Most have been referred to colleagues of mine, and I was just in town these past several days. I stopped by the Institute for a lecture. I'm surprised you didn't see me."

"You were acting as Lady Astrid's escort, I assume? Whitehaven must be paying you handsomely."

Astrid flinched. She hadn't considered Monte might be paid for his assistance. It was only logical. He had a gentleman's profession, but a profession it was, and he needed to earn his living. It depressed her to think she was merely a job. And a difficult one, by all accounts.

"And who pays you?" Monte countered. "I find it unlikely you have taken up the task of interrogating Lady Astrid for your own edification."

"I am both a peer and a medical professional. I see it as my duty to offer what expertise I can to the local populace. Being so nearby to Whitehaven, it is only sensible that I assist in this matter. Consider that the alternative is calling for a doctor from town."

"I *am* a doctor from town. The journey was not a hardship."

"Be that as it may, *I* have been appointed to this position and I will conduct my examinations as I see fit. You have said your piece, Dr. Montford. I suggest you cease your meddling and take yourself back to London."

Monte took a step toward Marvale. The earl had an inch on him height-wise, but Monte was younger, fitter, and possessed of arms strong enough to carry Astrid up a flight of stairs. His feet were set in a fighting stance, his expression icy. Marvale flinched.

"What, don't you know? I'm infamous in town these days. I gunned down a man in broad daylight. I'm surprised you haven't heard of it."

Marvale looked at Astrid. "Harboring criminals, young lady? Consorting with disreputable men?"

"On the contrary. We have provided Dr. Montford with a respite from the hordes of admirers requesting his services in the defense against footpads and other unsavory sorts. Please, follow me to the door. I will ask Crippens to fetch you a newspaper. You really ought to keep up on current events."

Monte accompanied her all the way to the door, glaring at Marvale all the while. They watched out the window until his carriage was out of sight.

"What an arse," Astrid muttered. "Do you think he's our murderer?"

"I wouldn't be surprised. He has no love for you and is a link between the Institute and Cliffsdale Asylum. And you will note he also made reference to my 'meddling.'"

"I will ask Lady Ophelia to watch and listen for anything regarding him. I'm visiting her this afternoon."

"What? No, you can't."

"I most certainly can, although I'm not certain what I am to wear, since you ruined my most slimming dress."

Monte blocked her path from the foyer. "I forbid it."

Astrid put both hands on his chest and shoved him out of

her way. Surprised, he stumbled backward, one hand splashing in the aquarium.

"You do not get to tell me what to do," she snarled. "And take care with my fish. I'm quite fond of them."

He grabbed her arm as she brushed past. "As a medical professional, I cannot allow you to harm yourself with those dangerous garments. The last time you were laced so tightly you could hardly breathe."

Astrid pried his fingers off of her and continued toward the stairs to her bedroom. "I must be in disguise, and Lady Ophelia will be expecting me. I have created a persona. I cannot simply change her. I will take the car today so I needn't walk."

"You will take *me*. I need to get into that potions room."

"Certainly not. You're known to them. You will ruin my disguise."

"Make a new disguise."

"Enough, Monte. I understand that you're concerned for me, but I'm determined to continue investigating."

"I have an idea. Please, will you hear me out?" His voice was quiet, but impassioned, his eyes softened to a cloudy gray.

She heaved a sigh. "Very well. Come into the parlor and sit."

"You will pose as my patient," he explained, planting himself close enough on the sofa to make her skin heat. "Our story is I liked what I saw on my survey and am bringing you on a visit to determine whether the asylum will suit your needs. When we are there, you create a distraction and I sneak into the potions room."

"No. You will be known as someone to watch for. Eyes will be on you at all times. We will both make the distraction. Lady Ophelia will go sneaking for us."

He frowned, but didn't argue. "Can you devise a way to let her know our plan and get her into the potions room?"

"I believe so. You know the location of the room?"

"Yes. It's on the first floor, not far from the entrance to the hospital wing."

"Good. I think I can devise a distraction that can gain us access, though it may depend on my disguise. What did you have in mind, if I can't be Miss Ada Anning?"

"We change your appearance again, but in a different fashion. Pick your largest dress and stuff it with as much padding as possible. But leave a bit of room for anything we need to smuggle out. You will be a retired performer. An actress, perhaps, or an opera singer. We dye your hair a streaky, clearly false blond. Darken your eyes and put them behind large spectacles. Bright colored cosmetics will further disguise you."

Astrid's mouth pursed in a thoughtful frown, and she jiggled her foot, considering the idea.

"I accept," she said at last. "Let me write a note to Lady Ophelia to say that Cousin Ada cannot visit."

Up in her room a moment later, she penned a short letter.

*Dearest Ophelia,*

*I regret to say that I have taken ill and Will not be able to visit. I am Extremely sorry to Miss you today. I Usually recover rapidly, So will not be Too long away.*

She rambled on about nothing, sprinkling in capital letters seemingly at random. It was a simple code, but Astrid doubted anyone would pay enough attention to notice, if they even bothered to read the letter. Ophelia would know the basic plan, and they could give her details when they arrived.

Astrid looked into her closet, examining possible disguise choices. It was time for a new persona.

## XX

# INVASION OF THE POTION SNATCHERS

**W**ITHOUT THINKING, Monte reached to lift Astrid from the hired cab, grasping her about the waist. The layers of padding squished beneath his hands, weakening his grip and causing her to slip just enough that she collided with him as he set her down.

She swatted him with her fan. "Always contriving to get me into your arms, you naughty boy."

Monte winced. She had settled on flirtatious opera singer? He stepped back with an awkward cough. "My apologies, madam."

She laughed. "Think nothing of it, *caro mio.*"

Her Italian accent was atrocious. She was going to be thought a courtesan faking her heritage to further a career on the stage. Good enough, he supposed.

He eyed her disguise before leading her into the asylum. She had puffed up her skirt with so many layers it resembled the crinoline fashions his mother had worn during his childhood. Strings of pearls wrapped around her neck, falling across

162

breasts she had thrust up and emphasized with a hopefully-not-unhealthful undergarment. Her haphazardly dyed hair was piled atop her head in a lofty updo, and chocolate-colored eyes peeped out from enormous, unfashionable spectacles.

"This will never work," he mumbled.

Even with the alterations, he could see the real Astrid. She carried herself with assurance, despite a slight waddle caused by the many skirts. The makeup couldn't hide her cheerful, round face and her sensuous lips. Nothing could diminish the gleam of defiance in her eyes.

Monte also had doubts about the healthfulness of his alternative disguise. She might not be crushed, but he feared she might overheat beneath so many layers, especially were she to exert herself, the way she was wont to do.

She had already sprung into action, and he hurried after her as she flittered up the steps.

"*Bellissimo!*" Astrid turned a full circle upon entering the foyer, her gaze on the ceiling. "*Molto bene!*"

"Might I be of some help?" asked a woman Monte recognized from his prior visit.

"Yes, indeed. My name is Dr. Ernest Montford. I was here on a visit not long ago. The lady is Signora Fiori, a patient of mine. A recent head injury has left her not quite herself, and we are considering this facility for her recuperation. I estimate she will need between three and six weeks of rest and care."

"Of course. I can get you the proper paperwork."

"Such a lovely spa," Astrid remarked. "As fine as the baths of Roma." She seized Monte by the lapel. "Come, darling boy, and show me all around."

He extricated himself from her clutches and addressed her with his best professional manners. "Madam, we must wait for an escort."

"Oh, posh! You, there!" She pointed at the woman who had greeted them. "Take this wrap. Signora wishes to explore!"

The woman took Astrid's shawl. "I shall send Nurse Blackwell to give the lady a tour."

Astrid's diva persona didn't wait on anyone. Monte chased her down, playing the harried physician desperate to rid himself of a difficult patient. Nurse Blackwell, who joined them momentarily, had a nonchalance that suggested she had seen this story played out many a time.

"Allow me to show you the music room, Signora," she said. "I believe you will find it much to your tastes."

"*Eccellente!*" Astrid once again grabbed Monte by his jacket, hauling him after her.

"Unhand me, madam," he commanded.

She turned so suddenly they collided once again. "Do not scowl, lovely boy. You shall grow wrinkly, and you are so very handsome. *Molto bello!*"

The laughter in her artificially darkened eyes nearly destroyed his self-control. He scowled all the harder, to cover up his desire to laugh or to kiss her. Ideally both.

Astrid leaned in and pressed her ruby lips to his cheek. "Ophelia likes to lie on the floor of the music room," she whispered.

Monte freed himself from her grip and scrubbed at his cheek with a handkerchief. Red lip paint stained the white cloth. Nurse Blackwell gave him a sympathetic look. He responded with the smile he would have liked to give Astrid. The nurse blushed.

In the music room, Astrid continued to expound on everything from the grand piano to the unsightly ceiling. Ladies around the room opened their eyes or turned from their books to observe the colorful newcomer. Monte hovered just out of arm's reach, backpedaling whenever she drew too close.

In the midst of an impromptu aria—if anyone asked, he would say the injury had affected her voice—he reached Lady Ophelia, who lay happily mumbling, apparently oblivious to the chaos.

Monte took a step backward, catching his foot on her outstretched legs, and tumbling to the ground in as inelegant a manner as he could manage without crushing his ally.

"Well done," Lady Ophelia giggled. "Though I'm afraid few were looking."

"Astrid plans to break into the hospital wing and cause a scene. The potions room is the first door on the left. Grab any notes and potions you can, and anything you think might be important." Louder, he said, "Dear lady, I'm so terribly sorry. Are you injured? I beg your forgiveness for my clumsiness."

"Oops!" she exclaimed. "Pretty men falling from the sky. Are you hurt, pretty man?"

He sat up. "I am unharmed, thank you. Please, allow me to help you to your feet."

Lady Ophelia hopped up without waiting for him to extend a hand, then thrust her hand out to help him. He declined the offer and climbed to his feet, eyes and ears locked on Astrid, who was warbling something that might have been Wagner.

Lady Ophelia cocked her head. "Do you hear an angel singing?"

Monte choked back a laugh, covering it up by clearing his throat. "Again, please accept my apologies, miss."

"Such strange, ethereal music." She took Monte's hand. "Show me where your music is, man from the sky."

Astrid had gathered a following of a half-dozen curious ladies, and the entire crowd was headed out of the room, undeterred by Nurse Blackwell's coaxing. Monte and Ophelia followed as the mob bowled through the halls, peeking into rooms, making noise, and gathering more excited patients.

The door to the hospital wing lay at the end of the hall, closed and guarded by a bored nurse. Monte left Ophelia to hide herself among Astrid's crowd and slipped over to the doorkeeper.

"Excuse me, miss." He flashed a winning smile. "Might I bother you for a bit of help?"

"Of course. What can I do for you?"

He steered her away from the door, facing the wall and speaking in confidential tones. "These ladies have taken it into their heads that I am some sort of prize. I can't approach them without some woman or other grasping at me in some improper manner."

"That does sound dire," she replied, her eyes gleaming. This was surely the most interesting thing that had happened to her in months.

"One of my patients is with them, but I can't get near enough to extract her. Do you think you might slip among them and draw her out?"

"Certainly!"

"Thank you, dear lady. I cannot express my relief that you should be so good as to come to my rescue."

"Nonsense. I shall only be doing my job."

They turned around together, and Monte pointed into the scrum. "There. In the yellow taffeta."

Astrid had reached the door. "What can be through here?"

"Oh, no!" cried the nurse, realizing she had neglected her post.

Astrid, naturally, continued on as if she hadn't even heard. The other ladies, emboldened by her daring, flooded after her into the hospital wing, pushing their way past Nurse Blackwell's gentle pleading, and her colleague's anguished cries. Astrid began to run, throwing open doors and shouting in bad Italian.

Monte joined the two nurses in chasing the ladies, shouting to every other member of the staff they passed to help them corral the runaways. Lady Ophelia had vanished, so he contrived to give her as much time as possible.

"Signora Fiori!" he shouted.

"Ah, *bello mio!* Come, see what I have found. This spa of yours has many offices. No place for a lady."

"But most interesting!" a young woman exclaimed.

"Yes, fascinating!" another woman joined in. "Let's see the kitchens next!"

"Signora, I won't stand for this unseemly behavior," Monte called over the clamor. "Tell these ladies to mind their nurses and return to their rooms."

"No, no, *dolce mio*. They were so bored. So sad. Look! I have brought music and joy!"

She began to sing again, with several other women joining in. Doctors and nurses torn from their usual duties joined in to usher the wild group out of the hospital wing. Astrid stopped in the doorway to the potions laboratory, her wide skirts obscuring the view of the room.

Monte seized her arm. "Madam, I am done with this. You have caused a scene. You have disrupted hard-working men and women. You have disturbed innocent ladies in their rest. You do not need a stay in an asylum. You need a stay in a gaol cell!"

Astrid began to scream Italian words at him. She talked so quickly he couldn't make out but a few phrases, but those he did pick up made no sense. Food, snippets of song, and nonsense words ending in Os or Is all intermingled in her tirade.

Lady Ophelia snuck up behind Astrid, a grin across her youthful face. Astrid's hands moved behind her back to collect whatever her friend had found. The transfer made, Monte stepped aside just enough to allow Lady Ophelia to slide past him and rejoin the crowd.

"Unbutton my top," Astrid whispered.

Monte stepped in front of her, shielding her from view, his fingers popping the top several buttons.

"This is highly irregular, madam." He dropped his voice to a whisper. "Usually when a woman asks this of me it is under vastly different circumstances."

Astrid spun around, stuffing papers and potions into her padded bosom. "You cannot take me away! They love me here! I am a star!"

"You are a star everywhere," he soothed her, patting her shoulders. "Come, dear one. Come away from here. Let's find you a stage where you can shine for more than a few ladies. This isn't the place for such a one as you."

After a few heaving sighs, Astrid turned around, her dress set to rights. Monte took her hand, and she followed him back to the main hall, her head down and her step sluggish.

Lady Ophelia bumped him as they walked, stuffing yet more potions into his pockets. She danced away, spinning with her hands in the air.

"Goodbye man from the sky! Goodbye lady of music! I shall see you in the clouds!"

"Nurse Blackwell," Monte called to the woman now left with the unfortunate task of settling all the other ladies. "We are leaving. I do not believe this facility is suitable for a lady of Signora Fiori's needs. Doors are not locked, windows are not barred, and the staff is neither trained nor equipped to halt an escapee. I'm surprised you haven't lost patients over the years. Good day to you."

Keeping a firm grip on Astrid's arm, he led her down to the foyer, snagged her shawl, and took her out to the waiting cab.

As the vehicle rolled down the drive on its journey back to Whitehaven, Astrid slumped against the back of her seat.

"Gracious, that was exhausting. Great fun, but mentally draining. Don't you agree?"

"I do agree it was exhausting, and your wild character made for excellent entertainment. I struggled not to laugh a time or two. I would not, however, term our escapade 'fun.' We are criminals now, you and I, and I wonder if we both ought not be committed." He ran a hand through his hair. "Lord, whatever possessed me to propose such a scheme?"

"You didn't want me to go alone or tight-laced. And I must say despite my initial misgivings, our combined talents proved most effective."

"I certainly hope so, because that incident is unrepeatable. From now on, they will be far more careful whom they allow in."

Astrid's shoulders slumped. "Sadly true. Miss Ada Anning might never see her cousin again."

"She may have to content herself with writing letters."

Her jaw set in that determined expression she so often wore. "Well, that remains to be seen. First we shall analyze our plunder. What did Ophelia give to you?"

Monte withdrew the handful of vials from his pocket. "Five potion bottles. You?"

"At least that many, and papers and a little notebook as well. I was too busy hiding them to get a close look. Would you like to dig them out of my clothing?"

Music to the ears of any rake, and torment to a man who had sworn not to ruin his best friend's sister.

"That would be most inappropriate, Lady Astrid."

"Simply Astrid, if you please. We have burgled an asylum together. I don't think we have a need for formality."

"Very well. Astrid it shall be."

"Might I call you Ernest?"

"No one calls me Ernest."

"Pity. I quite like it. Though I can't deny that Monte suits you. The real you, that is."

"Are you implying there is a false me? That is something, coming from a woman in the guise of an inept opera singer."

"The real Monte wants to dig through my clothing. He invented the opera singer scheme. The false Monte uses words like 'inappropriate' and thinks I bathe at the wrong time of day."

"You are mistaken, Lady Astrid. I promise you, there is only one Ernest Montford."

*He is simply at war with himself.*

## XXI

# A HARD NIGHT'S WORK

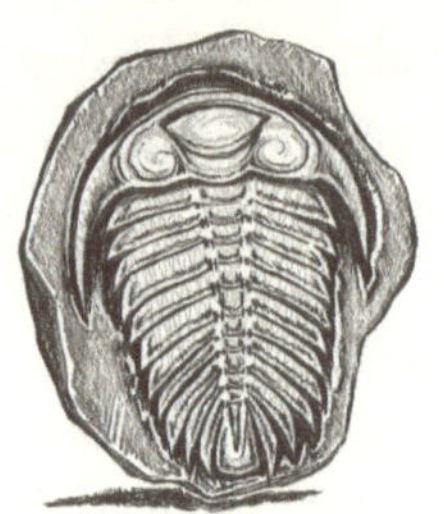

**A**STRID TURNED UP THE LAMP. Which was ridiculous, since the laboratory had no windows and was equally dark, day and night. Still, the late-night endeavor seemed to call for extra light.

She cleared the last of the papers from her desk, sliding them into a drawer, and dragged Grace's chair up next to hers. They would have a large, clean space in which to work.

The loot from the the raid on the asylum took the place of her usual piles. She had one stack of rumpled papers, weighted down with a small notebook, and eight potion bottles of assorted size and shape. If only Monte would arrive with the rest of the potions.

Astrid fiddled with a strand of hair, examining it for any remaining blond streaks. She hadn't liked the way she looked with the pale-gold locks. All those people who had said, "Pity you didn't inherit your mother's blond hair," were full of rot. She was meant for unruly brown curls. She also rather liked her blue eyes, and hoped they had returned to their natural state by now. When she had changed out of her opera singer costume, they had still been a strange, deep brown.

170

"Good evening, Lady Astrid."

"Hello, Monte." She had determined never to call him Dr. Montford again. She would force him into informality one way or another.

His eyes made a slow survey of her, head-to-toe and then back again. That penetrating gaze made her skin burn.

"You are looking restored to your usual self," he remarked.

"Are my eyes their natural color at last?"

He stared at her for much longer than necessary to answer such a question. "Yes."

"Good. I was feeling strange, not being myself."

His lips twitched upward. "I, too, prefer the real Astrid."

She quivered. Goodness, that voice. How could those soft, low tones create such a sensual whirlwind inside her?

"Have you brought the other potions?"

"Yes, and some things to help examine them."

Monte emptied the contents of his pockets onto the desk. He still wore the same dark gray suit as this morning. Even the waistcoat was gray. He had accessorized with a neatly done up bow tie. Proper. Dull. Not himself. Astrid missed the wild plaids and sloppy ascots.

"Have you read over the papers?" he asked.

"I only scanned them. They all looked like potion recipes, with much crossing out and rewriting. Experiments, perhaps. I'm not well-enough versed in potion making to determine for what purpose they are intended. Perhaps we ought to have told Grace about this. She may not be an expert, but she is by far more competent with potions than either Cal or I."

"I've been working with potions since before I went to University. I believe I possess enough expertise for our purposes. Besides, I thought you didn't want your brother to discover what we've been up to. If we involve Miss Fairfax in this matter, she is likely to tell him."

"Why do you say that?"

He frowned at her. Blinked twice. Then his brows rose in surprise. "You don't know."

"Know what?"

He shook his head. "It's not my place to tell you."

"What? No! You can't tell me I don't know something and then leave me alone in my ignorance! That's cruel."

"It would be ungentlemanly of me to divulge another's secrets. You must ask Miss Fairfax."

"Monte..."

It was no use. Ignoring both her and propriety, he took his seat and began to arrange the potion bottles. Astrid plopped down into the seat beside him and watched as he unrolled a leather pouch containing several scoops, picks, and empty bottles, plus a few small squares of cloth. He uncorked one of the potions and took a sniff.

"Sleeping draught. Used by the ladies in the main wing, I would guess."

He handed her the potion, and she studied it a moment.

"You can tell that just by sniffing?" She lifted the bottle to her nose. She caught a whiff of floral and a hint of cinnamon.

"Along with color and consistency, yes." He opened another bottle, held it up to the light, then sniffed it. "Basic health potion, I believe." He selected one of the metal picks, dipped it into the potion and touched it to his tongue. "Yes. For aches, pains, or other minor complaints."

Astrid's nose wrinkled as she sniffed the health potion. It had a vague odor of cow.

The third and fourth potions, in identical bottles with different colored corks, were both for relaxation. Monte said they varied only by potency. Astrid tried both smelling and tasting, but couldn't tell the difference.

Monte took his time with the fifth bottle. He sniffed with care, tasted it, and even dripped a bit onto one of the cloths to examine it further.

"This is entirely unfamiliar," he said. "Stranger yet, I can't even guess as to what its use might be."

"You usually can?"

"I can usually make certain assumptions based on the ingredients. I could possibly learn more if I were to take a larger taste. In this case, however, I'm loathe to do so, as we suspect some of these potions could be harmful."

Astrid had to stop herself snatching the potion from his hand. "Don't taste them at all, if you think they're poison!"

"One drop shouldn't be enough to cause harm. I can always drink that minor health potion if I'm concerned."

"I don't like it."

One corner of his mouth quirked up. "Be careful, Lady Astrid. You might give the impression that you like me."

"I can't possibly like you until you stop using my title."

Monte chuckled and set the unknown potion aside. "I shall strive to remember."

"I don't think you're as forgetful as all that. I think you do it deliberately."

"I do it without thinking. It comes out naturally."

He lifted the next bottle. He had an adorable little crinkle at the top of his nose when he was thinking. The way he squinted at things made her suspect he would benefit from a pair of spectacles.

He frowned and made a puzzled grunt as he passed the bottle beneath his nose. He cleaned one of his picks, dipped it, and tasted the potion.

His entire body jerked, and for a terrifying instant, Astrid was certain he had been poisoned. She grabbed for the health potion, prepared to pour it down his throat, if necessary.

"This is a narcotic!"

Monte took a deliberate second taste, rolling it around on his tongue before spitting it out into one of his little cloths. He slammed the cork back into the bottle. Astrid clutched the health potion.

His eyes grew icy, his jaw hard. "You were correct. They're being drugged."

"What is it?"

"An opiate-based potion. I've never seen the like, but I'm familiar enough with potions and with opiate medicines to determine what it might do. If I'm correct, this potion increases the negative effects of the original drug—morphine, perhaps— without enhancing its medicinal value."

"It's not a painkiller, then? What do you suspect it to be for?"

"Stupefaction. The potion will have a soporific effect, dulling the senses, making the patient biddable. Anyone ingesting it isn't likely to know who or where they are. Hallucinations are possible. It could be mixed with food or drink. A few drops in a glass of water would be enough, and it would take effect quickly."

Astrid thrust the health potion at him. "Please drink this. I don't want you falling over in a hallucinatory stupor."

The laudanum put her mother in such a state. Astrid and Cal checked on her every day, making sure she had food, medicine, and rest. And every day the sight of her in the thrall of the drug stabbed a little deeper.

Monte smiled. "I will be fine, but if it will ease your worries, I will drink it." He took the potion from her hand and downed the contents.

"Thank you. I feel better now."

"A funny thing to say, when I was the one drinking the potion. I think you do like me, Astrid."

"I think we have more potions to inspect." Her face flushed. Why had she turned up the lights so bright? Knowing he could see the color in her cheeks only made her blush harder.

"Quite."

Most of the remaining potions Monte declared harmless. One other was unidentifiable. He pushed the two mystery potions and the opiate into one corner of the desk, and the rest to the other side.

"We can use these or dump them, as you see fit. They are unimportant. The three suspicious potions should be evaluated by a potions master. Is there one at the Institute, or could Ayleston connect us with such a person?"

"We shall write him and ask, though I think your own grasp of potions rather masterful."

"Thank you, but I have studied only since my University days, while there are others who have mixed since childhood. Anyone could become as proficient as I, with diligent application."

"No, I think you have a particular talent for it. Certain people, I understand, are simply born with a natural affinity for potions."

"That's unscientific nonsense. It's a field of study, like any other. One cannot be born with the knack for chemistry or biology. One might have a mind suited to certain ways of thinking, but one must still apply oneself and learn. It is the same with potions."

"But potions are magic."

"We call it magic only because we do not yet understand how it works. I'm certain we will unravel the mysteries with time."

"It doesn't follow the laws of nature," Astrid argued. "Take an ordinary medicine, and you can alleviate certain symptoms. Mix up a proper health potion and, *bam*! It's one hundred times more powerful. Why? How? Drink an allure potion and people who've shown no interest are suddenly drawn to you. It makes no sense. It's beyond the laws of science."

Monte shook his head. "Potions may not be well understood, but they are predictable and repeatable. Someday our science will unlock their secrets."

Astrid sighed. "Why do you like to make everything dull?"

"It's not dull. Imagine all the things we could do if we understood the science behind serum."

A grin curved her lips. "I would bring trilobite specimens back to life so I could learn all the things we cannot from just a fossil. And perhaps I would keep a few as pets."

Monte shuddered. "Because that is what this house needs. Additional giant crawly things. Why can't you be content with the fish? They are pleasant and quiet."

"Bristles is very quiet. You would never know she was on you until you felt the little tickle of her hairy legs."

He cringed and shied away. "Gah! Enough! I am never entering your bedchamber again."

*Bugger.* That was the exact opposite of her desires. She needed a flirting manual. One with advice such as, "Do not taunt a man about his irrational fears."

"I'm sorry, Monte. For some reason I'm terribly fond of teasing you. You are so very serious, and I am not at all."

"You are perfectly capable of being serious, and I seem to remember making jokes in your presence."

"Yes, but only when I force them out of you with teasing and spiders. It's far easier to make you scowl. I do still wonder if you might be always hungry. You ate a stupendous number of cucumber sandwiches at tea."

"We were an hour late because of the visit to the asylum, and they are a favorite dish of mine. Regardless, I don't think I ate so many as all that."

"A dozen at least."

Monte checked his watch. "As fascinating as this scrutiny of my alimentary habits is, it is now quarter past eleven. I suggest we move on to the documents before today turns into tomorrow."

"I agree, if only because I think they will be tedious enough that we may fall asleep if we stay up too late."

He pulled the top sheet of paper from beneath the notebook

and perused it. "You may be right. Lists of ingredients don't make for compelling reading material. But we shall press on."

And press on, they did, though a half hour of reading told them nothing new. The recipes were innocuous, much like the majority of their stolen potions. Monte believed whoever had made the notes was experimenting with potency and working to make the effects last longer. Astrid began to regret interfering with someone's legitimate research, and vowed to find a way to return the notes and helpful potions to the asylum. Not all the nurses and doctors working there were evil.

The notebook turned out to be a chore. It was written in a scrawling hand that made it difficult to read. Potions were numbered rather than named, and few gave descriptions or full lists of ingredients. Explanations of their efficacy were vague. Most of the entries were dated, but they were also marked with curious combinations of letters and numbers. It took a dozen pages before Astrid grasped their significance.

She jabbed her finger at a line scribbled near the top of a page. "These are initials and dates of admission. MP, admitted on June the tenth, was given that potion and responded 'well.'"

Monte flipped back through several pages. "By Jove, you're right! Here she is again. These earlier results were 'substandard,' so it appears they improved the potions over time."

"Or maybe made them worse! 'Well' might mean she was in a stupor."

"JL415 is listed half-a-dozen times in just these few pages we have read. And EB501." He rocked back in his chair, letting the book fall from his hands. "Damnation! These women are lab animals for an unethical madman!"

"What do you think Fawdry is trying to accomplish with his experiments?"

"I haven't the foggiest. Nothing good, I can tell you that." He rubbed his temple.

"Do you have a headache?"

"Yes. And my eyes are tired. Perhaps we ought to turn in for the night. We can return to this notebook in the morning."

"It is already morning, I suspect."

He consulted his watch again. "Indeed. There's nothing more we can do at this hour. Please allow me to escort you to your room." He rose and offered her a hand up. His fingers were cold, but his voice was scorching, and his eyes liquid silver.

"Thank you." *Yes, please do. Then come inside and kiss me until I can't think straight and the rest of the world turns into nothing.*

They doused all the lights except the lantern hanging by the door, which Monte took up in his left hand, crooking his right elbow to allow Astrid to take his arm.

She reached for his hand instead, grasping it and twining their fingers together. His hand was freezing. The basement was chilly, she supposed, and Monte was one of those unfathomable people who were perpetually cold. Astrid ran hot. It fell to her to warm him up.

By the time they reached her bedchamber, his skin had warmed sufficiently that she no longer feared him in danger of imminent demise due to tasting all those potions. Was the rest of him still cold? She could deprive him of his clothes and find out, but the act of removing all his layers would make him colder yet. Whereupon she could save him with the heat from her own body, which was exceptionally warm just now.

She pushed open her door and tugged on his hand. He released her and took a single step backward.

"Goodnight, Lady Astrid."

"It's simply Astrid, and won't you come in?"

"I shouldn't."

"No, of course you shouldn't. Everyone knows that. But you are a rake, and you live for doing things you shouldn't."

"I am not, and I do not."

"You want to kiss me. You are dying to kiss me."

He didn't deny it. She stepped toward him, sliding her hands up his chest.

"Please won't you kiss me goodnight? A brief osculation shall suffice."

The rumble of his laugh delighted her all the more when she could feel his chest rise and fall beneath her hands.

"Lady Astrid, despite your attempt to make the exercise sound clinical and matter-of-fact, we both know it would be nothing of the sort. There is no such thing as a 'brief osculation' where you and I are concerned."

The lantern light glinted in his eyes. Her fingers found the edge of his waistcoat and grabbed hold, as if keeping him from fleeing, though he had made no attempt to escape her touch.

"What is there, then?" She tilted her head up, leaning closer until she could feel the warm current of his breath against her lips.

"A seething inferno of passion," he murmured, his deep voice sliding beneath her skin, liquefying her insides. "It will consume us, body and soul, until we are returned, ashes-to-ashes, to the earth from whence we sprung."

Her body tightened in anticipation.

"I should like that," she whispered.

His mouth crushed hers. She dragged him into the bedroom, where he dropped the lantern, backed her up against the wall, and proceeded to devour her.

Astrid pushed his jacket off his shoulders, and he squirmed out of it, leaving her free to unbutton his waistcoat and then his shirt. His own hands moved across her simple dress, popping buttons until he could tug it down and let it fall to a pool at her feet.

Monte pulled back enough to ogle her, standing there against the lovely, flocked wallpaper, in nothing but her combinations. Her skin flushed, her nipples hardened, and heat flared between her legs. That look. She would never get enough of that look on his face. Eyes blazing, lips parted. Wanting, yearning, needing. When he looked at her in that way, she felt powerful, desirable, and sublimely wanton.

"Goddamn, you are gorgeous."

She believed him. Tomorrow she might step out into the world and feel too short, too fat, too peculiar. But here, alone with him, she was the most radiant being in the universe.

His hands cupped her breasts, his thumbs teasing the nipples until they stood out, dark against the thin, white fabric. Pleasure bloomed throughout her body, stifling any worries, leaving only the Astrid of the beach. Wild. Reckless. Free.

She pried his shirt open and made her own exploration. Soft, pale hairs. Small, masculine nipples that stiffened beneath her fingers. Skin flushed and warm. His mouth found hers again, and she delved inside, tasting deeply, sating herself on the wet heat of him. He was going to give her everything. He would make her tremble and squirm and moan in pleasure.

Her fingers traced the helpful trail of hairs that ran down his abdomen, just in case she lost her way. She had the first button of his trousers undone when his hands gripped her wrists.

"Not tonight, beautiful. I haven't the potions necessary to safeguard against unintended consequences. You shall have to content yourself with a small sampling."

"Content myself?" She was afire with longing. Nothing but full satisfaction could content her. "I am bloody tired of contenting myself. I have contented myself for years, thinking about your clever hands and your unrestrained kisses. Laying in bed, touching myself, pretending it was you."

His hands dropped away. "I ought to have known. A woman of your passions cannot possibly have gone for so long without pleasure. Since you swear not to have taken a lover, it only makes sense you would practice self-abuse."

Astrid shoved at his bare chest. "That is an appalling term for it."

"It is an unhealthful practice that can lead to mental and physical disability."

"Nonsense. It doesn't do any of those things people say it does."

"Certain common beliefs are exaggerated, to be sure, but that doesn't mean they do not have some basis in reality. I have read decades of medical research on the subject, and I must advise you to refrain from such behavior as much as may be possible."

Astrid put her hands on her hips. "That smacks of hypocrisy. You can't expect me to believe that you never engage in this 'unhealthful practice.' Really, Monte? You?"

He coughed awkwardly. "I do my very best to find other ways to deal with such situations."

She snorted. "Such as?"

"Bathing in cold water appears to be the most effective remedy."

"I thought that cold baths were also prone to causing disability."

"Just so. It's best to avoid the situation entirely, though that cannot always be helped. Practicing general moderate habits can quell inappropriate thoughts, and modifying one's diet to avoid foods that inflame a body's appetites—"

"Cheese makes one lustful?" she scoffed.

"I didn't say that. But when one is trying to control one's behavior, it is best to keep the body in as healthful a state as may be achieved. A sensible diet is essential."

"It sounds to me that boring food makes a boring person. Besides, eating nothing but vegetables doesn't look to be working for you." She gestured at the bulge in his trousers.

"One doesn't fling off years of bad habits overnight. I can't imagine how bad my vices might have been had I not already been a sensible eater."

"You are crack-brained."

"I am not. Dr. Harvey has done extensive research on this subject, and—"

"On nutrition, or on masturbation?"

"Both. They are interconnected, as are all things. Foods loaded with spices, sugars, and fats—"

"Tasty things."

"Have a tendency to overstimulate the palate and the digestive system. And when one portion of the body is overstimulated, it can lead to overstimulation of other parts, including excessive amorous feelings. He has written an entire book on the subject, if you would care to read it."

"I read a bit of it already. Your Dr. Harvey sounds like a quack."

She regretted the words the moment they were spoken, but the damage was done. Fury blazed in his eyes.

"And Lady Lovelace was an inveterate gambler."

Astrid stiffened with a hot rush of righteous anger at this insult to her own hero. "Get out of my room."

Monte snatched up his discarded clothing. "I didn't want to enter in the first place, if you will recall."

"Oh, yes, you are so clearly here against your will."

"I didn't say that."

"It's all my fault of course, with my terrible habits, forcing you to entertain lustful thoughts despite you being the most insufferable prig in all Britain."

"First a rake and now a prig? You are rather inconstant in your insults, Lady Astrid."

"The former wasn't an insult, but if you are looking for more, I have plenty. Jackass. Oaf. Bleeding arse."

"Hellion," he shot back. "Minx."

"Strumpet?" she suggested. "Or should we go straight to 'whore'?"

Some of the fire went out of him. "Never that. I would sooner fault a cock for crowing than a woman for loving. Goodnight, Lady Astrid."

"But isn't that what you just did?" she sighed at his retreating form. "I can't understand you at all."

She sank onto her bed, drained of emotion, feeling nothing left but exhaustion and emptiness.

"Remedy for masturbation," she mused. "Have a shouting argument with the object of one's desires. Highly effective and much safer than a cold bath. Perhaps I should write a book."

# XXII
# SHOPPING AROUND

Monte pushed the salad around on his plate, unable to work up any appetite. "I finished the notebook this morning."

"Good." Astrid took a bite of cake, washing it down with a gulp from her glass of milk. He was certain she had chosen both foods to spite him.

"It was more of the same. Nothing that revealed their intent or the specifics of the potions."

"So Fawdry isn't stupid enough to spill his secrets in writing and leave them lying about for anyone to find. Not surprising."

"I packaged up the three suspicious potions, along with an explanatory note, to be sent to Lord Ayleston. You are certain he is to be trusted, yes?"

She glared at him over another bite of cake.

"I meant no insult. Since that man attacked me, I have been mistrusting of anyone connected to either the asylum or the Institute, and I don't know Ayleston as you do."

"He has been the greatest supporter of my career for years now. I would trust him with my life."

"Good. I will have the package posted."

A sullen silence fell over the table as they continued their meal. Astrid finished her cake, but didn't leave the table, choosing to remain staring at him while he picked at his lunch.

"Do you know where my brother is?" she asked some time later. "It's not like him to miss a meal."

"Ah, yes. He and Miss Fairfax have gone out. You missed everything because you were not at breakfast this morning."

"Someone kept me up late."

Monte winced. "I apologize for last night. I ought never to have kissed you."

Astrid rolled her eyes to the ceiling, her fingers clenching.

"And you don't want me to apologize."

"Not until you stop apologizing for all the wrong things. I don't want to talk about it. Tell me about my brother."

"He was particularly anxious this morning, over some trivial matter involved in the running of the estate. Miss Fairfax took him out for some relaxation."

"Out where?"

"On a drive. He was reluctant to leave the house, but she expressed eagerness to learn to drive the steam car, and he will deny her nothing."

"He could deny anything he wanted—" Understanding dawned in her eyes. "Oh! No, you can't be serious. Cal and Grace? Goodness. They're lovers, aren't they? That's the secret you wouldn't tell me."

"It is."

"But how could *they* not tell me? And they are always so formal in public. Always 'Miss Fairfax' this and 'Lord Caladay' that. How did you find out? Did Cal tell you?"

"Yes, but only recently."

Astrid frowned. "How long has their affair been going on?"

Monte hesitated before answering, and her expression grew hard.

"How long, Monte?"

"Three years."

Her jaw dropped. "Three years? No."

He nodded.

"How could I not notice? I feel like such a dolt. But, honestly, how could they not say anything? I am their most beloved sister and friend."

"For one thing, your brother is dreadfully afraid of causing a scandal."

"True."

"Secondly, he is fully devoted to Miss Fairfax and will take the utmost care for her reputation. Mostly, though, I believe they have enjoyed having a secret together. It has been something special and all their own."

"If they want something all their own, they could just have a baby like everyone else," Astrid blurted.

Monte couldn't help but laugh. "And a lovely dose of scandal to go with it."

"They ought to get married."

"I agree." He couldn't envision his friend being happy with any other woman. The obstacles in their way, however, were numerous and not insignificant. To a marquess, that was. Monte could marry Miss Fairfax and no one would care. The world was a strange, cruel place.

"This does explain many things."

Astrid's thoughtful frown made her upper lip plump out in an unintentionally enticing manner. Dammit, he needed to stop thinking about kissing her. Hadn't he caused enough trouble as it was?

"Oh?"

"Why Grace swapped with Elsie for the drafty corner room. It's just up the stairs from Cal's bedchamber. Why Grace and Cal often vanish at the same time. That has been happening for so long it seemed normal, and I always selfishly enjoyed the private time. Why they will both sometimes laugh at things that don't seem at all funny to me.

"I really do feel ridiculous for not knowing. For goodness sake, even the servants must know about it."

"You have a loyal household staff, all of whom seem fond of your eccentric family. I do not expect they would go revealing secrets to anyone."

"Hmph. Well, I'm going to talk to Elsie for certain. She ought to be most loyal to *me*, not to Grace or my brother. I wager she thought it great fun not to tell me. Everyone loves to tease me."

A grin tugged at Monte's mouth, and he fought to keep a semi-serious expression. "I can't imagine why that would be."

"Nor can I. I'm so very nearly perfect there is nothing one might possibly laugh about."

"Whereas I am but a poor fool whose foibles must be mocked mercilessly for the entertainment of all."

"Naturally."

She had the loveliest smile. Sweet, impish, and alluring all at once. Monte was relieved to see it again, and to have pushed away—however temporarily—some of the resentment from last night's argument. He dug into his lunch with renewed enthusiasm.

Astrid was devising a list of punishments to pay back Cal for his secrecy when Crippens appeared in the doorway, his customary grimace on his face.

"A Mr. Jones has called for you, Lady Astrid. I have shown him to the small parlor."

Monte had learned over the course of his stay here that the small parlor was where Crippens sent guests he didn't like—which was most of them. Monte was somewhat awed by the fact he had been shown directly to Cal's study.

Astrid's nose wrinkled. "I don't recall meeting any Mr. Jones lately. Did he bring flowers?"

"He did not."

She sighed. "See? Only Lord Smyth brings me flowers. I imagine I would marry him, were I a normal sort of girl."

Monte's jaw clenched. His own flowers counted for nothing, it seemed. What were hundreds of hand-picked weeds, after all, to a few big, flashy hothouse blooms?

"You are anything but." The words came out in a growl. Astrid gave him a look.

"Thank you for the unnecessary reminder." She turned her gaze to her butler. "Thank you, Crippens. I shall see this mysterious man now."

Astrid strode out the door, Monte trailing a step or two behind, as befitted a gentleman. It wasn't long before she turned, giving him that familiar look of annoyance.

"You needn't follow me. Go back and finish your salad."

"I was done. And what are the chances this is some innocent social call?"

"What are the chances you will only make things worse?"

"It would be irresponsible of me not to join you in meeting this questionable person who may play some part in our investigations."

"Nice excuse."

It was and wasn't. Yes, he believed she could take care of herself, particularly in the safety of the house, but he was still her sworn protector. Mostly, though, he was simply curious about the new intruder.

Jones looked like a law clerk or secretary. He stood a similar height to Monte, but appeared scrawnier. Monte couldn't tell if he was truly scrawny, or if his ill-fitting clothing made him seem so. His face was pallid, with a sharp nose and thin lips. He clutched a notebook and pen in his hand, and paced the room in the manner of a caged animal.

He jumped when they entered, then pulled himself together, squaring his shoulders and adopting the wide-legged stance of a man trying to look larger than his size. He cleared his throat, and addressed Astrid.

"Good afternoon, my lady. My name is Benjamin Jones. I am here as a representative of Lord Marvale."

"Ah, he has sent you to apologize? Excellent!"

Marvale's toady flinched. "Er, no. I am here to make observations. I am to follow you about during your daily activities and record your habits for his analysis."

"And if I send you away?"

"I was told by his lordship I am to insist upon it, as it is essential to his medical evaluation and for the good of your own person."

Astrid's blue eyes had gone as cold as ice. Her smile was predatory. "I'm terribly sorry to inform you, but I have shopping to do this afternoon. A great deal of very boring, very ladylike shopping. And I'm afraid you may have to wait some time before we can depart, as I am dressed for work and not for going out. I trust you don't mean to follow me to my bedchamber while I change?"

Jones turned red. "Certainly not! I shall wait for you here, and we may set out when you have finished dressing."

Monte took his turn staring down the unwanted visitor. "Now see here, my good man," he began, in his best stern doctor voice. "You can't possibly mean to be going out alone with the young lady. It is unseemly."

Monte loved using that voice. It commanded respect and told people he knew best and they had better listen. He used it on his patients because it reassured them he was giving his best professional advice. He used it on others to force them to take him seriously. Never mind that he clearly didn't know everything and sometimes felt a complete fraud. Better to at least sound like one knew what one was talking about.

"Are you Montford?" Jones snarled.

"I am."

"His lordship warned me about you. Said you were meddling."

"I have heard that word quite a lot of late." Monte looked the intruder over once more, assessing the chances of him carrying a weapon. One assault was more than enough.

"Why don't you gentlemen get acquainted while I prepare for the afternoon?" Astrid suggested. She held Monte's gaze for several seconds.

He nodded to show he understood. He'd keep an eye on the bastard.

Astrid took three-quarters of an hour to ready herself. It came as a surprise when she finally stepped back into the parlor. It had been so long that Monte had decided she had climbed out a window and struck out on her own. He wouldn't have blamed her if she had.

He'd made good use of the time by intimidating and interrogating the goon. Jones (the name was probably a lie) claimed to be a surgeon (definitely a lie), and he had worked for many years with Dr. Pierce in London, continuing to collaborate with him even now he had ascended to the Marvale earldom (an approximation of the truth). Jones possessed nothing in the way of medical knowledge. Monte had spent a good twenty minutes regaling the man upon the finer points of various dissections and surgeries he had attended during his medical studies, enjoying the green color that overtook his cheeks and the startled-hare look in his eyes. Jones stood his ground, however, which meant Marvale was paying him well or had him utterly terrified.

"I am *so* sorry to have kept you gentlemen waiting," Astrid cooed. She flittered into the room with the same wafting gait she had used with her diva persona. He hoped this new act would be less flamboyant. "You know how complex a lady's toilette can be."

Whatever had transpired during her forty-five minutes, she had spent maybe ten of them on her costume change, Monte decided. Probably the most time-consuming part had been cinching the laces of her too-tight corset. She was stuffed into one of those unsightly school mistress dresses again. He couldn't understand why she continued to wear them, since he knew she hated them as much as he did.

"Of course, Lady Astrid." Jones opened his notebook. "If you don't mind, might you tell me in advance where you intend to go this afternoon?"

"Oh, the milliner, the bookshop, the apothecary, and how many more I couldn't say. You know how it is when a lady goes out shopping."

"Of course," he repeated.

"Let's be off, then. Dr. Montford, you are accompanying us, are you not?"

"I wouldn't miss it for the world, my lady."

"Excellent. Come along, then. It's a good mile's walk into the village. My brother is out with the car, I'm afraid, but it's a fine day, so we needn't fret."

Jones scrawled something in his book, his brows scrunched in displeasure. Astrid could easily have requested to have the horses hitched to the Whitehaven carriage, but Monte suspected she took a perverse joy in making a man who didn't appear to ever step outside make the journey on foot.

The shopping trip was, as Astrid had predicted, very boring, though only to Mr. Jones. Monte found the excursion nothing short of hilarious. Astrid agonized over her many purchases, scrutinizing every item in every shop, and changing her mind multiple times before settling on anything. Most of the shopkeepers were surprised to see her out shopping for herself, but quick to help and eager to please.

She did her best to appear a practiced, though indecisive shopper, but Monte caught her uncertain glances and hesitant choices. Whenever possible, he offered surreptitious advice on colors, styles, and quality. At least ten times he had whispered, "Which do *you* like best?"

Now his arms were weighed down with packages. She had purchased a parasol, two fans, six handkerchiefs, and four pairs of gloves. Two boxes containing adorable hats dangled from his arm. A third hat was being custom made to her specifications.

She had even found jewelry—an ammonite fossil polished to a shine and hung from a delicate, silver chain.

Jones watched it all with the expression of a man who had been dragged down into the seventh circle of hell. He had written down every purchase in his notebook, along with shop name and time of the transaction. (The man was definitely some sort of clerk.) He had nothing else to record. Astrid was friendly and polite with everyone, as they were with her. She was dressed properly, purchasing proper things, and in all ways behaving like any other woman of means on a shopping expedition.

The bookstore, however, held the potential for trouble. They'd been inside for a quarter hour already, and Astrid had spent the entire time discussing the latest arrivals with Mr. Furbush, the proprietor. He had a number of things set aside for her perusal, including several scientific periodicals, two text books, and a stack of novels. For the first time that afternoon, Monte sensed no uneasiness in her as she considered the merchandise. Her smiles were genuine, her conversation easy.

Many of the books sounded interesting. Monte particularly coveted the shiny, new printing of the novel called *Treasure Island*, regardless of the fact it was ostensibly a book for boys and respectable doctors didn't become giddy at the prospect of a fantastical pirate adventure.

"Hold these, would you?"

Monte shoved the packages at Jones, who fumbled to accept them—wearing a look of shock and bafflement—because he was a man accustomed to taking orders. Burdened now only with the hat boxes, Monte joined Astrid at the counter. He grabbed for the book, his hand colliding with hers as she reached for it at the same moment.

"Oh, I'm sorry," she exclaimed, looking genuinely surprised. "Did you want that one?"

"If you don't mind."

She looked up at him, long, dark lashes framing her cheerful eyes. "You read novels?"

"I read everything."

"Oh." Her smile was one of smug satisfaction, but in the next instant it gave way to a grin so suggestive it knocked all the wind from his lungs. "Everything?"

Somehow he sucked in a breath, but it clearly was not of the healthful variety, because when he exhaled, the word that came with it was spoken in the husky tones of an unrepentant rakehell. "Everything."

Astrid turned pink. She was going to ask him about some of the things he had read. Maybe not here in the bookshop, but someday, when they were alone again…

*Please, God, do not let her ask about all the indecent things I have read.*

She turned her eyes on Mr. Furbush, her complexion settling back to its usual hue. "Dr. Montford would like that book, apparently, and I would like these four for certain, and the magazines. These, here, I am undecided on. What more can you tell me of them?"

Monte stepped aside to examine some medical journals while Astrid continued her conversation. Furbush liked her. Any fool could see it. He wasn't enamored, perhaps, but certainly interested. He was gentlemanly about it, too, keeping his words no more than friendly, and doing an impressive job of not looking too often at the place right between her breasts, where a button threatened to pop open. A bit of encouragement, and he would be sending hothouse blooms to rival Smyth's. Hadn't she said Furbush held some sort of title? For all her talk of being thought odd, she seemed to have plenty of eligible suitors.

Astrid wandered off to scan the shelves for something, so Monte took his magazines and returned to the counter to pay for his purchases.

"You're certain those are the ones you want?" Furbush asked, an odd note of sarcasm in his tone.

"Yes, why?"

"I thought it might have been hard to see anything through all your menacing glares."

"Pardon?" He hadn't been… Had he?

Furbush laughed. Not a spiteful laugh or a condescending one, but a true laugh of amusement. "Oh, you're in trouble, lad."

Lad? Monte bristled. Really. He was well past the age of majority, and Furbush couldn't be more than four or five years his senior.

The bookseller glanced over at Astrid, then back at Monte. "Heaps of trouble."

"Yes, I know." He held the other man's gaze. "I'd like to open an account here. I'm staying at Whitehaven for an indefinite duration."

"Certainly."

With financial matters settled, Monte reclaimed Astrid's purchases from Jones, who immediately began scribbling in his notebook. Hopefully about novels and science books and not about the way Astrid had distracted Monte to the point where he was unconsciously working to eliminate his rivals.

*They are not rivals. There is nothing between us.*

Lie.

*There mustn't be anything between us.*

And that was precisely the trouble.

# XXIII
# SOCIAL OBLIGATIONS

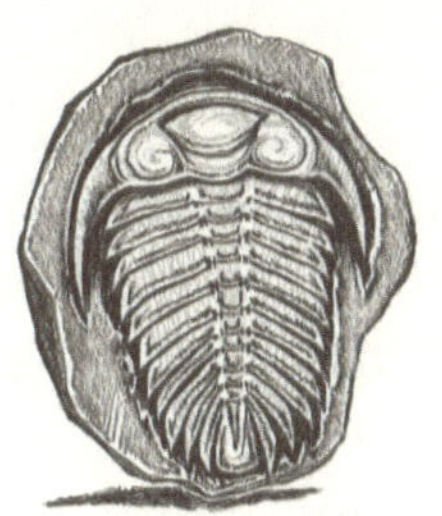

Thank goodness Marvale's man had come to spy yesterday and not this afternoon, because he would have witnessed Astrid in a semi-disheveled state, pounding on a gentleman's bedchamber door.

Even worse, when the door opened, what came out of her mouth was, "Monte, I need you."

Anyone of sense would forgive her for not thinking quite straight. Monte had abandoned his jacket and waistcoat, and his shirt was open at the top, exposing his kissable throat. His hair was rumpled, and he clutched his pirate novel, one finger marking his page. He had nearly finished, Astrid noted.

His hot gaze raked over her, taking in her unshod feet and the curls of hair tumbling all about. "Do you, now?"

"Yes." She was so caught up in staring at him it took an unseemly long time for her to explain herself. "I have dozens of accessories, and I haven't the slightest notion which ones to use. White gloves, or blue? Long or short? Do I take a handkerchief? Do I wear a hat, or only something in my hair? I need a fan, and shoes. I don't know how to do any of this."

Monte grinned at her, looking her up and down a second

time. "I can help." He put his book aside and followed her down the hall. "That is the dress you intend to wear?"

"Yes."

"It becomes you."

"Thank you. It's another of Lady Vayne's. Elsie made adjustments to the fit, and it seems the right size now. I like the bright blue color."

"As do I."

He hadn't lost all his rakish tendencies, because he entered her bedchamber without the slightest hesitation. His eyes flicked toward the terrarium, checking that Bristles hadn't escaped. Astrid looked away to hide her giggle.

Her room was a mess, with accessories scattered across all flat surfaces. Monte stepped over the five pairs of boots, scanning the array of choices with a frown.

"This is far more than you purchased yesterday."

"I know. I brought out many of my older things as well. As I said, I have no idea what I should choose."

"You had a London Season once, and you have attended events since then. Who helped you choose, if you didn't do it yourself?"

Astrid grimaced. "Everything was pre-chosen. Dresses were ordered from my mother's modiste, and they arrived complete with accessories. I never did more than select a color. But tonight I wanted to wear a dress that was comfortable."

"A sensible notion." He surveyed the room again. "You purchased none of these things yourself except what you selected yesterday?"

"Not a one."

"Are there any you are fond of?"

She shrugged.

"Right then." He stopped beside the desk, where she had set out all of her fans. He put aside the black lace and blue silk she had selected the day before, then flung the remainder to the floor with a single sweep of his arm.

Astrid gasped. Monte moved on to the gloves, repeating the procedure.

"What are you doing?"

"You wanted help. I'm helping."

"But…" She couldn't think of anything to say. She had already professed her ignorance of fashion matters. She stared in bewilderment as he discarded everything in the room but what she had bought for herself.

"There," he declared. "That should make your decision easier."

"But…" she repeated.

"Gloves, elbow-length or longer. Flowers, gems, or pearls in your hair. Put a handkerchief in your reticule, or if you feel brazen, tuck it inside your bodice."

Astrid ran her fingers over a pair of gloves. "But I don't know which colors suit. Or which hair ornaments match."

"Pick one up, try it on, look in the mirror." He gestured at her dressing table. "You have a large one, just here, in case you didn't know. Stand before it and you will see a reflection of yourself."

"I know how to use a bloody mirror!"

"Then you don't need further help."

"You are being deliberately obtuse."

"And you are being timid. The Astrid I know is far stronger than a mere pair of gloves."

"But I don't—"

"Care what anyone else thinks and will choose what makes you feel comfortable and pretty? Excellent. My work is done."

"Monte!" In her frustration, Astrid snatched up the nearest glove and swatted him with it.

"Do you intend to meet me at dawn? Despite recent insinuations, I am not an infamous duelist."

"Ugh!" She put a hand on his chest to push him away, then yanked it back when she realized how little separated her fingers from the warm flesh beneath. "At least tell me which boots to wear."

He frowned down at her array of footwear. "Haven't you any dancing slippers?"

"Yes, but they all hurt. They were made to make my feet look small and slender."

"That's idiotic. Why are your clothes so painful for you? Why did your parents never do anything about all this?"

Astrid turned away. "I never told them. People thought they were peculiar. I was even stranger, and I didn't..." She took a steadying breath. "I didn't want to make it worse. I tried so hard to fit in. But it's no use."

A painful stillness settled over the room. Even now it was no use. She couldn't be anything but different. She would be committed to the asylum, her dreams would be lost forever, and her brother would be left all alone.

Monte broke the silence. "Wear the black ankle boots. If you will excuse me, I had hoped to finish my book before I must dress for this ball."

Astrid spun back to face him. "Wait. You are going?"

"I am the son of a peer. I think I am sufficiently genteel to attend a social event at the home of a baronet."

"I..." She hadn't meant to insult him. "Of course."

"Excuse me." He gave her a nod and departed.

"Oh, hell."

Astrid rang for Elsie and plopped into a chair. The long, black gloves would do, she supposed. And the black fan. She stuffed a handkerchief into her decolletage, because she'd forgotten to buy a purse and her old ones were ugly—in her opinion.

One hour later, she sat in the carriage directly across from Monte, listening to the clop of the horses' hooves and dreading the evening ahead. He had prettied himself up for the ball with a fresh shave and slicked-back hair. His evening clothes were strict black-and-white except for the plaid ascot tie. He'd managed to get it properly knotted for once.

All afternoon she had fretted about his attendance. Marvale would be among the guests, she was certain, and he would be recording everything she did. She prayed there was nothing too unusual about her appearance. Elsie had said she looked properly noble, and had given her some sort of fashionable hairstyle. Astrid's plan had been to dance a few times in order to look normal, hang in the background at all other times to avoid notice, and speak as little as possible.

But Monte would be there. He would ask her to dance. It felt as inevitable as the sun rising each morning. She would have to accept—she wanted to accept—but then she would be in his arms, in public, in full view of the crowd, and everyone would know. They would see the wicked thoughts dancing in her head. They would know there was something between her and Monte, that they had done inappropriate things together. Everyone would know, because she didn't know how to hide her reaction to his touch.

Her only relief came from the presence of Grace at her side. Astrid had insisted upon bringing her as a companion, as if she needed a chaperone. What she really needed was a friend to turn to, in the event something went disastrously wrong. She also intended to force her brother and Grace to dance and interact romantically in a social setting. Step one in her make-them-spill-their-secret revenge plan. So far it was working as intended. Cal's eyes had grown huge when he'd first seen Grace in her beautiful ball gown, and his, "You are looking well tonight, Miss Fairfax," had come out low and gravelly. Now they were carefully eyeing one another across the carriage, holding back just enough that Astrid had to pay attention to catch them at it.

When at last they arrived, Monte helped Astrid down from the carriage, reinforcing all her worries. Even through the gloves, his touch sparked a tingle of anticipation. She separated from him as soon as she was able and hurried into the house.

His longer stride kept him right on her heels, and when she removed her cloak, he surveyed her completed outfit.

"You look lovely. Would you mind if I made one tiny suggestion?"

"Uh… no." *Now* he wanted to be helpful?

"Do you have a sentimental attachment to those pearls?"

"No." Her eyes narrowed. What was he about?

"Excellent."

He stepped up behind her and unlatched the necklace. The little hairs on the back of her neck stood straight up. He whisked the pearls away, and a moment later a chain slipped around her neck, its pendant settling just above her breasts. She looked down in surprise at her ammonite fossil.

"Now you look like you."

Astrid rounded on him. "How did you get that?"

His charming smile spoke for itself. "Your maid is a sweet girl."

"I will look weird," she hissed.

"No. You look beautiful."

"Do not dance with me."

"Pardon?"

"Don't do it." She hitched up her skirts and rushed ahead, determined to keep clear of him for the remainder of the night.

As the highest-ranking woman at the ball, Astrid found her plan for keeping in the background to be an impossibility. Everyone felt the need to greet her, and it didn't take long before her head began to throb from all the small talk.

She was eyeing the refreshment table longingly, when a familiar and unpleasant voice said, "Lady Astrid. How good to see you. Would you care to dance?"

*No. I would not.*

The false smile hurt Astrid's face. "Lord Marvale. How kind of you to ask."

"It's my pleasure." He took up her hand and led her onto the floor as the orchestra struck up a waltz.

*Yes. I'm certain it is. Bastard.*

"You are looking very respectable tonight," he simpered.

Astrid refused to thank him for such a barbed compliment. "As is appropriate for a ball."

She held herself stiffly, touching him as little as possible. Even the feel of his gloved hand against her back made her cringe. This, she suspected, was how Monte felt about bugs.

"Your modest jewelry choices are intriguing."

Monte was wrong about the ammonite, damn him. She looked weird. Also she had neglected to remove her nose ring. As usual.

"The diamond earrings were a gift from my mother upon my coming out," she replied, deliberately misunderstanding. "They are simple, but beautiful and elegant."

"And the necklace?"

"Purchased from one of our tenants, and a lovely reminder of the natural beauty of our homeland. Whitehaven prides itself on the care of and appreciation for God's creation."

*Argue with* that *you arse.*

He chuckled. "You have a quick wit, Lady Astrid. I cannot deny that. Now, I understand you went shopping yesterday. Why don't you tell me about it?"

*How about, "No."*

But rudeness wasn't an option, much as she would have loved to storm off and leave him standing alone in the middle of the dance floor. She gritted her teeth and waltzed, answering his obnoxious questions as briefly and civilly as possible.

The last strains of the music made her heart leap for joy. When she spied Lord Smyth heading for her, she beamed at him with such genuine gratitude that his head jerked and it took him several seconds to respond with a smile of his own.

"Lady Astrid. May I have the honor—"

"Yes, please!" She seized his hand, and they launched into the next dance, leaving Marvale to smirk at their backs.

"You are very animated tonight," Smyth observed. "Are you enjoying the ball?"

"I am now." She would dance every dance with Smyth if it kept her away from Marvale. "I enjoy dancing, so long as my partner is agreeable."

"We have that in common, then. Marvale was not an ideal partner, I take it?"

"It was like dancing with the much older man one is being forced to marry to save one's family from dire financial straits."

"Read a lot of novels, do you?"

"Yes."

"Don't have much interest in them, myself. I read the scientific papers, of course, with my position at the Institute, and I always want the latest news in the horse-racing world, but aside from that I get tired of all those words, you know."

"Mmm."

Monte was dancing with Grace. Astrid's eyes followed them across the floor. They made quite the dashing couple, perfectly dressed and polished, spinning elegantly through the steps. She was pleased to see them in good spirits. Whatever Monte was saying had Grace smiling. Excellent. Hopefully Cal would feel jealous and sweep her off her feet for the next waltz.

Smyth chattered on a bit longer and then fell silent, which was perfectly acceptable to Astrid. She smiled at her friends and let herself enjoy the dance.

At the end of the number, Smyth made a gracious bow. "Would you care for some refreshments, Lady Astrid?"

She glanced around to make certain Marvale wasn't about to pounce on her before answering. "Certainly. Dancing always makes me thirsty."

They made their way across the room, and had nearly reached a table of scrumptious-looking desserts, when their host intercepted them.

"Lady Astrid! I haven't had a proper chance to speak with you yet this evening." Sir Christopher beamed at her with his wide smile. A jolly man, short and slightly balding, he greeted everyone he met with gracious good cheer.

"Oh, hello, Sir Christopher. The party is lovely. Thank you for the invitation."

"No, no!" he exclaimed. "It is I who must thank you. So many prestigious ladies and gentlemen have joined us tonight, and I'm certain they only accepted the invitations because Whitehaven and his dear sister were coming. Is that not correct, Lord Smyth?"

"Not at all, my dear sir. Any of us would have been happy to attend so fine an event as you put on."

Smyth didn't sound sincere to Astrid's ears, but the excitable new baronet beamed.

"Thank you, thank you. Please, won't you have some refreshments? I am told the champagne is excellent, and we have potions of all sorts tonight. I'm so pleased they have become so widely available."

What he likely meant was "affordable." Astrid didn't understand the obsession with recreational potions. The idea of drinking something to make her feel not herself was repellant.

"Balance potion to improve your dancing?" a servant offered. "Stamina to ward off fatigue? Allure to catch the eye of that certain someone?"

Astrid caught herself before she turned entirely around to look for Monte. "No, thank you. Perhaps a glass of champagne."

She examined the food while she waited for the man to pour. There were three different chocolate confections, and she intended to eat them *all* because she was in an everyday, sensibly-cinched corset and not a medieval torture device. She reminded herself to write Lady Vayne a thank you note.

Astrid loaded a little plate with goodies and turned for her glass of champagne. Her hand hovered inches from the glass, when a man reached out and snatched it right out from under her.

"Here you are, Lady Arabella," he gushed. "A sparkling drink for the most sparkling of ladies in attendance tonight."

"Oh, I'm sure you exaggerate, Mr. Williamson."

"Not at all, darling lady."

Astrid watched the thieving couple wander off, forgetting that ladies didn't scowl. "Well, I never!"

Smyth pressed his own drink into her hand. "Here, Lady Astrid, take mine, and don't mind that barbarous man." He turned to the man pouring the potions and drinks. "You, there. Pour another glass of champagne."

"Y-yes, your l-lordship," the man stammered. His face had gone white.

"Don't worry. It wasn't your fault," Astrid assured him.

"T-thank you, my lady." He managed to pull himself together enough to pour Smyth a glass.

"Let's find a place to sit and eat, shall we?" she suggested.

"Of course." He followed her, carrying his own little plate with a single pastry on it. It wasn't even chocolate.

At least Smyth ate sweets. Monte would probably object to all the desserts, the silly man. Astrid wanted to see him eat some chocolate. She would feed him a bite of the richest, most sinfully delicious, melt-in-your mouth torte, and watch his eyes close in pleasure as the taste flooded his mouth.

Her eyes flicked down to the fan dangling from her wrist. Of course when she had need of it her hands would be full. She sipped her champagne instead, but it did little to cool her heated skin.

*Don't look for Monte. Don't look for Monte.*

She and Smyth found an unoccupied sofa and settled themselves down to eat. He was good enough not to place himself uncomfortably close.

"How do you like the chocolate cake, Lady Astrid?"

She had to quickly swallow a mouthful to reply. "It's excellent."

"Glad to hear it."

This led to a long speech on his own opinion of various pies, cakes, and biscuits. She nodded and made noises of agreement while she munched on her desserts.

The orchestra struck up another waltz. Astrid's fork froze in midair when she spied her brother and Grace, hand-in-hand, taking the floor. As fine a couple as Monte and Grace had been, they were nothing to Grace and Cal. The lovers moved as if born to be in each other's arms. Even when the overzealous Sir Christopher and his partner bumped them, they stumbled together, laughing together.

They had become one. Their faces were aglow, bodies pressed tightly, eyes locked on one another. In the midst of the crowd they were alone, nothing existing but their love and the music.

Astrid blinked away a tear.

"Lady Astrid?"

She had forgotten her companion. "I'm sorry. My brother is waltzing, and…" And what? She couldn't discuss Cal's private life with a near-stranger.

"I'm glad to see it," Smyth said. "He needs to move about in public as much as you do, and now he is marquess he will be desiring a wife. There are a few eligible ladies here tonight."

Cal didn't want an eligible lady. He wanted Grace, and it was so obvious Astrid couldn't see how the whole room wasn't staring.

"I'm acquainted with Lady Pamela Whitworth and Miss Dansby," Smyth went on. "I would be happy to make introductions if you and he have not already—"

A piercing shriek rent the air.

"Get them off! *Get them off!*"

## XXIV

# AUTHORITY FIGURES

Dancers scattered. The music stumbled to a halt. In the center of the room, Lady Arabella screamed, swiping at her clothes and her hair.

"Help me! Get them off me!"

Monte's dancing partner had just declared herself faint from the flurry of excitement, but he abandoned her to her imaginary complaints. He knew a real medical emergency when he saw one.

Cal, always the gentleman, had already rushed to the stricken lady's side. He appeared at a loss for what to do, but his arms were spread, ready to catch her if she swooned. Good man.

The same could not be said for Lady Arabella's own partner. He backed away, gaping at her in horror and doing nothing to aid her in her time of distress.

"Help me!" Arabella wailed again, arms flailing, tears running down her pale cheeks.

Monte caught her wrists, bringing her arms in front of her, keeping a firm grasp to prevent her hurting herself or another.

"Lady Arabella, can you hear me?"

"They're all over me," she sobbed. Her whole body twitched. "Please. Please help me."

He tried to inflect his voice with both authority and comfort. "Tell me what you see."

"E-everywhere," she gasped. "I can't… I can't…"

"She's mad," someone blurted.

"She's drugged," Monte snapped. Perfectly sensible ladies did not succumb to sudden hallucinations in the middle of a ballroom. "Whitehaven, help me carry her to a sofa. The rest of you, clear a path. Sir Christopher!"

"Yes, sir!" the baronet replied in an uncomfortably submissive manner.

"Send your servants to the kitchens. I want all your herbs and spices. Water. Brandy. Gin. Fetch the serum and all the mixing utensils from the potions table. And any pre-made medicinal potions you have on hand."

"At once!"

With Cal's help, Monte managed to convey the thrashing, weeping woman to a safe and comfortable location. Whispers of "mad" floated about the room. An older woman, whom he guessed to be Lady Arabella's mother, approached him, wringing her hands.

"Oh, my poor child. Whatever is to be done?"

"I will keep her comfortable here until I can make up a medicine for her," Monte assured the woman. "Can you tell me, has she ever suffered from anything like this in the past?"

"No! Certainly not."

"Has she been at all ill of late or seemed in any way altered in mood or behavior?"

"No. She has been in the best of health. Please, you must help her. Look how she suffers."

"I believe she has ingested a toxin that has brought on this fit. A health potion should revive her."

"A health potion cannot reverse madness."

Marvale. Monte spun to glare at the other man. "She is not mad."

"She is in the grip of a hysterical fit. Such things often occur with no warning. Madness does not always manifest itself as a slow decline."

Lady Arabella's mother fell to her knees at her daughter's side and began to sob.

"She was drugged, Pierce," Monte snarled, giving the man neither the courtesy owed to his rank nor his profession. "And well you know it."

A delicate hand brushed against Monte's back. Astrid. He could smell her jasmine-scented perfume. "I suspect she happened across a drink meant for someone else entirely," she said.

"I cannot imagine what you mean," Marvale replied. "The girl has succumbed to hysteria. A stay in a rest home will clear the problem right up. I suggest you remove yourself, Montford, and make way for a man who knows his business."

Monte abandoned the argument in favor of his patient, who had quieted, but continued to toss upon the sofa, mumbling. He patted her hand and spoke soothingly to her, trying to break through her delusions. He felt her forehead—normal— and checked her pulse—rapid, but not dangerously so.

"You are wasting your time, boy," Marvale scoffed. "You haven't the faintest notion what you are about."

Now that the initial shock of the incident had worn off, the assembly had grown curious, and ladies and gents alike crowded around for a look and listen. Monte decided to give them the entertainment they desired.

"I'm not certain you are aware, Lord Marvale, but I was elected a fellow of the Royal College of Physicians at age five-and-twenty. How long did you have to wait?"

Marvale, who was not a fellow at all, scowled. "Your fancy reformist notions may have attracted notice, but they cannot make up for a lifetime of experience. The girl is mad. I have worked in asylums."

"So have I. Also, I have examined the patient, whereas you have done nothing but stand about blustering."

A laugh came from the midst of the crowd.

An impassive expression settled over Marvale's face. "Perhaps you are correct."

The sudden capitulation and civility of his tone caused Monte to start. Astrid pressed against him. "What is he about?" she whispered.

"If you are correct," the earl went on, "and her illness has its root in a toxin, then it must be as a result of an inferior potion."

"Nonsense."

"Sir Christopher! Did your potions and serum tonight come from a reputable London dealer?"

"N-no, your lordship. They were purchased at a market. Made locally. The mixer tonight was one of the housemaids. She has a talent." His voice trailed off. "So they say."

"I rest my case."

Astrid jumped to Monte's defense. "Do you ever say anything based on scientific observations, Lord Marvale, or is everything that leaves your mouth mere conjecture?"

"What would a woman know of science?"

She smiled her icy-sweet smile. "More than you, clearly."

"Enough!" Cal's voice rang with all the authority of his rank, and the entire assemblage fell silent. "Marvale, you will apologize at once for the insult to my sister. The rest of you, clear a path."

The onlookers leapt into action beneath his withering stare. Marvale glared, but even he didn't dare to defy the marquess before the crowd.

"You have my apologies, Lord Whitehaven, Lady Astrid."

A trio of servants rushed through the newly-opened pathway, bringing trays loaded with the potion ingredients

Monte had requested. He took the tiny bottle of serum from a trembling, young housemaid, uncorked it and took a sniff.

Quality. He didn't dare taste it undiluted, but he dripped a single drop into a glass of water, swirled it about and drank it down.

"The serum is strong and pure. There is no chance for accidental poisonings there." He looked at the girl. "You mixed up potions tonight?"

"Yes, sir. Do you need me to make the lady a healing potion?"

"I will handle that, to treat her symptoms more specifically. But please make a sleeping draught to help her rest."

"Yes, sir."

Monte watched the girl out of the corner of his eye as he selected the ingredients he needed. The moment her hands touched the mixing tools, her trembling faded and her face settled into a look of concentration. She knew what she was doing.

He measured, poured, and mixed until his health potion had reached the color and consistency he desired. With limited utensils at hand, he was forced to strain the potion with a spoon, but he didn't think Lady Arabella's condition so severe it would make a difference.

"Whitehaven, grasp her head from both sides, gently, but firmly. I am going to administer the potion a spoonful at a time."

Cal's eyes betrayed not even a flicker of annoyance at Monte's continued use of his title. "I have her," he declared, looking and sounding every bit the marquess.

After three swallows, Lady Arabella ceased to twitch. By the time the glass was empty, she was sitting up and acting normal once more. Her gaze shifted between Monte and Cal, her cheeks flushing. "Er..." she began.

Her mother jumped in before she could say anything. "Lord

Whitehaven, how can we ever thank you for your gentlemanly care of my daughter?"

"Thank nothing of it, madam," Cal answered. "Any man in my position would have done so."

Monte almost snickered, catching himself and clearing his throat instead. "How are you feeling, Lady Arabella?"

"A bit dizzy, and weary, but not unwell. I'm not certain what came over me. I know I felt something awful was happening, but it has all begun to fade."

"You ate or drank something tainted, and it caused a hallucinatory reaction. The medicine will continue to destroy any remaining toxin in your system, and you needn't worry this incident will repeat itself. I do, however, recommend you retire for the night."

"Yes, I think that best," her mother agreed. "We have rooms here at my cousin's home, and I will see her to bed directly."

Monte tasted the sleeping potion that the housemaid had mixed up, confirming his appraisal of her talent. "Lady Arabella, this potion will help you sleep undisturbed tonight. Drink half of it, and retain the other half in case you feel you need extra rest again tomorrow night. I am staying with Whitehaven, and you may feel free to summon me if you have need of anything further."

Without further ado, Lady Arabella was whisked from the room by her mother and a trio of housemaids, all prepared to see to her comfort for the night. Monte tidied up the potions materials and handed them off, while Cal gave directions to the rest of the party. Within minutes, the orchestra had struck up a tune, the old food and drink had been removed, and new bottles of champagne were being opened in their place.

Cal crooked his finger at Astrid and Monte, beckoning them to follow. Grace scurried to join them.

Astrid's brows knit into a worried frown. "What is he doing, acting all high and mighty?" she whispered.

"He's growing into his role," Grace replied. "We had better follow."

"If he thinks he can simply order me about..."

Monte chuckled. "I don't think there is any concern there. No one can order you about, Lady Astrid."

"Marvale!" Cal stopped the man before he could slink out with a group of men to play billiards.

The earl looked the group over, but addressed only Cal. "Whitehaven."

"Your evaluation of my sister is over. This inquest is over. I will speak with the magistrate in the morning, and we will not hear any more of this. Is that understood?"

"Certainly. I would hate to part with any hard feelings between us. Consider my role in the matter ended."

Cal nodded. "Good evening."

Marvale nodded and departed, not looking back.

"Back to the party," Cal ordered. "Go enjoy yourselves." He walked toward a group of ladies. "Miss Dansby, would you care to dance?"

Astrid *hmphed*. "'Enjoy yourselves.' How can I? Blasted Marvale has ruined my mood, and now they've taken my chocolate cake away, and there isn't any more."

"Would you like to dance?" Monte asked.

Her eyes widened, then narrowed to angry slits. "No. And I told you not to ask me." She spun on her heel and stalked away.

Monte shook his head as he watched her go. He couldn't understand her. She enjoyed dancing. What was wrong with *him* that she would rather stand in a corner and sulk?

"Miss Fairfax, would *you* care to dance?"

Grace smiled at him. "Again? People will think there is something between us."

He took up her hand and led her toward the floor. "Nonsense. Anyone who saw you with Whitehaven can tell we haven't a fraction of the passion you two possess."

Her eyes drifted toward Cal. "He really is Whitehaven tonight, isn't he?"

"Absolutely."

"I'm so proud of him." She blinked away a tear. "And so unprepared for what comes next."

"You think he will leave you?"

"He must. He has a keen sense of duty and propriety."

"He'll learn to ignore it, if he knows what's good for him."

Grace's eyebrows twitched, a gleam of amusement in her eyes. "That's rather funny, coming from you."

"You think I don't know what's good for him?"

"I think you don't know what's good for yourself. We are so often blind to our own faults and foibles."

"I have many faults, Miss Fairfax, and I do my best to improve upon them, that I might do as little harm and as much good as possible."

"I know." She fell silent for a moment. "Oh, good, Astrid is dancing after all."

Monte turned to look, though he knew he shouldn't. "Not with Smyth again."

"No. Another young lord, heir to a barony, I believe. An eligible man. And not a fortune hunter. I wonder what his opinion might be on the wholesomeness of cheese."

"I wonder why you haven't used that saucy tongue of yours and simply demanded that Cal marry you."

"He needs to decide what he wants for himself, and whether I am to be a part of it."

"And what of what you want for yourself?"

Her dark eyes appeared almost black. "In this world, women rarely have the luxury of pursuing such."

Neither of them spoke for a long moment, each surveying the dance floor, watching Cal and Astrid, until Monte broke the silence with a curse.

"Bloody unfair, that."

# XXV
# WAITING IN VAIN

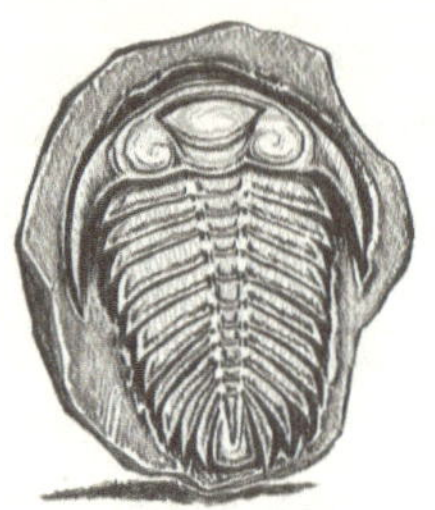

Astrid pressed her face to the glass, peering through the drizzle for any sign her brother had returned. The longer the afternoon wore on, the fewer minutes ticked by before she felt compelled to look again. She had tried everything to keep her mind occupied. First, she'd spent longer than usual reading to her mother. Lady Whitehaven had been as exhausted as usual, and probably hadn't heard a word Astrid said, but at least they'd had a few extra moments together.

Afterward, Astrid had done a bit of work, and finally taken a walk down to the beach in the rain. Neither had relaxed her mind. It was no use. She could concentrate on nothing else while her life hung in this strange limbo.

The clop of hooves and the rattle of the rigging announced the arrival of a carriage before the vehicle appeared out of the mist. It looked to be an ordinary hired cab, of the sort visitors often took when coming from the train station. But no visitors were expected at Whitehaven, to Astrid's knowledge. Could the steam car have broken down, leaving Cal stranded? Or had someone dropped by, unannounced? If Marvale had sent another man after last night, she would give him a piece of her mind.

Curious, and distracted from her worries at last, she hurried to the foyer and threw open the front door, right before the eyes of her astonished porter.

The cab rolled up to the front steps, and a woman emerged, swathed in a black, fur-lined cloak. She rushed up the stairs, tossing back her hood when she spied Astrid.

"Lady Vayne! Whatever are you doing here? Quickly, come inside before we both soak ourselves."

"Thank you." She raced the last few steps and through the door. She shook the water droplets from her cloak and handed it to the porter. "I'm sorry to intrude upon you like this, but I have important news, and I thought it best to convey it in person."

"Of course. Won't you come into the parlor?"

Crippens met the unexpected visit with his usual frown. "Shall I send for tea, my lady?"

"Oh, no, no." Lady Vayne waved him off. "I won't stay long. I have asked the cab to wait and convey me to the inn in the village when I am done."

"Nonsense!" Astrid exclaimed. "We have plenty of rooms. I insist you stay here. Crippens, I would love some tea, please. And if you could have Lady Vayne's things brought inside and a room prepared for her?"

"Certainly, Lady Astrid."

Lady Vayne smiled at her. "Thank you. I would never presume to intrude, but I'm certain this will be much nicer than the inn."

"It will, indeed. And I would never presume to turn down a visit from a friend. We are becoming friends, are we not?"

"We are."

They settled themselves on a sofa in the large parlor, Astrid plopping into her seat, while Lady Vayne slid gracefully onto the cushions, her skirts falling neatly into place. Astrid yanked her own skirt down to cover her bare feet. This didn't seem the time to discuss her dislike of footwear with her elegant friend.

"Welcome, Lady Vayne. Won't you tell me why you've come?"

"Please, call me Tricia, and firstly, tell me how you are? Have you resolved your troubles with the asylum?"

"My brother is out taking care of that as we speak. He believes he can use his position as marquess to put an end to the inquest. Given the way he commanded an entire ballroom last night, I am inclined to trust him."

"I'm glad to hear it. And is Monte still here? How is he? Fully recovered from his duel, I hope?"

"Oh, he was over that ages ago. You can't even tell it happened. But don't let him hear you call it a duel, or he will become more cross than usual. And he has been silent and morose all day. He didn't even say a word about my unwholesome breakfast, and that isn't like him. Perhaps he didn't sleep well. I know I didn't."

"Still sleeping alone?"

"Yes," Astrid sighed.

"What happened last night to disturb your rest?"

"We attended a ball."

Tricia's neatly manicured eyebrows arched and she waited for Astrid to continue.

"When this trouble with the asylum began, my brother took it into his head to take me to social events so everyone could see me behaving normally. He and our neighbors have colluded to host party after party, and invite as many titled guests as possible. Naturally, this includes Lord Marvale, whose house is a mere ten miles off. Throughout, I have entertained suspicions about him, but after last night, I believe he could be our murderer."

"Tell me more."

"A woman took a glass of champagne meant for me. It caused her to have a fit—screaming and hallucinating. If it had been me, there is no doubt I would be in the asylum today. Monte revived her, and everyone believes it was a germ from an unwashed glass or an incorrectly made potion. Marvale threw out the idea of an inferior potion when Monte insisted the cause of the fit to be poison." Astrid spread her hands. "So. There you have it. He has tried to poison me. No one else at the party has any connection to either the Institute or the asylum except Smyth, and I'm certain he isn't our villain."

"Hmm. Are you sure you aren't allowing yourself to be biased because he continues to press his suit? It's been in the papers, you know. Lady Astrid, who only loves science and had been thought a spinster, has been seen in the company of an eligible young lord. That and Monte's duel are the most widely written-up stories of the past week."

"Wonderful. And, no, I don't think myself biased. He is squeamish about blood and death. And while he is rather self-absorbed, I don't think him wholly a bad person."

Lady Vayne bit her lower lip, thinking. "Whoever tried to poison you—quite probably Marvale—is not working alone."

"No. There was that goon who attacked Monte."

"More than that. Let me tell you my news. Please, don't be alarmed, but my uncle, too, has become a victim."

"What? Oh, no!"

"He will make a full recovery. He is a cautious man, and has a daily potion regimen to bolster his health. Still, a poison slipped by his defenses and has laid him up at home. He is remaining abed for a time to rest and stay safe from any further attacks."

"Bugger," Astrid muttered.

"I agree. This is a bold move for our villains. If Ayleston were to die so soon after Dr. Stephens, it would rouse many suspicions. We were getting too close. You should also know Monte's attacker died suddenly, even after healing potions had been administered and the police informed us he was improving. He was to have been interrogated the next morning. We are told one of the potions may have been of inferior quality and caused a deadly reaction."

"Marvale."

Tricia nodded. "It makes me agree with your conclusions from the ball. He is a leader in this new potions reform movement."

"So Monte said. They are both on the Psychical Health Board."

"I know."

Of course she did. Lady Vayne seemed to know everything.

"Have you more information for me? Lord Ayleston must have learned something important."

"We've been gathering information on Fawdry. It took some digging, but we discovered he was a surgeon once, and lost his license for performing unnecessary procedures. He turned to smuggling, primarily serum and potions. We believe he supplied the Cliffsdale Asylum with illegal potions for years. During this time, he adopted his mother's name of Fawdry and began to move in higher social circles. Four years ago, he bought the asylum from the previous owner, for a paltry sum. I have notes here for you to read, but that covers the main points."

"Potions, then, link everything. Fawdry, Marvale, the experiments at the asylum."

"It would seem so. This will help us focus our study of the faction leaders. We will look for a connection."

A knock on the door announced the arrival of tea, and the ladies paused a moment to pour themselves steaming cups.

"And biscuits. Lovely!" Lady Vayne selected one and took a bite.

"These are my second favorite that Cook makes, after the chocolate."

"They are delicious. I have one more bit of information for you today, and, again, it is in the notes for you to read, but I will summarize. The potions you sent have been analyzed by an expert. The one potion is just what Monte thought, a morphia-based soporific. The other two appear to be variations of the same thing: a laughter potion."

"I've never heard of such a thing."

"It's a variation on a happiness-bolstering potion. Our expert says it will make the drinker laugh involuntarily. She believes these are longevity tests."

"So someone is trying to make people laugh uncontrollably for long periods of time? It must be a preliminary trial for something else. They are trying to make their drugs long-lasting, or even permanent."

"I'm inclined to agree."

"Perhaps Lady Ophelia had the right idea. Perhaps I should let them commit me and work from the inside." Astrid shook her head. "No. They would drug me senseless, immediately. I know too much already. We need Beth."

"Who?"

"Ophelia's friend Beth. She's in the hospital wing. If we could get her out, she could testify to the truth of what goes on in there."

"But who will be believed? The madwoman, or the respected asylum owner."

"The respected asylum owner who is a criminal?"

"You'll see if you read the notes, but most of our information comes from conversations with less-than-respectable people. It would be difficult to overturn the way the public sees him."

Astrid heaved a sigh. "Society is so idiotic."

"I agree. But we have made great strides, and identified several likely culprits. We will see this through. Now, let's finish our tea and discuss happier things. We can strategize later, when you have had time to digest all this new information. Tell me something fun about yourself."

"About myself? I, uh…"

*But everything about me is weird.*

Lady Vayne, though, she was weird herself, albeit in less

obvious ways than Astrid was. Perhaps she would enjoy some eccentricity.

Astrid kicked one bare foot from beneath her skirts. "I prefer not to wear shoes, or even stockings if possible." She lifted her right arm and began to unbutton her cuff. "And I have a tattoo of a trilobite."

"Really?"

Lady Vayne leaned in for a closer look. Astrid had begun to regale her with details of trilobite anatomy, when the door flew open.

"Astrid, it's done. You're free. I…" Cal stumbled to a halt. "Oh. Excuse me. I didn't realize you had company."

"It's quite alright. Cal, this is…" Astrid stopped herself and rose from her seat to do a proper introduction. "Lady Vayne, may I present my brother, the Marquess of Whitehaven. Cal, this is Lady Vayne. The late earl was her husband."

Cal bent over Tricia's hand. "A pleasure, my lady. I didn't know your husband, but I knew of him. A good man, I understand."

"Yes, he was. Thank you."

"What brings you to our home, Lady Vayne?"

"News from Lord Ayleston, and answers to Monte's potions questions."

Cal started. "You're a friend of Monte's?"

"Indeed. We met, oh, six or seven months ago, it must be."

His mouth twitched. "Is that so? I don't recall him mentioning you, but we have been uncommunicative of late. Will you be staying the night with us?"

"Your sister has insisted upon it."

"Excellent. I will leave you ladies to your chatting, and check that everything is being done to see to your comfort. You will have the best room in the house."

Astrid crinkled her nose at him, but he bowed and left without saying anything further.

"That was odd. He is up to something. I don't think I like

this new trend, where he is so very marquess-ish. Though, I suppose it has its uses. I needn't worry about being sent to Cliffsdale any longer. You heard him. I am free."

"I'm so glad. Now, why don't you tell me more about your trilobites?"

"Of course. Would you like to see my laboratory? Grace is down there, and I should like to introduce the two of you."

"That sounds wonderful."

Astrid led the way, trying to be as cheerful as Tricia but failing. She didn't feel free. She felt wary. Nervous. Marvale had ceded this battle, but he and his co-conspirators had a bigger goal in mind, one Astrid didn't yet know the scope of. All she knew was that she still stood in their way.

# XXVI
# BY YOUR LEAVE

"I HOPE YOU'LL CONSIDER coming back next week for the house party."

Monte frowned across his chicken stew. Was Cal talking to him? He hadn't been aware he was going anywhere. Was this a diplomatic way of telling him he couldn't remain here indefinitely?

"It will only be a three-day affair," Cal continued, "but it culminates with a fancy dress ball, and I know you enjoy those."

What Monte enjoyed was sneaking around and kissing the women who liked to use their disguises as an excuse for risqué behavior. Or he had done, once. He hadn't been to a masked ball in two or more years.

"Lady Vayne, would you be interested in joining us? I would love to have as many of Astrid's friends attend as possible. I will have an invitation sent to you."

"Why, thank you, Lord Whitehaven. I would enjoy that. I'm eager to see Astrid's dress. She had a long conversation with my modiste about it when she was last in town."

"Oh, you are the friend who took her dress shopping? I

must thank you for your assistance in that matter. That's not the sort of thing brothers are especially good at."

Monte glanced across the table at Astrid. Her eyes were fixed on her plate, and she attacked her steak as if worried it might still be alive. Given the redness of the center, it may well have been. He couldn't fathom why she wished to eat a half-cooked cow. He never ate beef, himself. Her dietary preferences mystified him.

He wanted to make a snide remark on the likelihood of her dinner getting up and walking away, just to see the irritable flash of her blue eyes, and hear her snappy comeback, but her grim expression held him back. She was unhappy. Lady Vayne's visit hadn't soothed her, nor had her release from the threat of the asylum. If anything, she looked more unsettled than she had at breakfast, or even at the ball last night. Monte had to wonder if *he* weren't the cause of her displeasure. They hadn't exchanged a single word all day. Had he made a serious error in judgment by insisting she choose her own accessories? She'd wanted nothing to do with him since then. Perhaps he should leave after all.

His stew was getting cold. Why did he never have any appetite when he was feeling anxious? He would pay for it later. He'd wake up at midnight starving and have to sneak down to the kitchens. Not a recipe for healthful eating.

The conversation trotted along without him, covering the house party guest list in great detail. Miss Fairfax put her superior mind to good use. She could recall an extraordinary number of details about the nearby estates, their owners, the owners' relations, and the merits of inviting them and for how long. She would make Cal a damned fine marchioness, if only he could see past outside expectations.

Unable to drum up any interest beyond what Astrid's fancy dress would look like, Monte forced down the rest of his stew and excused himself to return to his work.

He'd been at it all day, mixing potions in the kitchen,

taking notes, trying new recipes. His improvised medication for Lady Arabella had given him a few ideas. He'd made improvements to two of his regularly-prescribed potions, and he'd made progress on his formula to treat attacks of the nerves. It was almost to a point where he could ask Cal to try it out to test its effectiveness. He ought to have done this a year ago. Still, there would be new stresses now that Cal was embracing his title, and he would have need of it.

It was nearing midnight when Monte finally declared himself done for the day and packed up all his work. Finished potions went into his medical kit, and the array of ingredients went back onto shelves and into cupboards. The kitchen staff had been most accommodating with his poking about and taking up space. It was nice to be among people who didn't mind a bit of eccentricity.

Monte didn't bother to take a lantern, navigating the halls by the light of the sparse, low-burning lamps. He knew the house well enough by now that he didn't fear losing his way or tripping over an unexpected carpet.

He came up short several yards from his bedchamber. Light spilled from beneath the door. Was someone inside? He crept closer, listening for any sounds from within. The creak of the floor beneath his feet screeched in his ears.

Cal had put Lady Vayne in the next room down. He meant well with his notion that Monte needed to get some, and Monte did agree, to a certain extent. Having women thrown at him, however, was nothing but a nuisance.

It wouldn't be like Tricia to have snuck into his room. She was a passionate woman, certainly, but she was as much a lover of the charm and flirtation leading up to sex as she was of the act itself, and Monte had given her none of that this evening.

Which left one other possibility. One that set his heart to pounding and his palms sweating, swamping him with some wild emotion between fury and joy. He pushed open the door, equally dreading and craving her presence.

Astrid sat cross-legged on his bed, her feet bare, attired only in her nightgown, his copy of *Treasure Island* in her lap. Her loose curls gleamed in the gentle glow emanating from the hearth. God, did she look delectable. It was a shame he would have to toss her out.

She looked up at him, laid a ribbon between the pages to mark her place, and set the book on the bedside table.

"Please don't leave."

Her pleading tone caught him off guard.

"Leave?" What was she talking about? "This is my room. If anyone should leave, it should be you."

"Don't leave Whitehaven. I know you've discharged your obligation to my brother, but this affair isn't over yet, and I fear for your life if you return to London alone. You were already attacked once and I wouldn't be there to protect you if it happened again."

Bloody hell. Protect him? Far from being angry with him, she was fretting about his well-being? Of all the mad ideas. Protect him!

The last time someone had wanted to protect Monte, it had been a shy seventeen-year-old viscount offering to teach him how to fight off bullies. Now Cal's twin wanted a turn.

Monte could picture her stepping between him and an enemy, raising her fists, saying, "I'll get him for you, Monte." It was absurd and embarrassing and wonderful. It made him want to hug her and kiss her all over and whisper that, no, *he* would be the one protecting *her*. From anyone. Anything. Because she deserved a defender as fierce as herself. One who would treasure her for all that she was.

*Damn it all to hell.*

His heart was hammering so hard now he was certain she could hear it. His arms twitched, yearning to enfold her in a crushing embrace. Lord, but she had a knack for obliterating a man's resolve.

Monte deposited his medical kit on the floor and closed

the door behind him. He strode across the room and clambered up into the bed, kneeling before her.

"Who said I was leaving?" He loomed over her, hands splayed across the bedding mere inches from her luscious derrière. "This affair hasn't even begun."

Her lips curved in an impish smile and her dark lashes fluttered. "Actually, I believe the affair with Marvale began long before either of us had any inkling of it." The teasing words couldn't disguise her breathy voice.

"To hell with Marvale." His lips hovered above hers. "The only affair I'm interested in is the sort where you and I shag each other senseless."

Astrid wound her arms around his neck. "Well, what are you waiting for?"

"An invitation."

Her lips skimmed across his. "To The Honorable Dr. Ernest Montford." Fingers pushed beneath the collar of his coat, tugging it down over his shoulders. "From The Lady Astrid Wembley."

He caught her chin in his hand and kissed her thoroughly, teasing her lips open and stealing inside, drowning in the ravenous motions of her lips and tongue, until they pulled apart, breathless, eyes molten and faces flushed with desire.

"Please won't you shag me senseless?" Astrid finished.

He eased her onto her back and lay down beside her, hooking one leg over hers and nudging her knees apart. "It would be my pleasure."

But first, her pleasure. Always hers first.

He kissed her again, with soft, teasing flicks of his tongue against her lips. His hands pushed up her nightgown, running over her muscled calves. This was a woman who spent her days running around on the beach, or sprinting up and down the stairs between her laboratory and the library. He sat up enough to give himself a good look at the way her satin nightgown rose and fell over the contours of her body. A priceless gift, to be slowly unwrapped.

He wanted to laugh in the faces of all the idiotic men who would choose some fragile, dainty thing over such perfection. At the same time, he wanted to thank them for leaving her all to him.

"Christ, but you're magnificent."

Her cheeks were scarlet. "How can your compliments be so lovely when they are so wickedly blasphemous?"

"It's the way with us rakes, darling," he drawled. The words jerked him into reality, and he sat up abruptly. What the hell was he doing? Was he out of his mind?

"Hell. What has gotten into me? I ought to be throwing you out this instant."

"No, Monte, please don't. I like you this way. I want this."

He ran a hand through his hair. "I'm supposed to be respectable. I *must* be respectable. I can't help people if I'm not."

She sat up as well, and reached for him, her hand cupping his cheek, blue eyes soft and tender. Did she pity him? He didn't want her pity. He forced an authoritarian tone into his voice.

"No one wants a doctor who's a wastrel."

Her eyes went hard and then fiery hot. "*I* do."

He was undone. He was on her again in an instant, kissing her mouth, her cheeks, her throat. He shoved the nightgown higher and higher, hauling it over her head and casting it aside, feasting on the sight of her. She had gone pink clear down to the beautiful mounds of her breasts.

"Gorgeous," he murmured.

He licked one rosy nipple. Her head lolled back and she let out a throaty moan. His body tightened in response, and he repeated the motion, eager to hear what other noises she might make.

Her hands tugged at his clothes as he explored her, fumbling fingers undoing his loosely knotted tie and unfastening several buttons.

"Monte," she gasped. "Want to touch you."

He helped her get his waistcoat off and his shirt open. Warm hands splayed across his chest, then wrapped around to his back, pulling him down against her.

Monte smothered her with kisses, longing to taste every inch of her skin, heat pounding through his veins with her every tremble and sigh. He slid a hand up between her thighs, slicking his fingers across the warm, wet folds of her sex.

She moaned his name again, hips lifting into his hand. He teased her swollen bud until she writhed under him and dug her nails into his shoulders.

"Yes. Oh, Monte, right there."

He slid first one, then two fingers inside her, edging her ever closer to climax. Her fingers dug into the waistband of his trousers.

"Want you," she groaned. "Want to feel you. Inside me."

A bit of reality encroached on his pleasure. "Ah, not now, beautiful. I told you, I don't have the proper potions. But I won't leave you unsatisfied."

He redoubled his efforts, and she let out a deliciously erotic whimper.

"Then w-what were you doing?" she sighed. "In the kitchen? All day?"

"Research."

She'd been keeping track of him? He didn't want to dwell on the peculiar, bubbly sensation that knowledge created inside him. Instead he focused on her radiant body, her heaving bosom, and her parted lips.

"Monte." Astrid's expression morphed into a look of pure rapture as he carried her to the edge. "Oh." Her back arched, her whole body tensing then releasing in a shiver of delight. "*Ernest*."

Her moan of ecstasy made his entire body stiffen with desire. Hell and damnation. He would allow no one, ever, anywhere to use his given name except for Astrid in the throes of passion.

"Oh, Ernest, that was so lovely."

Monte pressed gentle kisses to the corners of her mouth.

*Just you wait, my sweet. I have so much more to show you.*

"*You* are lovely. From your tumbling curls to the tips of your toes, you are made for pleasure."

"What about you?" Her fingers ran along his thigh and traced the outline of his cock through his trousers. Monte sucked in a sharp breath. "How do I pleasure you?"

She popped open the buttons, one-by-one.

"May I look at you?"

He wriggled to free himself from the confining clothing, watching her eyes grow wide.

"Ooh." Her gaze moved from his erection up to his eyes, then back down again. "That is rather magnificent."

Damn, did she know how to make a man feel good.

"I only wish I could help to do something about it," she sighed.

"Pardon?"

"But I couldn't possibly ask you to show me." Her hand covered his, dragging it toward his aching cock. His fingers curled reflexively around the shaft. Astrid's hand tightened over his. "It being so very unhealthful and all."

Monte swore again. "Just stroke it."

She pumped his hand up and down. "Like this?"

"Yes," he hissed through clenched teeth.

He could have pulled his hand away. He should have pulled it away. But he had been too determined a rake and had gone too long without a woman's touch. He let her keep right on torturing him.

"Then what?"

"Harder. Faster."

Her fingers clenched around his, picking up the speed. His free hand clung to the bedsheets. All sanity had flown from his mind. There remained only the friction of his palm, the softness of her fingers clamped over his, and the gleam of excitement in her clear, blue eyes.

"You are a wicked, wicked woman," he gasped.

"Is that good or bad?"

"Good." His eyes closed involuntarily. "God, so good."

He couldn't stand it any longer. He jerked his hand from beneath hers and thrust against the sweet, smooth skin of her palm. Once, twice, and then he shuddered, the orgasm ripping through him, drenching her fingers with his sticky seed.

"Astrid," he gasped, rolling onto his back. "You are extraordinary."

She held up her hand to the light.

"This is terribly messy, isn't it?"

Being Astrid, she eyed his seminal fluid not with revulsion, but with a curious and scientific tilt of her head.

"Is it safe to taste?"

"Bloody hell," he murmured.

He was utterly wrecked, and yet one simple question from her lips and his body began to stir again. She was going to kill him. She was going to kill him and he would enjoy every second of it.

"I'll wash up."

She hopped from the bed and bounded over to the washstand, not seeming to care in the slightest that she was entirely naked. She wasn't just extraordinary. She was beyond anything he'd ever experienced. Monte managed to wriggle out of the remainder of his clothing as he watched her, but the effort exhausted him. By the time she doused the light and crawled beneath the blankets beside him, his eyelids were drooping.

"Now do we sleep snuggled together all night?" she asked.

*Now I send you back to your room like a responsible man would do and swear not to destroy the remaining shreds of your virginity.*

His traitorous mouth answered her in the affirmative.

# XXVII
# SURPRISES

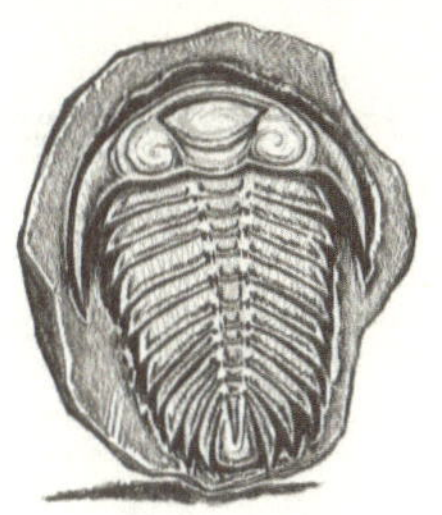

A SHAFT OF SUNLIGHT falling across the bed tugged Astrid from a deep slumber. It was time to rise. Cal and Grace would have breakfasted by now and would no doubt be lamenting how terrible she was at leaving her bed of a morning.

Even through her closed eyelids the sun seemed particularly bright this morning. So odd, when her window faced west.

Her eyes flew open. Good gracious, she was in Monte's bed. The entire household would be up and about at this hour. Elsie would know she had spent the night somewhere other than her room.

*I am ruined.*

The truth of it hammered in Astrid's chest. She swallowed a crazed giggle. The idea of ruination was both terrifying and thrilling. She didn't want any more trouble coming down on her head, yet she couldn't deny the satisfaction she took in her behavior. She was a worldly woman now. One who took matters into her own hands and made her own decisions. And oh, did she have a lovely, lovely man to shatter her reputation.

Monte looked delicious sprawled on his belly beside her, sandy hair mussed and creamy skin bared to her sight. She tugged down the blanket to see a bit more of him, revealing a tattoo that stretched across his back, much larger and more intricate than the one on his forearm. Startled, she gazed at it for several moments, admiring the artistry, before daring to run a finger over it.

"Beautiful," she murmured.

"Thank you."

Astrid jumped. "Oh! You're awake?"

"So it seems." There was laughter in his voice. "Please, feel free to continue stroking me."

Her fingers trailed down his back. "Is she any particular goddess?"

"Uh…"

"She does appear to be rising naked from the sea. But then she's also clutching a sword and a book, neither of which look especially classical."

"I was a bit worse for drink one night and decided this would be a good idea. I honestly don't remember what I said to the artist. But it turned out well, as far as I can tell, having only seen it in the mirror."

"She is lovely."

"Thank you. Again."

Astrid let her fingers continue to caress him. Why not seize the opportunity to enjoy his body, when she had touched him far more intimately last night?

"I think every scoundrel ought to have a naked goddess tattooed on his back."

Monte rolled over to look her in the eye. "I'm not a scoundrel."

"Bounder? Reprobate? Ne'er-do-well?"

"Nor those."

"You must be something. I can't have been ruined by a virtuous man."

Pain flashed in his gray eyes, and he rubbed his temple. "Lord, Astrid, I'm so sorry."

She flopped onto her back with a groan of frustration.

"I know, I know," he sighed. "And I promise you I won't apologize for what we did last night. I don't regret it, and I wouldn't take it back, given the chance. But I ought to have taken more care. I should have seen you to your room."

"I wanted to sleep here. And I don't care who knows it."

"I should go and announce it to your brother, then?"

Astrid winced. Cal would have an apoplexy. "I suppose not."

Monte slid from the bed and strode to the closet to fetch a dressing gown. Astrid found it difficult to maintain her annoyance with him while watching his naked backside. It seemed almost unfair that any man should be so beautiful.

She huffed her displeasure when he wrapped the garment around himself. It was a hideous, burnt-orange, paisley print, with big, fuzzy cuffs and collar. Plaid would have been better.

"You look nicer unclothed."

"I was getting cold." He picked up the fireplace poker and prodded the long-dead coals.

She held out a hand to him. "I'll warm you up."

Monte sighed, dropped the poker, and fetched her nightgown from the floor. "You'll go back to your room and get ready for breakfast." He tossed the dress at her, and she snagged it deftly from the air. "Good catch."

"We Wembleys are naturally athletic, you know. Mother is a champion tennis player. Or was, before her… illness."

"Cal mentioned her melancholia. Does she suffer physical ailments as well? There are many treatments available that—"

Astrid cut him off. "She does not leave her rooms." She would say no more. The hurt ran too deep, and she wouldn't be weak in front of him.

Monte nodded. "Of course. And I assume she has a physician."

"Yes. A well-respected one."

"Of course," he repeated. He crossed to the door and

yanked it open with unnecessary violence. "The hall appears empty. You ought to have no difficulty returning to your room undisturbed."

She wriggled into her nightgown and picked up his pirate novel, checking that the ribbon still marked her place. "You may come to my room tonight to fetch your book back."

She slipped past him into the hall, pausing just outside his door. A shiver raced down her spine. Monte was close enough to Cal to have been given a room in the family wing, but it was at the far opposite end of the corridor from her own door. Any number of people might appear before she reached her bedchamber, and she hadn't quite determined how much of a scandal she was prepared for. She needed Lady Vayne's sophisticated counsel, but the only advice that sprang to mind was Monte's.

*What do* you *want?*

She spun around and kissed him, lingering on his lips until the hairs on the back of her neck began to prickle with the certainty that someone was watching.

"Bring the potions," she instructed, and hurried off.

"Good morning, Astrid."

Astrid seated herself beside Lady Vayne and poured a cup of tea. A kitchen maid set a plate of toast in front of her.

"Your eggs will be ready shortly, m'lady. Shall I have Dr. Montford's bran cakes brought out as well?" Her cheeks turned pink.

Astrid tried not to react. Goodness, did all the servants know already? She would have to have a talk with Elsie.

"I haven't any idea when he will be down." Did that sound pompous? She'd meant to sound only indifferent. Astrid cursed under her breath. She was overreacting.

She needed to have a talk with her brother before he got wind of the rumors. Now that he was acting all high and mighty, she had no idea what he might do if she caused a scandal. Send her to a nunnery? Attempt to marry her off to the most easily available titled man? Demand Monte marry her himself?

That thought made her stomach do queer flip-flops. Part of her wanted to grab hold of him and shout, *Mine!* She shook the feeling off. She would sooner run away than let anyone force him into an undesired union.

Besides, if he ever had a mind to marry, she was certain he could charm the most beautiful and eligible ladies in the entire country.

Tricia sipped her tea, regarding Astrid in curious silence. Astrid blushed. Years of breakfasting alone had made her a terrible mealtime companion.

"I'm so sorry, Tricia. I haven't even said good morning. I was lost in my thoughts, I'm afraid."

An amused smile lit her face. "And how is Monte this morning?"

"Annoying, as usual," Astrid answered before she could stop herself.

Tricia laughed. "Most women find him charming."

"Oh, I'm sure. He can compliment very prettily. And his smile is devastating. But with me he is forever lecturing or arguing or apologizing."

"You fluster him."

"I don't see why. I'm certain he has slept with all sorts of…"

Her voice trailed off when he stepped into the breakfast room. She didn't know what he had been doing in the past twenty minutes, but it certainly wasn't readying himself for the day. He wore only trousers and a rumpled, white shirt, open at the neck. He hadn't shaved, and if he had run a comb through his hair he hadn't done a good job of it. He looked like he'd tumbled right out of bed and wandered downstairs.

"Yes? Do go on," he prompted.

"Er…" Astrid spluttered, flustered by his sudden and disheveled appearance.

He slid into the chair beside her. "About whom are we gossiping? Some scoundrel, no doubt?" His smile and the sly arch of his brows brought heat to her cheeks.

"Yes. One who arrives at the breakfast table in a shocking state of undress."

Monte's twinkling gray eyes looked her over, taking in the loose green dress with the stiff bodice laced over it and her hair twisted up into a messy knot. He couldn't see her bare feet under the table, but he probably suspected. She had no right to criticize his appearance.

"He sounds like trouble."

"Absolutely."

"You're right. I wager he's slept with all sorts of…" The intensity of his gaze sucked the breath from her lungs. "Ravishing beauties."

His words were exactly what she had meant to say, but on his lips they made *her* the ravishing beauty and not the odd girl who was maybe no more than a convenience.

The spell was broken by the arrival of the kitchen girl with their food and a fresh pot of tea.

"Thank you, Sally," Monte said when she set down the bran cakes.

The maid took in his negligent attire, turned scarlet, and gave him an awkward curtsy. "You're very welcome, sir. Enjoy your breakfast."

Astrid dug into her cheesy eggs. "He's probably slept with many serving girls, too."

"Undoubtedly," Monte admitted. "Scoundrels seldom turn down offers."

"I've heard scoundrels can be reformed," Lady Vayne remarked.

Astrid shook her head. "I don't believe it."

Monte scowled at her. "A change in habits can be achieved

with diligent application of the mind," he replied in his doctor voice. "Expending one's energy in healthful pursuits and mentally stimulating tasks can ward off the urges for unwholesome behaviors."

"Interesting. So, for instance, a whole day spent doing research would suppress any carnal desires?"

"In most circumstances, yes."

"But not all?"

"Some temptations are more difficult to resist than others."

"Is that a scientific fact?"

"It's a hypothesis based upon my observations."

"Hmm." Astrid waited until he was sipping his tea before replying, "I think this situation calls for extensive study. Stripping the facts down to their naked truth, so to speak."

Monte swallowed hard, but recovered quickly. "I would love to have the opinion of a respected lady scientist on the matter." His voice sank to a low rumble and he leaned into her. "Perhaps we might come to a mutual conclusion."

Tricia choked on her tea, which made Astrid think Monte must have said something incredibly shocking she didn't quite understand. She would demand an explanation later. This naughty flirting was great fun, and she hoped to improve her skills.

Monte straightened in his seat. "My apologies, Lady Vayne, for that horrendously inappropriate remark. Lady Astrid, I will refrain from begging your pardon, as I know it displeases you."

"Perhaps you might instead clarify your innuendo when we have a moment alone."

Tricia cleared her throat. "Ask him to demonstrate."

Astrid's eyebrows lifted. She cocked her head and looked at Monte. "Would you?"

"This isn't the sort of conversation we ought to be having among company."

"Then why did you make such a comment in the first place?"

"I wasn't thinking."

"Because you're a rake."

"Dammit, Astrid."

A loud throat clearing cut the argument short. Crippens stood glowering in the doorway. Astrid hoped he hadn't heard more than a word or two. Or heard talk that Monte had ruined her. Crippens had been with the family long enough that he might fling Monte unceremoniously into the street and never let him back in.

"Lord Smyth to see you, Lady Astrid. Are you at home?"

"Isn't it obvious I am?"

"But are you *at home* to callers, my lady?"

Astrid rolled her eyes. "I don't do that nonsense. Either I'm really at home or I'm not. I suppose I shall go see him." She glanced down at her half-finished breakfast. "But he will have to wait a moment."

"You should throw him out," Monte griped. "Only an ass would make a morning call this early."

Astrid's eyes flicked to the clock on the wall. "It's quarter to ten."

"Exactly. An uncivilized hour for socializing. Let me send him packing. It would be an honor to perform such a service."

"You're not even dressed."

"I'm as well-attired as you are. I intend to spend the day in the kitchens again, where it is hot and messy. There's no sense dirtying another suit."

"You will make the potions?" She didn't need to quirk an eyebrow to tell him what potions she meant, but she did it anyway, to indicate how serious she was.

"Yes, I'll make the dashed potions. Though I expect I will regret it later."

"No you won't." She scooped up a forkful of egg. "Crippens, please tell Lord Smyth that I will be with him shortly. And if he brought flowers, have them put in a vase."

"Of course." He nodded and departed.

Monte stared off into the distance. "Is there a grower nearby with a hothouse, or does he have all these flowers brought in from London?"

Astrid had no answer for that, but she wasn't certain he even wanted one. His odd, slightly wistful tone baffled her. In all honesty, she could do without more flowers. While she loved that Smyth thought her worthy of gifts, the house had no need for additional decoration and the flowers wilted so quickly. She would never forget his first bouquet, but the subsequent offerings lacked that special feeling.

She wolfed down the remainder of her breakfast, eliciting a comment from Monte on how rapid eating was bad for the digestion. She ignored him and excused herself, stalking off in annoyance. Whether her mood stemmed from his obnoxious remark or her own failure to argue about it, she wasn't certain.

She stopped only long enough to don stockings and shoes before meeting Smyth in the parlor. He stood at the window, staring out, hands clasped behind his back. When she entered, he made a slow turn in her direction, a smile growing on his face.

"Lord Smyth. What brings you here this morning?"

"You, naturally."

"Oh." Her face heated. Such statements were supposed to delight her, weren't they? Yet she felt not delighted, but awkward. Courtship, in her experience, was either insulting or embarrassing. Why couldn't she get the thrilling sort like in her novels?

"I enjoyed our time together at the ball the other night, and I have been wanting to see you again. I cannot stay but a short while, as I have business that needs my attention, but I wished to ask if I might take you to the theater when you are in town on Friday."

"Friday?" she echoed, trying to make sense of his statement. She was certain she hadn't said anything about plans to go into town.

"Yes, for the lecture? I assumed you would be in attendance."

"Oh, of course." His assumptions were based on old data. With circumstances being what they were, Astrid had thought to avoid the Institute for a time, particularly after Tricia's revelations about the attempt on Ayleston's life. "Things have been so busy here that I've hardly given it a thought," she lied. "What is the topic of Friday's talk?"

His thin lips puffed out a bit as he frowned. "Something about potions, if I recall."

Her heart leapt. The linking factor between Cliffsdale, the Institute, and Marvale's reform group. A potions lecture would draw out all the relevant parties and give her insight into who knew what and what their goals might be.

"Oh, yes, now I remember. I do intend to be there, and I would be happy to accept your invitation to the theater. You are very kind to offer."

"Not at all, dear lady." He took up her hand, bowed over it, and kissed it. His long moustache prickled her skin, and his lips were unpleasantly moist. She ought to be swooning over the attentions of a handsome and eligible man, but all her brain would think was that she'd rather be doing wicked things with Monte. "I must take my leave, but I look forward to our next meeting. Where will you be staying?"

"With a friend," she replied, plans for her visit forming even as she spoke. She had no intention of telling him or anyone beyond her closest allies where she would be.

He withdrew a card from his pocket and pressed it into her hand. His London address had been penned on the back.

"Send me a note when you arrive in town. I will come by Friday morning to escort you to the lecture. Do you prefer a horse-drawn carriage or a steam car?"

"It makes little difference to me. I expect I will meet you at the lecture, however, as I'm not certain when I will be getting in, and I may head straight to the Institute."

Smyth nodded. "I will meet you there, then, whereupon I will give you the details for dinner and the theater."

"That sounds wonderful. Thank you."

"You are most welcome. Friday can't come soon enough." He bowed again, but fortunately did not attempt to kiss her hand again before taking his leave.

Astrid sank into an armchair, her mind buzzing. This trip wouldn't be without dangers, but she couldn't pass up the opportunity to learn something. Everyone else would have to learn to live with her choice.

"You're certain you don't wish me to accompany you?" Grace gathered up the papers on Astrid's untidy desk and shuffled them into a neat pile.

Astrid bestowed a grateful smile on her best friend. After a morning full of arguments, it seemed the laboratory would be her afternoon refuge after all. Of everyone in the house, Grace was the only one accepting her plan without shouting. Even Lady Vayne had first met the idea with a horrified, "Absolutely not!"

Grace, though, was calm, even friendly. Astrid wondered if it were possible for her to be otherwise. It was her way. She took life's twists and turns in stride, keeping her head, maintaining order, always striving for optimism.

"I'm certain. Monte will be with me, and Lady Vayne has a large house where I might stay."

*Or where I might tell people I'm staying while I secretly sleep at Monte's flat.*

Shrewd brown eyes narrowed slightly. "Is that so? I have the distinct impression she has better things to do than act as chaperone."

"I don't need a chaperone."

"I would agree, were you going alone."

"I don't think you have any right to fuss over my reputation, in any event. Not when you've been bedding my brother for three years!"

Grace flinched. "Did Dr. Montford tell you that?"

"He let a few things slip, not realizing no one had ever told me. Once I put the pieces together, he confirmed it. I still feel foolish for not knowing."

"No one knew. Only Elsie and Cal's valet, and they are both sworn to secrecy. We wished to keep things private. What if your parents had learned of it? Cal was certain they would object."

"I can't see why. We all want Cal to be happy."

A half smile turned Grace's lips. "That I don't doubt."

"It's all true, then? You really have been lovers all this time?"

"It will be three years ago this Christmas."

"You ought to have gotten married by now."

Grace shook her head. "A lovely idea, but one abounding with troubles."

Astrid's jaw tightened. "Why? Cal is a marquess. He can marry whomever he pleases."

"Actually, I imagine he has less choice than most. His position puts him in a world of strict expectations."

"Stupid expectations."

Grace's lips pinched in a pained smile. "Life isn't always fair. We do what we can to make the best of it."

"Yes." Astrid chewed on her lower lip. Grace deserved the best of it, and the best wasn't sneaking around as Cal's secret mistress. "You'll take care of him while I'm gone? This new aura of authority about him unnerves me."

Grace only grinned. "He's growing up. It's been happening for years. You only noticed when that public insult to you caused him to snap. But it had been coming. With each little struggle he becomes a stronger, better man and I love him all the more for it."

"He cannot truly be better until he marries you." Astrid

would see it done. She didn't know how, but she would convince them. She wouldn't see two of her most beloved people heartbroken.

A tiny shake of her head was Grace's only answer. "You take care in London. Your enemies grow bolder, and there is much that remains unknown. Don't let your... *ahem*... other interests distract you."

Astrid feigned innocence. "I cannot imagine what you mean." Ugh. Once again, she sounded pompously defensive.

"Try not to spar with Dr. Montford too often."

"I've done very well today. This morning he told me I was eating so fast he feared I might do myself harm, and I just walked away. And then, only a short time ago, he called my plan 'foolhardy.' I did nothing more than scowl and leave." A sigh escaped her lips. "It was most unsatisfying."

Grace's tinkling laughter echoed off the laboratory walls. "I would never presume to tell you to stop arguing altogether, as it's clear you take great enjoyment in it. I caution you only to mind the complications that might arise from your impassioned association."

Astrid frowned. Grace didn't know. More and more it seemed no one did. She had spent the night in a man's bedchamber and gotten off scot-free. She wasn't ruined after all. How disappointing.

"I think our association is entirely reasonable," she insisted, attempting to rein in the pompous voice.

Grace laughed so hard she snorted. "Astrid, dearest, if you had wanted reasonable, you would have long ago married some ordinary, boring fellow."

"Well, I'm not going to marry anyone."

*I will simply have a torrid affair with Monte, and then after that...*

What? Imagining an 'after' proved difficult. She was so different now, and would become more different still. Grace spoke of Cal growing, and the same held true for Astrid. She'd become more comfortable in her own skin. More willing to express her true self in public. Less fearful of what the world might say about her. Slowly, she was learning to see herself the way Monte saw her. Her torrid affair was part of that. What did the real Astrid want? A place in a scientific society and Monte in her bed. And she couldn't imagine either of those desires changing, no matter how the rest of her did.

A knock on the laboratory door saved her from further introspection. "Come in."

One of the housemaids peeked into the room. "Beggin' your pardon, my lady, but you have a caller waiting in the large parlor."

A caller? So close to dinner? Certainly Smyth wouldn't have returned, unless there was some sort of emergency. And Astrid couldn't imagine Crippens putting him in the large parlor, even after all his visits.

"Mr. Crippens is seeing to the lady's needs, and he sent me to fetch you."

"Of course. I will go up directly."

Astrid excused herself and hurried toward the stairs, turning over the puzzle in her mind. What lady would come to visit her at all, let alone at such a peculiar time? Had a steam car broken down or a carriage overturned, and this was the closest place to seek shelter? No. The inn was a mere mile off. Anyone of sense would go there.

Astrid stepped into the large parlor to find a wisp of a woman in a pale green dress standing before the hearth, her arms crossed tightly over her chest. Ophelia turned red-rimmed eyes to her friend.

"Oh, Astrid," she gasped. "They… they've discharged me!"

# XXVIII
# MIDNIGHT CONVERSATIONS

Monte moved the stethoscope across the wall, searching for the clearest sound. This was, he brooded, the most appalling thing he had ever done. Eavesdropping on an enemy was one thing, but Astrid was a friend. More than a friend.

He didn't know what else to do. He needed to know what she was up to, and she wouldn't confide in him. After he'd snapped at her this afternoon for her dangerous, impulsive decision to return to London, she'd stormed out on him without a word. For the second time in a day. At dinner she'd been polite and aloof. She hadn't even mockingly offered him the cheese tray. Her silence was like a weight in his stomach. He yearned for her flashing eyes, her pink cheeks, and her sharp tongue.

If her disdain was the result of last night's tryst, he would never forgive himself. She hadn't asked to be ruined. No woman deserved that sort of shame.

He'd heard nothing, but that didn't mean there weren't whispers circulating about her that had yet to reach his ears. She had every right to hate him. He'd been careless, and he was never careless. Apparently he'd been respectable just long enough to forget all the rules of being a rogue.

And now he had a set of brand-new contraceptive potions he might never have a use for.

He shifted the stethoscope again, and Astrid's voice became more distinct.

"…won't leave her there."

"What…" Lady Ophelia's lilting voice faded in and out. "…do?"

"I'm not yet certain." Monte could hear Astrid clearly now. She must have turned toward the wall or stepped closer. He willed her to stay exactly where she was. "I've been pondering since you arrived, and I believe we must break into the asylum and free her."

Monte's fingers clenched on the stethoscope. That was what he'd been afraid of. Astrid feared nothing.

Lady Ophelia said something else Monte couldn't quite catch.

"I wish we could," Astrid replied. "But we need time to prepare. And because I'm leaving for London Friday morning, I'm afraid we won't be able to take any action until sometime next week."

"…rather wait than risk…"

"I agree. We have all of tomorrow to begin our preparations."

"…you have in mind?"

"We must make notes of everything we know. The grounds, the entrances. What we have seen of the hospital wing, and our best estimation of the layout of the remainder of it. We can at least determine locations of halls and staircases. The symmetry of the architecture will aid us with that. We must practice opening locked doors and windows and walking quietly. We must find appropriate clothing to allow us both stealth and freedom of movement."

"Heavens," Lady Ophelia sighed, her voice coming louder at last, "this is an enormous undertaking."

"Yes." A long silence passed. Monte could imagine Astrid's exact expression. Lips pursed, a small crinkle forming at the top of her nose as she frowned in thought. "We will need to procure potions as well. Health potions to protect us. Potions that could distract or disable an enemy. We will pay a visit to my friend Miss James. And perhaps we should ask…"

Monte couldn't tell if she turned away or let her voice drop, but he couldn't hear what, if anything, she said.

"I should let you get to bed," she said at last, her voice again loud and clear. "You must be exhausted. Let's meet here again tomorrow after breakfast, and we'll begin our preparations. I'm looking forward to learning how to pick a lock."

Lady Ophelia murmured something that sounded like a farewell, and Monte pulled back from the wall. He'd heard all he needed to.

He dropped the stethoscope back into his medical bag, considering all he had heard. He couldn't claim surprise. He knew Astrid well enough by now that such loyalty and bravery were only to be expected. Her plan was as sensible as could be hoped for, under the circumstances. She wouldn't be rushing headlong into danger. Instead, she would be rushing carefully prepared and practiced into danger. Which put his mind at ease not at all.

At least she wasn't running out tonight. He would sleep better knowing that. Assuming he slept at all without her beside him. The memory of last night had haunted him all day, leaving him aching with desire for a repeat performance. Even a quick kiss. A brief touch. Anything.

This wasn't how things usually went. He'd gotten enough satisfaction last night it ought to have blunted his lust. He ought to be relaxing with a drink, dispassionately contemplating his next move. Instead he was restlessly pacing the bedchamber beside hers, itching to grab up the stethoscope and press it to the wall again, just to hear her moving about the room.

Monte flung himself onto the bed.

*I am out of my fucking mind.*

For some indeterminate length of time he lay staring up at the ceiling, listening for sounds from the next room. Nothing. Not even a footstep or the creak of a floorboard. Most likely she'd already gone to bed. It was past midnight, after all.

Several times he almost rose and started for her room, thinking to retrieve his book. The excuse she had given him would get him to the doorway, if nothing else. But the thought of her slamming the door in his face kept him firmly on his back. If only he knew what was wrong, why she was acting strangely. Was she ill?

That thought made him sit up. She hadn't looked or sounded ill, but she had the sort of determined personality that would push on through sickness. If she were ailing, the best thing he could do would be to leave her to rest and check on her in the morning. If she argued with him at breakfast, he would know everything was fine. And if not, he would have to make her tell him what was troubling her.

He picked up his medical kit and listened at the door a moment before opening it and stepping out into the empty hall. No need to risk being caught sneaking about in an unused bedchamber.

What he needed tonight was a distraction to soothe his troubled mind. He mulled over the possibilities. Cal had turned in long ago. Either he was already asleep or was making love to Miss Fairfax. He wouldn't take kindly to an interruption. Thoughts of Astrid made it difficult for Monte to work or read. Playing billiards alone was boring. Drinking alone was pathetic. He needed a companion.

An idea sparked in his mind as he touched his key to the lock. He knew just the thing.

Several minutes later, he rapped on the next door over. A few moments passed before Lady Vayne answered his summons. She peered out, tugging her wrapper closed, a perplexed frown making a crinkle in her brow.

Monte brandished a bottle of wine and two long-stemmed glasses. "Good evening, Tricia. Care for a drink?"

Her dark eyebrows rose. "I hope this isn't some misguided attempt to make Astrid jealous."

"Astrid is fast asleep, I expect. May I come in?"

She opened the door wider. "You may as well, before anyone sees you and gets the wrong idea." She ushered him in, closing and locking the door behind him. "Or the right idea? I can't say I would be unhappy with a tumble, but Astrid is my friend, so if that's what you're about and you're doing it without her knowledge, best tell me now. Then I might only slap you instead of cracking you over the head with that wine bottle."

"It's not. I'm here for a drink. And a chat."

She waved a hand at the couch that occupied the small sitting area. "Why don't you have a seat?"

Monte popped the cork on the wine bottle and poured out two glasses, handing her one before lounging on the sofa as if he really were here for an illicit rendezvous.

"Lovely room you have, here."

It really was. Half-again the size of his, it had pale pink wallpaper and sturdy but feminine furnishings, including a beautiful writing desk and matching bookcases. It suited her perfectly. What he found most interesting was that it was both larger and more feminine than Astrid's room. It made him wonder if this one had originally been intended for her.

He sipped his wine, letting his gaze drift from the room back to Tricia in her wispy dressing gown, remembering what she looked like without it. Had it only been six months since their fling? It seemed like years.

She took a seat on the couch beside him, improperly close because he was occupying more than his fair share. She leaned over him, her own glass dangling negligently from her elegant fingers.

"What are you about, Monte?"

"Having a late-night drink with a lovely lady. As scoundrels are wont to do."

Tricia was too dignified to roll her eyes, but she gave him a sidelong glance. "This is why Astrid calls you insufferable."

"Indeed." He lifted his glass and took a long swallow. "And why suffer alone when I have a beautiful woman to inflict myself upon?"

Teasing her was fun. This uncomplicated flirtation was exactly what he had needed. He felt no urge to tear her clothes off, no fear he was ruining her, no sensation that his world was spiraling completely and utterly out of control. It was refreshing.

And a bit disappointing, because he would've liked to be lounging on a couch in Astrid's room, drinking with her and listening to her tipsy giggles.

Tricia settled against his side, and he draped an arm around her shoulders. There was something to this platonic cuddling. Something that warmed him inside the same way Cal's awkward hugs did. It was worth considering from a scientific perspective. He would study it. It could prove to be good therapy for sufferers of nervous disorders. His paper already had a title. *Embracing Health: On the Relief of Stress Through Non-sexual Bodily Contact*

"Why are you really here?"

He snapped out of his daydream. "Lady troubles."

Pink lips curved into a smile. "Don't they make potions for that time of the month?"

"Trouble with a lady."

"Personal or professional?"

"I don't know what to do about her. How can a woman who is terrified to choose a pair of gloves repeatedly fling herself into real danger?"

"You are worried about the lecture? I wired my uncle this afternoon. He is back to his usual duties, and assures me he has added security about the Institute. He is confident he can keep her safe, and we will be there with her."

"The lecture worries me less than her secret plan to break into Cliffsdale to rescue Lady Ophelia's friend."

Tricia stiffened. "What?"

"They were discussing it not long ago. She is proceeding rather sensibly, all things considered. She means to prepare, study, practice. But it remains a reckless plan, and I don't imagine she can be swayed from it."

"And what is your role in this plan?"

"Not to know of it."

Tricia's carefully manicured eyebrows arched. "You were spying on her? Be prepared for a tongue-lashing when she finds out."

Monte let his head fall back against the couch, gazing up at the ceiling. "Perhaps. She seems disinclined to argue with me anymore."

"Ah. Now we get to the crux of the problem." Tricia laid a hand over his heart. "Poor, poor Monte, all torn to pieces over a woman."

"I am not torn to pieces. I'm merely frustrated. And uncertain what I should and shouldn't do with her."

"You should be in her bed, Monte, not drinking with another woman. You two were flirting so nicely this morning. What happened since then?"

"She walked out to go see Smyth. Later, she came to see me and ordered me to accompany her to London. She ignored my complaints and left me without any argument. Ever since she's been cooly civil."

"Hmm. Yes. That does sound dire."

"Don't mock me, Tricia."

She sat up and frowned down at him. "Have you considered you might be overreacting?"

"What if she is furious over the liberties I have taken with her?"

Tricia's snort of disdain was surprisingly ladylike. "The only thing she's likely to be furious with you about is the fact that you are not currently in her arms, showing her what you meant by 'coming to a mutual conclusion.'"

"I don't think she's interested tonight."

Tricia shook her head. "Go to bed, Monte. Whether your own or Lady Astrid's is up to you, but I have finished my glass of wine and it is nearly one o'clock in the morning. I'm turning in."

"Very well." He shoved himself up off the sofa, and took the empty glasses and the half-full bottle. "What of her crazy asylum plan?"

"Unnecessary. She should leave that to someone else. I'll speak with my uncle. He knows men who are good at that sort of thing."

"Good at breaking into buildings? I'm entertaining more and more suspicions about your uncle and his friends."

She smiled as she nudged him toward the door. "Goodnight, Monte. Get some sleep."

"Goodnight, Tricia. Thank you for the talk."

"You're welcome."

She opened the door and pushed him out without another word. Monte sighed as it clicked closed behind him. A momentary respite from his problems, but few solutions.

"Monte?"

He spun toward Astrid's voice, nearly dropping the wine bottle. She stood in front of his door, dressed only in a flimsy nightgown, eyes wide with surprise.

"What are you… doing?"

Monte opened his mouth, but the only word in his brain was not one he ought to be saying aloud.

*Fuck.*

# XXIX
# INTERRUPTED

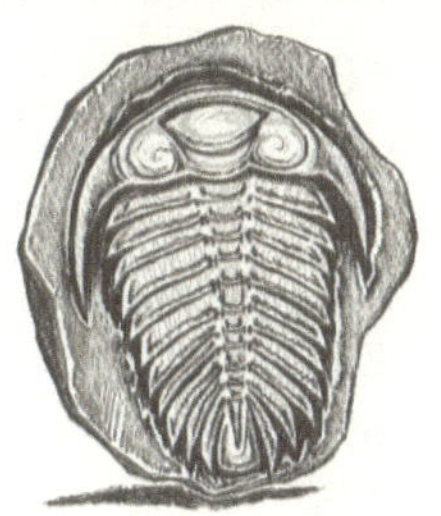

For a few awful moments Astrid was certain she had been cast aside for her prettier, more elegant, and more experienced friend. Then the shock subsided and her brain began to function again.

Monte's mouth hung open, his eyes round and panic-stricken, more fearful than guilty, with none of the false contrition she would expect of a man who would casually toy with her feelings.

"It's not what it looks like," he choked out.

"I know."

Gray eyes clouded over in confusion. "I'm sorry?"

"Look at you. You can't possibly have been engaged in amorous activities. Your hair is neat, your clothes are unrumpled. Well, all but your neckcloth, but it's clear you missed that portion of gentlemanly training."

"If I knot my ties properly, I feel choked. I keep them loose, or else tug at them until they become so. You know how I feel about painful clothing."

"Yes. Well, regardless, the remainder of your clothing is unmussed. You weren't misbehaving."

He took a step toward her, his gaze heating, traveling over her. Astrid's body tightened in response. Her nightgown wasn't transparent, but neither was it concealing, and now her nipples strained against the fabric. No doubt Monte was thinking of how she'd looked without it last night.

"You don't think I can misbehave while fully dressed?" The low growl of his voice sent a shiver down her spine.

"No. Any woman getting that close to you would be tearing your clothing off."

He laughed. "Perhaps you are more savage than most."

"Another reason I know you weren't misbehaving is both of those glasses are used, and part of the wine gone."

He frowned. "Which indicates I was in there for some time. With a companion."

"Yes. With Tricia, who is my friend. She would never steal away my lover. If you had gone in with nefarious intentions, she wouldn't have shared your bottle. I know her heart."

"Clearly."

"I also know yours."

That made him flinch. "Do you?"

"You are not and never were that sort of man. I call you a rogue, but that's because you were born for wildness and pleasure, not because you are hurtful or careless with the feelings of others."

An expression she couldn't define overtook his face. "And you would be hurt were I to take up with another woman."

"Of course."

Worse than hurt. She would be devastated. It would confirm all her fears of being an easy, convenient conquest and not the beautiful, powerful woman she felt when she was in his arms.

"Might I ask why, then, it is acceptable for you to entertain both my attentions and those of Lord Smyth?"

"Y-your attentions?" She blinked, wrestling with his

comparison of two relationships that to her mind were entirely unalike.

"Didn't I give you flowers? Take you shopping? Drug you with wild kisses? Those are attentions, aren't they? How many times has *he* kissed you?"

"None! He ought to know by now he will get nothing more than friendship from me."

"Doubtful. He would have stopped trying."

"But…"

Monte's eyes had turned steely hard. "He doesn't know, Astrid. Or, if he does, he still believes he can change your mind. The man wants you. Trust me on this."

"He probably wants my fortune."

"He may, but that's irrelevant. I've seen the way he looks at you. The way he talks to you. He is bewitched. Maybe even in love."

"But…" Astrid could only stare at him, her mouth agape.

Silver eyes softened to mercurial pools. "Is it still so hard to believe yourself desirable? Yes, you are not society's standard of a perfect woman. I'll tell you a secret. No one is. And another secret. Not all men are looking for that sort of woman. We are as varied as you are. Maybe they don't value you. But you *are* valuable. And I can't possibly be the only one to notice."

A sudden giddiness swept over her, and she suppressed a hysterical giggle that would merit another checkmark on his "reasons Lady Astrid might be confined to an asylum" list. His words were heartening and confusing. Emotions tumbled about, made worse by the late hour and the stress of her unresolved troubles. She couldn't sort through them.

"But you didn't come to me," she blurted, the painful doubts spilling out all at once. "Do you have regrets? Have you lost interest?"

"Have *I*?" In his shock, one of the wine glasses slipped from his fingers, and only Astrid's quick reflexes prevented a disaster. "I thought…" He lifted his hand as if to run his fingers through his hair, but his grip on the other glass prevented it. His hand dropped back to his side. "You've been avoiding me most of the day. I thought you were upset with me."

"But I didn't yell at you at all."

"I know. It was so abnormal I thought you might be ill."

"Ill?" This time she couldn't contain a snort of laughter. "Really? Do I look ill to you?"

"No." His voice dropped. "You look perfect."

Astrid trembled with desire, her lips forming a silent O.

"I'm a fool," he murmured.

"Me too."

He hefted the wine bottle. "Would you care for a drink?"

She glanced down at the glass in her hand. "Both these glasses have been dirtied."

Monte closed the space between them. "Who needs glasses?"

He took a swig directly from the bottle, then kissed her. She opened her mouth to him, tasting the dry, fruity liquid on his tongue as it slid over hers.

A moment later he broke the kiss to look at her, his gaze lit by the mischievous twinkle she so enjoyed. "See?"

Astrid set the wine glass on the floor and took the bottle from him. "My turn."

She tilted the bottle up and took a gulp, watching the flicker of amusement in his eye at her practiced motions. She and Cal hadn't stolen from the Whitehaven wine cellar for nothing.

She kissed him hard, mingling his taste with the wine, letting some of the liquid dribble down his chin and then licking it away.

His hands clenched on her nightgown. "Astrid," he groaned.

Encouraged, she tipped a few drops onto her fingers and smeared them across his cheek before pulling his head down to hers once more. The brush of her tongue over his cheekbone made him shiver.

"I want to do this all over you."

"Please," he gasped.

Her fingers made a new trail of wine along her neck. "And I want you to do it to me, too."

"Yes." He licked her clean, sucking on the sensitive flesh until tingles coursed up and down her body.

The creak of a floorboard caused them to spring apart. Good heavens, who else could possibly be up and about at this time of night? And what had they witnessed?

"Astrid?"

The dazed voice echoed in the silent hall, and her heart leapt into her throat. No. Not here. Not now.

"Mama?" She turned toward the footsteps, shoving the wine bottle into Monte's hands.

"Oh, Astrid, dear, it *is* you."

Lady Whitehaven rushed down the hall, her long, blond hair flying behind her. Even with her dressing gown not fastened quite right, her face creased with grief, and her eyes hazed with drugs, she was still heartbreakingly beautiful. Astrid had always found her so. Her mother was everything good and lovely, and it tore Astrid open to see her so heavy with sorrow, her mind clouded by the drugs that still could not fully soothe her.

There hadn't been an episode in weeks. Astrid had been hopeful things were improving. The wild look in the dowager marchioness' eyes dashed all those hopes.

"Darling, have you seen your father? I cannot find him anywhere."

Astrid gently clasped her mother's hand. "Papa is away. Don't you remember?"

"Oh, of course." She blinked. "I do wish he would hurry back. It's never the same here without him. Is he bringing Frederick home from school?"

"Cal is here, Mama. He's sleeping. It's very late. Let me walk you to your room."

"Yes, thank you, darling." She appeared to notice Monte for the first time. "What are you doing here, young man? I don't recall having met you."

Monte bowed to Astrid's mother, the wine bottle now on the floor behind him. "Dr. Ernest Montford, Lady Whitehaven. It's a pleasure to make your acquaintance."

"Montford." Her brow crinkled. "Oh, you are one of Frederick's school friends. He talks of you often. A doctor, already, at your age? You must be terribly bright. But, of course, Freddie wouldn't admire you so, if you were not."

"You are most kind, my lady."

"You have met my daughter Astrid as well?"

"Indeed."

"She makes her debut this spring. I hope she doesn't break too many hearts. She's a beautiful girl, don't you think?"

Astrid fought tears. These delusions grieved her, and for Monte to be subjected to them threw a hot rush of shame onto the agony.

"She is the loveliest woman I know," Monte replied. "Please, allow me to see you to your room. I would be neglecting my medical training were I to keep you from a proper night's rest."

Lady Whitehaven's features grew sorrowful. "I cannot rest well. The dreams are muddled and... terrible. Sleep does not calm me. Perhaps my tonic..."

Astrid guided her down the hall, murmuring soothing words, copying the soft bedtime ritual Mama had used on her as a girl. Monte trailed behind.

"I can recommend several different sleep aids, Lady Whitehaven," he said. His voice was quiet, but carried all the authority of his profession. "It would require a review of all your medications to determine the correct one, but I would be happy to do so at your convenience."

"Such a sweet boy," Astrid's mother murmured. "You

should get to know him, darling. He called you lovely, and just wait until he sees how intelligent you are. He will be dazzled."

Blinking hard, Astrid opened the door to her mother's bedchamber and escorted her inside. It took several minutes to get her settled and tucked into bed. Astrid adjusted the blankets and kissed her cheek.

"Sleep well, Mama."

"You are so good to me, darling. I'm sorry I am unwell."

"So am I. But you will get better." She gave her mother's hand a squeeze. "You *will*."

"How can I not, with you for a daughter?"

*Astrid Wembley does not cry. Astrid Wembley does not cry.*

"Goodnight."

She slipped from the room and made certain to lock the door. Monte waited in the hall, hands clasped behind his back, his expression somber.

"Are these episodes frequent?"

Astrid shrugged. "Sometimes. They can come several days in a row, or not for weeks. She slips in and out of lucidity and is often confused about where and when we are. Sometimes she does nothing but sit and stare, as if she cannot even see us."

He nodded, lips pursed. "She takes laudanum?"

"Yes. And the dosage has risen to levels that frighten me." She didn't know why she was confessing all this to him, except it relieved her to unburden some of her pain to someone who would listen.

"What else?"

"Potions. I'm not certain what they are, but her physician has prescribed them. I'd thought perhaps they were helping, but you saw how she was tonight."

"I meant what I told her. I will review all her medications and give you a recommendation for a sleep aid. It might be just what this other doctor has prescribed, but it might not. I should like to help in any way I am able. I will do all I can to ease her suffering. And yours."

Astrid nodded, her throat tight.

"If you will permit it, I would like to do a full examination of her health and mental state. If she is well enough, I know a potion that can wean her of her opiate dependency. It will take time, and she may still require other medications, but I'm hopeful I can do something for her."

"Thank you."

"The support of a loving family will also be of tremendous benefit."

Her eyes misted over.

*Astrid Wembley does not cry.*

Monte took up her hand. "Lady Whitehaven is a lucky woman to be in the care of so kind and brave a daughter."

Astrid choked as the flood burst through her carefully constructed walls. She couldn't be weak in front of him. She spun away and fled to her room, tears burning hot and furious trails down her cheeks.

# XXX
# THRILL OF THE HUNT

Tʜᴇ ʟᴇᴄᴛᴜʀᴇ ᴡᴀꜱ ᴀʟʀᴇᴀᴅʏ a terrible crush, and it wasn't due to begin for another half-hour yet. Monte steered Astrid toward the refreshment room, hoping for some strong tea to ease his pounding headache. Whose idea had it been to rise early enough to catch the 7:10 train?

"Monte, where are we going?"

Right. Hers.

"I need a drink."

Astrid freed her arm and stopped walking. "Don't you think it's rather early in the day to begin imbibing?"

"Tea."

"Oh. That does sound nice."

She turned tired eyes up at him. Even disregarding the lack of sleep, yesterday had been exhausting. Between the packing and the preparations, the entire household had wandered about in a state of perpetual stress. Cal had moped all day about his intention to choose a wife during his house party. He and Miss Fairfax wouldn't even look at one another. Astrid snapped at them both and repeatedly vanished with Lady Ophelia to practice lockpicking, wall climbing, or other unsavory things Monte didn't want to think about.

Monte had spent hours in conversation with Lady Whitehaven's physician, a spry septuagenarian who wouldn't step down or lighten his workload despite his age because he was the only licensed medical man in the village. He was a good man, and Monte liked him, old-fashioned though he was in his thinking.

It had been satisfying work, formulating a plan for the care of the dowager marchioness, but it had also been a day spent reliving the memory of Astrid's grief, knowing the intense pain that lay beneath her towering strength. It had also been a day he spent feeling wounded she wouldn't turn to him for comfort, then chastising himself for such selfishness.

"I can't dawdle too long," Astrid continued. "I promised Lord Smyth I would meet him here, and I don't want to hurt his feelings."

Her eyes betrayed her guilt and anxiety. Had she really not grasped the man's regard for her? Or had she been willfully blind and now regretted it?

"I intend to tell him I greatly esteem him, but only as a friend."

Monte's jaw tightened. *Greatly esteem. Ha! The man is a clod.*

"I can't understand why you like him," he grumbled, unable to squash his jealousy.

"He's nice to me. He is friendly and attentive, and he didn't hold a grudge after I publicly humiliated him. How many other men would do that? None, I wager."

"Any true gentleman would accept his defeat with magnanimity."

She snorted. "Ha! Think how you would feel if I had eviscerated you in such a manner."

One corner of Monte's mouth curved into a smirk. "Lady Astrid, you could never humiliate me in public."

She stiffened. "Of all the arrogant—"

He held up a hand to halt her. "You misunderstand me. Certainly, you are capable of besting me in various intellectual debates. I would not, however, suffer humiliation were I to lose to you."

"Oh?"

"I would feel a slight embarrassment, I expect, but that would be overwhelmed by the pride of witnessing another display of your wit and determination."

Her cheeks turned beautifully pink. "What gives you the right to take pride in my accomplishments?"

"Nothing but my regard for you. It brings me pleasure to see you rise above your naysayers."

"Even if you are among them?"

"We don't always agree, but I welcome any attempt to prove me wrong. I know you are always up for a spirited argument."

She cocked her head, and her eyes took on a flirtatious gleam. "Well, pay attention next time I prove you wrong, because I'm certain you shall sulk instead of behaving magnanimously, thus proving yourself not to be a true gentleman, but a rogue, just as I have said. And there you have it. I was right about you all along."

Monte gave her a rather ineffective scowl, struggling not to laugh. "I question your convoluted logic."

"You question everything I do, Dr. Montford. It's your favorite pastime."

He stepped closer and let his eyes rake across her body. "Second favorite."

"Lady Astrid!" Lord Smyth hailed her, striding toward them.

Monte cursed to himself and backed away. "Your escort, my lady. Have fun."

"I'm not here for fun, I'm here to learn something."

"I find learning new things can often be fun."

She frowned at him as if he'd said something inappropriate, though he hadn't meant it as an innuendo. For once.

The refreshment room did have tea, thankfully, but by the time Monte returned to the lecture hall, every seat was full. He leaned against the back wall, adopting a casual posture as he scanned the assembled crowd for any signs of suspicion. Astrid sat beside Smyth, poised with pen and paper, ready to take notes on the lecture and reactions of audience members. Tricia was tasked with encouraging arguments about potions reform. Ayleston had his eye on the Institute members. Monte was left to focus his attention on Astrid.

Twenty minutes in, he realized he wasn't the only one. The young man watching her was also standing, just behind the last row of seats. He was a nondescript type, neither short nor tall, sporting ordinary brown hair and ordinary clothes. He stood like a fighter, however, with hands free and a wide, stable stance. Monte could find no obvious signs of a weapon, but the man's frock coat could easily conceal a gun or a knife.

The lecture ran on for near to two hours, during which Monte contemplated a dozen different ways to kill the man, if necessary. Bashing him over the head with a chair seemed the best choice, though it would require everyone standing up.

When the final applause at last died down, Monte rushed forward to put himself between Astrid and the suspicious character. Interrupting Lord Smyth's dowry-chasing courtship was an added bonus.

"Lady Astrid, are you ready for our afternoon outing to the museum?" Thank God for prior plans. He would simply hurry them along.

Smyth gave him an exasperated look. Astrid's nose wrinkled as she frowned at him.

"We needn't rush off so quickly," she argued, a note of irritation in her voice. "I had hoped to take a bit of refreshment first, and Lord Smyth and I haven't yet discussed our plans to visit the theater this evening."

"We will be attending a performance at the Savoy," Smyth announced, plenty loud enough for dozens to hear, including the man who had been watching Astrid. "You mentioned you are staying with Lady Vayne at her home near Berkeley Square?"

"Yes, that's correct."

"Excellent. I shall come by with the carriage at seven."

"I thought the performance wasn't until nine," Monte argued.

Smyth turned up his nose. "We need plenty of time to drive through crowded streets, and, naturally, we wish to be early enough to see and be seen."

"You could go on foot. It can't be even two miles, and Astrid is an excellent walker." Monte quirked an eyebrow at her, and she bit her lip to keep from giggling at the horrified expression on Smyth's face.

"Certainly not! That is entirely inappropriate and unsafe for a lady, as well you know."

"I suppose the carriage it is, then. And speaking of our transportation, we ought to be off, Lady Astrid. Lady Vayne's carriage will be awaiting us outside."

He offered his arm, and she accepted his escort, though her stiff posture and pinched brows betrayed her displeasure.

"I wanted to stop in the refreshment room," she hissed. "It was sweltering in there, and I'm parched."

"We need to get out of here," Monte replied, keeping his tone confidential. "There's a man spying on you."

"What?"

"Don't look for him, just keep walking. We'll collect Tricia and talk about it in the carriage."

Her head bobbed a fraction, but her scowl remained firmly in place.

"Describe the man," Lady Vayne ordered, the moment the carriage jerked into motion.

"Unremarkable. Young. Brown-haired. He stood like a fighter, so he could be a hired thug."

Tricia's skeptical dark eyes bored into Monte from across the carriage. "And what was so suspicious about his behavior?"

"He was watching Astrid."

"Describe it."

"He looked at her. Repeatedly. Sometimes with his whole body, but usually with his eyes only."

"Couldn't he merely have been glancing at her because she was a woman in a room full of men?"

"No."

"How do you know?"

"He was looking at *her*, Tricia. Only her. I can't describe it any better."

Astrid leaned forward, resting her elbows on her knees. "What do you think he wanted?"

"To kidnap you? Kill you? Frighten you off? How should I know? I'm not a bloody spy."

"Maybe I'm simply so beautiful he can't keep his eyes off me." She grinned at Monte as she spoke, her eyebrows twitching coquettishly. Monte's heart sang. She spoke in jest, of course, but her tone was breezy, confident. She had begun to believe in herself.

He favored her with his most dazzling smile. "I have that problem every time I see you. But, then, I don't usually stand about looking ready for a fight."

"Actually..." Tricia teased.

Monte glared at her, sinking back against the cushions.

"We will remain vigilant," Lady Vayne added, her voice once again sober and authoritarian. "But unless we see anything more, I would advise you not to worry about it. You are overprotective, Monte. Which isn't a terrible thing, but it's something to keep in mind."

The ladies appeared satisfied with this pronouncement, but Monte knew what he had seen. While they lunched and wandered among exhibits and antiquities, he trailed behind, his head on a constant swivel, judging everyone who dared cast a glance in their direction. Twice, he caught a glimpse of a profile he thought may have been his suspicious person, but before he could ever take a second look, the man would be gone. By seven o'clock that evening, he was so agitated he followed Astrid out the door and all the way up to Smyth's carriage.

"Take care of her," he demanded.

Smyth shook his head with that same look of exasperation. "Relax, Montford. What sort of villain do you take me for?"

"I'm not worried about *you*."

"I'm not certain whether to be relieved or insulted by that."

"Just watch out for her."

"Monte, nothing is going to happen," Astrid insisted. "Perhaps you should go home and rest. I know you must be nervous after what happened in the park last time we were in town. If you promise to stay inside, I'll let you know the moment I arrive home."

He had to blink at her for a moment before he could speak. She was doing it again, trying to protect him, and it was so bloody adorable he wanted to kiss her, right there in front of Smyth and his driver, and the people passing on the street, and Tricia's butler who was waiting impatiently for him to return to the house.

"Enjoy yourself, Lady Astrid."

"Thank you. I shall."

Monte watched the carriage start off before bounding up the stairs into the foyer.

"Are you ready?"

Tricia regarded him with raised eyebrows. "I'm not going to the theater, Monte."

"Very well. I shall walk by myself." He reached for his hat and checked the knife he had stashed inside his coat.

"Oh, good grief," she grumbled. "Let me fetch a wrap."

"And a good pair of opera glasses."

Quite a good pair, as it turned out. From Lord Ayleston's

excellently situated private box, Monte trained them on Astrid, checking that she seemed in good health and spirits before beginning a systematic sweep of the area about her. He lingered a bit to take in the new, pale blue dress that hugged her curves in spectacular fashion.

"You do realize everyone can see what you're doing? You're only adding fuel to the rumors."

"There are rumors Astrid is being watched?"

"No, but there are rumors you are in love with her."

He lowered the glasses and turned to frown at Lady Vayne. "I esteem her greatly." The words sounded stupid, even to his own ears.

Tricia laughed. "Oh, Monte, you are so terribly transparent."

"I'm worried about her, Tricia. I truly believe someone is following her."

She rested a hand on his arm. "I know. I'm sorry. Go ahead and keep spying, if it eases your mind."

Monte lifted the opera glasses to his face and returned to his task, moving outward from Astrid's position in an ever-widening circle. His entire body jerked when a familiar face appeared in the corner of his vision.

Tricia's fingers tightened on his biceps. "What's wrong?"

"He's here. The same man. He is seated well behind her, near the door. If she should leave her seat for any reason…"

Tricia reached for the binoculars. "Let me see."

Monte helped her pinpoint the man, watching her mouth tighten as she considered the situation.

"Do you recognize him?" he asked.

"No, but that doesn't mean much except to say he doesn't move about in the same circles I do, nor is he a regular visitor to the Institute."

"A thug, then. He means her harm."

"Monte."

"You can't deny this is suspicious. Don't even try."

"Smyth is with her. Keep an eye on the man, and if he

moves toward her, or does anything that suggests dangerous intent, we will rush to her side. But he may be no more than an observer, in which case it's better not to reveal we have discovered him."

Monte did his best to heed her advice, but as intermission approached, he could no longer contain his anxiety. He sprang from his seat, dropping the opera glasses into Tricia's lap. "You must excuse me. I need to check on Astrid."

He raced from the box, taking the stairs two at a time up to the gallery behind her seat. Showgoers were filing out, and he skidded to a halt to avoid crashing into the mass of humanity moving in the opposite direction.

Astrid was nowhere to be seen, though he expected she would be out shortly in search of refreshments. Her departure time had cut into dinner, and she would be hungry and thirsty. Sure enough, a few moments later she appeared on Smyth's arm, smiling and chatting. Monte slid toward the entranceway, his hand delving beneath his coat in case he had need of the knife.

His quarry appeared momentarily, shuffling along with the rest of the crowd, angling toward Astrid and Smyth. Monte inched along behind, waiting to make certain of the man's intent before confronting him. The thug kept his distance, but the direction of his movements and the turn of his head left little doubt of his target.

Monte wormed his way between several people to come at the man from behind, seizing the collar of his evening jacket and hauling him to a stop.

"Who are you and what do you want?" Monte snarled.

The man jerked and spun, flinging Monte into a pair of chatting dandies, who cursed him and shoved him into yet another theatergoer. Shouts rose from the crowd as more people began to push and shove. A fist flew, striking a glancing blow across Monte's cheek, but he was fixated on Astrid's pursuer. He barged through the melee, heedless of whom he was thrusting aside. When a large man barred his way, Monte threw a punch without hesitating, barreling over the fellow and leaping upon his target.

The two men tumbled to the floor amidst the screams of gentlewomen. Monte slammed a knee into the man's kidneys, then rolled him onto his back, pinning him down and putting the knife to his throat.

"Who the hell are you? What do you want with her?"

"Ayleston," the man choked out.

The name startled Monte, and in his moment of surprise the thug—or whoever he was—caught Monte's wrist in a viselike grip, twisting it and disarming him in one smooth motion.

"I work for Lord Ayleston," the man growled, still gasping a bit. "I'm a bodyguard. Now, get the hell off me, Dr. Montford."

# XXXI
# DISCOVERIES

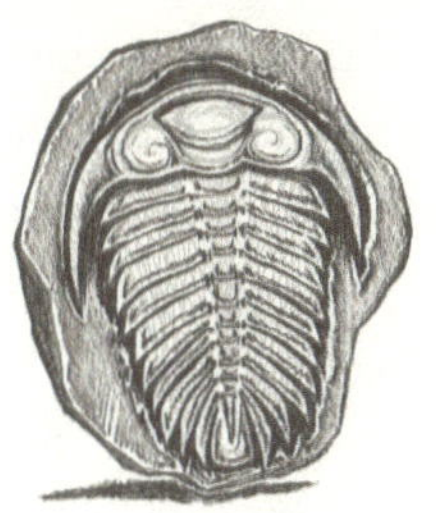

ASTRID SPREAD HER PAPERS across the dining table, scanning her scribbles as she bit into her scone. The information she wanted was here. She could feel it in her bones. It was only a matter of sifting through the notes for the pieces that fit together. After a surprisingly successful fitting of her gowns for Cal's house party, she felt a renewed sense of purpose. She would sit here and stare at yesterday's notes until she had her answers or die trying.

Well, no, probably not that. But she was determined nonetheless.

She took another bite of scone. Delicious. The blackcurrant jam had just the right ratio of tart to sweet, and it paired perfectly with the brisk Assam tea. Lady Vayne's kitchen staff was unrivaled.

*Focus, Astrid.*

"Ah, Dr. Montford."

Astrid's head snapped up when Tricia spoke, her eyes going directly to Monte's.

"So glad you could join us at last." Tricia smiled at Monte. "What kept you today?"

An acute sense of shame for causing a ruckus in a theater? Fear of a scolding from his lady friends? Not that Astrid intended to scold him. She thought it had been rather dashing, the way he had leapt onto the supposed ruffian in order to save her. Silly, but dashing.

"Work matters."

Of course. He had a job. One she had kept him from far too long. While dragging him into danger. And now she was staring at him. As if she could read his thoughts if only they locked eyes long enough.

*Focus on the* papers, *Astrid.*

Monte crossed the room with deliberate steps, his gaze never wavering until she forced herself to look elsewhere.

He took the seat beside her and poured himself a cup of tea. As usual, he declined any milk or sugar, but before drinking he pulled a small, metal flask from his coat pocket and tipped a bit of clear liquid into the cup.

"A potion," he replied to the ladies' raised eyebrows. "I have a headache."

"Again?" Astrid turned worried eyes on him. "Are you certain you are well, Monte? You've had far too many headaches of late. As a doctor you ought to know better than to neglect your own health."

Nothing in his looks suggested he was unwell. His complexion was good, when one ignored the slight bruising across his left cheekbone, and his eyes were bright and clear. His clothing was tidy, and even his necktie was better than usual. She rather liked the vibrant purple plaid of his waistcoat, though even someone of her limited fashion sense could tell it wasn't *en vogue.* It was inspiring, the way he embraced his own personal style.

"I'm not neglecting my health. I'm fine. A bit more stressed than usual, is all."

"Are you eating? Sometimes you don't eat when you're upset. That's not healthful."

The hint of a smirk tilted his lips. "Now you're lecturing *me* on my dietary habits?"

"Well." She tossed her head, making her unpinned curls bounce. "It's nothing less than you deserve."

Astrid dropped her eyes back to her notes, re-reading her latest list as she finished her scone, and helping herself to one more cup of tea. Monte wasn't going to eat the scones, or the jam, or the little baked cheese bites. The remaining choices were unacceptably few. She dumped her cucumber sandwich onto his plate. He made no comment, but gave her a smile that caused a swelling of warmth in her belly.

"What have you ladies learned from yesterday's escapades?" Monte inquired.

Astrid brushed crumbs from the page. "Very little. I was able to write out a list of men who possessed strong opinions on potions matters. I've been trying to compare that with my previous notes to get some idea of which faction they might support and whether they might be conspirators, but..."

She paused, rearranging the papers once again, her eyes lingering on the faction lists she had made from Ayleston's observations. The names at the top nagged at her. These men annoyed her. Loud, blustery sorts who could rile up others but who inspired few. She couldn't imagine either of them garnering enough loyalty to out-vote Ayleston. They were merely showmen...

"Puppets!" Astrid blurted.

Monte made a grunting noise and swallowed. "What?"

"They're nothing more than puppets. The faction leaders. They were never intended to be serious competitors for director of the Institute. The factions are all nonsense." She put her lists side-by-side and picked up her pen, circling anyone in either faction who had professed solidarity with the potions reformists. "Look at this. These are the men in both factions who agree with Marvale."

Monte and Tricia moved closer, watching Astrid's pen

scratch across the page. Her heart raced. This was it. The connection she had been searching for. A short time later, she made a final circle, then set down the pen, admiring her handiwork.

"There it is. The whole story."

"I'm beginning to follow you," Monte murmured, bending over the page, "but I'd like to hear you tell it."

"Count the number of circled men. Add to them the men on our list of 'bribables.'" She snagged another list and laid it beside the other. "This puts you one vote shy of a majority."

"One vote that could be gained by putting a loyal man in your place."

"Exactly. *This* is the real faction. The potions reformists. Marvale is pulling the strings. It all makes sense. He is a quiet man. Unassuming. He keeps to the background, watching. He lets others do his dirty work. But he is intelligent. Devious. Ruthless."

"He's so good at keeping the attention off himself he escaped the Imperial Potions Company collapse with relatively minor losses," Tricia said. "Most of his colleagues faced either criminal charges or financial ruin. He slunk away and spent the past two years slowly picking himself back up."

Monte grimaced. "And murdering convenient relatives to inherit an earldom."

"Possibly, though I've never heard rumors to that effect."

"He's been putting himself more in the public eye recently," Astrid pointed out. "He hosted that ball. He's begun speaking up at the lectures."

"He joined the Psychical Health Board," Monte added. "He has stepped up as a champion of potions reform. All within the last six months."

"He used his connection to Cliffsdale to send Fawdry after me, but Fawdry is too reclusive and wrapped up in his unsavory experiments. Marvale had to step in himself. But he backed down when Cal challenged him. He can't push too hard or he risks showing his hand."

Tricia steepled her fingers against her chin. "He is our mastermind, then, not just a participant. It may be difficult to accuse him, though, if all the crimes have come at the hand of underlings."

"Yes," Astrid agreed. "The man is no fool. Look at the faction list again. The men near the top are closest to the faction leaders, those at the bottom more loosely associated. The bottoms of both lists are full of circles. Marvale owns those men. He can change their loyalty should either faction begin to grow too large. I would bet he pushed the faction leaders to make noise in the first place."

"Which would mean he has been planning this for more than a year," Tricia mused.

Astrid nodded. "Do you know when the membership vote will be?"

"According to my uncle, voting is always in early December. Every three years they vote for director, and every year they vote whether to expand membership—which rarely happens. Due to Dr. Stephens' passing, a special vote for the single opening will take place one month prior in order to have full membership for the December vote."

Astrid let out a gasp. "Good heavens, it's nearly the end of October. I had no idea my vote was so imminent."

"Damn," Monte swore softly. "No wonder he's growing bolder. He's running out of time. At least Ayleston is sending guards to look out for you. And himself, I assume." He looked thoughtful for a moment, then asked, "Where does Smyth fall in these lists?"

Astrid pointed. "Bribeable. I've seen nothing to suggest he cares at all about the ambitions of any of those other men, but he does lack money."

"Do you think he would sell you out for a bribe? Even after courting you?"

"I don't know."

"He would come into a great deal more money by marrying you than he's likely to get from Marvale. I advise you to string him along until after all the voting."

"Monte, that's terrible! I don't want to break his poor heart. Besides, I already told him we will just be friends. It's quite obvious I will never marry."

Monte turned back to his cucumber sandwiches. "Yes. Quite."

· · · ✺ · · · ·

Monte contributed next to nothing to the dinnertime conversation with Lord Ayleston. Which suited him perfectly fine. Watching Astrid explain her now-refined theory was a delight. Her cheeks glowed and her hands waved in animated motions as she rehashed her lists and her analysis of the situation. He could have listened for hours. A bit disconcerting, that.

Dinner concluded the way it always did, with him declining all offers of sweets, alcohol, and cigars. Astrid swiped an extra chocolate bonbon and stashed it in a handkerchief. She caught his eye as she did so, raising one eyebrow, daring him to comment. He winked at her instead, causing her mouth to drop open in shock, then snap shut in outrage when he laughed. Such beautiful, pouting lips she had.

To be honest, Monte saw no reason to stop her from taking extra chocolates. It was clear she was in good health, and if she ate any less she might lose her lovely figure.

Even small as their gathering was, the men and women went their separate ways when the meal ended, and he spent an awkward quarter of an hour wandering Tricia's library, pretending to search for a book while trying not to inhale the smoke from Ayleston's noxious tobacco products. Ayleston apologized for not specifying he was giving Astrid her own personal guard, Monte apologized for attacking said guard, and the two men spent the remainder of the time muttering about the weather.

Both Monte's lungs and his mind were vastly relieved when Ayleston finished the cigar and decided to take his leave.

"I would be happy to give you a ride to your home, Dr. Montford," he said, sliding his arms into his greatcoat and donning his hat.

"Ah, thank you, no. I prefer to walk."

What Monte really preferred was to have a moment to talk to Astrid, to ask if she wanted to come home with him. Every time he looked at her he thought of their night together. Each moment that passed by without touching her brought more fantasies of how he might get her alone and what he might do when he managed it. He knew her interest hadn't waned. Her eyes had been all over him from the moment he'd walked through the door at tea time.

Fittingly, given the muddle his life had become, Astrid herself dashed all his hopes.

"You can't walk, Monte! Not when you've already been attacked once in this city and we've established Marvale is growing desperate. I won't stand for it. You must take the carriage."

"Why don't you take my carriage, Dr. Montford," Tricia offered. "Then my uncle has no need to go out of his way and you can put Lady Astrid's mind at ease at the same time."

Ayleston eyed his niece suspiciously, guessing at the reason for her interference, but gave in with a sigh. "Please be cautious, all of you, and let me know when you intend to return to Whitehaven. I will feel safer with you all away from crowds and strangers."

"I promise to make certain Monte doesn't do anything dangerous," Astrid said with a grin.

"And I promise to follow Lady Astrid and protect her when she *does* do something dangerous," he retorted.

Ayleston shook his head and turned for the door. "You youngsters. All the same."

"Well." Astrid clapped her hands together the moment the door closed behind him. "Shall we send for the carriage? I'm ready to go to your flat."

Monte stared at her for a moment. "Er, yes. Let's."

"Have fun," Tricia laughed. "I will send the carriage to pick you up in the morning. You can join me at church and repent of your sinful ways."

"Repent?" Astrid scoffed. "I'm not going to feel sorry about it." Her eyes flicked upward to meet Monte's. "Are you?"

"Not a chance."

"Good."

They clambered together into the elegant Vayne coach a short time later. Monte barely had time to open his arms before she was on him, smothering him with hot kisses.

"Oh, gracious, Monte, it's been *forever*."

"Only a few days." A few days that had felt like forever.

"You haven't even tried to kiss me. You've been neglectful."

She teased the corner of his mouth, then slipped higher, creeping up to his cheekbone. Pain lanced across his face when she pressed her lips to the bruised area. He'd opted not to rub a healing salve on it, figuring he had only gotten what he deserved.

Astrid pulled back at once, apologizing. "Does it hurt very much?"

"I'll live."

"You were in the papers again, you know."

His muscles clenched. "Is that so?" He didn't want to talk about it. He wrapped an arm around her waist, urging her closer. All he wanted was to kiss her and forget the rest of the world existed.

True to her intractable nature, she didn't comply, shifting to sit beside him. "What's wrong, Monte? You've been irritable all weekend, and today you're worse than ever, no matter how you try to hide it. Are you nervous about Marvale, or is it something more?"

"It's nothing. Come kiss me again."

"No, I think I'll sit here until you tell me."

"Astrid," he sighed.

"I remember what it said in the paper. 'Hyde Park duelist Dr. Ernest Montford has been involved in yet another wild to-do, this time instigating a brawl at the Savoy theater. Three men reported injuries, and several women swooned, though it is unknown whether the cause was the fisticuffs or the sight of so notorious a personage. The melee is thought to be tied to the affections of a certain eccentric woman, though this columnist believes the lady has set her cap at a far more eligible man.' Well, this 'eccentric woman' does not 'set her cap,' and she is going home with *you* tonight, so you have no reason to fret."

"I have plenty of reasons." Like the seven patients who had baldly stated they would no longer be seeing him. Or the nasty letter from one of his colleagues on the Psychical Health Board. His letter to Dr. Harvey had gone unacknowledged. Worst of all was the somber rebuke from several distinguished gentlemen at the Royal College of Physicians.

Everything he had worked for was in peril. If the press continued to paint him as some unhinged ruffian he risked losing his fellowship, or even his license to practice. All the strides he had made would be ignored, all the good he had hoped to do would be nothing but a fantasy.

Astrid's fingers closed over his. "Monte, you look terribly distressed. Won't you tell me so I can help?"

"You can't help. Can you restore my reputation? Convince the world I'm not a scoundrel?"

She scoffed at that. "Everyone who knows you knows you aren't really a scoundrel. You're a good man with something of a wild streak. And I think it wouldn't be so noticeable if you would stop trying to keep it under such rigid control. Or if there weren't, you know, dangerous people about."

Monte stared out the window of the carriage, his amorous urges squelched by the melancholy. He couldn't drink himself into a stupor, as that would only exacerbate the problem. Astrid had rejected his request for another kiss. A madman wanted them all dead. The crisp, clear autumn night mocked him. A gray, bone-chilling drizzle would have suited his mood far better.

Astrid's fingers traced soft trails across the back of his hand. "Shall I taunt you about your constant refusal to eat sweets?"

Absurd, darling woman. Her gentle voice was sweeter than any food could hope to be.

"Or your unnatural hatred of cheese?" she continued.

The need to defend himself made him turn back to look at her. "It's not unnatural. Cheese makes me ill."

"It does?"

"Yes." The carriage pulled up in front of his door, and he helped her step down, explaining all the while. "As a child, I would vomit whenever I was made to drink milk. Even small amounts of cheese could upset my stomach. On one notable occasion, an honored guest visited from France, bringing some runny cheese dish with him. I ate it out of politeness, only to cast up my accounts before we reached the last course. I was not invited to dine with the adults again. Milk, cheese, cream, I can't ingest any of them."

"It's an allergy then?"

Monte unlocked the flat and waved her inside. "I don't believe so. An intolerance of some sort. I could perhaps eat some varieties of cheese, but as I detest it, I see no reason to experiment. I can eat most things cooked with milk as an ingredient, along with some yogurts, and butter doesn't bother me."

Astrid let out a long breath, a strange guilty expression in her eyes. "Thank goodness for that."

"Why do you say that?"

"I, uh…" She plopped down into one of the two old chairs at his dining table. "Well, if you must know, I asked my cook to add extra butter to your cucumber sandwiches, because I was concerned you weren't getting enough fat in your diet."

Tightness gripped Monte's heart, and when it ebbed he was no longer the man he'd been before. Something inside him had cracked, leaving him vulnerable in a way he feared but was powerless to resist. It was as if someone had pried open his chest, removed his heart, and offered it to Astrid. *Here*, the thudding beats of the organ seemed to say. *This belongs to you now.*

He trembled with the hope that she would take it, cherish it, give him hers in return. And with the fear that she might instead have no use for it.

Astrid's blue eyes peered out at him from beneath fluttering lashes, full of concern and compassion. "I'm sorry?"

Monte blinked. Right. The sandwiches. There his heart went again, hammering with excitement over her concern for him. "Don't be. It was kind. And they are delicious."

"You're certain you're not angry? You have a peculiar look on your face. I promise I only meant to keep you healthy and happy."

Over and over. No matter what he did, from public scandals to intimate private moments, she was there, helping, protecting, caring. His own parents had never been so devoted to his well-being. Astrid was outdoing even Cal, who had long held the distinction of being the one person Monte would trust with heart and soul.

It was her nature. She was the sort of woman who would befriend someone after a single, brief meeting in an insane asylum. Who insisted upon kindness toward a man who was almost certainly after her fortune. Who tucked her mother into bed at night, even though her heart broke a little each time. She gave of herself, expecting nothing in return, and often where it was undeserving.

"Here. I brought you something," she said, opening the tiny purse tied to her dress. The worried crinkle above her nose hadn't disappeared. "Perhaps it will make you laugh, because I know you don't want it, but I wanted to give it to you anyway. I hope you will at least taste it, if only to tell me how disgusting and unhealthful it is." She unfolded her handkerchief and the little chocolate bonbon rolled out onto the table.

Monte did want to laugh, but the sound caught in his throat, tangled in a swell of emotion. "Astrid, I—"

"You don't want it. I understand. I respect your personal food choices."

*I love you.*

The words hung there, on the tip of his tongue, terrifying and wondrous. The force of his longing for her left him staggering. He needed her, body and mind. Her laughter, her tears. Her determined spirit and her gentle heart. He craved all that was Astrid with a passion that defied reason.

*Tell her, you fool.*

He pushed the thought away. *God, no. She doesn't want that sort of complication in her life.*

She lifted the bonbon toward her lips. For the first time in his life, he envied a bit of chocolate. "Shall I eat it, then?"

Monte grabbed the second chair and pulled it around next to her, sitting so close his legs were touching her skirts. "On rare, special occasions I have been known to indulge in a small sweet."

"Oh."

He loved the shape of her mouth when she made that sound. He loved the delicate curve of the hand that brought the chocolate to his lips. The salty taste of her skin as he licked her fingers. The husky groan his reaction drew from her throat.

Oh, God. Now he was groaning, too, because this chocolate—her chocolate—was exquisite beyond any he'd ever tasted and he needed to suck every last drop from her fingers. He felt the shiver of her hunger vibrate out to her fingertips.

She was golden, honeyed perfection. He wanted more of her. All of her. He slid off the chair onto his knees.

"Monte?"

"Your chocolate was delicious, my darling, but I find myself in need of sweeter fare." His eyes sought hers, his breath catching at the desire shimmering in their depths. Smooth silk caressed his palms as his fingers curled under the hem of her skirt. "May I?"

## XXXII

# CARPE DIEM

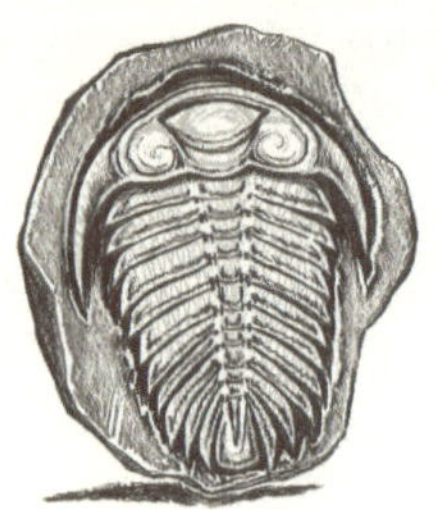

"**Y**ES, MONTE. PLEASE."

Those three words seemed to be the only ones she could remember how to say. She must have repeated them five times over, in varying orders. She couldn't recall. Her brain had wandered off somewhere. Scattered across the floor, perhaps, with her stockings and garters.

It didn't matter, anyway. Not when Monte was trailing scorching kisses along her bare legs, while his fingers did delicious things to her insides.

Now, without warning, he tugged her to the edge of the chair and put his mouth to her sex, tasting and teasing her right where she wanted it most. Astrid sagged against the back of the chair, rendered helpless by the sensual onslaught. His tongue swept a languorous circle over her clitoris, the slowest, dreamiest caress imaginable, as if he had all the time in the world to drive her out of her mind.

"Ernest," she gasped, adding the intimacy of his private name to this most intimate of acts.

"Sweeter than the chocolate," he murmured, then returned to his unhurried exploration of her person.

Astrid's fingers clutched at the sides of the chair, her only anchor in a churning sea of sensation. Her whole body twitched, tightening, yearning for release. Words tumbled from her mouth, begging him for more, for everything, until the orgasm took her in a perfect, shuddering storm.

Muscles unclenched. Her breath heaved in and out of her lungs, and her arms fell limply to her sides. She said his name again, a whispered exhalation of contentment.

Monte eased out from between her legs and rose, helping her up from the chair and guiding her toward the bed. His soft, cozy bed. It looked a lovely spot to curl up with him. Just the place for her still-trembling legs. When he lay her back and kissed her she could taste herself on his lips, the flavor strange and erotic.

"That, love, was only the first course." He crooked a finger through the neat bow tied between her breasts, tugging it loose, slipping the lace from the first of the hooks that ran down her bodice. "Convenient design."

"It's so I can be elegant and still dress myself."

"I love it." The fierceness of his voice caused another tremor inside her.

One-by-one he popped her laces free, his fingers criss-crossing down her chest, leaving a trail of heat everywhere they touched.

"And stiff boning," he observed. "Good support. Do you have a corset underneath?"

"No."

"Excellent."

He pried open the bodice, grinning his admiration of her filmy chemise. Hands cupped her breasts. His mouth came down to tease one nipple. Astrid threaded her fingers through his dark blond hair, loving the way it looked all tousled.

"Such a difficult choice you present," he said against her bosom.

"Hmm?"

"Do I stay and continue slowly undressing you, or do I leave that to you and go ready the potions."

Astrid dropped her hands to his shoulders and pushed him off. "Potions. Tonight you are ruining me once and for all."

Wicked pleasure glinted in his eyes. "As my lady desires."

She shimmied out of her skirts and her underthings while he gathered what he needed. Even naked her skin felt warm, her entire body humming with arousal. The air seemed to crackle with excitement. Soon, so soon, she would have him under her hands, over her body, and deep inside her.

Monte returned shortly, carrying a tray with two glasses of wine and two small, metal flasks. He paused a few steps from the bed to gaze down at her with his liquid silver eyes. His tongue ran over his lower lip.

"Damn, but I adore your body. I could make love to you every night and still never be satisfied."

Astrid could feel the blush racing down her neck and spreading across her chest. He hadn't even needed the words, delightful as they were. All he ever needed to do was look at her and she felt beautiful. Beautiful for her own self, tattoo and nose ring and round belly and all.

He set the tray on the bed beside her. "Your potions, my dear."

"Do they need to be mixed with wine?"

"No. They're prediluted. One swallow will last you a full twenty-four hours. Yours is the flask with the rose."

Astrid picked it up, uncapped it, and took a gulp. The potion had a slight citrusy tang, but otherwise seemed like plain water.

"So, no accidental children?"

"Exactly."

"And what is the second potion for?"

"Me." He opened it and took a sip. "The same thing, only formulated for a man."

"Are both potions necessary?"

"No. I just like to be extra careful." A shadow passed over his face. "There was a girl, once, who lived near me, and I adored her in that half-innocent way only a boy just beginning to grow to manhood can. Some bastard got her with child. People were cruel. She couldn't afford potions and died giving birth. It… left an impression. Now I give these potions out for free to anyone who asks for them."

Of course he did. Gracious, but he was a sweet thing. Always trying to do good, her Monte.

"That's very kind of you."

He shrugged, a bit of a faraway look still in his eyes, and she worried she may have ruined the mood.

"If that's all with the potions, then why the wine?" she asked.

His smile returned at once. "Ah. Well, you can drink it, if you like. Or we can play that game of yours we missed out on the other night." He dipped a finger into one of the glasses and flicked wine onto her chest. "How clumsy of me. I suppose I shall have to clean that up."

Astrid put out a hand to stop him. "Oh, no. Not yet. First you get out of those clothes. Fair is fair."

"Yes, ma'am."

It was remarkable, really, how quickly a gentleman bent on seduction could divest himself of his garments. In a trice, he was naked and atop her, licking away the droplets of wine and threatening to spill the rest of it across his sheets in his enthusiasm.

Astrid laughed and smeared the dry, red wine across his shoulder, his jaw, his arm, anywhere she could conveniently reach. When she had first thought of this, she had meant it to be seductive, but it was also fun and funny. They were grinning, laughing, teasing, and groping, all at once.

This was something she'd never anticipated. Sex wasn't only hot and hungry. It could be silly, cheerful, playful, joyous. And still hot. Her body was wild for him.

A laugh ringing in her ears, she pulled his mouth down to hers and kissed him as eagerly as she ever had. His hands raced across her skin, tracing her curves, delving between her legs to check she was ready for him. His rigid shaft rubbed against her thigh, eager to be inside her. She lifted her hips, yearning for him.

"Yes, please."

When he entered her with one swift thrust, it sent a wave of shock all the way up her spine. The sensation was tight and strange, not quite bad, but not good either. Until it was. Until it was better than good. Until all she could think of was the incredible feeling of him filling her, while his fingers and mouth touched her and coaxed all her mad cravings to the surface.

"Ernest," she moaned. "Oh, God, Ernest."

"I love the way you say my name," he purred, thrusting again, deeper, harder, making her back arch and her hands clutch at his shoulders. "I love everything about you. God, you are so fucking perfect."

He didn't even seem to notice his vulgar language. He just kept sliding. In her. With her. Astrid moved in time to his every thrust, straining for release with every muscle within her, climbing higher and higher until they were both soaring to new heights of pleasure, tumbling toward a wondrous crash. When the world shattered, she took Monte with her, feeling his tightening body, hearing his groan of ecstasy, unable to identify the place where her pleasure stopped and his began.

They collapsed together, sated and sweaty, arms wound tightly around one another. For several long seconds they lay there, too spent to separate, each content to bask in the warmth and comfort of the other.

Monte moved first, rolling over, and then settled her into the crook of his arm. His free hand brushed her hair back from her face.

"That, darling, is what I meant."

Astrid ran a finger over the tattoo on his arm. "It was a successful experiment, in my opinion."

"Very."

"We must be scientific about it, though," she said, trying her best to sound serious. "And I'm certain you know what that means."

"Yes." His grin was mischievous and laughing and as happy as she had ever seen. "Any good experiment is repeatable."

# XXXIII
# SCORCHING

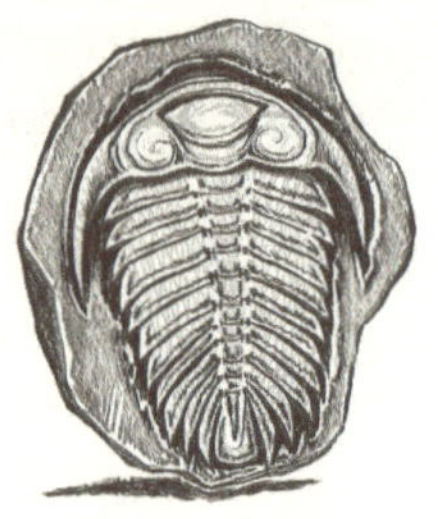

Sleep was impossible. Astrid dozed a bit, but they'd gone to bed so soon after dinner she wasn't yet truly sleepy, and her mind was abuzz with everything that had happened and the implications thereof.

*I am a worldly, sophisticated woman.*

She nearly laughed aloud. She wasn't sophisticated. She would forever be socially awkward, scientific, unladylike Astrid. And, somehow, that was fine.

Whom did she need to impress? Not Ayleston. She had his recommendation to the Institute. Her work spoke for itself. Her friends were odd enough to appreciate her eccentricities. Monte picked flowers for her, worshiped her body, and vowed to protect her like some absurd, medieval knight. She continued to grow more comfortable in her own skin. Slowly. It could be a lifelong process.

She was happy. That was all that truly mattered. Despite Marvale and his plots and threats, she continued to seize bits of joy in her unpredictable life.

This was one of those joys, this fascinating man at her side. Monte slept soundly, curled up against her. Any time she

290

moved he huddled closer. He was probably chilly. They hadn't lit a fire, and the apartment was cold. There was a draft coming from somewhere behind her, but she hadn't worked up the desire to check on it. Monte was too distracting.

She couldn't study his handsome figure beneath the blankets, but she could touch him all she wanted. He was hard and lean beneath his smooth skin, probably due to his austere diet and strict attention to maintaining bodily fitness. He tasted good. Or, at least the little exposed bit of his shoulder did. As good as his mouth and face and neck, and everywhere she'd kissed thus far. There was quite a lot of him left to explore.

She pressed her face close to him, inhaling deeply. He had an indefinable scent all his own, overlaid with the mingled smells of his soap and shaving lotion. A hint of lemon. A touch of something that reminded her of potions, a remnant of his experiments. A bit of… smoke?

Astrid sat up abruptly, her nose sniffing for the intrusive odor. Unmistakably smoke, and coming from somewhere near the window.

The curtain burst into flame, and she let out a shriek, shoving Monte so hard she nearly knocked him from the bed.

"Monte! Monte, wake up! Fire!"

"Fucking hell!" He scrambled from beneath the blankets, grabbed a nightshirt from a hook on the wall and flung it at her. "Get out! Get out now!"

Astrid yanked the garment on over her head, stuffing her feet into her boots while her eyes darted about the room, looking for anything she might wish to save. Monte's medical bag sat on the table, and she seized it in one hand. Across the room, flames crawled up the wall and slithered to the floor, spreading unnaturally fast. Fueled by a potion, perhaps, or a chemical accelerant. Arson.

"Go, go, go!" Monte pushed her toward the door. He had donned another ugly dressing gown and carried an armload of books.

Together they dashed out into the darkened streets of London, quiet at this hour in this neighborhood, the only two people moving in a sea of silence.

Monte thrust the books into her arms and pushed her toward the door of the next flat over. "Bang on that door until someone wakes up. Then alert the neighboring buildings."

Astrid fumbled with the armload, startled and confused, while he raced toward a third door, the one leading to the upper floor apartments. "Monte, wait. What?"

"Do it!" He vanished through the door, back into the burning building.

"Monte, no!" She took two steps after him before stopping herself. She had to alert the neighbors. He would be back. He would.

She pounded on the door, clutching the medical kit and the books in one arm. No answer came. She tried again, using her whole fist, hammering as hard as she was able. A third time. A fourth. Her bruised hand flew again, when the door at last swung inward.

"Fire," she gasped.

The inhabitants of the flat, a middle-aged man and his wife, hurried out to join her in the street, a box of valuables and a stack of photographs clutched in their hands.

"We must wake the neighbors," Astrid directed. "Alert the fire brigade."

They joined her in sounding the alarm, waking others and sending several boys running for help. Where was Monte? Astrid dumped her pile of his things on the curb and flung open the door to the upstairs, only to be met by a stampeding herd of children. Arms filled with dolls, books, food, and clothing, they tore down the stairs, followed by their pale, terrified parents. Monte wasn't with them.

Astrid grabbed the father's arm. "Where's Dr. Montford?"

"Helping Mrs. Adams. No, don't go in there. Young lady!"

She ignored the cries and flew through the door, her feet

pounding up the stairs. Acrid smoke pricked her eyes and burned her lungs. Hazy, sweltering air closed around her, obscuring her vision.

"Monte! Monte, where are you?"

"Goddammit, Astrid!"

The furious words were among the sweetest she had ever heard. He materialized in front of her, one arm around a stooped, white-haired woman, walking her down, step-by-step, his other arm struggling to contain a squirming lapdog.

"Astrid get out of here! The whole damn place could come tumbling down on you."

"Not without you." She yanked the dog from his arms, allowing him to pick up Mrs. Adams and run the rest of the way down and out into the safety of the night.

The inhabitants of the flaming building gathered together down the street, holding one another and their few prized belongings, watching everything else they owned go up in smoke. Astrid returned the yapping creature she had helped save to its owner, who settled the dog against her chest, petting its curly fur and quieting it with a gentle voice.

That task accomplished, Astrid turned a slow circle, feeling the need to do something, but uncertain what form that something might take.

"Sit." Monte's doctor voice was as commanding as she had ever heard. He pointed at the curb where she had dumped his books. His medical bag was in his hand, his stethoscope around his neck. "Don't get up. Don't run away. Don't try to do anything. Not until I have checked you."

"Checked? What?"

But he had already moved on, stooping to talk to his neighbors, looking into their eyes, listening to their breathing, asking after their health. Astrid sat beside the gaggle of jabbering children, gathered up Monte's books, and watched.

One-by-one, he moved down the line, treating every person who had been exposed to the fire, checking for burns, taking pulses, and distributing spoonfuls of healing potions. He was amazing. Gentle, yet authoritative. Thorough. Caring.

Astrid hugged her knees to her chest and looked over the books he had saved. His most treasured possessions. They were all novels. Not a single medical book, not even Dr. Harvey's text. These were stories of pirates, explorers, and adventurers. Well-loved volumes he must have read dozens of times over.

The flickering light from the burning building illuminated his profile. He knelt in the street in an appalling, paisley dressing gown, murmuring soothing words to a frightened little girl.

"That hurt in your chest that's making you cough, this potion will make that go away. One spoonful, no more."

"But I read in the papers 'bout how somebody got killed from drinking potions."

"That's not this. I would never give you anything dangerous. It's a vow one must take to become a doctor. To only help people."

"Does it taste bad?"

"Yes!" This from her unhelpful oldest brother.

"It does," Monte said, "but a brave girl can handle it, and I can tell you are especially brave."

She shook her head.

"Oh, you are. Being brave doesn't mean you're not afraid. It means you can be strong regardless." He handed her an empty spoon. "Here. You make certain your dolly takes her medicine, and I'll give you yours."

The girl swallowed her potion, and Astrid blinked away a tear. This was what he lived for. Helping people. Saving lives. Being a hero. He loved tales where good triumphed over evil and the world was saved. He might not be a world traveler who fended off pirates or a soldier fighting a dozen enemies barehanded, but he set out every day to make the world a better place. To care.

No wonder he was so determined to reform himself. So

frustrated by gossip and scandal. Astrid stared at the firefighters working to quell the blaze, not really seeing more than a blur. She had mocked all his complaints, not realizing how deeply the rumors pained him. And now, here she was, making it all worse. A blotch on his pristine reputation. Sitting in the street wearing nothing but his nightshirt. Anyone with a lick of sense would know exactly what they had been doing.

"Astrid, what's wrong? Are you hurt?"

Monte pressed the stethoscope to her chest. Lost in her thoughts, she hadn't even noticed him sit down beside her. Everyone was looking at her. At them. Formerly pale faces glowed with renewed color. The girl's coughing had subsided. Mrs. Adams was smiling and petting her little dog.

Astrid brushed his hand away. "I'm fine."

He thrust a spoonful of potion at her. "Drink this."

Astrid lifted her eyes to his. "Only if you do. Heroes need care, too."

"I'm not a hero."

"Yes, you are."

The girl tugged on his sleeve. "Dr. Montford? Are you scared to drink the potion like I was?"

"No, he's simply stubborn," Astrid replied.

He glared at her and swallowed the potion. "Happy?"

"Yes, actually."

He measured out another spoonful of thick, brown liquid and held it out to her. "Drink it."

The boy was right. It tasted awful. But it did ease the lingering discomfort in her chest.

"Dr. Montford?" the girl asked again.

"Yes?"

"Who is that lady?"

*Oh, no.*

Dozens of answers flitted through Astrid's head at once. *My whore.* No, never. *My mistress.* Not in front of children. *My friend.* Safe enough, but an obvious lie. *Lady Astrid Wembley, sister to the Marquess of Whitehaven.* Scandalous. *Famous opera singer Signora Fiori.* Silly.

"My wife. You may address her as Lady Astrid or simply 'my lady.'"

Astrid fought to wipe the look of shock from her face. Of all the things he might have said, that one would have never occurred to her.

"Oh, so that's why you've been away so long," the oldest boy remarked. "You were getting married."

Monte avoided another outright lie. "I've spent most of my time with Lady Astrid's family."

It was a plausible story. It avoided scandal. Protected both her reputation and his. But what would happen after she was gone? How would he explain? It made her queasy to think about. She had brought all this trouble down on him.

The rumble of a carriage over the cobblestones caused her to look up. The resplendent Vayne coach pulled up beside the bedraggled crew, eliciting gasps from the adults and shouts of excitement from the children. Tricia stepped down, looking shockingly elegant given the rush and the late hour.

"Monte. Astrid." She hurried to grasp both their hands. "I'm so relieved to find you well. I came as soon as I heard. I will, of course, put you both up for the night. What else can I do to help?"

Monte nudged Astrid toward the carriage. "You should go. I need to help everyone find shelter for the night, and then I will join you."

"How many are we?" Tricia asked before Astrid could protest.

"Mr. and Mrs. Cole and Mrs. Adams makes three," Monte replied. "Six in the Mason family. An even dozen with you, Astrid, and I."

"The carriage seats six. We will need to make two trips, but I have room in the house for you all."

Amidst the flurry of "thank yous" and "oh, we couldn't possiblys," Astrid pulled Monte aside.

"I'm so sorry."

He pulled her into his arms. "No, darling, don't blame yourself. I know you suspect foul play, but the men who did this deserve the blame. You're a victim, not a culprit."

"No. I mean, yes. That's not what I was talking about. I'm sorry for un-reforming you. For putting you at risk for more scandals. For making you have to lie to these good people."

His grip relaxed, and he leaned back just enough to look her straight in the eye.

"Ah."

The single syllable hung in the air between them. Awkward. Painful. Unable to stand the silence, Astrid opened her mouth to speak, but Monte stopped her with a finger to her lips.

"I think I finally understand why you reject all my apologies. Now I'm rejecting yours. Don't be sorry. I'm not."

He walked her to the carriage, helping her climb inside with the other ladies and the two youngest children. The men and the older boys watched and waited. Before Monte released her, he pressed a kiss to the back of her hand.

"Goodnight, my lady."

The carriage door swung closed and the vehicle lurched forward. Astrid slumped against the cushions, exhausted, her emotions in a tangle.

"Well," Mrs. Adams said, fingers stroking her curly-haired mutt, "it's about time that boy brought home a nice girl. Smart, tough, kind. Much better than all those hussies he used to bed. I hope he keeps you."

# XXXIV
# PARTY PLANNERS

"**O**NE WOULD THINK IT WAS Christmas time, with all this cooking and cleaning and decorating." Lady Whitehaven's eyes followed yet another member of her domestic staff scurrying by with an armload of ribbons. She frowned. "It's not Christmas time, is it?"

"No. Nearing All Hallows Eve."

"Of course."

This was as lucid as Monte had seen the dowager marchioness. The fact she had even come into the drawing room this afternoon spoke for itself. His potions were helping. Well, not *his*, precisely. He'd adapted the recipe from Dr. Harvey. Besides being an astounding nutritionist, the man was a leader in the drive to stem the rampant overuse of opiates. Monte was determined to write him again once all the scandals had died down.

He'd begun to question the doctor's views on limiting sexual intimacies, however. Monte couldn't keep his hands off Astrid. During the last three days he'd kissed her in nearly every room in this enormous house, fondled her in almost as many places, and spent every night in bed with her. All it had

298

done was leave him happy and energized. And hungry for more.

"I'm glad Astrid will have a party to attend," Lady Whitehaven continued. "I worry for her. She worked so hard to be social during her Season, but she never managed to attract the right sort of people. She never once complained, though we could tell she was unhappy. That's why we never pushed her to try again. But she meets so few men and women her own age now, and I can't bear to see her lonely."

"She isn't. She has lovely friends."

"I do hope she has fun at this party. You will dance with her, Dr. Montford? She loves to dance, but she will never go looking for gentlemen to fill her dance card. You must set the example."

"It would be my pleasure."

"Thank you. Do you think you might walk me to my room? I have quite exhausted myself."

Monte took hold of the marchioness's arm and helped her from the couch. Too thin, this woman. He would give the cook a few recommendations for simple ways they might pad her diet.

Despite her illness, Lady Whitehaven was a striking woman. Her daughter's opposite in body shape, but with an equally beautiful face. The same cheekbones, same nose, same crystal blue eyes. The resemblance was unmistakable.

"Did I tell you, young man, how I came to live in this country?"

Monte smiled. "You did, my lady. Your father was an ambassador, and you met a young man during your year in London."

"I did. It was so fortunate when I happened to miss that train on our way home to discover he was staying in the area. He was generous enough to get me a room at his hotel."

Polite words for, "We moved in together." It had been an enormous scandal. Monte had found newspaper clippings about it in the library, right beside the wedding announcements and mentions of Astrid and Cal's birth. It was also one of the reasons certain people regarded Astrid with suspicion. She wasn't the first bold, independent woman in the family.

"You find yourself a love match, young man. No money, no title, nothing at all can compare to that."

"I believe you." If only Astrid weren't put off by the idea of marriage. If only she felt the way he did.

"Remind me to mention it to Astrid and Frederick before this party begins. They might meet a special someone." She paused and closed her eyes. "What were we speaking of?"

Monte helped her into her room, where her lady's maid waited to assist her into bed. "Many things, Lady Whitehaven. Don't fret if you don't recall them. We shall speak again soon. Rest well."

He checked his watch. Forty-five minutes out of her bedchamber, including rational conversation. It was worth reporting to Astrid. Each bit of improvement lessened the weight on her shoulders.

He found her and Lady Ophelia in the laboratory with piles of hairpins, practicing picking locks on the doors and cabinets. Miss Fairfax sat at Astrid's desk, organizing papers.

"Interesting research," he commented dryly.

Astrid dropped the pins she was holding. "Bugger! Now I shall have to start all over again. Why did you have to sneak in here, Monte?"

"I thought practicing stealth might be a wise plan, since it seems we will be engaging in some criminal enterprise in the near future."

She hadn't said a word to him regarding her intention to rescue Lady Ophelia's friend from the asylum. He suspected her of wanting to protect him.

"I can't imagine why you would think that."

"Oh, Astrid, don't be silly," Grace sighed. "It's obvious he knows what you're planning. What's the point in pretending? Why don't you simply talk to him?"

"Have you talked to Cal? Or are you both pretending nothing is happening?"

Grace stood abruptly. "Excuse me."

Astrid's shoulders slumped as she watched her friend leave. "Oh, Monte, I don't know what to do. They're both so miserable. And so stubborn."

"That trait is endemic to this house. Why do you insist upon doing this?" He gestured at her makeshift lockpicks.

Astrid gave him a look of exasperation.

"We can't leave Beth there." Ophelia's voice was soft, shy, but determined. She glanced up at him for only an instant before returning to her task.

"Exactly," Astrid agreed. "Nor the other women. We must rescue them and expose the asylum for what it is."

Monte rubbed his temple, another headache growing. "Didn't Tricia enlist some friend of her uncle's to undertake the task for you?"

"Ayleston's man is unavailable. His wife recently gave birth and he is needed at home."

"I see. And you intended to keep me in the dark about your plans?"

Astrid glared at him in silence.

"She did," Ophelia murmured, still looking down at her own lock.

"Why?"

Astrid's jaw clenched. "Because I knew you would object."

"Damn right I object!" Monte shouted.

"You think it's too dangerous."

"Yes!" He threw up his hands. He couldn't convince her. He knew he couldn't, but neither could he stop himself trying.

"You don't think I'm competent enough—"

"You are entirely too competent!" he interrupted "That's the trouble. You do whatever you set your mind to. And in this instance, you've set your mind to breaking into an enemy stronghold. That building is full of who knows what horrible things. And horrible people! I'm certain they've added guards. Even if Fawdry is too fixated on making illegal potions to pay attention, Marvale knows how bold you are."

She folded her arms beneath her breasts. "So I should do nothing, then."

"I didn't say that."

"But you will try to stop me."

"I didn't say that, either." Monte didn't think he stood a snowball's chance in hell of stopping her. She would sneak out without him. That was what truly terrified him. That she would put herself in danger and he wouldn't even know until it was too late. "Please. Let me help."

"Help?" She stared at him, and even Ophelia looked up.

"I can make potions. Defensive potions to fend off attackers. Health potions to protect us from anything harmful we might breathe in or touch. Potions to counteract the drugs those women have been given. I can make an antidote to that opiate potion. I will need to steal a few drops of your mother's laudanum to do it."

"I don't think she'll notice."

"No. Actually, I came here to tell you how well she was doing. She's resting now, but she spent the better part of an hour speaking with me in the drawing room."

"Oh. Thank you." Astrid's eyes shone with fragile hope, her smile wavering slightly. "Every little bit you do for her means so much to us. I will make certain you receive full compensation for all your time."

"No. Please. There's no charge." *No charge for family.*

"Don't be ridiculous. This is how you make your living. We've kept you from it far too long already. How much has Cal been paying you?"

"Nothing. I've asked for nothing, and I will turn down anything he offers."

"What? Monte."

Lady Ophelia climbed to her feet and inched toward the door. "I should… go. Now. Excuse me." She dashed from the room, closing the door behind her.

"Monte, you can't be doing all this work and not be paid for it."

"I'm not here to work. I'm here…" *For you.* "Because I want to be here."

"You deserve something. We're interfering with your life." *You* are *my life.*

Oh, God. He was so far gone, and he didn't know whether to spill his heart out to her or to continue suffering in silence. How did other men handle this? Had Cal spilled his heart to Miss Fairfax? He may well have done. And now he was on the cusp of losing her forever.

"It's no trouble."

Silence. Suffering. Like a proper gentleman.

Astrid was having none of it. "Oh, of course. No trouble. It's not like you had your flat burned to the ground a few days ago. Or dueled a ruffian in broad daylight."

"For the last time, it was not—"

"A goddamned duel. Yes, I know."

"Could we talk about something else, please?" His eyes darted about the room for something to save him, and to his amazement, something did. "Say, is that the entire collection of *The Comprehensive Guide to Medicinal and Potional Uses of the Flowers of the British Isles?*"

She twisted to follow his gaze. "Er, yes. My parents did a lot of botany. But it's out-of-date. From at least ten years ago, maybe more."

"No matter." Monte brushed past her, reaching for the thick index volume. "The information I need shouldn't have changed in that time. I've been meaning to look up a few things related to the experiments I've been doing." He opened the book to find a small flower pressed between the pages. "What's this?"

Astrid reached to take the book from him, but he turned away, flipping more pages, finding flower after flower carefully preserved.

"It's full of flowers," she blurted. "I'm sorry. I didn't think anyone would need it."

The front cover fell open, and a paper fluttered out. Astrid snagged it out of the air and placed it back into the book. His own handwriting stared up at him.

"These are my flowers?"

"Yes."

"How many?"

"Dozens. One from every bouquet."

He swore softly. "I thought you didn't care for them."

"I loved them."

"Do you save Smyth's flowers too?"

She shook her head. "Only these."

"Why?" Monte's palms were sweating so badly he thought he might drop the book. He closed it and stuffed it back onto the shelf. "What makes my sad little flowers special?"

"You picked them all yourself. It must have taken an hour."

"More than."

"You told me I deserved them. Simply for being me."

He seized her hand. "You did. You do. Why the devil haven't I brought you flowers every day? Or chocolates? Or taken you to the theater?"

"Because we've been worrying about asylums and murderers?"

"Because I'm a bloody fool."

She flattened her free hand on his chest. "No. You are sweet. You scare off fortune hunters and spies. You punched a man for me. You fought a duel while protecting me."

"I was stalking you, and it wasn't—"

She pressed a finger to his lips. "Shut up and kiss me, Monte."

He did, losing himself in her unsurpassable sweetness. Mere moments passed before he had her up against the bookshelf, kissing her as if his life depended on it, hiking up her skirts while she fumbled with the fastenings on his trousers.

"Astrid, darling." She wasn't wearing any drawers, the saucy wench. As if she had been anticipating this. "Oh, fuck, Astrid, I want you so much."

She had torn off his necktie and her mouth was all over his throat, sucking greedily, branding his skin. "You have… a very… naughty mouth."

"Yes. What shall I do with it today?"

The door opened.

Monte froze.

"You son of a bitch!"

Monte scrambled to put his clothing to rights. Astrid, predictably, jumped between him and Cal.

"Don't you dare touch him!"

Cal's furious gaze swept past her. "I trusted you, you bastard!" Pain sparked behind the anger in his blue eyes. Betrayal. Monte's chest ached.

Astrid stormed toward her brother, glaring up at him, her ferocity undiminished by her short stature. "This is none of your business."

"None of my business? I am the head of this family."

"Please," she scoffed. "I'm five minutes older than you, Cal. I'm a grown woman who can make her own choices. You have no right to tell me what to do."

"I have every right! I am the Marquess of Whitehaven, and I am responsible for every man, woman, and child in this household, not to mention those in the village and in all the surrounding areas. It is my duty to protect you all."

"I don't need protecting."

"Obviously you do!"

"Why? Because I'm a 'Lady'? Because I must preserve my virtue so it can be sold to the highest bidder?"

"I would never!"

"You're a hypocrite, Cal. You sneak around with Grace for three years, and for what? So you can thrust her aside for someone 'better'? That's appalling."

His features contorted in pain. "It's not like that."

"Oh? Then what is it like?"

He looked away from her, staring at some unknown spot beyond the wall. "I have duties. Responsibilities. You don't know, Astrid. You don't know the expectations and the necessities of my position."

"What horse shit. Either you're too cowardly to stand up to society's expectations, or you don't really love her."

Cal's face had gone a ghostly white. "You don't understand."

"Get the hell out of my laboratory, and get the hell away from Grace. You don't deserve her."

The siblings stared at one another, all six feet plus of Cal withering beneath his sister's censorious gaze.

"You're right." His voice was quiet, and deadly calm. "I don't. Excuse me." He turned and strode off, but not before Monte caught a glimpse of the utter devastation etched on his face.

Monte spun toward Astrid. "Does your brother have a gun?"

"What?"

"Does he?"

"Er, yes. Hunting rifles, of course, and a pistol in his study, I believe." When Monte whirled to leave, she grabbed his arm. "You can't think he would—"

"That man has been on the verge of a nervous breakdown for months now. I won't chance it. Please excuse me."

He took the stairs to his room two at a time, grabbed a potion, then raced back down, jumping the last several stairs, ignoring the faces of the staff gaping at his wild behavior and state of dishabille. He flew through the door of the study, not bothering to knock.

Cal sat at his desk, his head in his hands. He didn't look up.

"Give me the gun."

"Monte," Cal sighed.

"Give it to me."

Slowly, Cal's eyes lifted to meet Monte's. He opened a drawer and extracted a small revolver, sliding it across the desk. "It's not loaded."

Monte snatched it up regardless and tucked it into his pocket.

"I'm not stupid, Monte. I know how I can get. The ammunition is locked away. Only Crippens has the key. I'm not going to off myself, in any case." His gaze dropped back down to the desk. "Though I'm still debating whether to murder you."

Monte flattened his hands on the desk, leaning toward his friend, speaking softly. "Would it help if I told you I love her?"

Cal didn't look up. "Maybe today you do. What about next week? Three months from now? You can't undo this, Monte. How is she supposed to find a husband?"

"She has stated in no uncertain terms she has no intention of marrying."

"And what of her recommendation to the Institute? Ruin her reputation and she might lose her place."

A seething fury built in Monte's chest. "No man would lose his place due to such an affair, and neither should she."

Cal breathed a heavy sigh of despair. "That's not how the world works."

Monte slammed a fist against the tabletop. "The world is wrong, goddammit!"

Cal jumped at the outburst, and his head jerked up. Wide blue eyes locked with Monte's, commiserating in silence.

"Yes," he said at last. "It is. But we have to live in it."

Monte leaned in closer still, reaching across the wide desk to grasp Cal's hand. Forget gentlemanly behavior. They were a team. Inseparable. "We can change it."

Cal chuckled mirthlessly. "How do you propose we do that?"

He gave Cal's hand a squeeze. "You can start by marrying Miss Fairfax."

"I wish I could."

"I understand the process to be relatively straightforward. Post the banns, go to church, say your vows. Done."

"But what of the consequences, Monte? The gossip. The scandal. How can I bring that upon my family, especially after all that has happened with Astrid? I have a duty to them. I have a duty to the people that rely on the reputation and prosperity of this estate. My ancestors were an odd bunch. Hermits, eccentrics, wastrels. There's a reason we have a reputation for madness. The estate suffered for their peculiarities. My father worked his entire life to undo the damage and to make it what it is today. I can't destroy his legacy. I can't put my own selfish desires ahead of my responsibilities. I've already made such a mess of things. We're in all the papers. The whispers of madness are worse than ever. I can't even prevent my best friend from ruining my sister."

Cal pulled away, slumped in his chair, and squeezed his eyes shut. His mouth twisted in an expression of physical pain.

Monte started for the liquor cabinet. "Let me get you a drink."

"Doesn't help. You know that. You're a doctor."

Monte poured himself a glass of brandy and Cal a glass of water and brought them both to the desk. Taking the potion from his pocket, he added three drops to the water before handing it to his friend.

"Drink up."

Cal cocked a blond eyebrow. "What is it?"

"Something to settle your nerves. I've been working on it for… well, since we were seventeen, to be honest."

"All this time? For me?"

"Of course for you. At first I thought I would make a cure, but that's proven impossible so far. I switched to focusing on the symptoms, and I think this will help. I hope it will."

"I've tried all the therapies, Monte, I really have. Nothing has been working. Not even the meditation. It's all too much. I can't live up to all the expectations."

"You don't have to. We're all here to help. Now, drink." Cal drained the glass and Monte set the potion bottle in front of him. "Three drops to one glass of water. When it gets like this, where you can't function."

"How soon should I expect to feel better?"

"I have no idea. This is all an experiment."

"Oh, so I'm at the mercy of a mad scientist?" A trace of levity in his tone suggested to Monte the potion's effect began within seconds. "Or have I just been poisoned? I should have known better than to trust the backstabbing knave who can't keep his filthy hands off my sister. You promised, Monte. You vowed not to touch her."

"I didn't know she was your sister."

"What are you talking about? Didn't I introduce you and say, 'This is my sister, Astrid'?"

"Long before that. Years ago. When I met her down by the beach."

Cal's big eyes looked even larger for the shock. "Years ago? Oh, God. Are you telling me *Astrid* was your mystery girl? The one you were so obsessed with you had to look for her every time we came near this part of the country? You went on and on about her lips and her…" Cal cringed. "Eew, Monte, she's my sister. That's revolting!"

"Not to me."

"God." He rubbed his temple. "Go on out of here, Monte, before I decide to murder you after all. Your poison seems to be working, so you needn't check back until it's killed me. In the meantime, I have a mess of correspondence to attend to, and four new bicycles to inspect."

"Bicycles?"

"My esteemed sister has decided to host a sporting competition as part of the house party. It was my fault. She handles household accounts and approves things such as purchases of food and other necessities. I gave her free rein to buy all decorations and supplies for the party. She decided a bicycle race was a necessity."

"It sounds better than Charades."

"Oh, good, you'll participate then? You can show off for the ladies."

"There's only one lady for whom I wish to show off."

"Stop, please. Don't touch her again. I'm still trying to scrub the image from my mind. Honestly. In the middle of the day? Up against a bookcase? You're such a rake, Monte."

"So your sister tells me."

Cal shook his head. "Right. You stop touching Astrid and help me with all these ridiculous games she's coming up with, and I think maybe everything will work out. My only other concern is Marvale."

Every muscle in Monte's body clenched. "Marvale is coming here?"

"He's a neighbor. I did consider not inviting him after how he treated her at the last event, but Astrid insisted."

Monte flexed his fingers. Cal would look just right with a broken nose and blood running all down his front. "That man will be here. Living under the same roof."

"Astrid said she felt more comfortable knowing where he was and what he was doing."

Monte leaned over the desk once more, glaring down at his friend. "You ought to have refused."

"One does not simply refuse Astrid, as I imagine you are aware."

All too aware.

"That man is a danger to her. I should have your head for this."

"And I should have yours for dishonoring her." Cal shuffled through papers, selecting one and turning it so Monte could read it. "Astrid's sporting competition. Bicycle race, beach running, rock climbing, stick fencing, and various other feats of strength and skill. I will meet you on the field of battle." Cal stood, straightening his shoulders, the marquess once again. He extended his hand. "May the best man win."

"Fuck you, Whitehaven. You know I don't stand a chance."

"Beat me at any event and I will cease pestering you about Astrid."

Monte grasped his hand. "Consider it done. Now, if you'll excuse me, I must go shout at her for letting that man come here."

"Good luck. I'll send along a chaperone."

"Go to hell."

"I'll meet you there."

The banter cut straight to Monte's heart. The potion worked. It had brought Cal some measure of relief from the melancholia. He paused in the doorway.

"I love you, Cal." Maybe it was better to say it aloud after all. "I'll always be here for you. My feelings for Astrid haven't changed that. I would propose to her, if I thought she would have me. Regardless, I will love her until the day I die. I will never be the same man I once was. Please excuse me."

# XXXV
# PLAYING GAMES

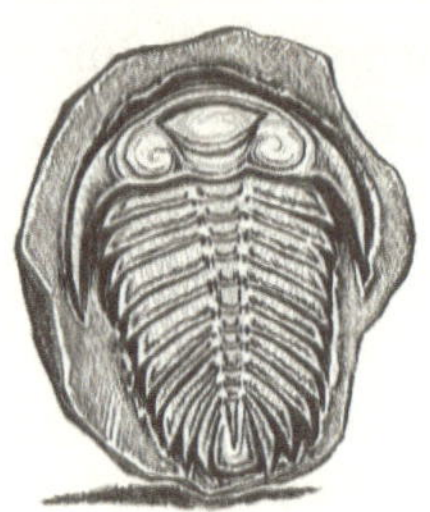

Astrid toyed with the silk flower pinned to her dress. Would anyone notice if she happened to knock the pin out and lose the embarrassing thing? Everyone, probably. It was a big, bright red rose. Curse Grace and her ridiculous prize idea.

Giving the winner of each contest a flower had seemed perfectly reasonable until Cal had chivalrously handed over his beach running prize to Lady Arabella Hetherington. Ever since, all the gentlemen had bestowed their winnings on their chosen victims. Two other ladies wore her brother's prizes for cliff climbing and stick fencing. Perhaps it had been a mistake to base so many events around their childhood games.

And then Smyth had won the bicycle race.

Naturally, he had presented his fake rose to Astrid with a bow and a flourish, and now she was stuck wearing it while everyone looked at her and whispered. Why had he done that? She'd told him they could only be friends, but during the two days of the house party he had been courting her more ardently than ever. Marvale watched the whole thing with a sneer on his face, probably hoping she would make a fool of herself and put her position at the Institute in jeopardy. It would save him the trouble of murder, and he struck her as the sort of man who preferred a tidy solution. If he had noticed "Mr. Thompson" the bodyguard watching him, he had given no indication.

Cal fiddled with a bit of ivy in the silk flower basket. "I propose we give out flowers to the winners of tonight's indoor games, as well. The ladies have had no chances to win, and that seems grossly unfair. What do you all think?"

He was met with a chorus of approval, Astrid among the voices. Maybe Monte would be able to win something at last.

For someone who took regular exercise and had once carried her up a flight of stairs, he was appallingly bad at sporting contests. He'd put up a good showing in the stick fencing, until Cal disarmed him in the final bout with two quick flicks of the wrist. In all the other events he'd been soundly defeated.

This evening, after a spectacular crash during the bicycle race, he sported yet another colorful bruise on his face and held his left arm gingerly. Stubborn man he was, he wouldn't hear of taking a healing potion.

He did have a knack for puzzles and guessing games, however. He'd been among the best at Twenty Questions, and no one would play Dictionary with him any longer, after he'd trounced them all several times over. If Cal had awarded flowers for those games, perhaps Astrid would have another one to wear.

Or perhaps not. Monte hadn't so much as touched her since Cal had caught them tearing at one another's clothing in the laboratory. He'd been too busy striving—and failing—to assert his manliness through games of sport. He looked at her though, and often. With that all-over gaze that heated her skin and turned her brain to jelly. Her performance during the guessing games had been less than stellar.

"We will start with riddles, and see where that takes us," Cal declared. "I will begin. 'Three little letters, a paradox to some. The worse that it is, the better it becomes.'"

"Pun," Grace replied immediately.

*Cheaters.* Grace knew Cal too well and shared his love of wordplay. That answer was far too obvious.

"Very good, Miss Fairfax. Would you be so kind as to supply us the next riddle?"

"Halo of water, tongue of wood, skin of stone, long I've stood. My fingers short reach to the sky. Inside my heart men live and die."

*Castle.*

Astrid had heard that one before and didn't answer, giving the others time to figure it out. She had no desire to win. Having to select and bestow a flower would be even more embarrassing than wearing one.

It took no more than a dozen riddles to make it clear this game would be a tight contest between Grace and Monte. Even Lord Ayleston, who was a riddling sort of man, couldn't keep up. Skipping over riddles they already knew was of limited help. They each possessed an uncanny knack for puzzling out unfamiliar riddles.

"I'm running out of riddles," Grace declared when it looked as though the rest of the party was growing bored. "I shall have to write new ones if we are ever to play again. This one is simple, but it's all I can come up with. 'If you cut my head, I become a lord. If you cut my tail, I'm fruit. If you cut both, I'm with you. What am I?'"

Monte thought for a moment. "A pearl. Earl, pear, ear. I, too am running out of puzzles. I'll leave you one more, and if you can answer it before the others, I shall concede the victory to you."

She nodded. "Let's have it."

He cleared his throat and spoke, looking not at Grace, but at Astrid. "If you break me, I do not stop working."

Astrid sucked in a breath. She knew this riddle.

"If you touch me, I may be snared."

His gray eyes bored into her. His voice was deep and husky.

No. He wasn't directing this at her. He wouldn't. Not in front of all these people. That was a scandalous, rakish thing to do, and he was reformed.

"If you lose me, nothing will matter."

Astrid shivered.

"Heart," Grace answered, her voice softer than was her custom. "Too easy."

"Congratulations, Miss Fairfax." Monte's gaze hadn't wavered. "Please choose a flower and bestow it where you will."

Grace plucked the bit of ivy Cal had been toying with and handed it to him. "For choosing my favorite game and suggesting the prizes. You have my thanks, Lord Whitehaven."

"My pleasure, Miss Fairfax."

His eyes were locked on Grace in a fashion eerily similar to Monte's. Astrid longed for a fan to cool her flushed cheeks, but she didn't carry one as a matter of course. Her pulse raced. A hand touched her elbow and she jumped.

"Excuse me, Lady Astrid," Smyth said. "I hoped you might join my team for Charades. I expect you to be an excellent performer. I think together we will have a good chance to win a flower or two."

"Oh. Um. Yes, that would be lovely." Ugh. Parties. Why did people enjoy events where one was obliged to accept a man's invitation or be counted unforgivably rude?

Enough alcohol had circulated through the room for the guests to feel relaxed and amiable, and the group plunged into the next game with vigor. Astrid passed on all food and drink. She'd been selective and sparing at dinner. There would be no repeat of Marvale's hallucinatory potion tonight. Her stomach was gurgling something fierce.

A drink to calm her nerves would have been welcome. She hadn't felt so on display since her Season. Everyone supposed it was Astrid, smiling and participating in the games, but this was as much an act as Signora Fiori had been, and she feared the brittle facade would crack under all the scrutiny.

She wished she could sit quietly in a corner with a book, like Ophelia had done most of the evening. But the life of a wallflower wasn't possible for Astrid tonight. Not at her own party, while under the shadow of a deadly intrigue.

Smyth hovered, polite and gentlemanly, but his eyes always on her. Marvale chatted with Ayleston as if they were old friends, both men more interested in Astrid than one another. And Thompson watched them all, weapons likely at the ready.

She could handle their attentions. It was Monte's behavior she thought might break her. All evening he flirted with the ladies, laughing and flattering them, using the games to make comments and double entendres just short of scandalous. Comments directed at *her*.

Was she imagining things? Perhaps she read too much into the little flicks of his eyes in her direction. Perhaps he only looked at her because she was staring. And yet, with every innuendo she overheard she caught him looking past his companions. Catching her eye. Melting her with the power of his smolder.

"You seem distracted, Lady Astrid."

Marvale's frosty voice cut like a winter wind, and she suppressed a shiver. How had he gotten so close without her noticing? Was Thompson nearby? Why hadn't she thought to hide a knife in her bodice?

"For a woman who professes unladylike tendencies, you appear to have attracted some surprisingly ardent admirers."

Astrid turned to face him, more comfortable when she could see his hands. She estimated the distance between her knee and his groin and gauged her ability to bring the two together while hampered by her fashionable skirts. She was short and the evening dress left her arms free. A downward punch might prove more effective.

"I beg your pardon, Lord Marvale, but that sounded to my ears like an insult. I do hope that isn't the case, as I would hate to have to turn you out of my home."

"On the contrary. It was merely an observation that your behavior is at odds with your prior assertions. After all, what could be more feminine than toying with the affections of multiple gentlemen? Classic womanly wiles."

Astrid's leg twitched. If ever a man deserved a knee to the privates, it was he. If it weren't for the audience, he would be writhing on the floor and she would be enjoying every second of it.

"I believe this conversation is at an end. Good evening."

"You are flirting with scandal, Lady Astrid," he said to her retreating back, loud enough for several others to overhear.

Astrid struggled with many of the mannerisms of gently-bred ladies, but she knew how to spurn an offensive man. She strode away with her head held high and inserted herself into the game Monte and his crowd of ladies were playing. Her dour mood served her well, and she was very near to becoming the last person to crack a smile until Monte leaned close and whispered, "Shall I strangle Marvale with his own necktie, or use mine?"

She laughed, and Lady Ophelia took the prize. Ophelia plucked a flower from the basket and handed it to Monte, the only man she had actually spoken to outside of the games. When not putting on a performance, Astrid's friend was painfully shy.

She also looked exhausted. Astrid looped her arm through Ophelia's. "I can't believe how late it's gotten."

"Indeed. I find I have grown quite weary. Would you be so good as to walk me to my room? I should hate to go astray in this large house."

Monte gave them a nod and a knowing look. They had all agreed to go nowhere alone. His eyes drifted across the room. Searching out enemies. "Sleep well, ladies."

Astrid inclined her head. "Goodnight, Dr. Montford. We will just say goodnight to a few more friends, and then we will be on our way."

It took several minutes to take their leave of Ayleston and Grace, who were bandying about ideas for advertising Astrid's first geological lecture. Cal was at cards with Lady Arabella and her parents and could no more than turn for a quick peck on the cheek. Astrid let her finger brush over the ivy pinned to his lapel. She took it to be a good sign when his eyes turned at once to Grace.

Astrid looked around for Tricia, only to spy her slipping from the room on Monte's arm, their heads bent together in a conspiratorial manner. Lovers bound for a tryst, everyone would assume. They were drawing the gossip away from Astrid and onto themselves. Good people. Devoted friends. She could want for no better allies.

Monte awaited her outside her bedroom, lounging against the wall, legs crossed at the ankles.

"Door's locked."

"Of course it is. Isn't yours?"

"It is, and I appear to have misplaced my key. I don't know what to do about it."

"My cue to leave," Ophelia said. She gave Astrid a squeeze and scampered a few doors down to her own bedchamber.

"Didn't you conceal your key on your person as I did?" Astrid fished in her bodice for her own key, enjoying the hungry look this brought to Monte's face.

"I believe I did. Would you help me look for it?"

"It's the least I could do. Won't you come in?"

They slipped inside and she locked the door behind them. Monte grabbed a chair and wedged it underneath the handle.

"Did Marvale threaten you?"

"Indirectly. I think he wishes to destroy my reputation. Murder will be his last resort."

"A logical plan. The more crimes he commits or instigates, the greater the odds he'll be caught. Better to rid himself of you another way."

"I expect him to try to tarnish my name at the masquerade

tomorrow night. With four times our current number in attendance, word of any scandal will spread far and fast."

Monte frowned. "Do you want me to leave? I will suffer another night without you to help protect you."

"No. Please stay. We've been overly long apart. I felt I was staring at you altogether too much this evening."

His mouth ticked up. "I liked it. You were radiant tonight."

"It was all an act. I wanted to roll my eyes at all the casual chatter and kick Marvale in the bollocks. Instead, I had to play perfect lady. It was exhausting."

"Then we'd best get you to bed at once." He slipped his arms around her waist. "You would have looked beyond radiant crushing that man's testicles. Go ahead and do it next time. I will gaze at you in adoration and praise your beguiling courage to all my lady friends. It will become the fashion to give bastards their due."

"You are a silly man." She looked up at him with an affectionate smile and brushed her fingers across his cheek.

Monte played with the silk rose on her chest. "I'm sorry I was unable to win you a flower. I did try."

Her thumb grazed his latest bruise. "I know. You did win at Dictionary, before Cal declared there should be indoor game prizes."

"That's because I have an unnaturally large vocabulary and extensive knowledge of Latin and Greek. It's the result of my profession."

"Ah, but you also have enough mischief in you to invent clever and enticing false definitions." Her lips skimmed over his. "You needn't win anything for me. I prefer your kisses to any flower."

They moved toward the bed, discarding clothing with each step. Monte flopped onto the bed and Astrid straddled him, licking her lips as she gazed upon his nude form.

His hands grasped her hips. "I would rather win you than all the prizes in the world."

*Win me as a lover? You've done that. Win my heart?*

Butterflies danced in her stomach.

*Have I won yours?*

Those questions were too heavy to contemplate on a night such as this, so she distracted herself by bending over him for a long and thorough kiss.

"Come and claim me, then," she breathed.

His smoky gaze caressed her. "It would be my pleasure."

# XXXVI
# VOULEZ-VOUS DANSER

*A* GENTLEMAN DOES NOT *answer the door half-naked.*

The knock came again, more urgently.

Monte moved toward the door, buttoning up his trousers as he went. No one in this house considered him a proper gentleman, did they? Not after all the scandals in the papers and three days of non-stop flirtations. If he were wrong about his visitor, it would just be one more blurb for the gossip sheets. He no longer cared. Since having his flat burned to the ground, he'd been doing some deep thinking. He wouldn't be going back to London.

*Thud. Thud. Thud.*

"For the love of God, Astrid, I'm coming."

He yanked open the door and froze. It was, fortunately, Astrid standing there, dressed in the most astounding gown he had ever seen. The cream-colored fabric clung to her breasts and hips, displaying them to their full advantage, and the neckline was deliciously low. It was the embroidery, however, that left him stunned.

An ocean floor had been stitched all along the hem and down the train. Intricately sewn ripples of sand pooled at her feet, swaying with her every movement. Among the needlework rocks and plants were dozens of trilobites, miniature to large, each one a scientifically accurate rendering of a specimen or photo from her laboratory. More trilobites trailed up the dress in an S-curve that swung across the skirt, over her hip, and around to end beneath her breasts with a jeweled *terataspis*. Never had a spiny, multi-legged beast looked so beautiful. Never had a dress screamed its owner's name with such clarity.

"Astrid. You look—"

"A mess, I know."

*Stunning. Brilliant. Perfect.*

Yes, her hair was all over, and her bare toes peeped out beneath the hem, but he wouldn't have changed anything for the world. If only he had a camera to capture her like this forever.

"Are you going like that?" she asked. Her greedy eyes ran up and down his bare chest.

"Certainly not! I'm a rake, not a barbarian."

She grinned at his description of himself. "Pity."

"No one wants to see me shirtless. I don't have an especially impressive physique."

That drew a frown. "Given your love of tartan prints I'd hoped you might at least wear a kilt."

"No one wants to see me in a kilt, either. I have knobby knees."

"Monte, I've seen you in the altogether, and you do yourself an injustice."

"Believe it or not, most people of my acquaintance prefer to observe me fully clothed."

"You are a beautiful man. Tricia agrees with me. I'm certain many of the other ladies would, too, if they saw you undressed."

He gave her a playful tap on the nose. "You, my darling, have an eye for skinny men."

"Oh, well, if you want to gain weight, you should eat more cakes and things."

"And be unhealthful? No, thank you."

She crossed her arms. "I eat cakes."

"And I have no wish to stop you so long as your health does not suffer for it."

"Most people eat cakes."

He shrugged. "I don't particularly enjoy sweets."

"You are quite peculiar."

"Yes. Is it also peculiar that we are having this discussion in an entirely cordial fashion?"

"Shall we argue instead?" The gleam in her eye matched the eager tone of her voice.

"Not just now. Why don't you tell me why you're here."

"Ah, yes." She heaved a sigh. "Would you please help me choose accessories? I know you prefer I select things myself, but I don't know fashion as you do, and don't want any talk of my oddness. I mean to thwart Marvale's plans, whatever they may be."

"No matter what you choose, there will be others in odder costumes. That's the purpose of a fancy dress ball, after all. To be wild and unusual. My recommendation is your ammonite necklace, and a few pearls in your hair. Nothing else."

"Nothing? What about gloves? People will see my tattoo."

"Let them."

"I'm guessing you don't want me to take out the nose ring, either."

"Correct. Simple is best. Change nothing. Let your beautiful dress do the talking."

"You like it, then?"

"I love it. It needs no accessorizing."

"Right. Necklace. Pearls. Thank you."

"You're welcome."

"Oh, what about shoes?"

He waggled his eyebrows at her. "I dare you to go barefoot."

"Only if you wear a kilt with nothing under it."

"Another time, then. Wear matching slippers—cream or pale green—so long as they are comfortable. You will wish to dance. I must finish dressing now. Will you save me the first waltz?"

She looked into his eyes for a long moment. "I will."

"Thank you. I'll see you shortly."

He watched her bound off down the hall. She needed no accessorizing, no alteration. She was perfection, all by herself. He would add only one thing: his ring on her finger. He would steal a moment alone with her tonight, to tell her how he felt. To ask for her hand. If she didn't want him, so be it. But he needed to try.

The way she looked at him and the way she had held him last night made him hopeful. She cared. He knew that down to his bones. But did she love him?

Monte slipped back into his room to finish preparing. He shaved again and trimmed his moustache. Brushed a bit of potion into his hair to keep it in place. Put on a crisp, white shirt beneath his suit. Everything was flawless, save for his necktie. Astrid would be disappointed if he tied it up snugly.

For too long, he fidgeted in front of the mirror, making minuscule adjustments no one would ever notice.

*Get on with it, man. She won't have you if you're standing around fussing over nothing like a ninny.*

He locked up his room, double-checking it was secure before slipping the key into a waistcoat pocket. He didn't go directly to the stairs, but walked to Astrid's room and knocked on her door.

"She's downstairs already."

"Lady Ophelia." Astrid's friend had dressed herself up like a candle, complete with a hat that resembled a flame. "You look luminous."

"Tyger, tyger, burning bright."

"Ah, are we insane again this evening?"

"The best people usually are."

He offered his arm. "Allow me to escort you to the ball, my lady, and request the honor of a dance."

She looked up at him with an impish smile. "Will you not be partnering Lady Astrid for every single dance?"

"We're trying to keep our names out of the gossip sheets, I'm afraid."

"Well, I hope you enjoy yourself, even so."

"I will do my best."

The jangle of metal-on-metal caused him to turn toward the servants' staircase. Miss Fairfax stepped into the hall in full Indian dress, a collection of gold bracelets bouncing around her slender wrists. Her sari was bright red silk, edged with a swirling, organic pattern embroidered in delicate gold thread. A gold band was woven into her upswept hair, and matching jewels decorated her ears and throat. She looked regal as a queen and as beautiful as Monte had ever seen. He bowed to her.

"Miss Fairfax. You are dazzling." He extended his other arm, and the trio descended toward the ballroom.

"Thank you. I own no fancy dress costumes, so I seized the opportunity to wear my sari. I'm proud of this half of my heritage, and I have few occasions to display it."

"It would make a lovely wedding gown." He winked at her.

Her smile was radiant. "You are a meddler, Dr. Montford."

"Helpful, I believe you meant, Miss Fairfax. Cal will faint when he catches sight of you. Be prepared to catch him. I shouldn't like to have to tend a head wound this evening."

Cal, fortunately, was made of sterner stuff than Monte had indicated, and didn't faint away. He did, however, abandon his gaggle of admirers and slice his way across the ballroom to her side. The sprig of fake ivy was pinned to his lapel.

"Gracie. You look astounding. Might we talk a moment?"

Monte released Miss Fairfax into his friend's care, let Ophelia slip away to huddle with Astrid in the corner, and went to rescue the ladies who had been left in the lurch by the marquess.

It was freeing to be a flirt again. His quest to be respectable had caused him to grow antisocial. He hadn't realized how painful it had been repressing behavior that came naturally until Astrid had coaxed it out of him.

Best of all, not only did she like Monte the rake, but he could use that side of himself to her advantage.

Over the past three days, he had learned which ladies—and gentlemen—were most likely to spread gossip, who was worth talking to, and what they all really thought of the Wembley twins. He now knew Lady Arabella didn't want to marry Cal, though her mother desperately wanted it. He knew that while Lord Smyth had recently fared well in some mysterious investment, he was still seeking to improve his financial situation. And he knew Miss Dansby was quite a wicked young lady in secret. Her spare room key was now among his possessions. He was contemplating tying a ribbon to it and presenting it to Astrid with a note reading, "I am forgoing the bed of a lovely young woman all for you."

As he approached, Miss Dansby lowered her mask just enough to catch his eye. He could read the question on her face. *Why didn't you come to me last night?* The mask rose a split second later. She was dressed in red-orange velvet, with a fluffy tail pinned to her bustle and tufted ears perched atop her hair. A vixen.

Fascinating girl. Quiet. Subtle. Worth talking to.

"I can't imagine what he sees in her." Lady Pamela Whitworth, queen of the gossipy young ladies, made no attempt to modulate her voice as she gawked openly at Cal and Grace. She and a number of her friends had donned Elizabethan garb for the evening's festivities. "She is so foreign and brown."

"She's his mistress, obviously," replied one of Her Majesty's ladies in waiting.

Monte sauntered closer, mulling over possible ways to defend his friends.

"I hope he marries her," said Lady Arabella. "Then my mother will stop throwing me at him."

"Men don't marry women like that, do they, Dr. Montford?"

Monte feigned ignorance of the conversation. "Women like what, now?"

"That Miss Fairfax. She is foreign and all but a servant."

He waved a hand. "Irrelevant. All that matters is that she is among the most beautiful and accomplished ladies in the room. She's in the running for first waltz."

Lady Arabella raised her carefully plucked brows. "First waltz?"

"I make a habit of dancing the first waltz with the most beautiful woman in the room."

Lady Pamela frowned at him. "Isn't that an impossibility? Surely any woman of merit will have the dance long claimed."

He gave a lazy shrug. "I've cut in before. I can do so again."

"Shocking! No wonder you are in all the papers. Now, tell the truth, whose bed were you in last night?" She sounded so like a reporter that Monte looked down at her hands, expecting to see a pen and notebook.

"My own."

"Nonsense. Was it that Lady Vayne again? Is she a candidate for your first waltz?"

"She is beautiful, certainly," Monte replied.

Miss Dansby's mask lowered once again. "Don't be daft, Lady Pamela. He means to dance with Lady Astrid. Anyone with a whit of sense can see he's obsessed with her."

"Of course he is," Lady Pamela's friend laughed. "He has few prospects, and she is terribly wealthy."

"Both true," he conceded. "Though, again, irrelevant. My regard for her would be the same were she no more than a farm girl."

He took note of which ladies erupted into giggles, assuming he was joking.

"Miss Dansby, are you engaged for the quadrille? It appears the dancing is about to start."

"I am not, thank you."

The group of gossips dispersed to find dancing partners. Monte hoped the worst of them would have their feet trod upon.

He took Miss Dansby's hand and joined the crowd gathering on the dance floor. Astrid remained in the corner talking to Lady Ophelia. He tried to make eye contact as the dance began.

"Those women are fools," Miss Dansby sniffed. "You're mad in love with her, and all they see is money."

"When one is brought up to view all of life as a financial transaction and one's own self as a commodity, it's difficult to think otherwise."

"A harsh commentary on the state of society."

"Yes."

They fell silent, taking a moment to enjoy the dance and put their unpleasant acquaintances behind them. Miss Dansby was first to speak again.

"May I have my key back?"

Monte favored her with his best flirtatious smile. "I rather like having it."

"But you have no intention of using it. I admit I wasn't entirely certain when I gave it to you."

"Have I earned your respect, then, or your censure?"

Her grin was crooked. "A bit of both. Now I'm decided I will make an effort to get to know Lady Astrid better. You're an interesting man, therefore she must be equally interesting."

"I should be happy to encourage the connection. One cannot know too many decent people."

"Thank you, Dr. Montford."

"Monte," he corrected.

"And you may call me Miss Dansby. Until I get my key back."

Monte laughed, and they spent the remainder of the dance in happy silence. When the number came to an end, he bowed over her hand and kissed it.

"Thank you, dear lady, for the most pleasant dance I have experienced in quite some time."

Her eyes sparkled with amusement. "You say that, and yet you are already looking for your next partner."

"Guilty."

True to her promise, Astrid was moving his direction, her sea-floor dress trailing out behind her as she strode purposefully across the floor. The toes of her rugged walking boots flashed with each step. Adorable woman. Every little thing she did made him more in love with her.

"Lady Astrid, what a brilliant dress!"

She skidded to a halt in front of the bookseller. "Oh, Mr. Furbush. Hello. Thank you."

"Did you design it?"

"I had the beginnings of the idea and supplied the example photographs, but my modiste did the rest. It's amazing, and she ought to be world famous for it."

"I have never seen its equal. It well-nigh screams your name. Would you care for a dance?"

Monte stepped up behind the man and cleared his throat noisily.

Furbush turned. "Montford." He gave a nod. "Of course. You have long had this dance claimed, I presume."

"You presume correctly."

He bowed to Astrid. "Another dance, then."

She was beaming. "Yes, absolutely."

"Excellent. Excuse me." As he turned away, he had a near collision with Miss Dansby. "Oh, I beg your pardon, Lady…?"

"Miss. Dansby. And you are Lord…?"

"Mr. Furbush. Would you care to dance?"

"Yes, please."

"Fascinating woman, that Miss Dansby," Monte remarked, placing a hand on Astrid's back and drawing her close. "I think you two could be friends."

They swung into motion with the other couples, letting the rhythm of the music infiltrate them, moving as one through the steps of the dance.

"I would never have guessed being threatened with incarceration in an asylum would throw me into the path of so many interesting people," Astrid said. "Life is so strange. Three men asked me for this dance, Monte, can you believe it? Three! And not one of them a fortune hunter. Well, perhaps Smyth is. I'm still not certain."

"I'm only surprised it wasn't more. As I informed the rumor-mongers, I always dance the first waltz with the most beautiful woman in the room."

The sun glinting off ocean waters couldn't match the brilliancy of her eyes in that moment. "I am not the most beautiful woman in the room, but I rather feel like I am."

His hand tightened on hers, and he edged scandalously close. "And that is all that matters. You feel beautiful. You *are* beautiful. I couldn't care less what anyone else might say. Their opinions, their standards mean nothing. Beauty is inside you. It's inside us all if we dare to let it shine. Tonight, to me, you are perfect. You will always be perfect."

"Monte." Her hot breath scorched his neck where his badly-tied ascot gaped.

Giving in to a wildly inappropriate impulse, he let his fingers trail down her back, grazing the sublime curve of her backside. No ridiculous bustles obscured her alluring shape, no restrictive undergarments crushed her waist to unnatural proportions. The neatly inked lines of her trilobite tattoo stood out from her pale skin, visible to all. She was no more and no less than her true self.

"Don't step on me with those boots," he whispered. "I'm wearing my good dancing shoes."

The touch of pink that rose in her cheeks only made her lovelier. "The slippers pinched."

"I'm glad of it. I suspect you of not liking them, even if they fit."

"I wobble in the heels."

"I take it back, then. You ought to wear them whenever I'm near so you might wobble directly into my arms."

"You're ridiculous."

"Yes."

Monte spun her, feeling the swish of her dress against his legs. They were far too close for propriety and it was marvelous. He didn't care who was watching or what they thought. The other couples around them had faded to nothing more than part of the scenery. The world was an inconsequential, distant thing.

This was all there was. Him. Her. The dance. Their bodies joined as one. Lovers moving in perfect, erotic bliss.

"I adore you," he murmured. "I could dance with you until the rivers ran dry and the mountains tumbled down around us."

Her hand slipped down from his shoulder to his chest. "Ernest," she murmured. His heart thumped. Her fingers clenched on his waistcoat. "Darling, that sounds terribly unhealthful."

A laugh burbled up from inside him. He thought his heart might burst for love of her. "I don't care."

"I will make certain we pause for food and drink." Dark lashes fluttered. "And to go to bed."

His body tensed, arousal flaring. "I will never neglect our bed, love. But first, we dance. I am claiming your last waltz. And everything in between."

"You can't do that."

"I can, and I will."

"No." She shifted into a more respectable posture. "Marvale is watching."

Monte faltered. "Damn." He relaxed his grip on her. The small amount of space it created felt like a mile separating them. "The last waltz, though, is mine."

Astrid's nose twitched and she grinned impishly. "You can wrestle Lord Smyth for it. In the nude. The ladies will like that, and if they say they don't they're lying."

"Now who is ridiculous?"

"You, still."

"Stop being so cheeky, or I'm going to kiss you in front of all these people."

"Oh, the horror!" She sobered quickly. "But, Marvale. Scandal. The Institute."

"How dare they interrupt my courtship."

Her blush spread clear down to the swells of her breasts. He was one hundred percent, unquestionably proposing to her tonight.

Separating from her at the close of the dance left a physical ache in his chest. He kept hold of her hand overlong, pressing a kiss into her palm.

"When you can spare a moment, might I have a word with you in private?" The ease with which the words flowed surprised him.

"Of course."

Her eyes flitted around the room. Was she contemplating an escape right now? He only needed a few minutes. They could be out and back in the space of a single dance.

But then another gentleman approached her, asking for a dance, and Monte had to let her go. He could not deprive her of her beloved dancing time. Not when she had garnered well-deserved attention.

"That is a curious dress," the gentleman said. "Word is you study these... bugs?"

He sounded skeptical, but Astrid launched into an

explanation that would probably span multiple dances, glowing with confidence.

Monte slipped away to go flirt with the wallflowers. They deserved attention, too, and all he wanted at this moment was to stand in a corner and watch his love.

# XXXVII
# SO TRULY TURNED OVER

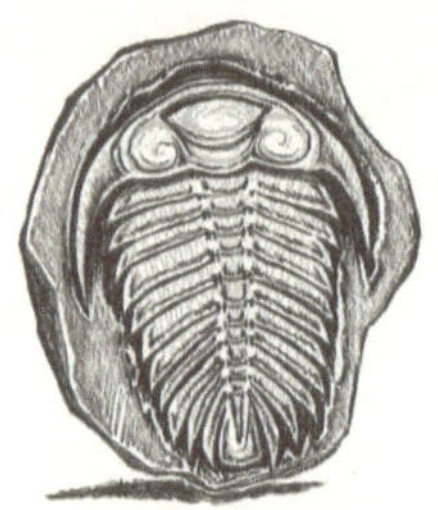

Now she knew. This was how it felt to truly enjoy a ball. Dance after dance, she whirled around the room, in a comfortable dress she loved. She stomped about in her inappropriate boots, and her feet didn't hurt one bit. Were these men all after her fortune? Was she boring them with talk of trilobites? Were the fashionable ladies sneering beneath their masks? She didn't care.

Others might be dressed up as Marie Antoinette or Cleopatra, but she was here as herself. She wasn't here to please anyone. Not her parents, not Lords and Ladies, not Marvale or Ayleston or anyone associated with any institute or asylum. And in not pleasing anyone, she had pleased herself. She pleased her friends and her family. Her brother had gushed about how happy she looked during their turn together.

She could say the same for him, watching him bow to end yet another dance with his beloved Grace, daring anyone to comment. No one would condemn the marquess in his own home, but whispers abounded and there would be talk tomorrow. Her heart swelled with pride. He knew. And still he defied them all.

"Lady Astrid. I believe this is my waltz." Lord Smyth offered his hand.

Astrid had no idea. She'd been dancing with anyone who asked rather than relying on a dance card as she ought to have done. With a nod, she accepted his hand and took her place facing him.

"I think after this dance I must pause for a rest or I will wear through my shoes."

That was nonsense, of course. These boots had carried her miles along cliffs, beaches, and city cobblestones.

"I would be happy to walk you to the refreshments. Your brother has provided excellent champagne for the occasion."

"Thank you."

What she really wanted was to find Monte and see if he still wished to slip away for a moment. She hadn't imagined it, had she? When their dance had ended she'd felt so certain of things. All his stolen glances and riddles about hearts, his murmurings in bed about winning her, they had all been leading to this. He loved her. He meant to propose.

Away from his touch, doubts had crept in. Perhaps she'd been swayed by the unchecked hedonism of their dance. The music, the laughter, the warmth of his body—had she allowed those things to sweep her up into a romantic fantasy conjured from her own fevered imagination?

She brushed too close to another couple, and something jabbed her arm.

"Ooh." She winced a bit, but the tiny burst of pain had already begun to pass.

If Monte had proposed right then, during or after the dance, she would have accepted. Maybe she would be in his arms now, instead of...

"What's the matter?"

She looked up at Smyth. "Oh, nothing. Someone bumped me."

Her head tilted. She stared at him. Gracious, but he was

handsome. More so than any man here. How had she not realized that before? Had she overlooked that exquisite nose? Or the golden swirls in his dark eyes?

His perfect mouth turned downward in a slight frown. "Lady Astrid?"

Astrid clung to his coat, struck by a sudden sensation of flying or falling. Yes, falling. Head over heels.

"Oh, Lord Smyth." She was breathless. Wonderfully breathless.

He gripped her tighter, keeping her moving through the steps of the dance, but prepared to assist her should she falter. "Are you feeling faint? Do you need to sit down? Shall I fetch you some water or wine?"

"No." She let herself lean against him, her fingers worming their way beneath his necktie to caress his skin. "Dance with me. Dance with me all night."

"Lady Astrid?" He sounded dreadfully concerned for her. So loving. So wonderful.

"I love you," she sighed. She wanted nothing more than to hold him, kiss him, breathe him in. To be with him always and forever.

He jerked and his steps slowed. Was he truly startled by his irresistibility? What a lovely, humble man.

"You *what?*"

"I love you. So very much. So very dearly. I can think of nothing but you. Wanting you. Needing you."

"You don't want me."

She wound both her arms around his neck, not caring that they were no longer waltzing properly. "I do. I do. Oh, so very much."

"You do not."

Such a deep, stern, masculine voice. The poor man didn't believe her. How could he be so blind to his own magnificence?

"I do. I love you dearly. You must believe me."

He steered her into a turn, putting a bit of distance

between them and the nearest couple. "You don't love me. You love Montford."

Something sparked inside of her. "Monte?"

"Yes, 'Monte.' The man who had you panting in his arms during the first waltz. Remember him?"

"Yes." Thinking of Monte brought strange, conflicted thoughts into her head. Thoughts that made no sense at all, because she couldn't want him, could she? Not when she was here with Smyth who was… was…

"You love him," Smyth said, sounding sure of himself. "This ridiculous scheme never stood a chance. He's always been the one you wanted."

"Scheme? What? I don't understand. I love you. I do."

"What is my given name?"

She hesitated far too long, groping for the memory. It began with a G, she thought. "Giles?"

"Gideon."

"Gideon." It sounded so nice on her tongue. "I shall remember it forever."

"What is Montford's name?"

"Ernest," she answered immediately. "The Honorable Dr. Ernest Ambrose Montford, FRCP."

"I rest my case." He wove them between whirling dancers, not halting their waltz, but heading for the edge of the dance floor. Did he not wish to dance with her?

Astrid blinked rapidly, trying to clear out the confusion in her head. "That doesn't mean—"

"When is his birthday?" Smyth continued.

"August the fourth."

"What is his favorite color?"

"Plaid. Well, green especially, but he'll wear plaids in all colors. He also favors hideous paisley dressing gowns."

Smyth shook his head. "I think the fact you've seen his dressing gowns speaks for itself."

"Oh." Her cheeks burned.

"Forget that. What is his favorite food?"

"Cucumber sandwiches."

He twirled her to a halt, just past the other dancers. "How does he take his tea?"

"Strong, without cream or sugar."

"What does he want most out of life?"

"To be a hero. To save everyone who needs help."

Smyth released her, officially ending their dance. "No. What does he long for? With all his heart and soul?"

That spark jolted again. "Me. He wants me."

"You love him."

"Yes."

*Yes! A million times, yes!*

Now she saw it there was no denying the truth. Monte was wedged deeply in her heart. Permanently stuck. She would love him forever. She reeled with the shock of it.

"Gracious."

Her head spun like a runaway carousel. Why was she here with Smyth and feeling such wild longing for him? Tearing her eyes from his took all her willpower. She loved him. She did. Did it even make sense to love two men at the same time? Her brain was a mess of fog.

She tried to keep Monte in her mind, since that's what Smyth wanted, but Smyth was *here*, and his eyes were so magical and his lips so ripe.

"Kiss me," she begged, lunging for him once more.

He put both hands on her hips, creating a painfully large space between them. "Lady Astrid, I believe you may have been drugged."

Drugged? Was that what this fuzziness was? How? "But I haven't even tasted the refreshments yet."

Smyth reached up to grasp both her wrists, gently prying her hands off of him and turning her around. "Let me escort you away from here, my dear, and we'll talk."

Not looking at him cleared her mind enough for her to

realize that she did not, in fact, want to kiss him in the middle of a ballroom. What would Monte think? Where was he, anyway? Smyth put a hand to her back and took a firm grip on her arm, guiding her from the room.

"This way," she gestured. "We can use my brother's study."

"Does he keep his best liquor there?"

"Yes."

"Good. I could use a strong drink."

Smyth released her the moment they were through the door. He waved at the desk. "Have a seat. Would you like a drink?"

"Please." Anything to settle her. She sank into Cal's big chair, her feet dangling several inches from the floor.

"Try not to look at me. I think it's helping."

"Yes. Not touching you is helping also. I feel less out-of-control."

A few moments later a hand appeared, setting a tiny glass with a very ladylike portion of brandy on the desk. Astrid glared at the finger's-width of amber liquid. Monte would have poured her a proper serving. And then ranted about the perils of overindulging. After all, if one wasn't careful, one might end up with a naked goddess tattooed on one's back.

"Something funny?" Smyth had that concerned voice again.

"Do you have any tattoos, Lord Smyth? I mean, Gideon. It *is* Gideon, correct?"

"It is. And, no, I do not have any tattoos."

He sounded rather repulsed by the idea. Annoying.

"I have one." She stuck out her arm to make certain he could see it. "Do you like it?"

"It looks highly professional."

He hated it. Doubly annoying. Was she allowed to be annoyed at the man she loved?

She swallowed half the brandy in one sip. Of course she could be annoyed. Monte annoyed her all the time. It felt wrong with Smyth, though. She wanted only to be loving him, worshiping him.

Astrid fixed her gaze on the desk. Yes. Something was very wrong here. These feelings weren't normal. More than that, she couldn't say.

Behind her, Smyth coughed. "Lady Astrid, I'm afraid I owe you an explanation and an apology. Would you be so kind as to hear me out?"

"Of course."

"Thank you. As I'm certain you know, given your investigative prowess, my finances have not been what one might desire for the heir to an earldom. Risky investments have harmed the estate, and my father has cut my allowance severely. Several poor choices of my own also contributed to my financial difficulties."

"I'm sorry to hear that."

"Yes, well, an offer came along that would put an end to my troubles. A significant sum for a simple task. Smear the name of a young lady."

She turned to face him, needing to see the remorse in his expression. "Me."

"You." He looked away, clasping his hands behind his back. "I jumped at the chance. The woman who had disgraced me before a room full of my colleagues? I wanted revenge. The goal was simple enough. Woo you until you fell prey to my charms and then cause a scandal. Compromise you, jilt you, slander you." He shrugged. "The details didn't matter as long as I made you look bad. Anything that would keep you out of the Institute.

"I honestly believed it would never get that far. I was certain you would be thrown into that asylum. But your brother grew a pair of bollocks… Er, excuse me. That was a poor choice of words. He began to throw his title around, and they let you off."

"So you drugged me with a love potion? Is that why I feel this way?"

"No! No, I didn't. I've grown to respect you. You're not at all what others have said. You are intelligent and determined. A hard worker. You deserve Ayleston's recommendation. But Marvale has been pressuring me. Making threats. I didn't know what to do other than to keep up the courtship. I doubted I could win you away from Montford, but I told myself I would do my best, right up until the vote. In more optimistic moments, I thought maybe I could beat him and Marvale in a single blow. I would win you for myself and be secure with your fortune."

"Who drugged me, if you didn't?"

"Marvale, I assume. He's been here throughout the party. He knows how hopeless my suit is. He, or more likely someone doing his bidding, slipped a love potion into your food or drink."

"I told you, I haven't had any refreshments. I last ate at dinner."

"Perhaps it was then. How long have you felt this so-called love for me?"

"Forever, of course!" Astrid swallowed the remainder of her brandy, trying to clear her mind. "No, that makes no sense. Let me think. I was looking at you, looking up into your eyes, and I was amazed at how beautiful they were. While we were dancing. You were asking after my health, or something of that sort." Her eyes widened. "Oh! That poke. When someone bumped into me. They must have jabbed me with a poisoned pin or dart."

Her shoulders sagged in relief. Her brain still worked. Her emotions were a gnarled mess, but she could think.

"That must have been it. I'm sorry, Lady Astrid, for causing you this grief. I'm sorry for courting you under false pretenses. I'm sorry you don't truly love me." A moment later, he chuckled. "No, I'm not sorry for that. I'm glad of it. You and Montford suit far better. I shall find myself another heiress. But please believe I hold you in high regard and I did and do firmly believe you to be an excellent woman and a fine choice of wife. I would have married you, never ruined you."

"Never? But aren't you tempted? Don't you want me? Don't you want to fling me against the wall and have your way with me? You must not love me as I love you."

"I'm a gentleman, not a rake like your boy Montford. Let me take you to him. I think that might help ease this ridiculous love talk. Why don't you lead the way? Then you need neither look at me nor touch me."

"A good idea, I think. I'm growing tired of loving you already."

"A positive sign."

They returned to find the ballroom in an uproar. Music was playing, but few couples were dancing, and groups of men and women all around were gathered in animated conversation. Some looked shocked, others angry. The chatter was so loud Astrid couldn't make out a word.

She scanned for Monte. He was no longer lounging by the far wall, nor was he among the dancers. Had he gone for refreshments? She waded through the sea of guests. How difficult could it be to find a man dressed head-to-toe in green and blue plaid?

"Lady Astrid, you must be so devastated!"

She turned toward the voice. Lady Arabella's mother looked down at her in dubious sympathy.

"Pardon?"

The lady gave a jerk of surprise. "You don't know? Oh, dear."

"Know what?"

Oh, God. What had happened? Where was Monte? Was he hurt? Dead? Her limbs trembled. No. No. He couldn't be. He could not. It would destroy her. She wanted to grab this woman by the shoulders and shake her, scream at her to say where he was. She would do anything to have him back safe.

"It's your brother, my dear."

Cal? No, not Cal, either. He was her twin. Her flesh. They couldn't be parted. Not like this. Not permanently.

"I know you were hoping to snare an earl's heir, but with such a scandal…" She reached out to pat Astrid's hand, but Astrid pulled away. "No one blames you, of course."

"Tell me what has happened."

"Lord Whitehaven has eloped. Run out on his own party with that Indian servant girl."

Astrid's hammering heart began to slow. Cal and Grace had run off. That was all? No maiming? No death? She nearly laughed in relief.

"Miss Fairfax isn't a servant," Astrid said defiantly. "She is an upstanding and accomplished woman of gentle birth and Whitehaven loves her. He *should* marry her."

"Well." Lady Whatever-her-name-was stuck her nose in the air. "I can see why they call this family peculiar. I'm glad my daughter will not be a part of it."

Astrid felt a pang of sympathy for poor Arabella.

"You haven't seen Dr. Montford, have you?"

"Who?"

Astrid gritted her teeth. They had been under the same roof for three days now. He had saved Arabella from the hallucination potion at Sir Christopher's party. She knew who he was. Second sons of barons were beneath her, apparently. Horrid woman.

Astrid stormed off without another word.

*Cross off one guest for the next ball.*

Smyth hurried after her. "I'm sorry your brother has made such a mess of things."

"My brother is doing what he should have done long ago. I'm happy for him and furious at all those who dare to think ill of him for it."

"Er, yes."

"Help me find Monte." She couldn't relax until she had found him. A part of her still feared him to be dead somewhere, or lying broken and bleeding on the ground, moaning her name in anguish.

"Have you considered he may have gone after them?"

She stopped in her tracks and turned to look at Smyth. Another rush of not-love ran through her. "Why would he do that?"

"He's Whitehaven's best friend, isn't he? He's just the man to chase them down and prevent an ill-advised alliance."

"He would never! Monte loves my brother. He would never separate him from his beloved. He wouldn't even contemplate such a thing."

Smyth shrugged. "You know him better than I do."

"If anything, he would help."

"Let's go ask the doorman, then, and see if anyone assisted the fleeing couple."

Her porter was busy with a steady stream of people leaving the party, most chattering excitedly about having witnessed a scandal firsthand. The butler, though, was standing by the aquarium, keeping tipsy people from touching the fish while supervising their exit.

"Crippens, could you tell me what actually happened with Lord Whitehaven and Miss Fairfax?"

"They departed not long ago, my lady, before this premature rush to leave. They took the steam car. I'm told he has a special license in hand and intends to return in a day or two."

"They planned this ahead of time."

"It seems that way, my lady."

"Well. How very devious. I don't think Cal has been so sneaky since we were children. Was Dr. Montford helping them?"

"Not to my knowledge. He departed on foot just before the clamor resulting from his lordship's disappearance. I must say, my lady, he looked in terrible distress."

"Distress?" Her heart began to race again. "Was he injured? Bleeding?"

"Not physical distress, my lady. He looked grief-stricken. As if he had received some dire news."

*No.*

He had seen her with Smyth. That had to be it. She had broken his heart. He would hate her forever. Nausea turned her stomach.

"Which way did he go?"

"Toward Whitehaven village, I believe."

*Please be at the tavern. Please be at the tavern and not on a train to London.*

"Thank you, Crippens."

She whirled back toward the party, grabbing Smyth's arm. "Help me find Lady Ophelia. She is likely to be in a corner, watching and not talking."

"Whatever I can do to help. I owe you for my deception."

Astrid paused. "I have a better idea. Find Marvale. Tell him all about how much I love you." She was growing accustomed to the effects of the potion. The words sounded almost silly now. "Lie if you must. Tell him how well his plan is working tonight."

"And what will you be doing?"

*Collecting my allies. Using this distraction.*

"Finding Monte and going after my brother, of course. I need Ophelia as a chaperone."

"But I thought you approved of Whitehaven's elopement."

"I've changed my mind. Everyone is in hysterics. He ought to do things properly."

"You are wiser than he."

*You are a fool and I wish this potion would stop making me swoon over your eyes.*

"Perhaps in some ways. Goodnight, Lord Smyth."

"Goodnight, Lady Astrid. I wish you luck."

"Thank you. And might I ask, do I have your vote for membership to the Institute?"

He bowed to her. "Absolutely."

Astrid watched him go, then sliced through the crowd toward Ophelia's flame hat. It was now or never. The plan was going into action. By morning Ophelia would have Beth and Astrid would have evidence against Fawdry and Marvale.

*And with any luck, a fiancé too.*

# XXXVIII
# A NIGHT OUT

**P**<sub>LINK</sub>.

The champagne in Monte's glass rippled. How, when his world had frozen?

*Plink.*

A droplet on his dancing shoes. A wet trail down his cheek.

*Plink.*

Dr. Ernest Montford, noted rake and notorious Hyde Park duelist, stood in the middle of a ballroom, crying.

Whispers echoed in his ears.

"I heard her say she loves him."

"It's an excellent match, especially at her age."

"I think she might kiss him, right in front of us."

Monte could see Astrid's face, eyes shimmering with desire. He could read the words on her lips. *I love you. Kiss me.*

Impossible. This made no sense. Only moments ago Monte had been so certain of her affection. Now… nothing but confusion and pain.

The world continued on without him. Astrid ducked out of

the room with Smyth. The chatter changed to something about Whitehaven. People walked, talked, danced.

Monte could only stare at the empty place where Astrid had once been, frozen but for his tears. Didn't they see him? Didn't they feel his shattered heart? He was all but a ghost. Alone with his sorrow.

He had no one left to care.

*Plink.*

He didn't know how he managed to leave the party, but somehow he escaped the house and walked the mile to the tavern. He stumbled in, fell into a chair, and sat there until someone brought him a drink.

*Plink.*

Monte scrubbed away the evidence of the stray tear with the sleeve of his coat. He was a fool. God, he was such a fool.

He stared down into the mug of ale, nearly full. He didn't even have the heart to drink. How could he have been so wrong? He'd spent years seeking out women who wanted nothing more from him than some fun and pleasure, yet he couldn't see one in front of his face. He had seen her through the haze of his own emotions and misunderstood everything.

When had things changed between her and Smyth? It must have been during the house party. He'd been so focused on his own desires and plans. He'd flirted too much with the other ladies. Astrid would naturally believe herself free to look elsewhere.

"Dearie, you look a wreck." The buxom barmaid pulled up a chair beside him.

"A wreck, eh? I feel worse." Heartbroken. And something more. As if his emotions had spiraled beyond his control. As if all logic had fled the world, leaving him in some strange alternate reality of despair.

"Want to tell me what's wrong?"

"I've lost the love of my life."

She sighed in sympathy. "Because of your heart troubles?"

Monte shook his head. "The only heart troubles I have are emotional. That was a story. Nonsense. I didn't want you that night because I wanted her. Only her. And now I've lost her. To a man who had the sense to court her properly instead of arguing with her and seducing her. I'm a fu… dashed idiot."

"You're not dying?"

"Only of a broken heart."

The barmaid harrumphed. "Where is this girl of yours? Did she run off with the other fellow?"

Monte gestured with his head. "Back at the house."

"The party? She's a lady, then."

"Yes."

"Well, I doubt she'd approve of you bein' in a sorry little tavern, cryin' into your ale, even if it is the best ale in the county. You oughta go back. Fight for her."

"I thought I did. I thought she preferred me to any other." He let out a bitter laugh. "I have a ring in my pocket, if you can believe that. I'd hoped to be engaged by now. For all I know she's engaged to someone else instead. The rest of the world thinks them such a splendid couple."

He put his head in his hands. "Dammit, I don't know if I ever told her I loved her. I thought she knew. And the way she looked at me…"

*She was in my arms. Touching me. Teasing me. She was mine.*

Monte straightened, looked at his companion and took a long drink. "It doesn't make any sense. They were only casual friends, and I—we—were more. Dearest friends. Lovers. It's as if someone swept her away and replaced her with a changeling, and now my Astrid is gone forever."

"Astrid? Lady Astrid, sister to the marquess?"

"The same."

"Well, either you needn't cry any longer, dearie, or you're about to have your broken heart stomped on, because she just walked in."

"What?"

Astrid's voice reached his ears before he could even get halfway around. "Ernest Montford, how dare you jilt me?"

The marvelous dress was gone, replaced by a voluminous gray cloak, and what looked like trousers underneath. Her boots were the same, however, and her hair remained in its elegant updo.

"Astrid?"

Her brow was creased, her expression anxious, though her posture suggested annoyance. This assumed, of course, he knew how to read her. He wasn't certain of anything any longer. Life was like a fantastical waking dream.

*Please, God, let this be a nightmare.*

He would give anything to wake up in his bed. Or better yet, hers.

"We had an agreement. You wanted to talk in private. I was saving the last waltz for you. You vanished."

"So did you." With another man. She wore no ring on her finger. If Smyth had proposed, he hadn't given her a love token.

"Not to a tavern a mile away to flirt with a barmaid whose dress barely covers her." Astrid cocked her head in that thoughtful way of hers. "Actually, that's a nice little dress. Do you think it would look good on me?"

"Ravishing."

She blushed. This was the Astrid he knew. The one he had thought might be able to love him. Had he imagined everything in the ballroom? Why was she here now? His heart was pounding and his palms were slick with sweat. Just looking at her brought more tears to his eyes. Why was he so damned hysterical over everything tonight?

She held out a hand to him. "Can you come along with me, or are you too drunk?"

"I haven't even finished one glass."

"Good. Let's go. I need you."

How? Why? What for?

He dumped whatever coins were in his pocket onto the table, hoping it would be enough.

"Good luck, dearie," the barmaid called. "Go a little easier on the champagne next party."

"I'm not bloody drunk," he muttered.

Even so, the brisk autumn air hit him like a slap, making him instantly more alert and level-headed. He'd come unhinged tonight. Was this what happened to every man who suffered a broken heart?

Beside the tavern, Lady Ophelia waited with three bicycles. Like Astrid, she wore a cloak and trousers. His medical bag was looped over the handlebars of the tallest of the cycles.

"Tonight?"

Astrid nodded. "The timing is perfect. Everything is chaotic because of Cal's elopement."

Monte stumbled, which wouldn't help his claim of sobriety. "Wait, what? Cal eloped?"

"Yes. He and Grace walked out on the party and drove away, bags packed and special license in hand."

"Good for them. At least two people will be happy tonight."

"In all the excitement, I don't even know if anyone realizes we left. If they did notice, they will assume I'm chasing after my brother. That's what I told Lord Smyth." A faraway look flashed in her eyes for a split second. Monte's heart constricted.

"I also told him to keep Marvale occupied. We're as safe as we can get and prepared as we can be, assuming you have all the potions we discussed."

"They're in the bag."

"Good. Let's be off. There's no time to waste."

He watched her swing herself up onto one of the bicycles—a bicycle suspiciously well-fitted to her size.

Ophelia straddled the new prototype safety bike Cal had tried out the other day, to the derision of most of the other young men. Low to the ground, with near-equal wheels, it rode smoothly and mitigated the risk of flying over the handlebars.

Monte's shoulder was still sore from his crash. He was lucky he hadn't broken anything or suffered a serious head injury. As a medical professional, he approved of the new design. He also believed both cyclists and equestrians ought to wear padded helmets. Not that he expected anyone to heed such outlandish advice.

"A bicycle race." Monte mounted his own vehicle and pushed off. "What a convenient excuse to buy your own ride and have extras on hand for your partners in crime."

"Yes, it was."

The glow of a potion-fueled streetlight illuminated her profile, giving him a glimpse of her satisfied smile. He loved that she proudly admitted to her scheming. He loved that she was outpacing him already and would scoff if he suggested she slow down or switch to the safety bicycle. He had to fight for her, dammit. He would claim that moment in private and plead his case.

Ultimately, however, the choice was hers. If someone else made her happy, he would go away and let her be. America needed doctors, too.

Astrid led on, like the stalwart she was, showing them where to stash their cycles to avoid the night watchmen that strolled the asylum grounds.

"I know the best place to crawl through the hedgerow," she whispered. "Stay close to me, because it's difficult to find it in the dark."

Good grief, how many times had she snuck out here in the middle of the night to determine that? Had he been asleep in her bed while she dashed about on a bicycle? Entirely plausible.

The ladies had to leave their cloaks behind, and Monte removed his coat, draping it over the handlebars. He felt a pang of loss, knowing the rest of his suit would probably be ruined. His budget for frivolous clothing was limited and he could spend nothing until he had established a new home and office.

The necessary potions for their operation went into the

pockets of his waistcoat and trousers, and he brought along his stethoscope as both a spying device and a medical one. His sleeves he rolled up to the elbows, revealing the tattoo etched into his skin.

"Into whatever houses I enter, I will go into them for the benefit of the sick."

Astrid looked over her shoulder at him. "What was that?"

"Nothing. Take a swallow of this, then pass it on to Lady Ophelia. It will help protect against poison."

She took the bottle and drank. "I could have used this earlier."

"What do you mean?"

"I'll explain later. When we're done here, I'm claiming that moment in private."

"Astrid, if someone has harmed you..." He sucked in a breath when she laid a finger across his lips.

"I'm well. Don't fear. Are you ready?"

To break into an asylum and put them all in danger? Not at all. But to follow Astrid? To help the women suffering under Fawdry's mistreatment?

"Yes," he said. "I am."

# XXXIX
# THE SECOND FLOOR

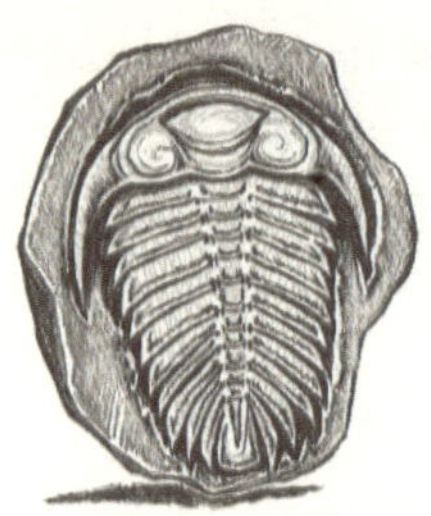

THE CHUNK OF GLASS FELL AWAY, landing on the grass with a dull thud.

"Be careful," Monte warned. "Not only is that edge razor sharp, but it may hold traces of the acid potion. Even a drop of it could burn right to the bone."

Astrid wanted to be annoyed with him for being patronizing, but she had said, "be careful," herself at least three times while he applied the potion to the window. They were both jittery.

She eased her hand through the small opening, found the latch, and flipped it open. They were in.

The cluttered office made for tricky navigating in the dark. Astrid bashed her shin on an unseen chair, and Monte scattered a stack of papers, causing a flutter of noise that made her heart leap into her throat. The trio gathered at the door, listening for any sounds from the hall beyond.

"I wish we had a potion of invisibility," Astrid whispered.

"I've found nothing in my studies to indicate such a thing is possible." Monte somehow managed to maintain his doctor voice with his words barely audible.

"Ah, but how would you know? Maybe someone has discovered it and is sneaking around watching us all while keeping the secret to himself."

"Or herself," Monte suggested.

"A woman would put it to better use."

"Rescue forays into asylums?"

Astrid felt a tug on her sleeve. "Sorry to interrupt the flirting," Ophelia murmured, sounding quite the opposite.

Enough stalling. Astrid steeled her nerves, then put her hand to the doorknob and twisted. There was no turning back now.

The darkened corridor stretched out before them, empty and silent. Splotches of iridescent paint intended for emergency navigation marked each doorway and both ends of the hall, but did little to illuminate the space. Hand-in-hand, the trio moved deeper into the asylum, following their improvised map to the staircase that would carry them to the higher floors.

The first floor mimicked the one below, and they didn't pause to look it over before continuing up. At the top of the stairs, a heavy door barred the way, locked to prevent unauthorized entry.

"Bugger." The whisper slipped from Astrid's lips. "We didn't practice in the dark."

Ophelia squeezed her hand. "Let me."

She knelt on the top step and began to work at the lock. Astrid could see no more than dim shapes and flickers of movement as her friend worked. Each scrape and click of the pins made her jump. Monte's hand was cold against hers. She wanted to pull him close to warm him up. Or perhaps merely for the comfort of his embrace. He stood stiffly beside her, not leaning in as he had so often of late.

She heard him exhale in relief when the lock gave way. Ophelia rose and pushed the door open just enough for them to slip through.

By now, Astrid's eyes had adjusted, and she could see

the outlines of the doors lining the walls. She counted down, guessing at which would open upon the room she had glimpsed from outside. She led the way more than half-way down the hall, pausing before the door she wanted. Several more terrifying minutes ticked by as Ophelia worked on the lock. Astrid had to release Monte's hand to wipe her sweaty palms on her trousers.

A mumbling noise beyond the door made her jump so badly she stumbled. Monte's arm prevented her from falling, and his warm breath brushed her earlobe.

"We have found your troubled women. They are moments away from our help."

The door swung open. Ophelia clambered to her feet, taking up Astrid's hand again. Her breathing was rapid, and she trembled.

The room beyond was a dormitory, with four beds along each side. A single small lamp hung beside the door. Monte lifted it down and turned it up just enough to illuminate the faces of the patients.

Most of the women slept soundly, but a few tossed and turned, and one mumbled into her threadbare sheets. Ophelia stopped by the foot of one of the beds, staring, her hands tightening on the metal frame. Astrid looked down at the pale, underfed woman huddling beneath the worn blanket.

"Is that Beth?"

Ophelia nodded. The tears on her cheeks sparkled, reflecting the lantern light.

Monte sat on the edge of the bed, waking Beth with gentle hands, helping her to sit up. Beth blinked in confusion, her eyes glazed by drugs. She made no protest when Monte measured out a capful of his special potion and fed it to her.

Astrid shivered. How often were these women given strange substances? Was it such a common occurrence that they would drink anything without question? Or were they simply too stupefied from the opiates to object?

"Ph-phee?" Beth's eyes, beginning to clear, fixated on Ophelia.

Ophelia dropped onto the bed, wrapping her arms around her friend and sobbing against her chest.

"Phee, it is you." Trembling fingers lifted to stroke her hair. "H-how? Why? Oh, Phee, you shouldn't be here!"

"Miss, do you have something warm you could put on over your nightgown?" Monte asked.

Beth shied away. "Who are you?"

"These are my friends," Ophelia replied, indicating Monte and Astrid. "We're here to help you and the others."

Monte pressed a second potion bottle into Astrid's hand. "Help me wake the other women. Give each one a capful. It should clear their heads long enough to get us out of here."

"There are more of us."

They all turned to look at Beth.

"In the room across the hall. Also the room beside the Doctor's suite, where his favorites stay."

"His favorites?"

"Those who have been here longest. They obey. We… sometimes don't."

Monte moved on to the next bed. "We will get as many out as possible."

They worked quickly, waking the patients one-by-one and helping them to drink the potion. As frail as Beth was, she was sturdier than most. None of the others spoke, and several remained in their beds, too terrified to move, even when Monte used his most soothing voice.

Astrid pulled the stethoscope from around his neck and tucked it down the back of her trousers. "Maybe that will help. I think they may be afraid of doctors."

"And justifiably so. Lady Ophelia, can you open the room across the hall while we finish here?"

"Yes." She helped Beth to her feet, and the two women disappeared out the door.

Astrid and Monte managed to get all but two of the women to their feet, draping them with whatever extra clothing and blankets they could find. It wasn't much, and none of the women had shoes. They wouldn't be able to walk the miles back to Whitehaven. She would find them a safe place to wait and go back for the carriage. They could squeeze eight at a time inside, if necessary. And her home was large enough to hold everyone until Monte could find safe homes or proper hospitals for them.

The sound of a distant door opening made Astrid turn. Was Ophelia done already?

"What the devil?" a gruff voice echoed down the corridor. Fawdry.

Monte swore and raced for the hall, Astrid on his heels. Over by the staircase, a lamp flared, lighting the corridor so brightly she had to squint. Fawdry stood in the center of the hall in his nightshirt, a woman in a clingy nightgown hanging on his arm.

"You," he snarled. "Marvale predicted you would be trouble. What do you think you're doing, trespassing on my property?"

Monte stalked toward him, his jaw clenched with rage. "You will let these women go or you will rot in prison for the remainder of your days."

Fawdry threw open a door. "Ladies!" he shouted. "Protect me!"

Eight scrawny, glassy-eyed women rushed into the hall, a few still tangled in their bedclothes. They formed a line in front of Fawdry, shielding him from Monte's wrath.

"What have you done to them?" Monte snarled.

"They were madwomen. Now they are my companions. I have calmed them and given them purpose."

Footsteps thundered up the stairs, and a man appeared at Fawdry's back. "Sir. I heard shouting."

"Fetch the constable and alert the men outside to be ready. We have intruders."

Astrid shifted from one foot to the other. She had a knife in her boot. Monte had claimed to have a potion that could temporarily blind an assailant. They could fight their way out, if necessary, but how could they get the women out with them? She inched closer to Monte. Ophelia was behind her, holding Beth's hand. The other women huddled in the background.

"Give it up, Fawdry," Monte said. "These women are free of your poison. They will testify to the truth of what you are doing here."

"We will." Beth's voice was shaky but filled with determination.

"I do only good here, isn't that true, ladies?"

The women surrounding him nodded.

"You have turned innocent people into mindless slaves!" Monte snarled.

Fawdry only laughed. "And how will you convince the world of that, Dr. Montford? You? Embroiled in yet another scandal? With only the word of a few mentally unstable women to support you?"

Monte continued walking toward him with slow, measured steps. "There is nothing scandalous here. I was summoned by Lady Ophelia to come to the aid of her friends. I have found them in a state of malnourishment and potion-induced stupor. You will be reported to the Psychical Health Board, among other authorities, and your license to run this institution will be revoked."

"You would sound more convincing were you not intruding in the middle of the night and consorting with indecently dressed women. But, I suppose we shall leave it up to the constable to decide. How will you explain your presence to him? How did you gain entrance to this facility?"

"I let them in."

Fawdry spun around to gape at the nurse who had come to stand behind him.

"Ah, Nurse Blackwell," Monte greeted her. How did he

always manage to remember everyone's name? "Lovely to see you again."

Nurse Blackwell addressed Fawdry, but glanced over at Astrid. "Several of us have harbored suspicions regarding this floor. A box of misplaced potions and papers was returned to us not long ago, with a kind note thanking us for our good work on behalf of the patients. It warned us some suspicious potions had been discovered in the workroom. Since then, I've been watching. I don't yet know the details, but I know you're up to nothing good. This week I work nights. What better time to bring help?"

"You're as daft as the rest of them."

"Give it up, Fawdry," Monte repeated. "You are exposed and without allies."

Fawdry's eyes narrowed in anger. "That is where you are wrong. Ladies."

The women all straightened, ready to jump to do his bidding.

"Kill him."

## XL

# MORTAL PERIL

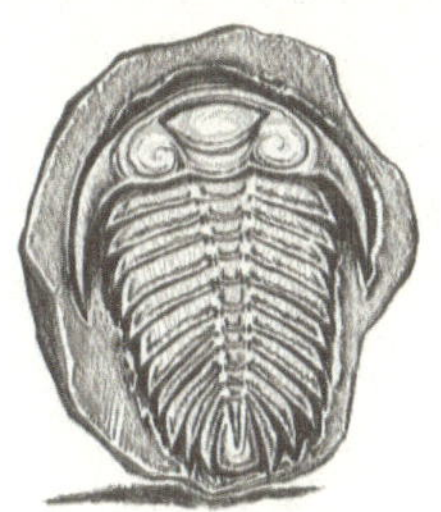

MONTE HESITATED. Astrid saw the way his body tensed, freezing with indecision. The women were wild and dangerous, but innocent. By the time he raised his fists to defend himself, they had swarmed him, and he collapsed in a heap, the women clawing and pummeling him.

Astrid didn't realize she had screamed his name and drawn her knife until the writhing mass of humanity was at her feet. She had no chance against the mob. They were in a drug-induced frenzy. Her eyes snapped to Fawdry.

He flinched beneath the force of her rage and ducked behind his mistress, or whoever she was. Astrid flung the woman aside like a rag doll and slammed Fawdry against the wall. She brandished the knife.

"Call them off."

His eyes were wide with fear, but he didn't respond. Behind her, his gang of narcotized women howled in fury, while Monte cried out in pain.

"Do it!" she demanded.

"Astrid," Monte gasped.

Her hand trembled, tightening on the knife. She wouldn't

lose him. She slammed the blade into Fawdry's arm, and he screamed in agony. Astrid yanked the knife free and pointed it at his chest.

"Call them off now, or I will put this straight through your heart."

"Stop," he gasped, clutching at his wound. Then, louder, "Stop. Leave him be."

The howling ceased. Astrid spun around, pushing through the dazed women to kneel beside Monte's crumpled from. His clothes were torn, his arms streaked with blood. She rolled him onto his back. Pained-filled gray eyes gazed up at her.

"Astrid." His features contorted in anguish simply from forming her name.

She dug through his pockets, in search of a potion he had promised to bring along. In his trousers, she found the small rubber bottle that held the acid potion and the remedy they had used to revive Beth and the others. She tossed that to Ophelia, along with the bottle she still carried.

"Give the potion to these women. Get them free of his spell."

"They'll need…" Monte took several gasping breaths before he could finish. "A double dose."

"Hush."

She resumed her search with both hands, tucking her knife under her knee to prevent anyone using it against her. Monte's waistcoat had several small pockets, including the one where he usually kept his watch. She slipped her fingers into it, recoiling in shock when one poked straight through a ring.

Tears welled in her eyes. He *had* meant to propose. He ought to be holding her right now, smiling and celebrating, not lying broken on the floor.

Blinking rapidly, she checked the next pocket, locating at last the little glass vial filled with yellowish liquid. A potent healing potion, he had called it. Astrid popped the cap off and put the bottle to his lips.

"Save some," he said after several swallows.

"No." She stared him down until he had drained the bottle.

Within seconds he was sitting up, though still wincing. Astrid pressed his stethoscope to his chest and listened to his heart, not because she could discern anything of medical importance, but simply for the comfort of hearing it beating.

Her gaze flitted repeatedly to Fawdry, who still stood by the wall, clutching his wounded arm. His mistress hung on his good shoulder, silent, but surprisingly loyal. It made Astrid wonder if he'd used a potion on her, too. Nurse Blackwell barred the path to the stairs, looking ready to wrangle anyone who tried to pass her, just as she would have handled an unruly patient.

Astrid turned to Ophelia and Beth, watching them distribute the potion to Fawdry's victims. The women looked baffled and scared. Some were crying.

"It will take more than a potion to heal them," Monte said. "They will need rest, food, possibly other medications, a real doctor to care for them."

Astrid covered his hand with her own. "You're a real doctor."

"That I am." He struggled to stand, allowing Astrid to assist him. "Miss, er, Beth? Pardon, I don't know your proper name."

"I haven't one I wish to use. Beth will do."

"Of course. Do you know where Mr. Fawdry keeps his records and correspondence?"

"No!" Fawdry lurched toward them. Astrid waved the knife at him and he stumbled. "You are intruders. Criminals. I will see you behind bars!"

Beth pointed at a door, and Ophelia pulled out her hairpins. "I'll open it."

"No!" Fawdry stepped away from Astrid's reach, trying to skirt around Monte instead. "You can't go in there."

Monte leaned heavily on Astrid. She turned to support

him, but the moment Fawdry came within arm's length, he straightened up and threw a solid punch, knocking the asylum owner to the floor.

"Sit down and shut up."

"Yes, Fawdry, do. You are good for little else."

Astrid whirled at the sound of Marvale's contemptuous voice. Nurse Blackwell flattened herself against the wall as the earl pushed past her, prodding Lord Smyth with a gleaming revolver.

A burst of potion-induced joy rushed through Astrid at the sight of her artificial beloved, followed by a jolt of very real terror. She waved a hand at Ophelia, urging her to shoo the asylum residents into the safety of a nearby room.

"I'm so sorry," Smyth said. His dark eyes shone with fear and remorse. "He knew I was lying."

"Such devotion you inspire, Lady Astrid," Marvale sneered. "I can understand it somewhat. You are quite the determined adversary. Still, I will not be thwarted."

He shoved Smyth, sending him stumbling into Monte, who pushed him roughly aside.

"Sorry, Montford," Smyth mumbled.

"Go to hell."

Marvale laughed. "Yes, this will do nicely. While I *had* hoped my potions would cause your lovers to destroy one another at the party for all to see, a murder-suicide in a lunatic asylum will suffice." He swung the revolver back and forth between Monte, Astrid, and Smyth. "The question is, who kills whom?"

Monte tensed beside her, shifting his feet into a stable stance and clenching his fists. Astrid gripped his wrist to prevent him charging at Marvale.

"You poisoned the champagne, you bastard!" Monte shouted.

Marvale gave him a malevolent smile. "Just a little

something to make your emotions difficult to control. Fawdry invented it, but I question its effectiveness."

"I ought to tear your balls off and shove them down your throat!"

Astrid clutched him tighter.

Marvale chuckled. "Or perhaps it works after all. I think you will be my murderer, Dr. Montford. With your wild reputation, no one will be surprised you became unhinged enough to kill both Lady Astrid and yourself. But, first, your rival." He cocked the pistol and took aim.

Monte jerked free from Astrid's grasp and hurled himself at Smyth. Her scream of terror was lost beneath the crack of a gunshot. The bullet slammed into the wall several inches above Monte's and Smyth's tumbling bodies.

"Monte!"

He was already leaping to his feet. He caught Astrid's arm, trying to force her behind him.

"Get out of here. Take Smyth and go." His eyes were fixed on Marvale, blazing with fury.

Astrid grabbed onto the back of his waistcoat. She wouldn't let him rush headlong at Marvale. Her mind raced. She still had her knife in hand, but throwing it would do no good, and she was well out of striking distance.

Marvale met Monte's glare with an irritable frown. "You're out of your mind. Why protect your enemy?"

"*You* are my enemy. I'd rather see her happy with someone else than let you harm a single hair on her head." He took a deliberate step forward. "Go ahead, do your worst."

Smyth grabbed his shoulder. "Are you daft, man? It's you she loves. Don't let him shoot you."

Astrid flung her knife. Marvale dodged easily, but it bought her a few, precious seconds. What else could she do? Did Monte have the potion that could blind a man? Did it spray? Her heart pounded. She knew something that did. She let the smooth fabric of his waistcoat slip from her fingers.

Marvale leveled the gun at Monte. "Very well. I shall deal with you first."

"Run, Astrid." Monte braced himself to charge.

"Never. Not without you."

Astrid plunged her hand into the pocket of his trousers, finding the small, rubber bottle. Marvale's thumb pulled back on the hammer.

Monte sprang. Astrid thrust out her foot to trip him, at the same time lifting the bottle and squeezing with all her might. A stream of acid potion arced from the metal tip, splattering Marvale's arm and hand. He howled in agony. The revolver clattered to the floor, sizzling where the caustic liquid had eaten through it.

She ran to retrieve her knife, pointing it at her wounded and disarmed enemy.

"Surrender," she demanded.

Marvale crumpled to the ground, cradling his ruined hand and whimpering.

# XLI
# A WORD IN PRIVATE?

Monte hardly had time to process everything that had happened before Astrid hauled him to his feet, her hands fisting in his shirt.

"Don't you ever try to die for me again, Ernest Montford, do you hear me? Never." Tears shimmered in her ocean-blue eyes. "Don't even think about it."

"Astrid." He pulled her into an embrace. Her head fell against his shoulder, and he held her close, basking in her warmth and breathing in the scent of her. His ribs ached with every breath, but he welcomed the reminder he was alive and they were together.

He was winding a strand of her hair around his finger when the sound of footsteps pounding up the stairs made them both jump. A crowd of men rushed into the corridor: three night watchmen, a burly man who must have been the constable, Lord Ayleston, and Thompson the bodyguard. Thompson sported a nasty gash on his left temple. He glared down at Marvale.

"Your work, Montford, or the lady's?"

"You need to ask?"

Astrid turned to meet Thompson's eyes and he nodded to her. "Shoulda known you didn't need a bodyguard."

"What happened here?" the constable demanded.

"Constable Scully!" Fawdry's lady must have sensed an ally, for she spoke for the first time that evening. "That hussy stabbed my husband!" She pointed an accusatory finger at Astrid and scampered to Fawdry's side.

"Someone married him?" Astrid mumbled. "Huh."

Monte bent to whisper in her ear. "Perhaps there's hope for me yet."

Her lips curved in the slightest of smiles. "Perhaps."

It was enough encouragement to set his heart to racing.

Lord Ayleston made a quick survey of the situation and stepped in to take control of the matter. "I believe you will find, Constable Scully, that Lord Marvale has been engaged in a number of illegal activities, in which he has been assisted by Mr. Fawdry, among others." He darted a glance at Smyth. Monte felt Astrid flinch in his arms.

"I'm given to understand their correspondence and other incriminating papers can be found in that room," Smyth replied, gesturing at the office. One of Ophelia's hairpins jutted from the lock. "I can testify to what happened here tonight, and I have other evidence of his wrongdoing that I would be happy to disclose in confidence."

But not in public. Selfish bastard. What all had he done, and did Astrid know about it? The way she smiled at him made Monte want to put a fist through his face. Or walk away and let them be.

"Do you love him?"

Astrid's gaze jerked back to Monte, and she blinked several times. "Oh. Pardon. It's difficult not to stare at him. It's only synthetic love. I was dosed with a love potion. It's quite tiresome."

He pressed his forehead to hers. "Of course. Forgive me. My nerves are frazzled tonight."

"I understand completely." Her voice dropped to a whisper. "Bloody Marvale and his bloody potions."

Another burst of rage welled up inside Monte. Now that he understood the reason for his unsettled state of mind, it was easier to combat the wild emotions. He let the anger fuel his resolve to set things right, and further checked it by focusing on Astrid.

He ran a finger down her cheek. "I would love to kiss you, but there is much work yet to be done. Will you assist me?"

"Any time. You need only ask."

It took the better part of an hour to finish distributing potions to all the second floor patients, then see them tucked into bed as safely and warmly as was possible under the circumstances. Monte promised a few extra coins to the watchmen to stand guard in the hall for the remainder of the night. They didn't seem to care who paid them, so long as they got their money. Not the best of helpers, but better than nothing.

Exhausted and aching, he closed the last door behind him and looked to his friends and allies who waited in the hall.

"I will need to return in the morning with another round of potions, and begin a full medical evaluation of all of the patients. It may be days or weeks before they can be released, and some may have conditions that require permanent medical care. I would also like to interview the entire staff. No one who knowingly assisted Mr. Fawdry should be allowed near these women."

"We will be reviewing all of Fawdry's papers in the coming days," Ayleston replied. "What we have found tonight of his correspondence with Marvale is damning enough to bring in additional help from London. They were conspiring to create a new authority to control potions use and commerce, and meant to drug people into agreement, if necessary."

"Order!" Marvale snarled. He and Fawdry were both in cuffs, ready to be taken to the nearest gaol by the constable and his men. Nurse Blackwell had bandaged up Marvale's wounds, but he still looked to be in pain. Monte wouldn't be offering him any medications. "I mean to bring order to a world that has none. The new Potions Control Board is to rein in the wild excesses, prevent war, and put all the power of potions under the control of a single, well-run, global organization."

Astrid glared at him. "While murdering people and destroying their minds? I think we prefer chaos, thank you very much."

"You are all fools."

Constable Scully prodded him. "And you are still under arrest, your lordship. Come along now."

"I will see they both receive the punishment they deserve," Ayleston promised. "I also expect this institution will be shut down shortly."

"No!" Monte blurted. "There are women here with no place to go, or in need of a great deal of medical care. You can't put them out on the streets or into another asylum that may prove equally horrific."

Ayleston's brows knitted together. "What do you propose?"

"I'll buy the asylum."

It would bankrupt him. He would be forced to beg for donations of clothes and blankets for the patients and dig for serum on the grounds to make medicinal potions. The asylum would be painfully understaffed without Fawdry's people. If the wealthy convalescents stopped coming due to Fawdry's arrest or Monte's own tainted reputation, he would fail these women who needed him. But he had to try.

"I will outbid you."

Monte's head swivelled toward Astrid. "You will what?"

"Whatever you are willing to pay, I will pay more. This will be my asylum."

He stared at her, slack-jawed.

"I propose a partnership. I put up the funds and you provide the expertise."

Every man in the room—whether friend, enemy, or complete stranger—was staring at him. They knew enough about his financial situation to understand exactly why Astrid had made her offer. Investors backed businesses every day, and this was no different. Yet they would judge him forever if he allowed a woman to pay his way.

He thrust out his hand. "I accept."

Astrid's fingers closed around his. Monte shook her hand, but didn't let go.

"I have a proposal for you, as well," he murmured.

A tremble ran through her. He couldn't determine whether that was a good sign, or bad. Certainly, she knew what he was about. He'd seen her flinch away when she'd found the ring in his pocket. It was entirely possible she wanted nothing to do with marriage. But he couldn't live with himself if he didn't ask.

"Do you wish to claim that moment in private?"

"I have no need of privacy." Monte dropped to a knee. Let the whole world listen in. He wasn't ashamed. "I love you, Astrid Wembley. From your tattoo to your strange pets to your room full of trilobites, I love you. I love your clever mind and your brave heart. There is no one more determined, no one more loyal, no one more beautiful, inside and out. You are a champion by my side and a goddess in my..." He coughed, softening his planned words for public consumption. "My arms. You frustrate me, challenge me, and make me a better man. If a husband isn't what you want, I will understand and respect that, but I must ask, with all the love in my heart, will you marry me?"

Her hand tightened around his. Watery blue eyes peered down at him. "Let me tell you what I want, Ernest Montford. I want to see icky bran cakes at the breakfast table every morning. I want to keep pretending I haven't noticed how many more vegetables Cook has incorporated into our meals. I want to tease you about spiders and cheese. I want to watch you caring and helping and saving people. I want to go to bed every night knowing when I wake you will be near. I want to love you forever. And I emphatically, irrevocably want to marry you."

Heart racing and eyes tearing up, he pressed a kiss to her hand.

Astrid pulled her hand away, leaned in, and kissed him hard. "I love you, Monte. Only you. Don't ever forget it."

"Never." He cupped her face between his hands and kissed her back.

# XLII
# ENDINGS AND BEGINNINGS

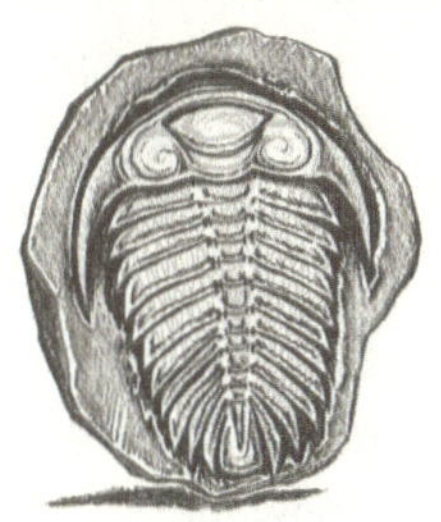

February 14, 1885

Tʜᴇ ʙʀᴜꜱʜ ʀᴀɴ ɪɴ ʟᴏɴɢ, smooth strokes, teasing the last few tangles from Astrid's long curls. This wasn't a typical occupation for a marchioness, but it was for a devoted mother. For these few, quiet minutes, Astrid was content to be nothing more than Linnea Wembley's little girl. Even if it did make her a little misty-eyed.

"It was so good of you two to delay your wedding until my health would permit me to attend. I know it must have been frustrating not to be married promptly."

"Um…" Astrid mumbled. Monte had moved into her bedroom the day after proposing. Life had been blissful. She felt color rising in her cheeks just thinking about it.

"Not like that, darling. As passionate as you are, I would only be surprised if you *hadn't* anticipated your vows."

Astrid blushed harder. Did other people's mothers comment on their intimate life?

"I meant you must wish for everything to be official. To

be able to go out in society as husband and wife and to know nothing can separate you."

"Nothing *can* separate us. We need no outside approval, welcome though it may be. We need only our minds and our hearts."

Astrid could see her mother's beautiful smile in the mirror. "Ah, my spirited girl. I forget you are older and wiser than I was when I married your father. And you are more right than you can know. He may not be here with us any longer, but he will never leave me."

Bittersweet tears welled in Astrid's eyes. She didn't fight them. She'd had time to reflect these past months, and had determined she needed a new mantra. Astrid Wembley *did* cry sometimes, but that didn't make her weak. It made her human. It meant she loved and was loved in return.

Her mother began to twist her hair up into a complicated knot. "Your Monte is a sweet boy. Though I still don't understand this nonsense about dueling. Don't laugh so, darling. It makes you shake, and I want to get this just right."

"Yes, Mama." She closed her eyes and let herself savor the moment.

Her hair was near perfection when a knock sounded on the door.

"Come in."

Elsie entered with a single red rose and a slip of paper. "A note for you, my lady."

Astrid's mother poked another pearl-tipped pin into her hair. "From your fiancé, no doubt."

"Yes." Astrid read the paper with a smile.

*A flower, my Valentine,*
*For you to wear.*
*I'm down in the chapel.*
*Come marry me there.*
*-Your Monte*

She pushed up out of her seat, though the last few pearls hadn't yet been added to her coiffure. "It's time to go."

Perhaps her mother was right, after all. She was tired of waiting. And her unhelpful brother had kept Monte away from her for the last three days.

"One more thing." The dowager marchioness threaded the rose into Astrid's hair and then stepped back to take a look. "Perfect. Slip into your shoes and we shall go."

"I prefer to go barefoot."

Her mother shrugged. "Very well. Only don't let the minister notice, or he will surely faint, and then we shall have to reschedule."

"There will be no rescheduling. Monte will revive him, if necessary."

Mama kissed her cheek. "Congratulations, my love." The two women linked arms and headed downstairs.

Astrid forgot everything the moment she saw Monte. Dashing and roguish in formal black, he wore a properly knotted necktie for once. True to himself, however, he finished the ensemble with a green and blue plaid waistcoat. Their eyes locked across the chapel, and it was all she could do not to run down the aisle and throw her arms around him.

His heated gaze melted her. She'd been feeling beautiful in her trilobite gown, but now she was a shining star, loved with an intensity matched only by her own passion for him.

She sailed past her dearest friends. Ophelia and Beth, looking happy and well-fed. Lady Vayne and Lord Ayleston, seated among a small delegation of fellow Institute members. Miss Dansby, who appeared to be using a book to flirt with Mr. Furbush across the aisle. Lady Arabella, here without her mother, sitting improperly close to Lord Smyth and giggling. Perhaps he'd found himself a suitable heiress at last.

Last, but certainly not least, were Lord and Lady Whitehaven, the perfect picture of elegant nobility, waiting with Monte at the altar. They would always be Cal and Grace to her.

Astrid took Monte's hands before the assembly. The press of his perpetually cool fingers warmed her insides. The adoration on his face made her heart leap with joy. Afterward, she couldn't recall any of the words the minister spoke. Even the vows were hazy. What she remembered was the shimmer in Monte's eyes and the tremble of emotion beneath his ardent voice. The trickle of a happy tear down her mother's cheek. The loving smiles from her brother and sister-in-law.

Happiness filled the chapel, and as Astrid kissed her husband before all those she loved best, a new mantra came to her.

*Astrid Montford will never fight alone.*

# EPILOGUE

August 14, 1887
Day One of The Second Annual Women's Open-Air Science Symposium
Whitehaven Women's Recovery Centre and Research Hospital

"**Y**OU ALLOW YOUR PATIENTS to walk to the beach?" Dr. Harvey posed the question in a matter-of-fact manner, but his face betrayed his skepticism.

Monte clasped his hands behind his back as he walked. "We do. I've found the fresh air and exercise to be enormously beneficial to sufferers of a variety of ailments. The patients are supervised, of course. I wouldn't risk anyone's safety. We have an enclosed garden for those who aren't well enough to leave the grounds."

"Very interesting."

"Freedom of movement is one of many things that set us apart from a typical asylum environment. Many of these women would otherwise be confined entirely indoors, or even in a single room." Monte gestured at the construction in the distance. "As you can see, we are building a large beach house to accommodate swimmers and beachgoers. It will have rooms for our patients to change in and out of bathing costumes, a large porch where they might rest out of the sun, and a shelter in case of inclement weather. It will also provide an indoor location for scientific symposia. The success of this particular event has Lady Astrid wishing to hold others of a similar nature. And while she prefers the out-of-doors, we can't always depend on the cooperation of Mother Nature."

"She is paying for these improvements? I was given to believe she owns this property."

"She does and she is."

Monte braced himself for the inevitable disapproval. He'd feared crushing disillusionment since the moment Dr. Harvey had accepted the invitation to visit. It was bad enough he'd had to acknowledge over the years that many of the man's theories were wrong, some even absurd.

"She seems an interesting woman. I look forward to meeting her."

Monte exhaled in relief. "Follow me, then. The current lecture should be ending momentarily."

The two men walked on, pausing at the edge of Astrid's makeshift amphitheater. A few chairs had been provided, for those who needed them, but most of the audience sat upon logs, stumps, and boulders. Others had spread out blankets, and some simply rested in the sand.

"We are not the only men here," Dr. Harvey noted with some surprise. "And there are children present."

"Many of the women have brought along their families. Our speaker, for instance." Monte gestured to the current lecturer, who walked back and forth as she talked, her youngest child resting in a sling against her chest. "Mrs. Elle Ainsworth, master potion maker and the genius behind the technique of extracting serum from soil. That's her husband down the beach supervising the rest of their brood and half-a-dozen others besides."

Belatedly, Monte realized this might not have been the best thing to mention, as Mr. Ainsworth appeared to be leading the children in some sort of mock battle, shouting and storming sand fortifications.

Dr. Harvey, fortunately, only laughed. "I can see where you acquired your reputation for rebelliousness, Dr. Montford. You seem to surround yourself with unconventional people."

And his wife was not least among them. Astrid had developed an almost uncanny ability to sense when he was near. She slipped from her seat to join him, settling the toddler in her arms onto her right hip.

"Foss," the boy declared, thrusting a rock toward Monte's face.

"I've been teaching him how to spot fossils," Astrid explained.

"Ah." Monte peered at the rock, adjusting his spectacles. He'd yet to become entirely accustomed to wearing them, but he couldn't deny he enjoyed the way Astrid would fog them up and slowly pull them off before kissing him. "Lovely fossil, lad." He ruffled the boy's dark hair. "Astrid, darling, please allow me to present Dr. Patrick Harvey. Dr. Harvey, Lady Astrid Montford, with our rambunctious nephew."

Astrid handed the child over to Monte and extended her hand. "It's a pleasure, Dr. Harvey. Monte has spoken so well of you."

"The pleasure is mine, Lady Astrid. This looks to be quite the event you have here."

She beamed. "Oh, yes! We have doubled our attendance from last year. We have women from all walks of life who have come to learn and share their knowledge and love of science."

"I'm happy to hear it. The education of our womenfolk is of great advantage to society. What better foundation for a child than both a mother and a father who value knowledge and learning?"

"True, but my goal is to celebrate and promote the accomplishments of all women, young or old, married or unmarried, childless or dripping in youngsters. We all have much to contribute, whether to our families, the world at large, or merely our own satisfaction. Our work has value. We have value."

Monte didn't realize how tightly he was holding his nephew until the boy squirmed in his arms. Monte set him down to toddle off toward his mother. It had been an instinctive reaction to hold him close, a need to embrace someone as fiercely as he wished to embrace Astrid right at that moment. Dear God, did he love her. Every day she grew stronger, wiser, and more beautiful. To the rest of the world she was still peculiar and unladylike, but to him she was, and always would be, perfect.

After a lengthy discussion of Astrid's work with trilobites and the study of the ancient Earth, Dr. Harvey excused himself, needing to be on his way. Monte walked him back toward the hospital, catching his wife's eye as they departed.

*Wait for me here?*

She pointed to the far side of the half-built beach house.

*Meet you there. Even better.*

"A spirited and fascinating woman is Lady Astrid," Dr. Harvey said.

"I wouldn't have it any other way."

"And what of your work, Montford? Have you made progress on the hysteria cure? You mentioned it in several of your older letters."

"Ah, well…" Monte began. "The truth is, it doesn't exist."

"There is no cure?"

"There is no hysteria. We misdiagnose other ailments. We call women hysterical when they are simply suffering from stress brought on by too restrictive an environment or are victims of traumatic circumstances. We call them hysterical because they don't fit into our pattern of 'respectable womanhood.' It's a sham, and I will never again consider it a legitimate diagnosis. I am happy to argue further and show you my research, if necessary."

"Write a paper, my boy, and I shall read it. I cannot guarantee I will agree with you, but I promise to give it my consideration."

"Thank you. And I can tell you that I *do* have a medicine to treat melancholia and attacks of the nerves. You may have heard mention of that. Lord Whitehaven recently publicly endorsed it at a meeting of the Psychical Health Board as part of a statement on the need for greater awareness of and research into mental health issues."

Dr. Harvey smiled. "You are doing good work, my boy. Thank you for the tour and the chat. I can see myself out. You ought to return to your wife. She appeared eager for a word in private."

Monte didn't need to be told twice. He rushed back down to the beach, past the crowd returning to take luncheon in the garden, clambering through the construction to find Astrid tucked inside a little cove, stretched out atop a blanket, awaiting him.

He dropped to the ground beside her, slung an arm around her shoulders, and pressed a kiss to her brow.

"I am so damned proud of you," he said. "I know that must sound ridiculous, but I can't help it. Everything you've accomplished, the way you state your case so defiantly, knowing many will shun you. You are an inspiration."

Astrid beamed at him. "Those who matter don't shun me. And you don't sound ridiculous at all. I'm proud of you, too. You've done so much good here. You impressed your physician hero. I could see it in the way he looked at you. You can stop being nervous about that."

"I wasn't..." Monte shook his head and sighed. "Yes, I was. I was craving his approval, I suppose. I would have felt a fool if I had wasted a lifetime admiring someone who hates all the work I've done."

"He seemed a good man. You needn't agree with everything he says to admire him. After all, I love you dearly and I still think your bran cakes are revolting."

He laughed. "And I think you mad for keeping a pet spider in our bedroom. Yet I still wish to make love to you, right here, on the beach."

Her arms wound around his neck and her lips brushed his cheekbone. "I know you do. Why do you think I brought a blanket?"

Monte drew her close. Their lips joined and their bodies melded together, the physical manifestation of their inseparable hearts.

# THE END

# ABOUT THE AUTHOR

Award-winning author Catherine Stein believes that everyone deserves love and that Happily Ever After has the power to help, to heal, and to comfort. She writes sassy, sexy romance set during the Victorian and Edwardian eras. Her stories are full of action, adventure, magic, and fantastic technologies.

Catherine lives in Michigan with her husband and three rambunctious girls. She loves steampunk and Oxford commas, and can often be found dressed in Renaissance festival clothing, drinking copious amounts of tea.

Visit Catherine online at
*www.catsteinbooks.com*
and join her VIP mailing list for a free short story.

Follow her on Twitter @catsteinbooks,
or like her page on Facebook @catsteinbooks.

# ALSO BY CATHERINE STEIN

## The Earl on the Train

*An earl with a problem.*
*A woman with a plan.*
*The journey of a lifetime.*

## How to Seduce a Spy

*A barmaid with a rare talent.*
*A spy on a mission.*
*A love neither can resist.*

## Not a Mourning Person

*A determined widow.*
*An ancient curse.*
*Crime and passion.*

## Eden's Voice

*Football, mechanical dragons,*
*industrial espionage, sexy*
*romance. Welcome to fall in*
*Ann Arbor.*

Available at your favorite online retailer.

*www.catsteinbooks.com*

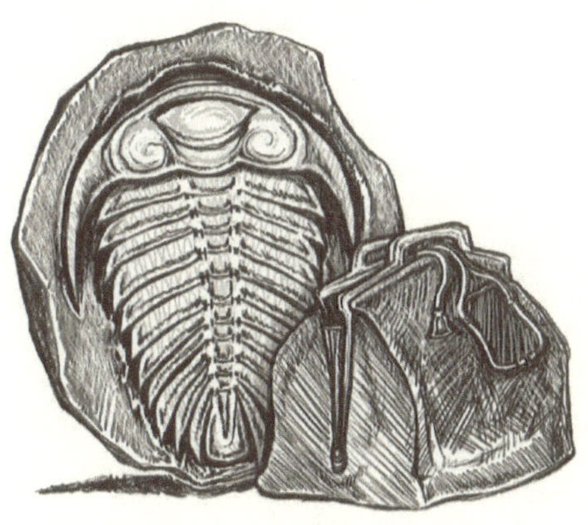

Thank you so much for reading.
If you enjoyed the book and are so inclined, I would love for
you to leave a review. Happy readers make an author's day!

I love hearing from readers,
so feel free to contact me on social media, or email:

*catherine@catsteinbooks.com*